MY BOYFRIEND IS A MONSTER

#3

My Boyfriend Bites

OR
ONCE BITTEN, TWICE SHY

DAN JOLLEY

Illustrated by ALITHA E. MARTINEZ

GRAPHIC UNIVERSE™ · MINNEAPOLIS · NEW YORK

STORY BY
DAN JOLLEY

ILLUSTRATIONS BY
ALITHA E. MARTINEZ
WITH ADDITIONAL SHADING BY ESTHER SANZ

LETTERING BY
BILL HAUSER

COVER COLORING BY
ELDON COWGUR

Graphic Universe™
A division of Lerner Publishing Group, Inc.
241 First Avenue North
Minneapolis, MN 55401 U.S.A.

Website address: www.lernerbooks.com

Main body text set in CCWildwords. Typeface provided by Comicraft Design.

Library of Congress Cataloging-in-Publication Data

Jolley, Dan.
       My boyfriend bites / by Dan Jolley ; illustrated by Alitha E. Martinez.
          p.   cm. — (My boyfriend is a monster ; #03)
       Summary: Seventeen-year-old Vanessa Shingle finds her New Mexico town invaded by vampires and learns it may not be a coincidence that gorgeous Jean-Paul McClellan has turned up in her love life.
       ISBN: 978–0–7613–5599–1 (lib. bdg. : alk. paper)
       1. Graphic novels. [1. Graphic novels. 2. Horror stories. 3. Vampires—Fiction. 4. Vampires—Fiction.
5. New Mexico—Fiction.] I. Martinez, Alitha E., ill. II. Title.
   PZ7.7.J65My 2011
   741.5'973—dc22   2010028723

 Manufactured in the United States of America
1 – BC – 7/15/11

Chapter 1

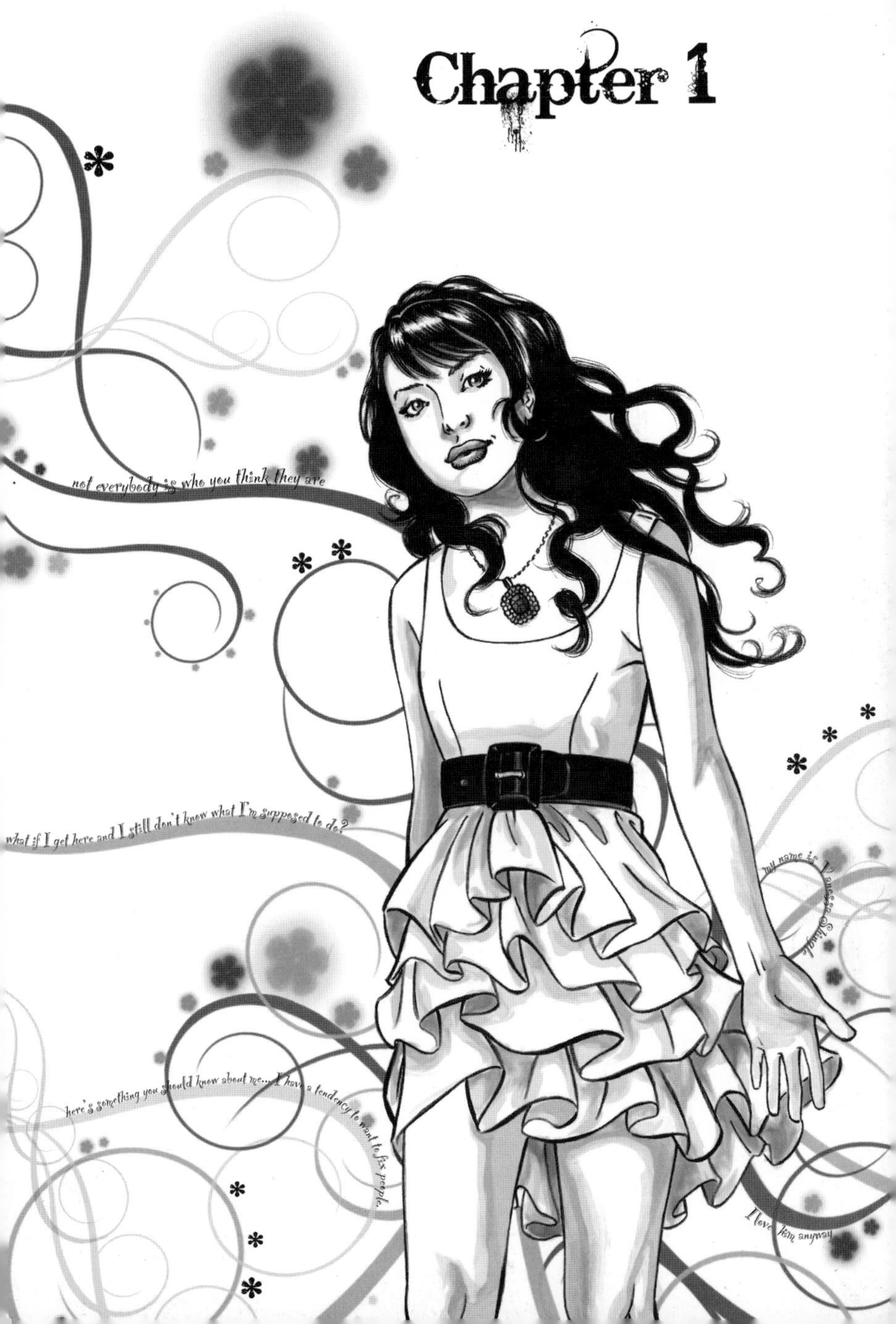
not everybody is who you think they are
what if I get here and I still don't know what I'm supposed to do?
my name is Vanessa Shingle
here's something you should know about me... I have a tendency to want to fix people.
I love him anyway

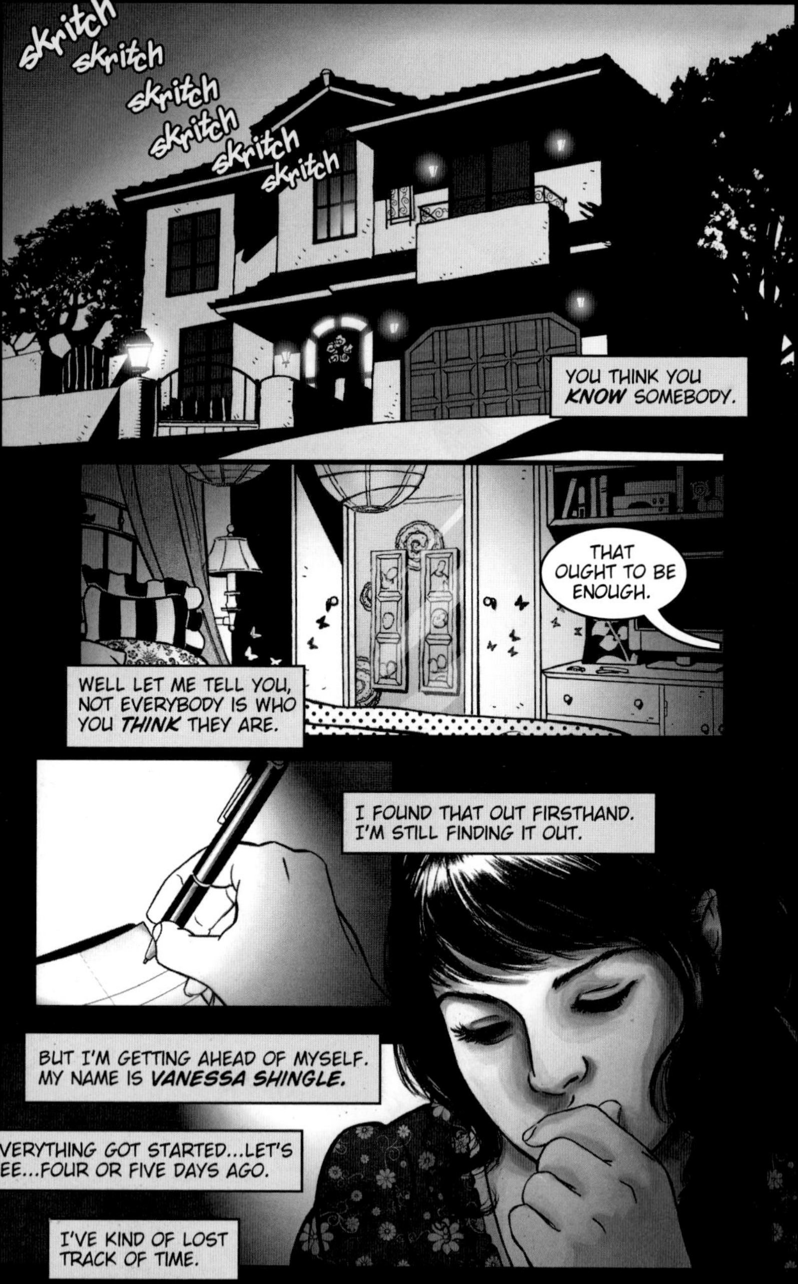
skritch
skritch
skritch
skritch
skritch
skritch
YOU THINK YOU KNOW SOMEBODY.
THAT OUGHT TO BE ENOUGH.
WELL LET ME TELL YOU, NOT EVERYBODY IS WHO YOU THINK THEY ARE.
I FOUND THAT OUT FIRSTHAND. I'M STILL FINDING IT OUT.
BUT I'M GETTING AHEAD OF MYSELF. MY NAME IS VANESSA SHINGLE.
EVERYTHING GOT STARTED...LET'S SEE...FOUR OR FIVE DAYS AGO.
I'VE KIND OF LOST TRACK OF TIME.

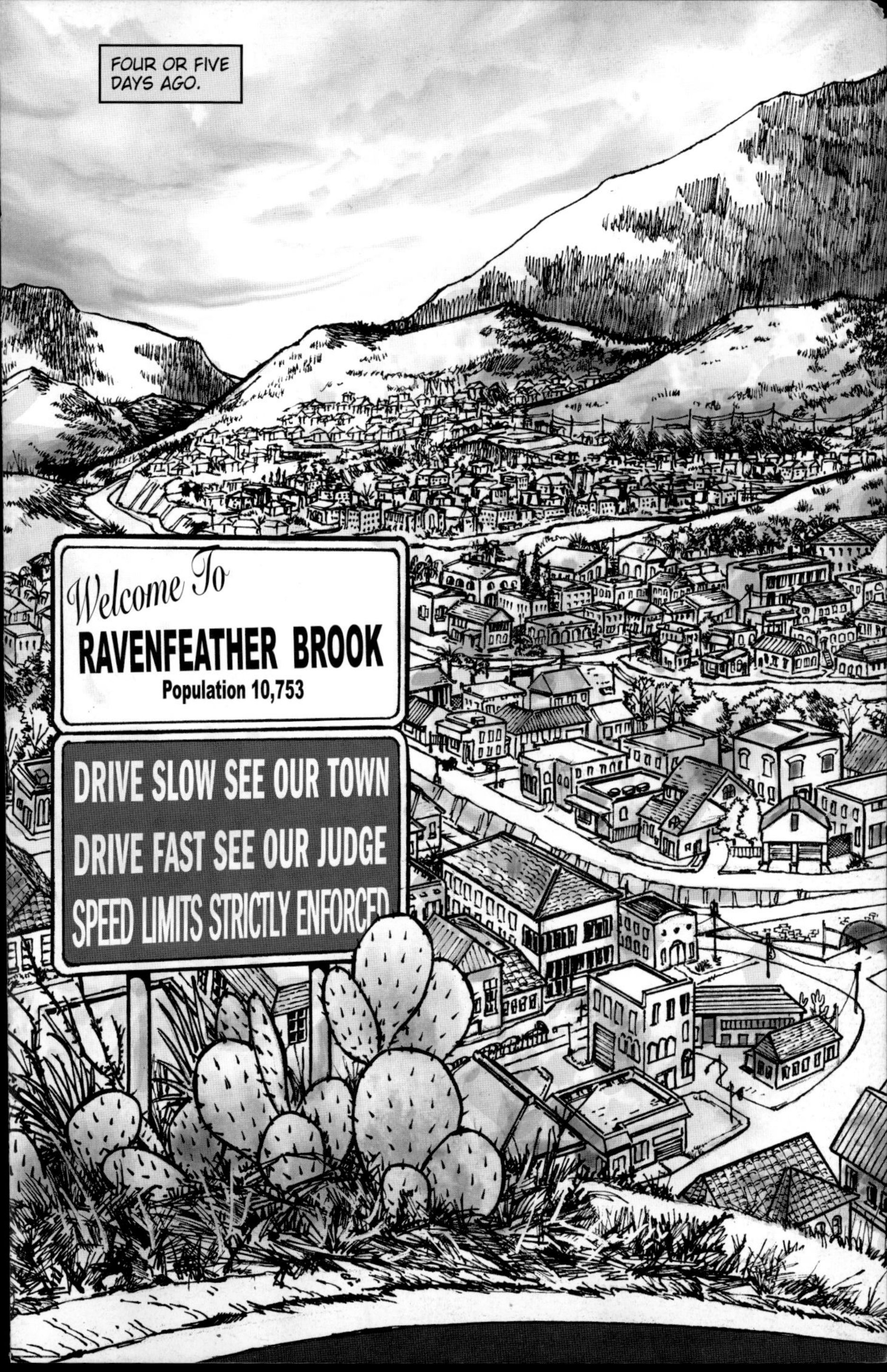
FOUR OR FIVE DAYS AGO.
Welcome To
RAVENFEATHER BROOK
Population 10,753
DRIVE SLOW SEE OUR TOWN
DRIVE FAST SEE OUR JUDGE
SPEED LIMITS STRICTLY ENFORCED

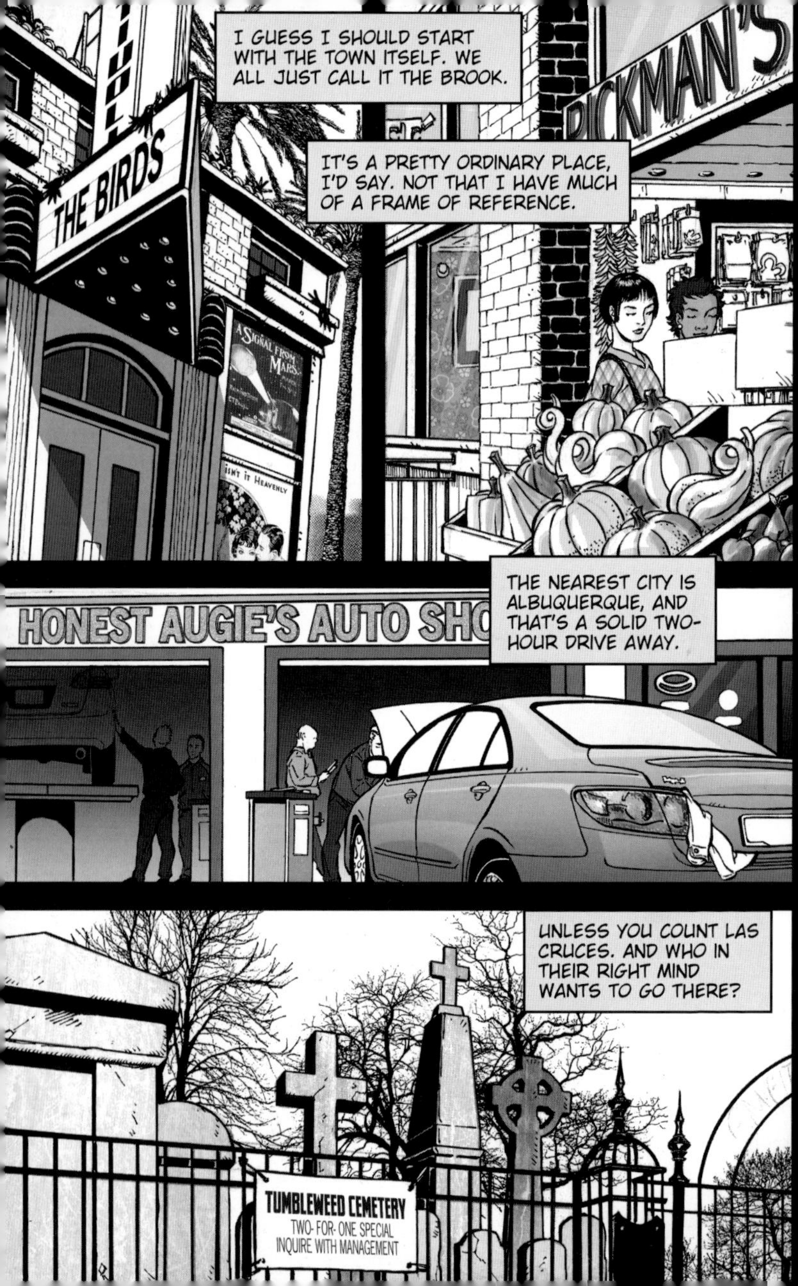
I GUESS I SHOULD START WITH THE TOWN ITSELF. WE ALL JUST CALL IT THE BROOK.
THE BIRDS
IT'S A PRETTY ORDINARY PLACE, I'D SAY. NOT THAT I HAVE MUCH OF A FRAME OF REFERENCE.
A SIGNAL FROM MARS
ISN'T IT HEAVENLY
HONEST AUGIE'S AUTO SHO
THE NEAREST CITY IS ALBUQUERQUE, AND THAT'S A SOLID TWO-HOUR DRIVE AWAY.
UNLESS YOU COUNT LAS CRUCES. AND WHO IN THEIR RIGHT MIND WANTS TO GO THERE?
TUMBLEWEED CEMETERY
TWO-FOR-ONE SPECIAL
INQUIRE WITH MANAGEMENT

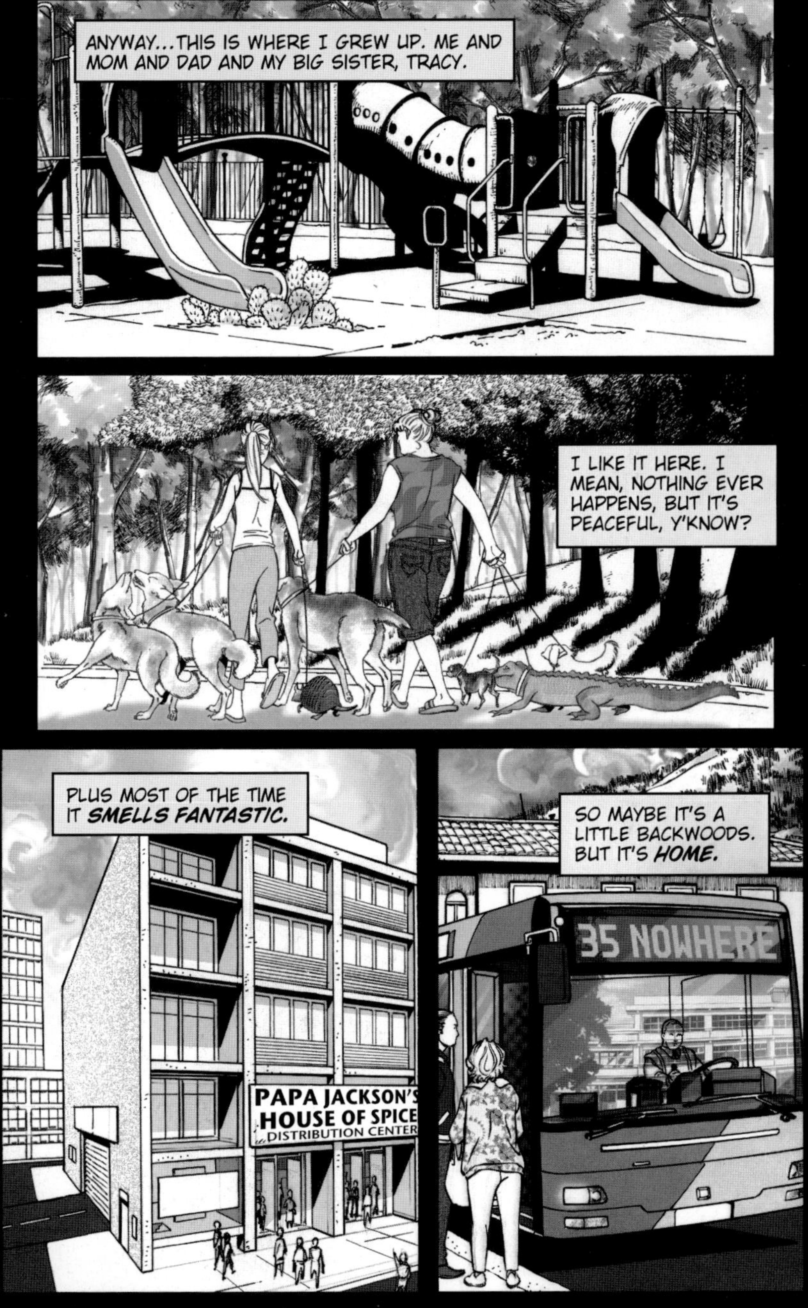
ANYWAY...THIS IS WHERE I GREW UP. ME AND MOM AND DAD AND MY BIG SISTER, TRACY.
I LIKE IT HERE. I MEAN, NOTHING EVER HAPPENS, BUT IT'S PEACEFUL, Y'KNOW?
PLUS MOST OF THE TIME IT *SMELLS FANTASTIC.*
PAPA JACKSON'S HOUSE OF SPICE DISTRIBUTION CENTER
SO MAYBE IT'S A LITTLE BACKWOODS. BUT IT'S *HOME.*
35 NOWHERE

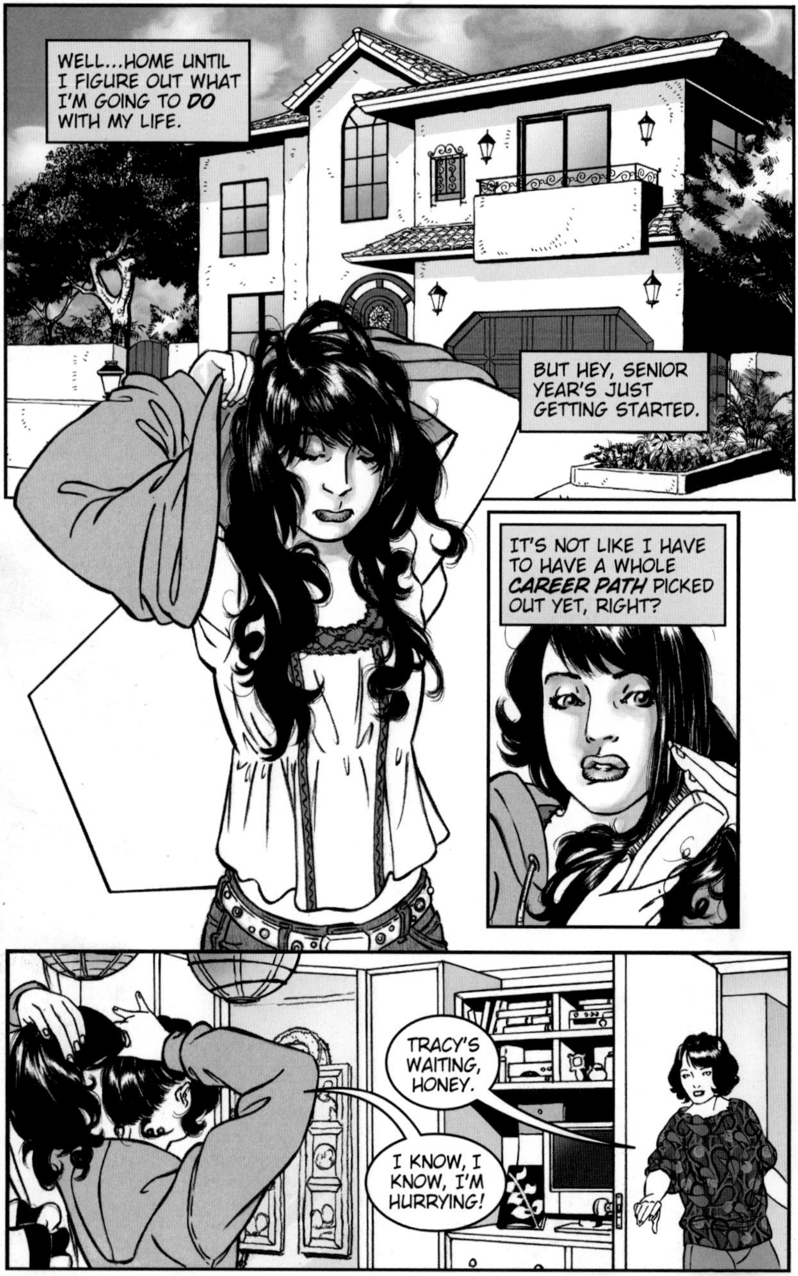
WELL...HOME UNTIL I FIGURE OUT WHAT I'M GOING TO *DO* WITH MY LIFE.
BUT HEY, SENIOR YEAR'S JUST GETTING STARTED.
IT'S NOT LIKE I HAVE TO HAVE A WHOLE ***CAREER PATH*** PICKED OUT YET, RIGHT?
TRACY'S WAITING, HONEY.
I KNOW, I KNOW, I'M HURRYING!

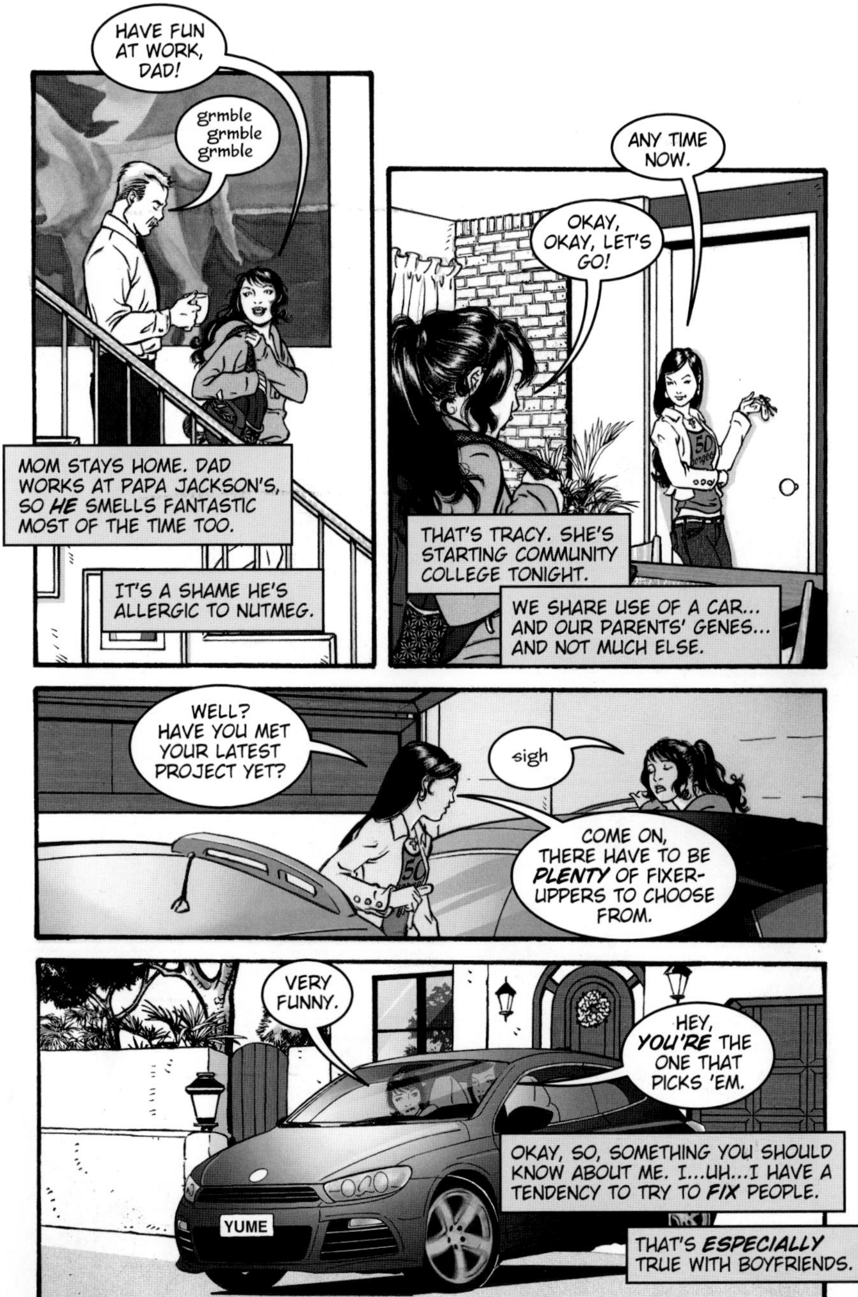

HAVE FUN AT WORK, DAD!
grmble grmble grmble
MOM STAYS HOME. DAD WORKS AT PAPA JACKSON'S, SO *HE* SMELLS FANTASTIC MOST OF THE TIME TOO.
IT'S A SHAME HE'S ALLERGIC TO NUTMEG.
ANY TIME NOW.
OKAY, OKAY, LET'S GO!
THAT'S TRACY. SHE'S STARTING COMMUNITY COLLEGE TONIGHT.
WE SHARE USE OF A CAR... AND OUR PARENTS' GENES... AND NOT MUCH ELSE.
WELL? HAVE YOU MET YOUR LATEST PROJECT YET?
sigh
COME ON, THERE HAVE TO BE *PLENTY* OF FIXER-UPPERS TO CHOOSE FROM.
VERY FUNNY.
HEY, *YOU'RE* THE ONE THAT PICKS 'EM.
YUME
OKAY, SO, SOMETHING YOU SHOULD KNOW ABOUT ME. I...UH...I HAVE A TENDENCY TO TRY TO *FIX* PEOPLE.
THAT'S *ESPECIALLY* TRUE WITH BOYFRIENDS.

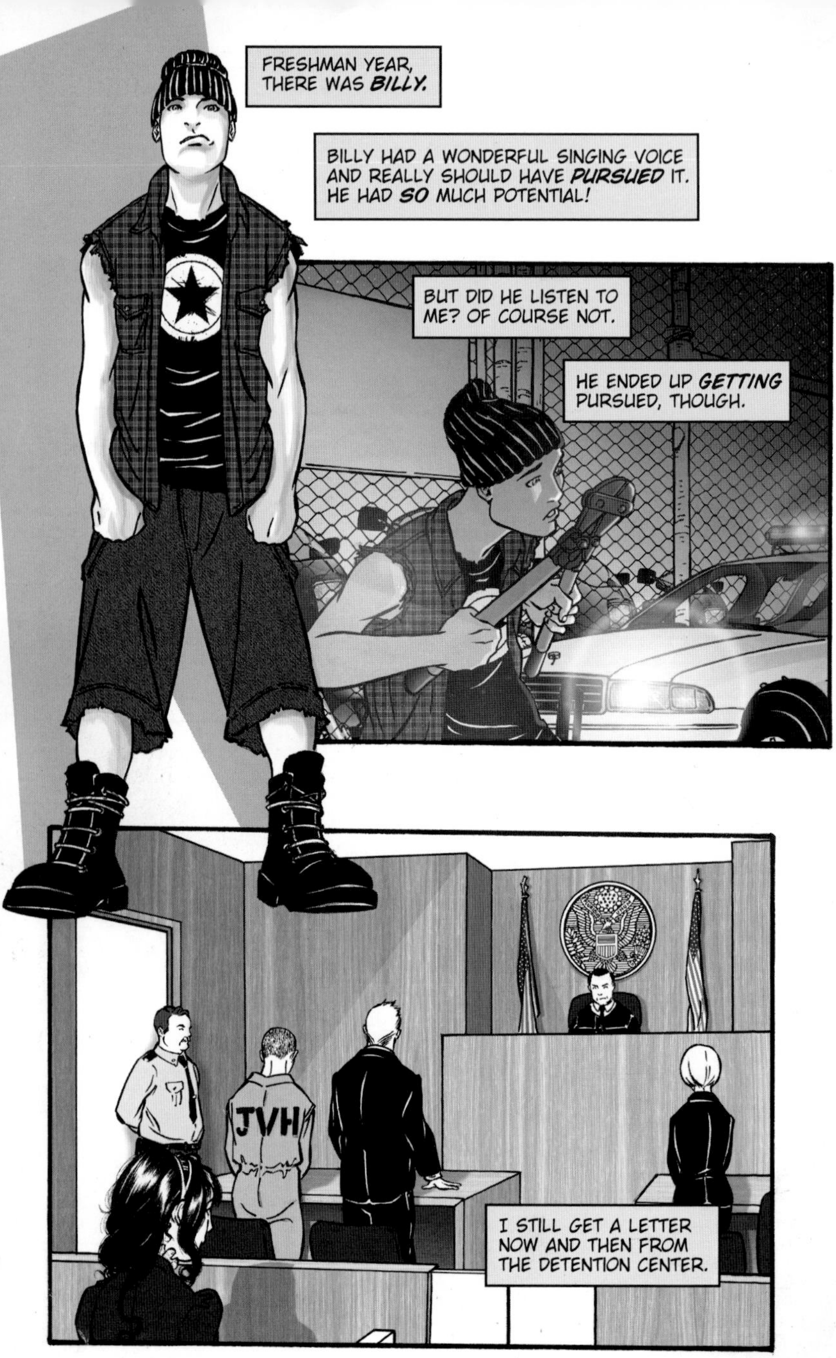
FRESHMAN YEAR, THERE WAS BILLY.
BILLY HAD A WONDERFUL SINGING VOICE AND REALLY SHOULD HAVE PURSUED IT. HE HAD SO MUCH POTENTIAL!
BUT DID HE LISTEN TO ME? OF COURSE NOT.
HE ENDED UP GETTING PURSUED, THOUGH.
JVH
I STILL GET A LETTER NOW AND THEN FROM THE DETENTION CENTER.

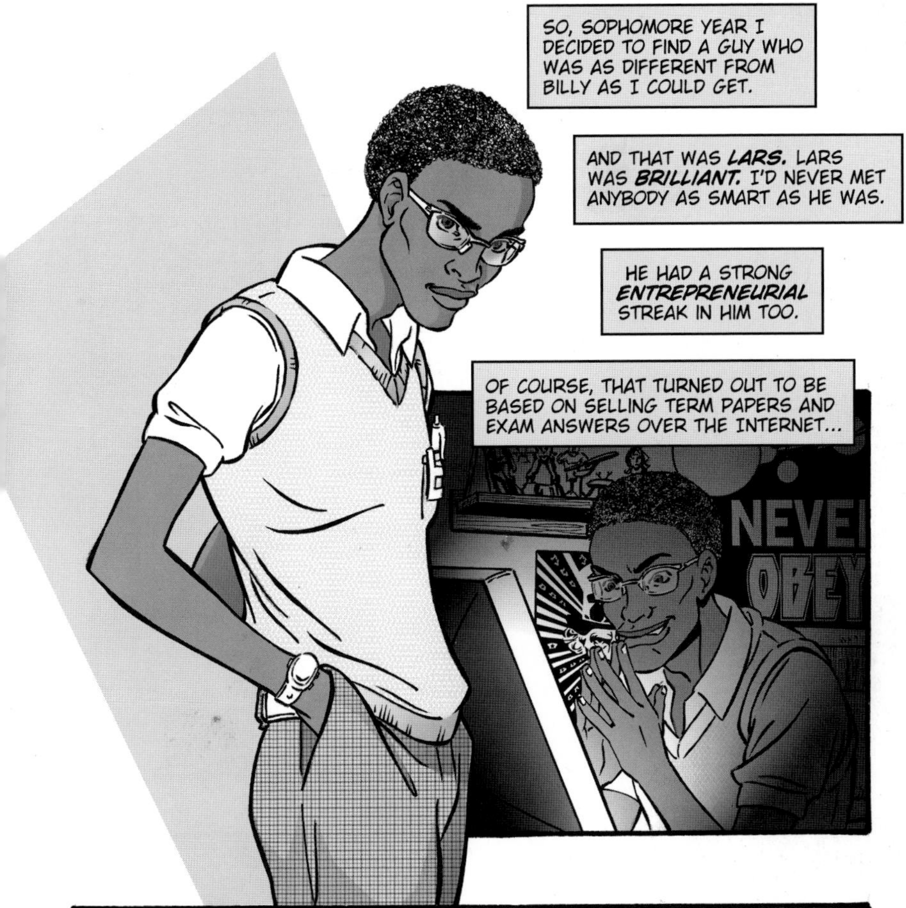
SO, SOPHOMORE YEAR I DECIDED TO FIND A GUY WHO WAS AS DIFFERENT FROM BILLY AS I COULD GET.
AND THAT WAS LARS. LARS WAS BRILLIANT. I'D NEVER MET ANYBODY AS SMART AS HE WAS.
HE HAD A STRONG ENTREPRENEURIAL STREAK IN HIM TOO.
OF COURSE, THAT TURNED OUT TO BE BASED ON SELLING TERM PAPERS AND EXAM ANSWERS OVER THE INTERNET...
NEVE
OBEY

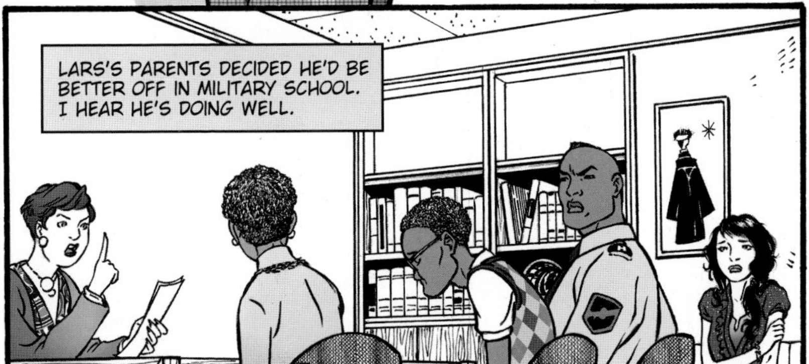
LARS'S PARENTS DECIDED HE'D BE BETTER OFF IN MILITARY SCHOOL. I HEAR HE'S DOING WELL.

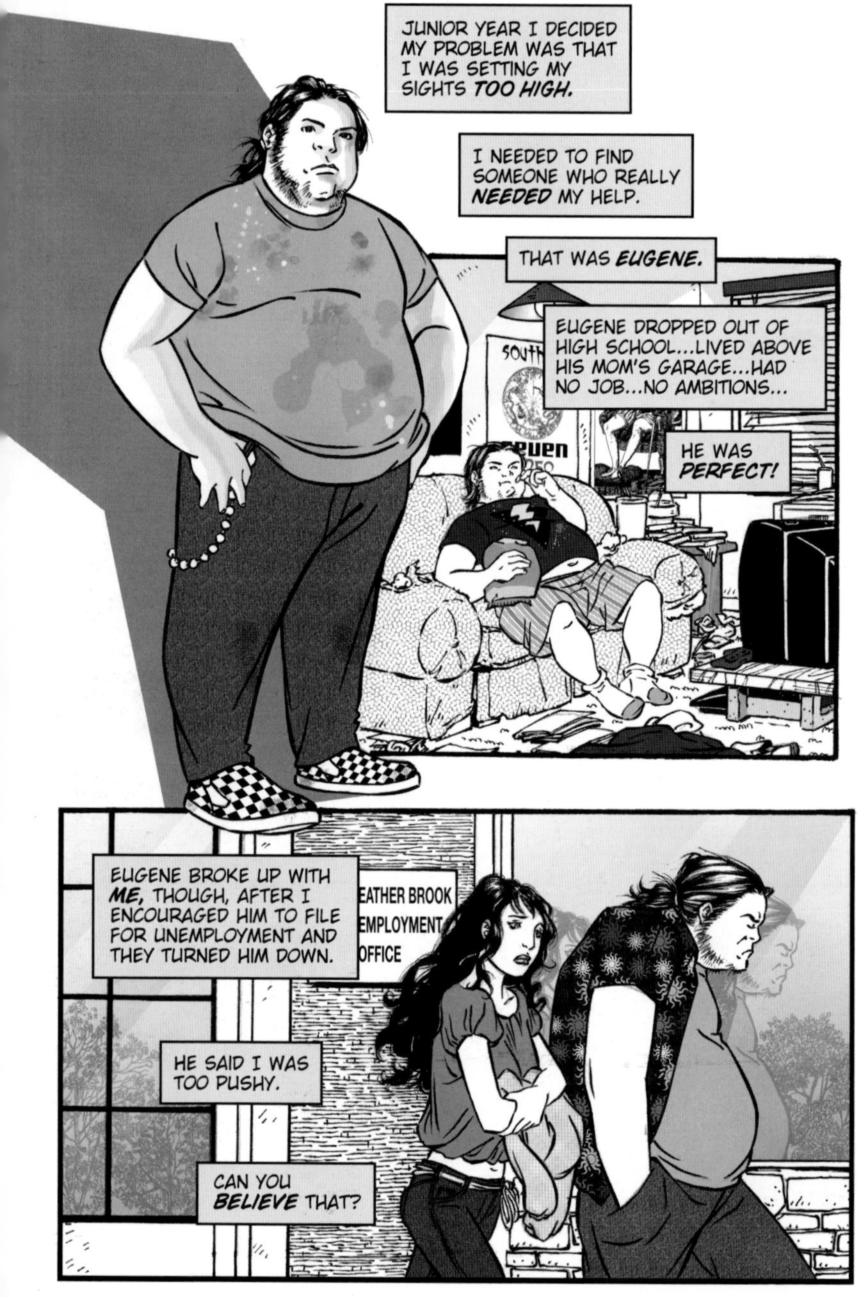
JUNIOR YEAR I DECIDED MY PROBLEM WAS THAT I WAS SETTING MY SIGHTS TOO HIGH.
I NEEDED TO FIND SOMEONE WHO REALLY NEEDED MY HELP.
THAT WAS EUGENE.
EUGENE DROPPED OUT OF HIGH SCHOOL...LIVED ABOVE HIS MOM'S GARAGE...HAD NO JOB...NO AMBITIONS...
HE WAS PERFECT!
EUGENE BROKE UP WITH ME, THOUGH, AFTER I ENCOURAGED HIM TO FILE FOR UNEMPLOYMENT AND THEY TURNED HIM DOWN.
EATHER BROOK
EMPLOYMENT
OFFICE
HE SAID I WAS TOO PUSHY.
CAN YOU BELIEVE THAT?

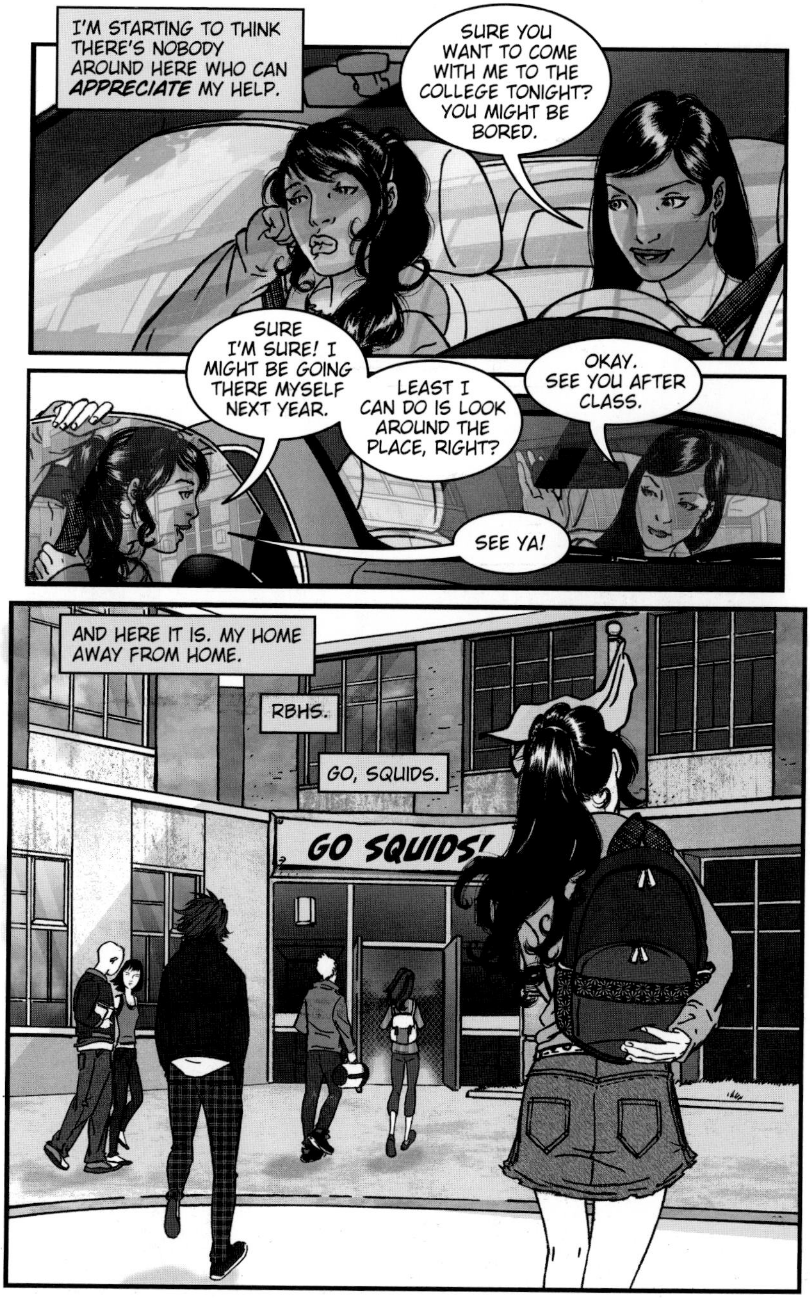

I'M STARTING TO THINK THERE'S NOBODY AROUND HERE WHO CAN *APPRECIATE* MY HELP.
SURE YOU WANT TO COME WITH ME TO THE COLLEGE TONIGHT? YOU MIGHT BE BORED.
SURE I'M SURE! I MIGHT BE GOING THERE MYSELF NEXT YEAR.
LEAST I CAN DO IS LOOK AROUND THE PLACE, RIGHT?
OKAY. SEE YOU AFTER CLASS.
SEE YA!
AND HERE IT IS. MY HOME AWAY FROM HOME.
RBHS.
GO, SQUIDS.
GO SQUIDS!

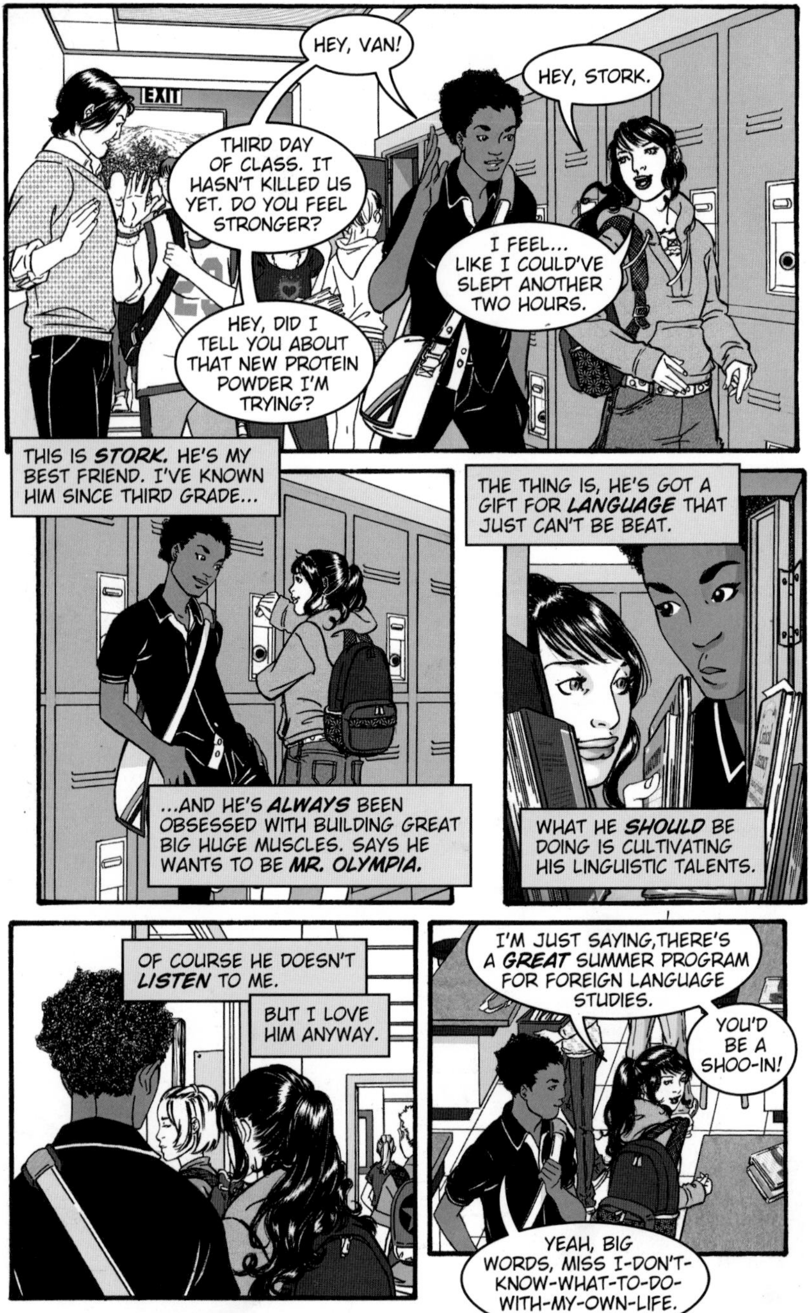
HEY, VAN!
HEY, STORK.
THIRD DAY OF CLASS. IT HASN'T KILLED US YET. DO YOU FEEL STRONGER?
I FEEL... LIKE I COULD'VE SLEPT ANOTHER TWO HOURS.
HEY, DID I TELL YOU ABOUT THAT NEW PROTEIN POWDER I'M TRYING?
EXIT
THIS IS STORK. HE'S MY BEST FRIEND. I'VE KNOWN HIM SINCE THIRD GRADE...
...AND HE'S ALWAYS BEEN OBSESSED WITH BUILDING GREAT BIG HUGE MUSCLES. SAYS HE WANTS TO BE MR. OLYMPIA.
THE THING IS, HE'S GOT A GIFT FOR LANGUAGE THAT JUST CAN'T BE BEAT.
WHAT HE SHOULD BE DOING IS CULTIVATING HIS LINGUISTIC TALENTS.
OF COURSE HE DOESN'T LISTEN TO ME.
BUT I LOVE HIM ANYWAY.
I'M JUST SAYING,THERE'S A GREAT SUMMER PROGRAM FOR FOREIGN LANGUAGE STUDIES.
YOU'D BE A SHOO-IN!
YEAH, BIG WORDS, MISS I-DON'T-KNOW-WHAT-TO-DO-WITH-MY-OWN-LIFE.

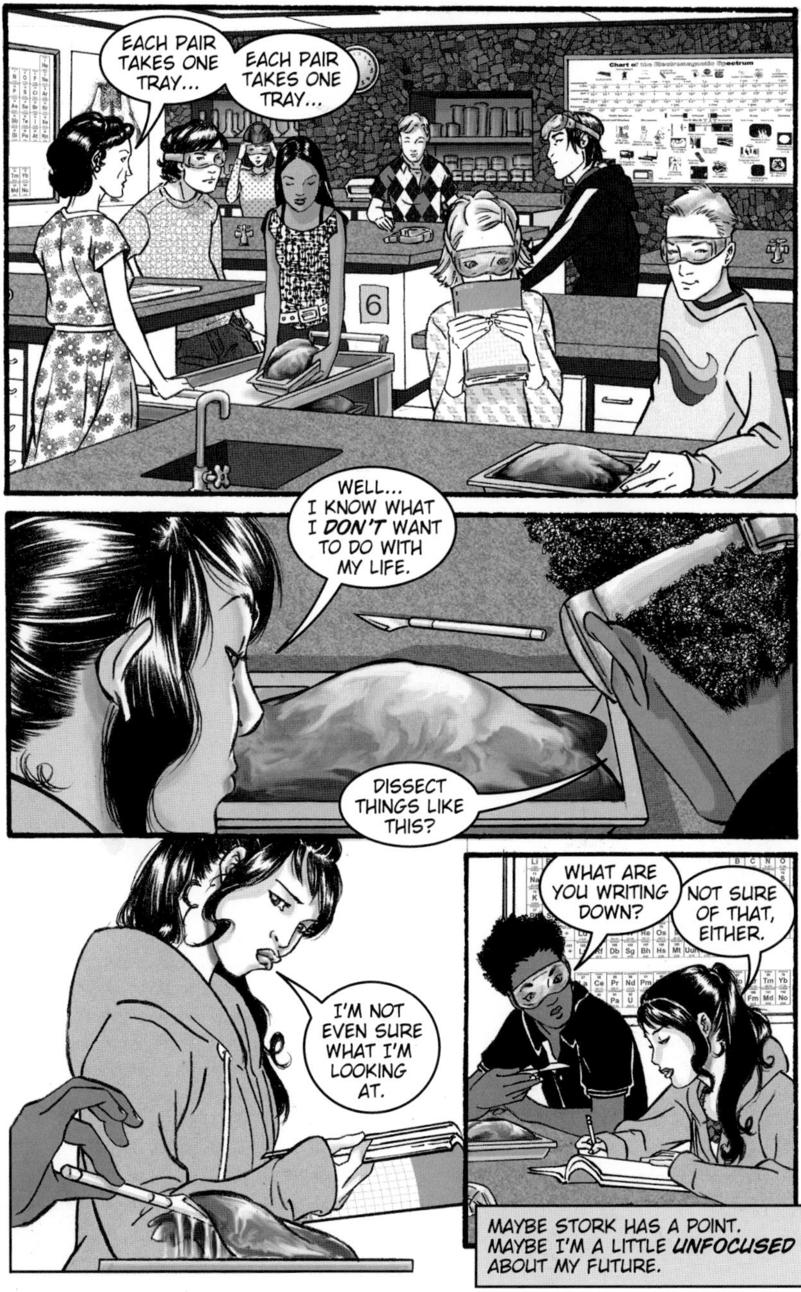
EACH PAIR TAKES ONE TRAY...
EACH PAIR TAKES ONE TRAY...
WELL... I KNOW WHAT I DON'T WANT TO DO WITH MY LIFE.
DISSECT THINGS LIKE THIS?
I'M NOT EVEN SURE WHAT I'M LOOKING AT.
WHAT ARE YOU WRITING DOWN?
NOT SURE OF THAT, EITHER.
MAYBE STORK HAS A POINT. MAYBE I'M A LITTLE UNFOCUSED ABOUT MY FUTURE.

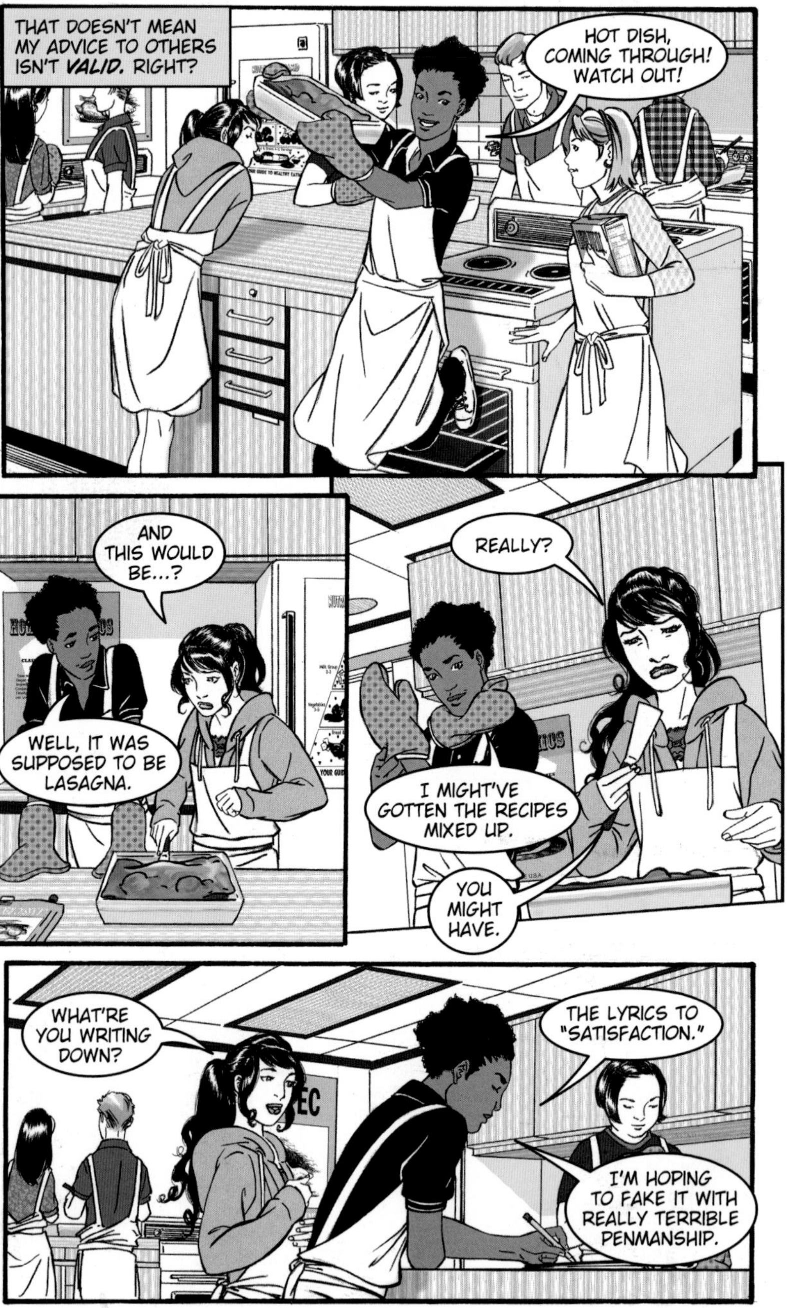
THAT DOESN'T MEAN MY ADVICE TO OTHERS ISN'T *VALID.* RIGHT?
HOT DISH, COMING THROUGH! WATCH OUT!
AND THIS WOULD BE...?
WELL, IT WAS SUPPOSED TO BE LASAGNA.
REALLY?
I MIGHT'VE GOTTEN THE RECIPES MIXED UP.
YOU MIGHT HAVE.
WHAT'RE YOU WRITING DOWN?
THE LYRICS TO "SATISFACTION."
I'M HOPING TO FAKE IT WITH REALLY TERRIBLE PENMANSHIP.

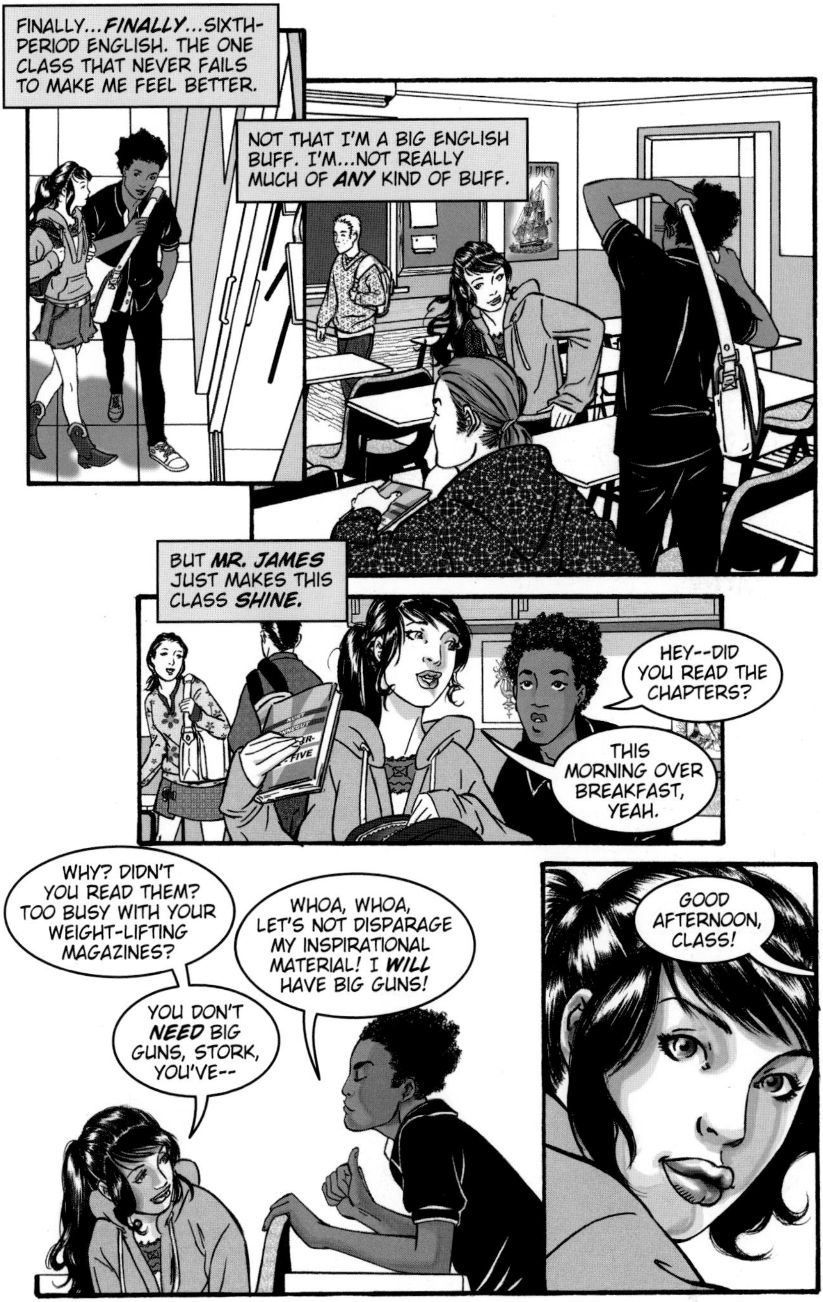

FINALLY...*FINALLY*...SIXTH-PERIOD ENGLISH. THE ONE CLASS THAT NEVER FAILS TO MAKE ME FEEL BETTER.
NOT THAT I'M A BIG ENGLISH BUFF. I'M...NOT REALLY MUCH OF *ANY* KIND OF BUFF.
BUT *MR. JAMES* JUST MAKES THIS CLASS *SHINE.*
HEY--DID YOU READ THE CHAPTERS?
THIS MORNING OVER BREAKFAST, YEAH.
WHY? DIDN'T YOU READ THEM? TOO BUSY WITH YOUR WEIGHT-LIFTING MAGAZINES?
WHOA, WHOA, LET'S NOT DISPARAGE MY INSPIRATIONAL MATERIAL! I *WILL* HAVE BIG GUNS!
YOU DON'T *NEED* BIG GUNS, STORK, YOU'VE--
GOOD AFTERNOON, CLASS!

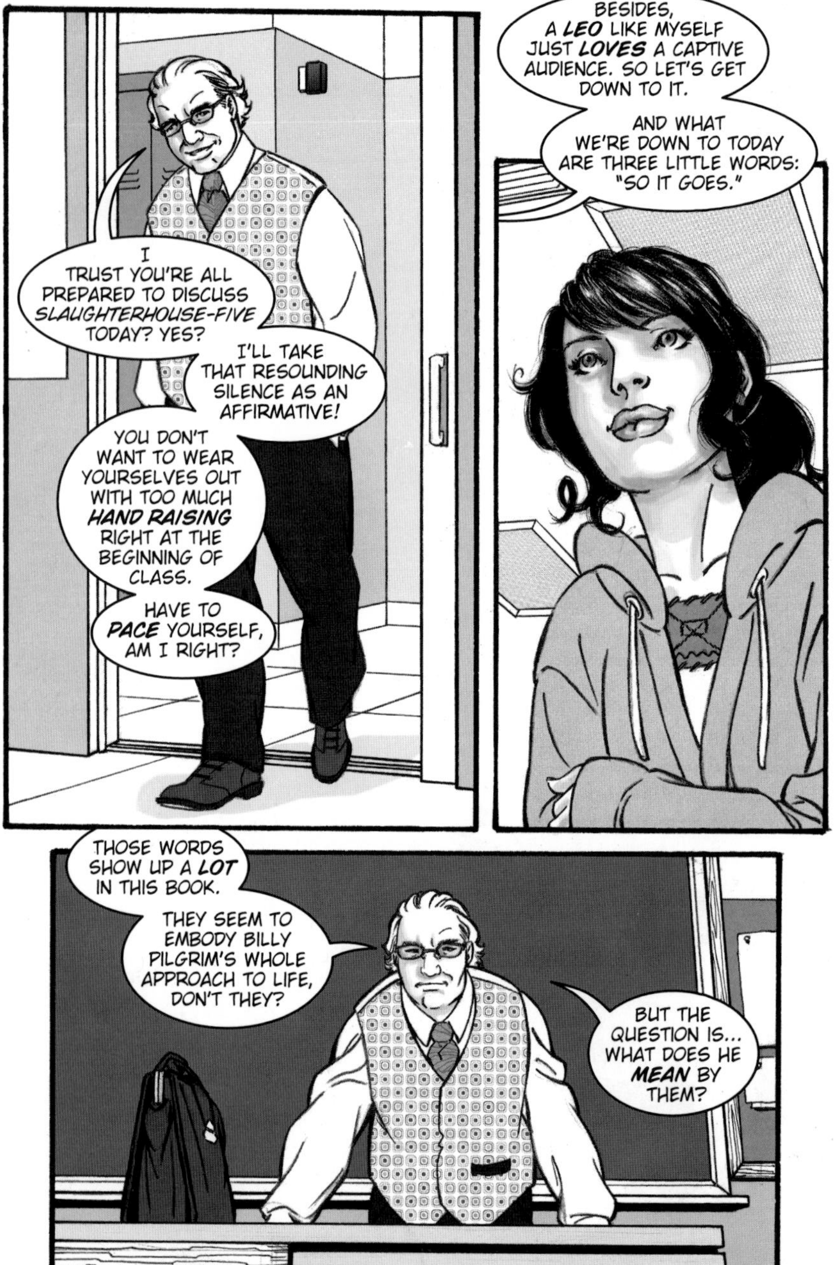
I TRUST YOU'RE ALL PREPARED TO DISCUSS *SLAUGHTERHOUSE-FIVE* TODAY? YES?
I'LL TAKE THAT RESOUNDING SILENCE AS AN AFFIRMATIVE!
YOU DON'T WANT TO WEAR YOURSELVES OUT WITH TOO MUCH ***HAND RAISING*** RIGHT AT THE BEGINNING OF CLASS.
HAVE TO ***PACE*** YOURSELF, AM I RIGHT?
BESIDES, A ***LEO*** LIKE MYSELF JUST ***LOVES*** A CAPTIVE AUDIENCE. SO LET'S GET DOWN TO IT.
AND WHAT WE'RE DOWN TO TODAY ARE THREE LITTLE WORDS: "SO IT GOES."
THOSE WORDS SHOW UP A ***LOT*** IN THIS BOOK.
THEY SEEM TO EMBODY BILLY PILGRIM'S WHOLE APPROACH TO LIFE, DON'T THEY?
BUT THE QUESTION IS... WHAT DOES HE ***MEAN*** BY THEM?

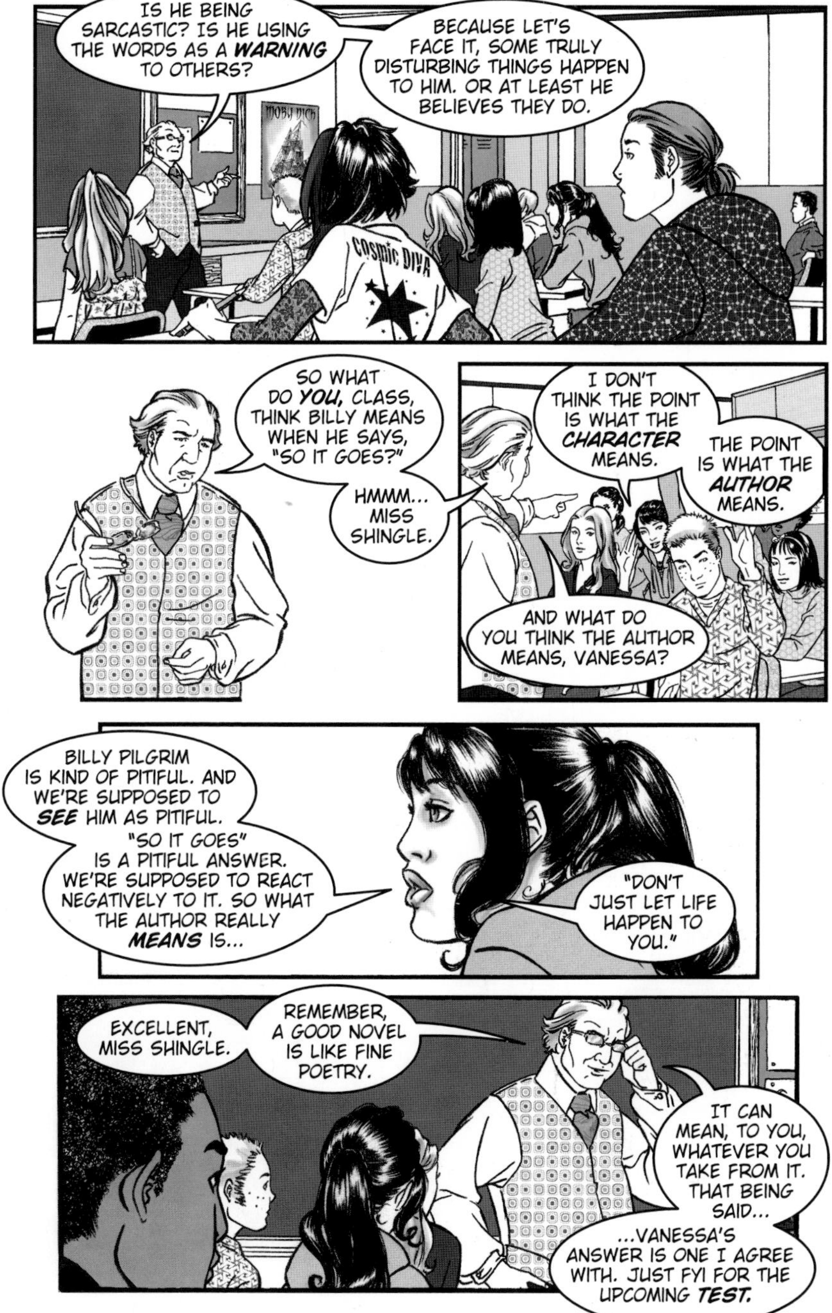
IS HE BEING SARCASTIC? IS HE USING THE WORDS AS A WARNING TO OTHERS?
BECAUSE LET'S FACE IT, SOME TRULY DISTURBING THINGS HAPPEN TO HIM. OR AT LEAST HE BELIEVES THEY DO.
MOBY DICK
COSMIC DIVA
SO WHAT DO YOU, CLASS, THINK BILLY MEANS WHEN HE SAYS, "SO IT GOES?"
HMMM... MISS SHINGLE.
I DON'T THINK THE POINT IS WHAT THE CHARACTER MEANS.
THE POINT IS WHAT THE AUTHOR MEANS.
AND WHAT DO YOU THINK THE AUTHOR MEANS, VANESSA?
BILLY PILGRIM IS KIND OF PITIFUL. AND WE'RE SUPPOSED TO SEE HIM AS PITIFUL.
"SO IT GOES" IS A PITIFUL ANSWER. WE'RE SUPPOSED TO REACT NEGATIVELY TO IT. SO WHAT THE AUTHOR REALLY MEANS IS...
"DON'T JUST LET LIFE HAPPEN TO YOU."
EXCELLENT, MISS SHINGLE.
REMEMBER, A GOOD NOVEL IS LIKE FINE POETRY.
IT CAN MEAN, TO YOU, WHATEVER YOU TAKE FROM IT. THAT BEING SAID...
...VANESSA'S ANSWER IS ONE I AGREE WITH. JUST FYI FOR THE UPCOMING TEST.

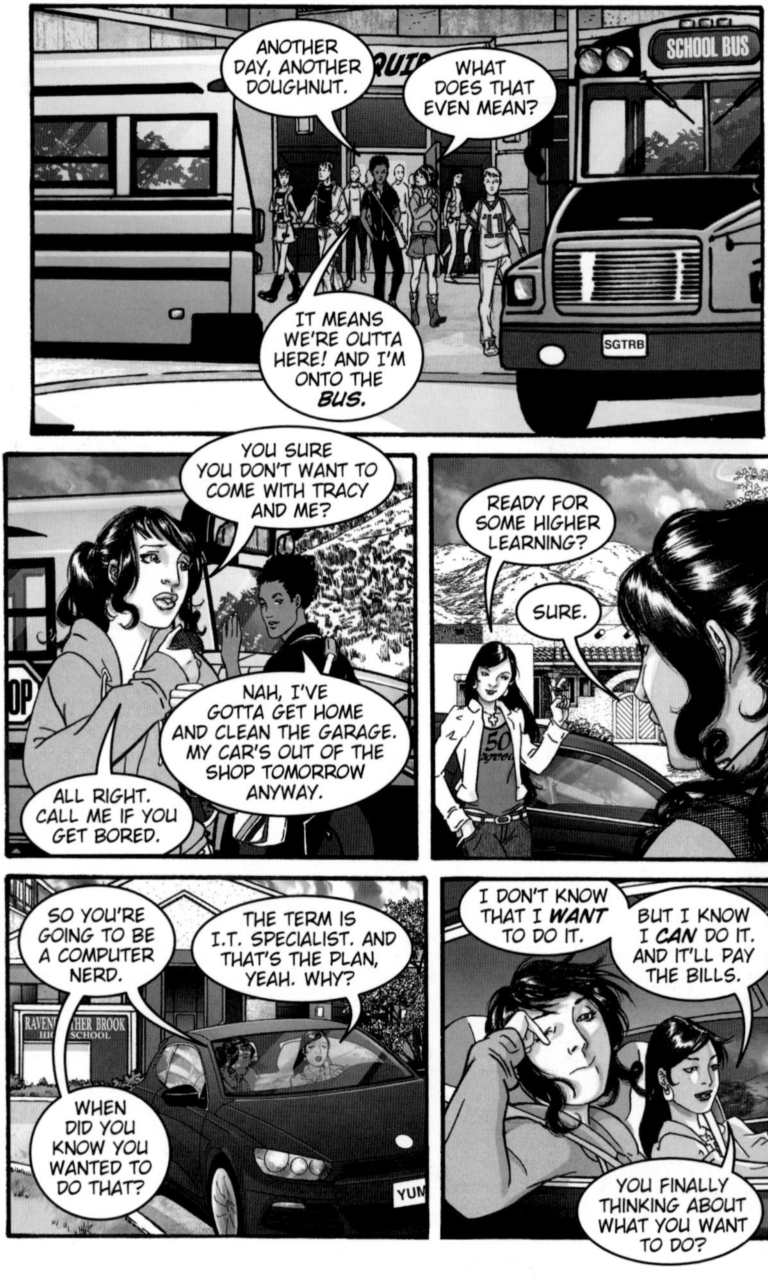

SCHOOL BUS
ANOTHER DAY, ANOTHER DOUGHNUT.
WHAT DOES THAT EVEN MEAN?
IT MEANS WE'RE OUTTA HERE! AND I'M ONTO THE *BUS.*
SGTRB
YOU SURE YOU DON'T WANT TO COME WITH TRACY AND ME?
NAH, I'VE GOTTA GET HOME AND CLEAN THE GARAGE. MY CAR'S OUT OF THE SHOP TOMORROW ANYWAY.
ALL RIGHT. CALL ME IF YOU GET BORED.
READY FOR SOME HIGHER LEARNING?
SURE.
SO YOU'RE GOING TO BE A COMPUTER NERD.
THE TERM IS I.T. SPECIALIST. AND THAT'S THE PLAN, YEAH. WHY?
WHEN DID YOU KNOW YOU WANTED TO DO THAT?
YUM
I DON'T KNOW THAT I *WANT* TO DO IT.
BUT I KNOW I *CAN* DO IT. AND IT'LL PAY THE BILLS.
YOU FINALLY THINKING ABOUT WHAT YOU WANT TO DO?

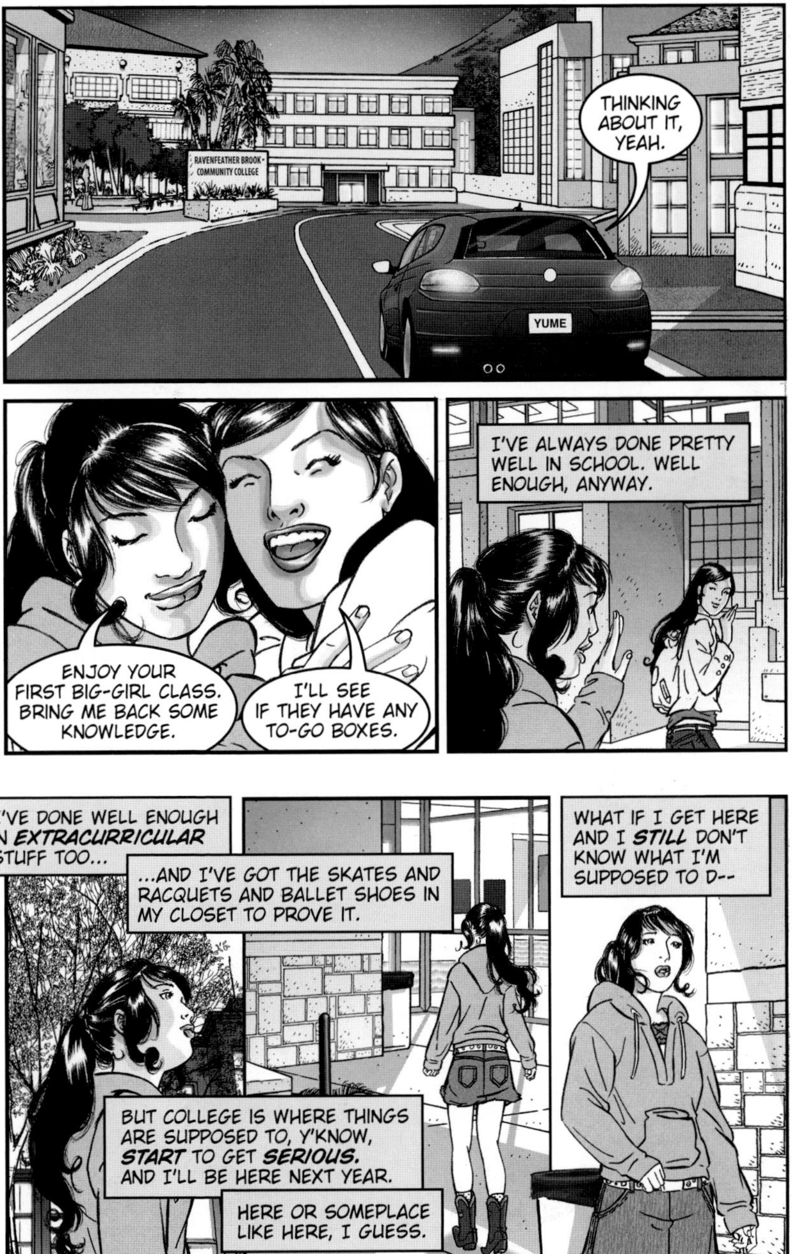
RAVENFEATHER BROOK COMMUNITY COLLEGE
THINKING ABOUT IT, YEAH.
YUME
ENJOY YOUR FIRST BIG-GIRL CLASS. BRING ME BACK SOME KNOWLEDGE.
I'LL SEE IF THEY HAVE ANY TO-GO BOXES.
I'VE ALWAYS DONE PRETTY WELL IN SCHOOL. WELL ENOUGH, ANYWAY.
I'VE DONE WELL ENOUGH IN *EXTRACURRICULAR* STUFF TOO...
...AND I'VE GOT THE SKATES AND RACQUETS AND BALLET SHOES IN MY CLOSET TO PROVE IT.
BUT COLLEGE IS WHERE THINGS ARE SUPPOSED TO, Y'KNOW, *START* TO GET *SERIOUS.* AND I'LL BE HERE NEXT YEAR.
HERE OR SOMEPLACE LIKE HERE, I GUESS.
WHAT IF I GET HERE AND I *STILL* DON'T KNOW WHAT I'M SUPPOSED TO D--

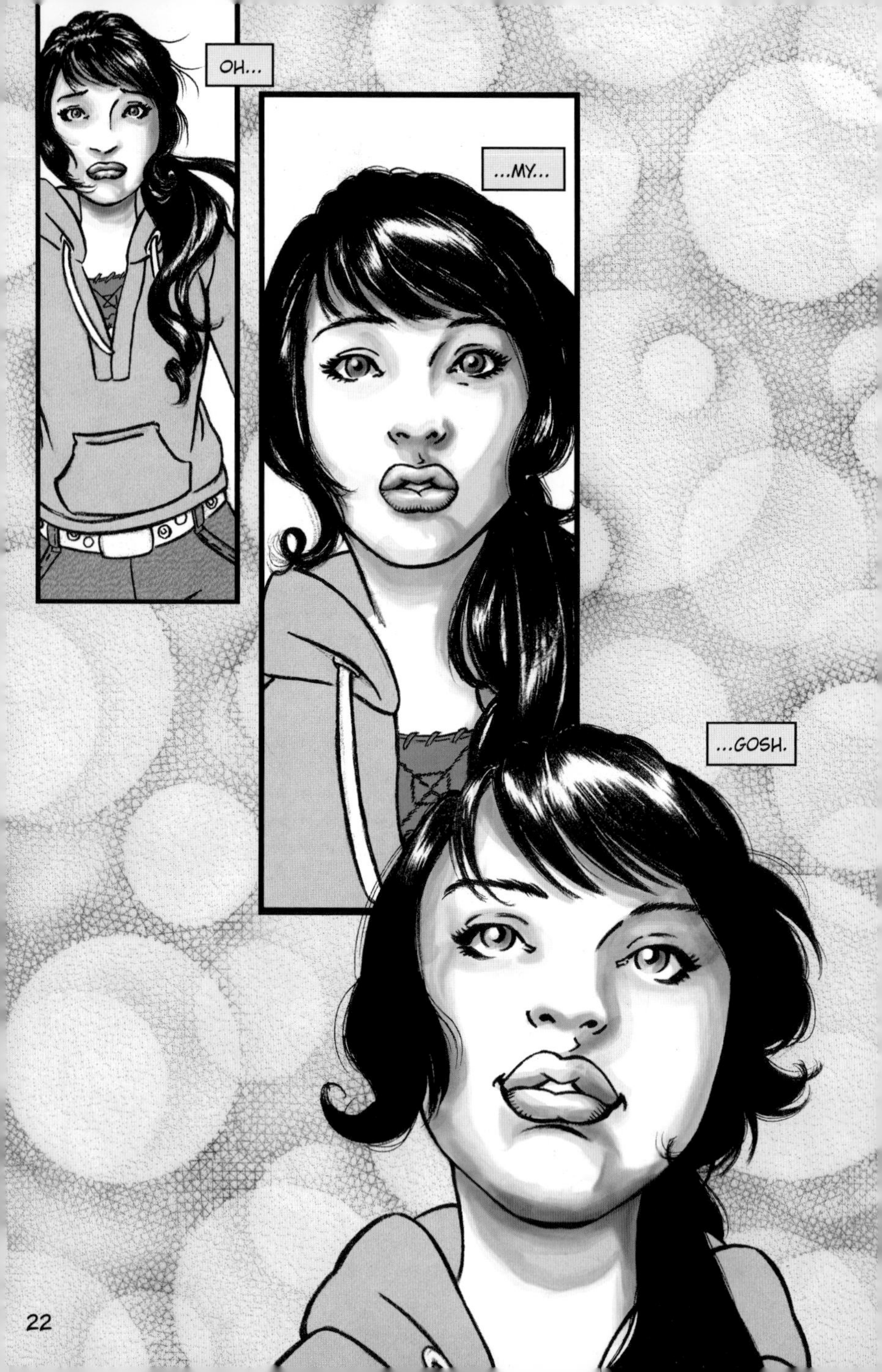
OH...
...MY...
...GOSH.

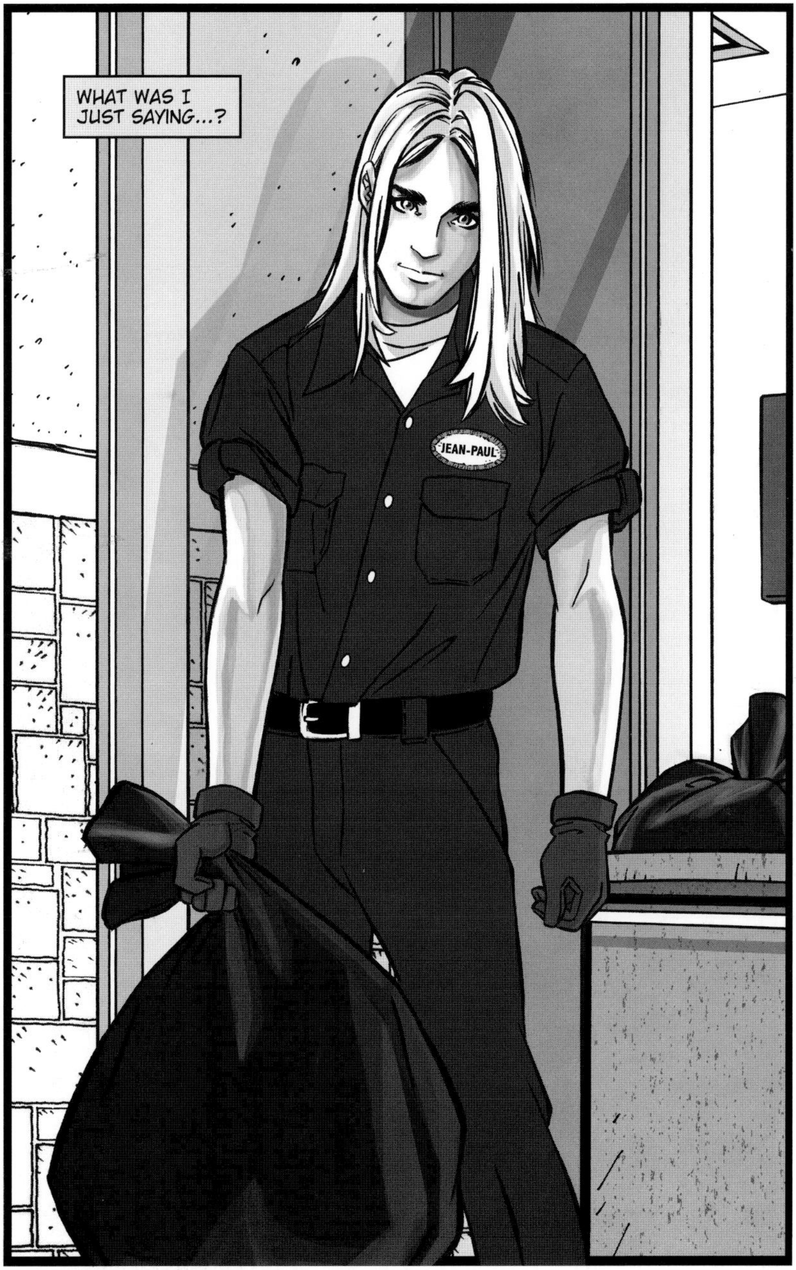
WHAT WAS I JUST SAYING...?
JEAN-PAUL

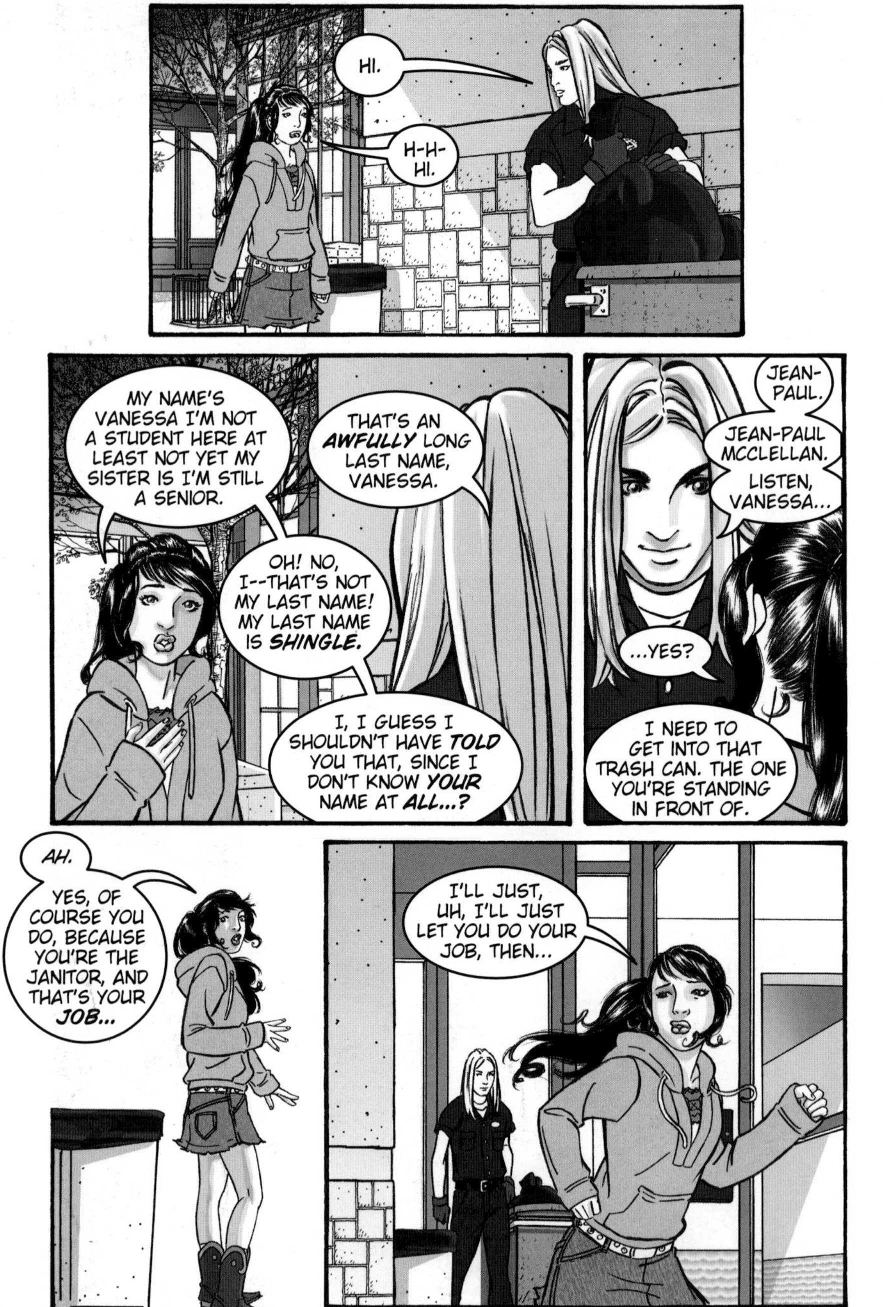
HI.
H-H-HI.
MY NAME'S VANESSA I'M NOT A STUDENT HERE AT LEAST NOT YET MY SISTER IS I'M STILL A SENIOR.
THAT'S AN AWFULLY LONG LAST NAME, VANESSA.
OH! NO, I--THAT'S NOT MY LAST NAME! MY LAST NAME IS SHINGLE.
I, I GUESS I SHOULDN'T HAVE TOLD YOU THAT, SINCE I DON'T KNOW YOUR NAME AT ALL...?
JEAN-PAUL.
JEAN-PAUL MCCLELLAN.
LISTEN, VANESSA...
...YES?
I NEED TO GET INTO THAT TRASH CAN. THE ONE YOU'RE STANDING IN FRONT OF.
AH.
YES, OF COURSE YOU DO, BECAUSE YOU'RE THE JANITOR, AND THAT'S YOUR JOB...
I'LL JUST, UH, I'LL JUST LET YOU DO YOUR JOB, THEN...

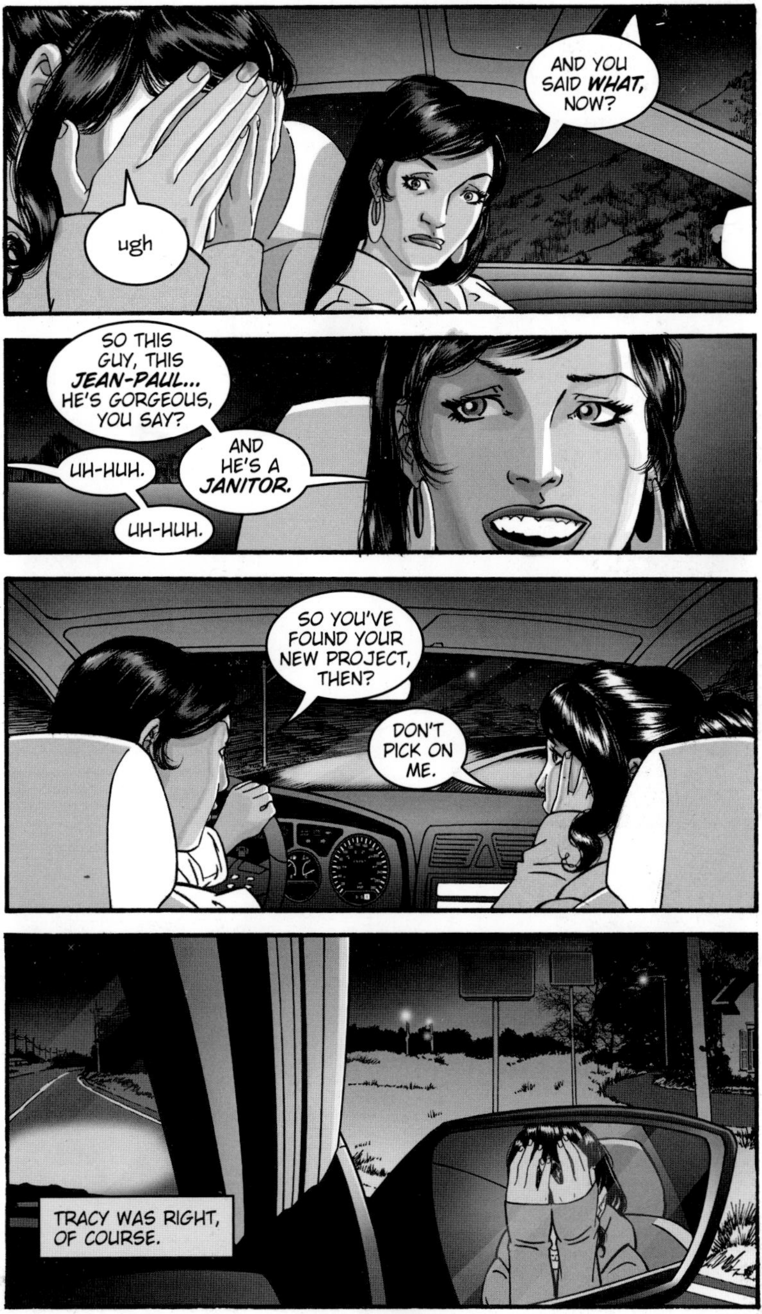

AND YOU SAID WHAT, NOW?
ugh
SO THIS GUY, THIS JEAN-PAUL... HE'S GORGEOUS, YOU SAY?
UH-HUH.
AND HE'S A JANITOR.
UH-HUH.
SO YOU'VE FOUND YOUR NEW PROJECT, THEN?
DON'T PICK ON ME.
TRACY WAS RIGHT, OF COURSE.

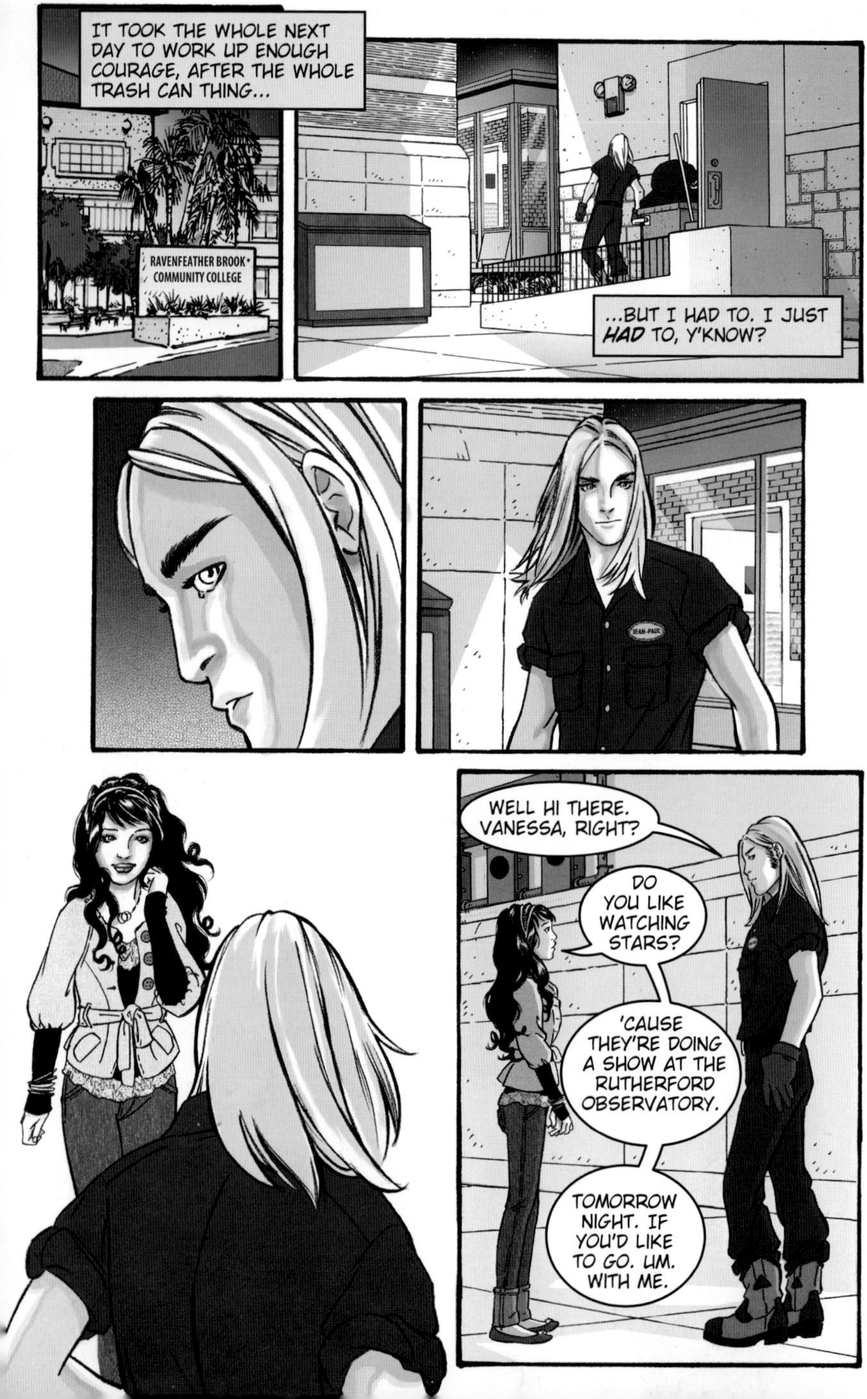

IT TOOK THE WHOLE NEXT DAY TO WORK UP ENOUGH COURAGE, AFTER THE WHOLE TRASH CAN THING...
RAVENFEATHER BROOK COMMUNITY COLLEGE
...BUT I HAD TO. I JUST *HAD* TO, Y'KNOW?
JEAN-PAUL
WELL HI THERE. VANESSA, RIGHT?
DO YOU LIKE WATCHING STARS?
'CAUSE THEY'RE DOING A SHOW AT THE RUTHERFORD OBSERVATORY.
TOMORROW NIGHT. IF YOU'D LIKE TO GO. UM. WITH ME.

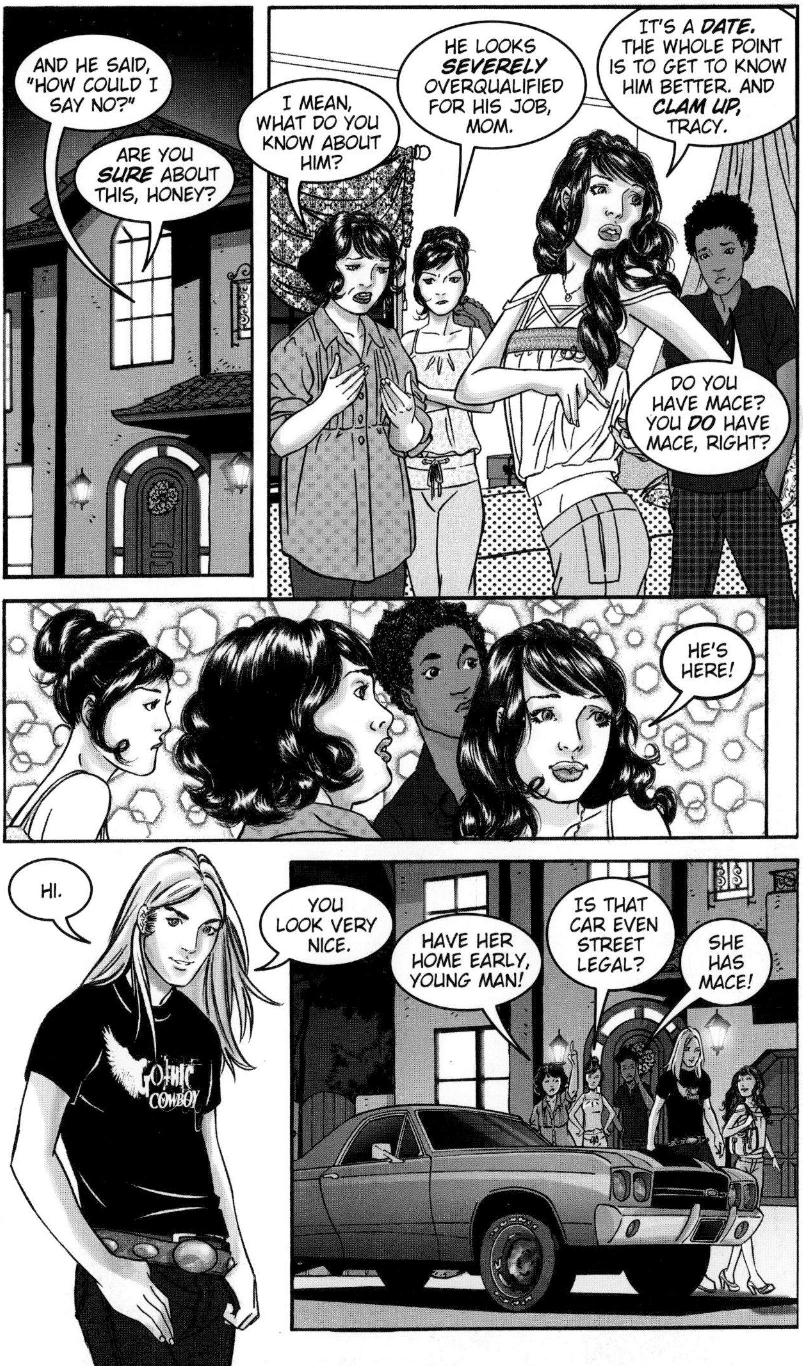

AND HE SAID, "HOW COULD I SAY NO?"
ARE YOU **SURE** ABOUT THIS, HONEY?
I MEAN, WHAT DO YOU KNOW ABOUT HIM?
HE LOOKS **SEVERELY** OVERQUALIFIED FOR HIS JOB, MOM.
IT'S A **DATE.** THE WHOLE POINT IS TO GET TO KNOW HIM BETTER. AND **CLAM UP,** TRACY.
DO YOU HAVE MACE? YOU **DO** HAVE MACE, RIGHT?
HE'S HERE!
HI.
YOU LOOK VERY NICE.
HAVE HER HOME EARLY, YOUNG MAN!
IS THAT CAR EVEN STREET LEGAL?
SHE HAS MACE!
GOTHIC COWBOY

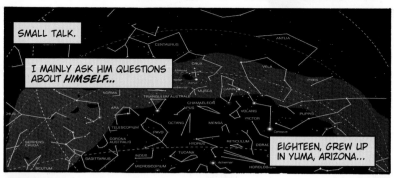

SMALL TALK.

I MAINLY ASK HIM QUESTIONS ABOUT *HIMSELF*...

EIGHTEEN, GREW UP IN YUMA, ARIZONA...

...AND JUST SORT OF DRIFTED FROM ONE JOB TO ANOTHER, LETTING THE WIND TAKE HIM WHEREVER IT CHOSE TO.

THIS WAS KIND OF A BUNGLE ON MY PART, I THINK.

HOW DO YOU MEAN?

WE SHOULD BE SOMEPLACE WHERE WE CAN TALK. I WANT TO KNOW MORE ABOUT YOU...

...YOU CAN ASK ME ANYTHING YOU WANT.

WELL... AFTER THE SHOW...

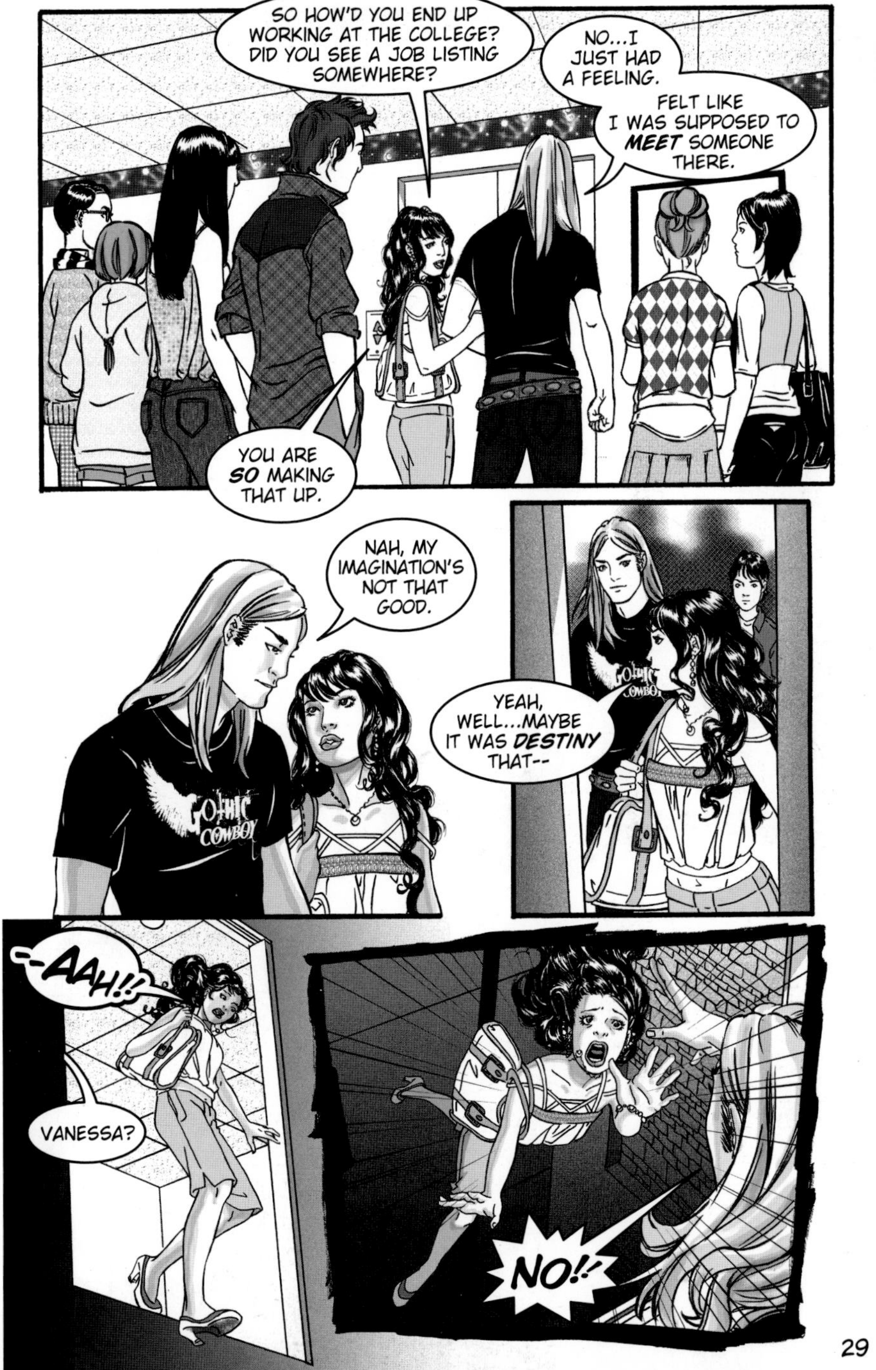
SO HOW'D YOU END UP WORKING AT THE COLLEGE? DID YOU SEE A JOB LISTING SOMEWHERE?
NO...I JUST HAD A FEELING.
FELT LIKE I WAS SUPPOSED TO MEET SOMEONE THERE.
YOU ARE SO MAKING THAT UP.
NAH, MY IMAGINATION'S NOT THAT GOOD.
YEAH, WELL...MAYBE IT WAS DESTINY THAT--
--AAH!!
VANESSA?
NO!!

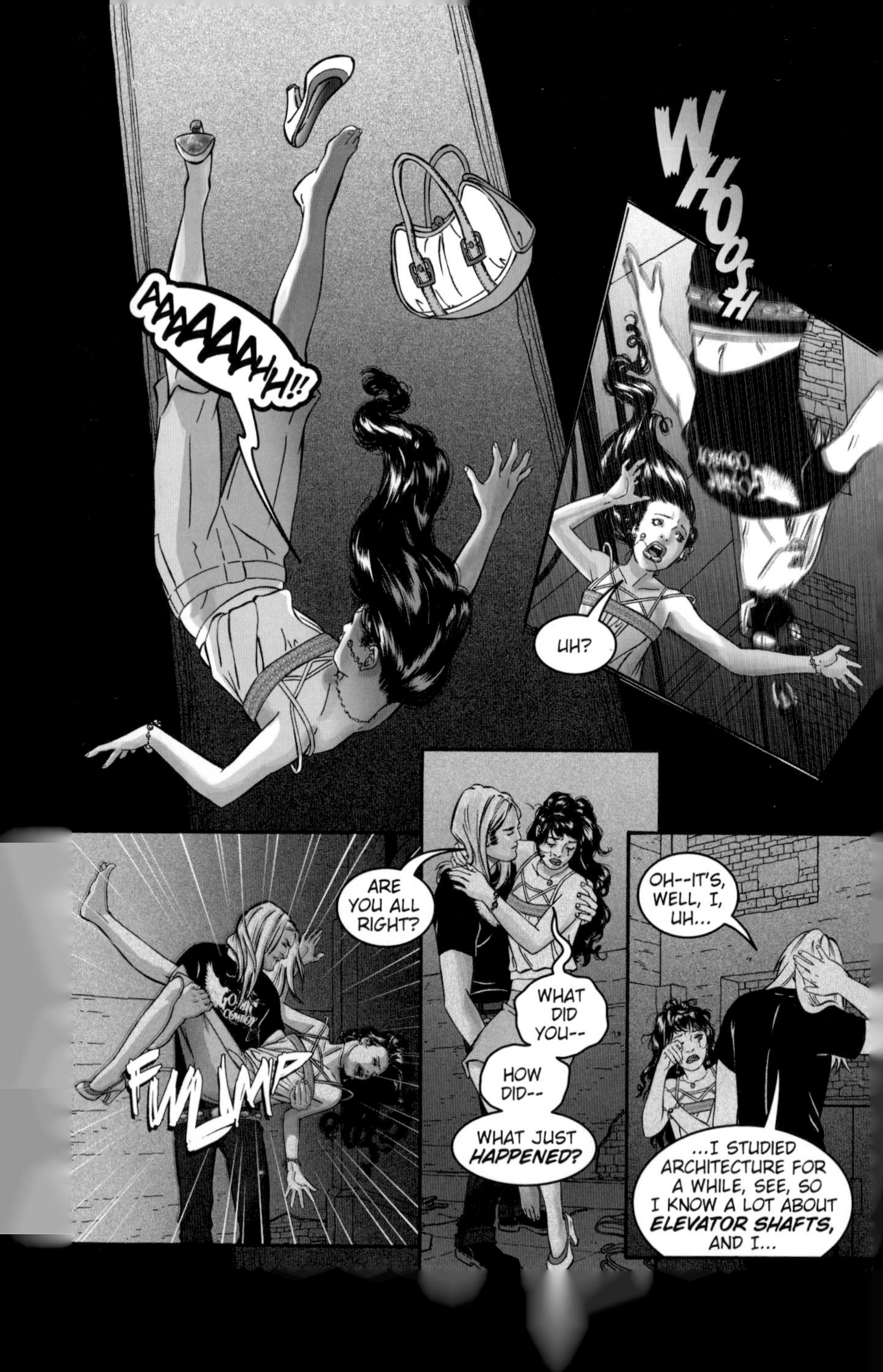
AAAAAAAHH!!
WHOOSH
UH?
FWUMP
ARE YOU ALL RIGHT?
WHAT DID YOU--
HOW DID--
WHAT JUST HAPPENED?
OH--IT'S, WELL, I, UH...
...I STUDIED ARCHITECTURE FOR A WHILE, SEE, SO I KNOW A LOT ABOUT ELEVATOR SHAFTS, AND I...

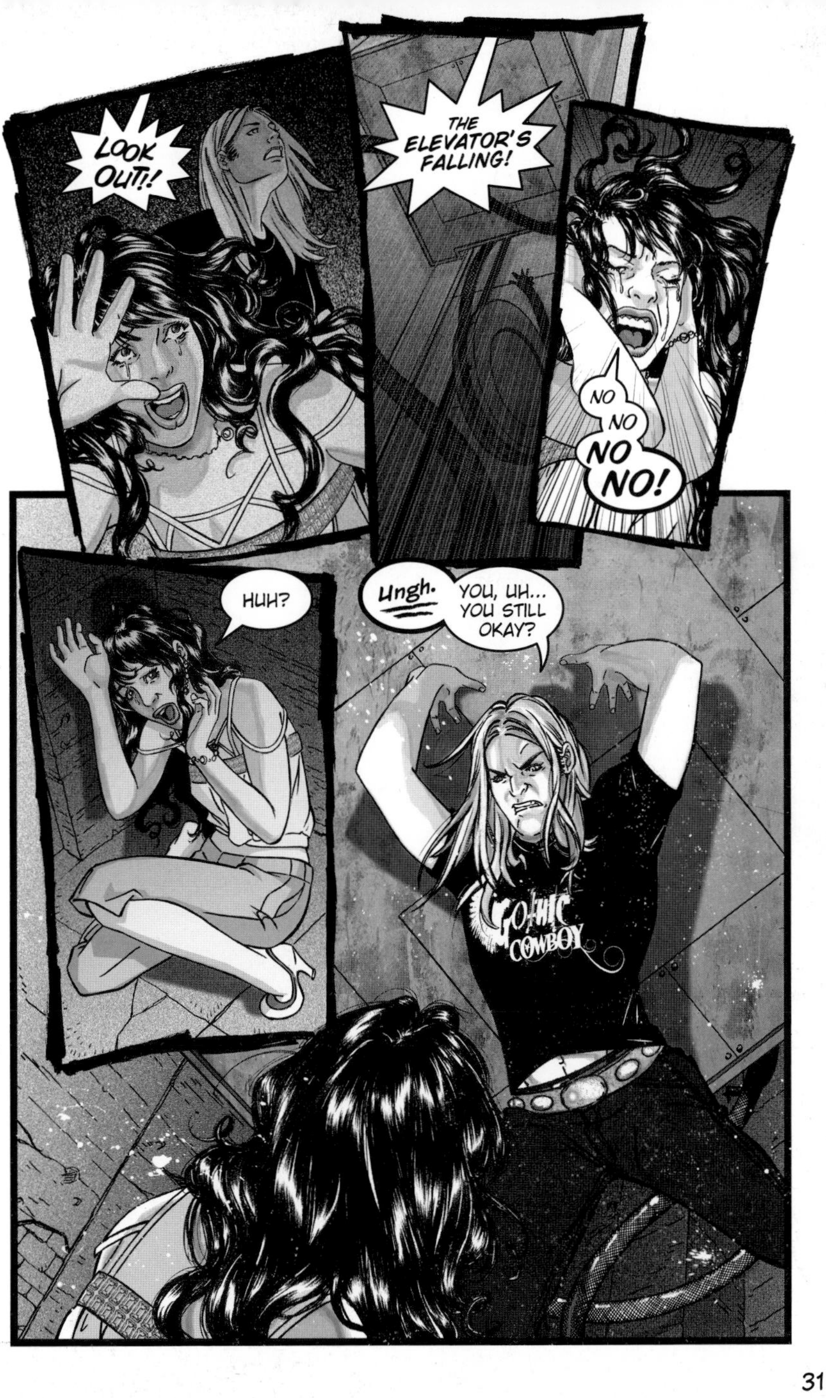
LOOK OUT!!
THE ELEVATOR'S FALLING!
NO NO NO NO!
HUH?
Ungh.
YOU, UH... YOU STILL OKAY?
GOTHIC COWBOY

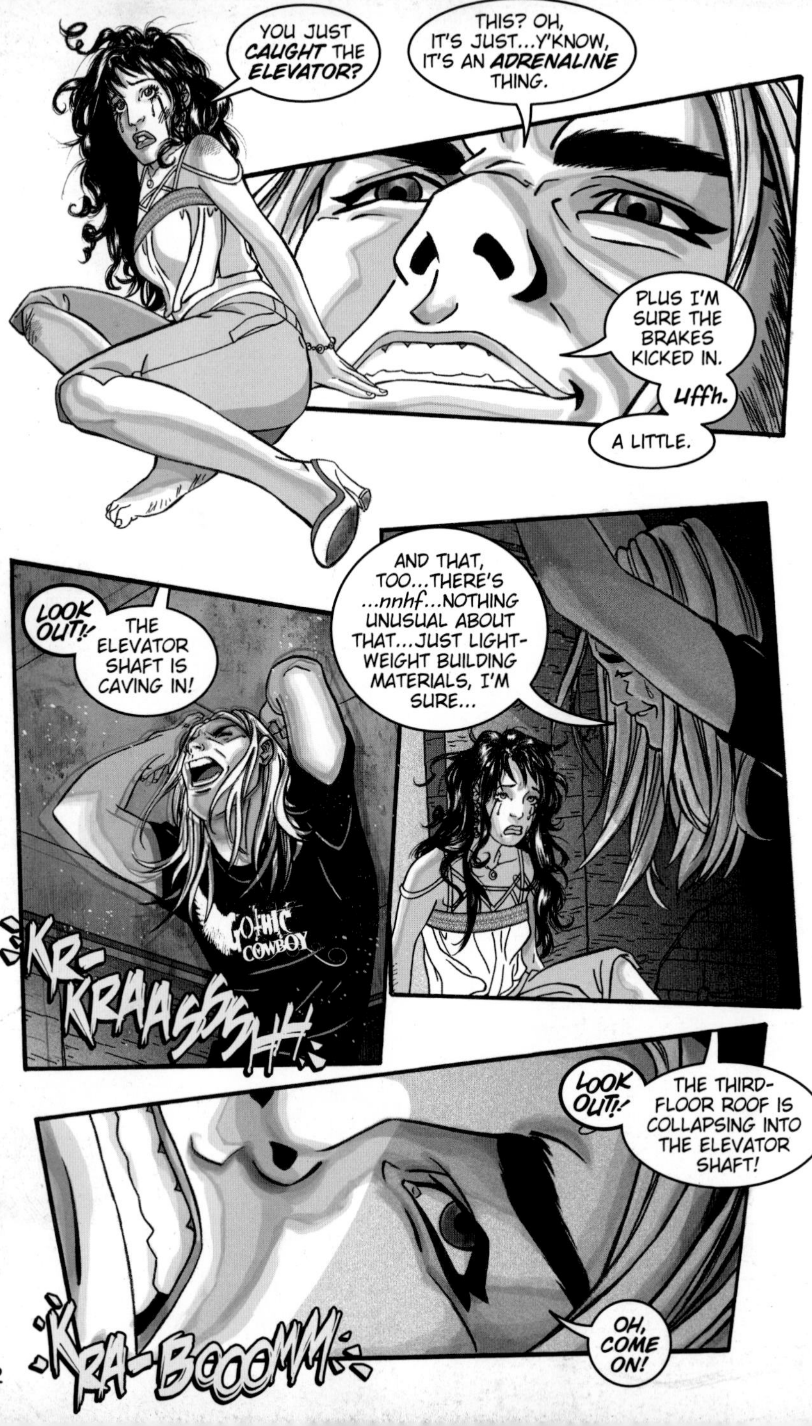
YOU JUST CAUGHT THE ELEVATOR?
THIS? OH, IT'S JUST...Y'KNOW, IT'S AN ADRENALINE THING.
PLUS I'M SURE THE BRAKES KICKED IN.
Uffh.
A LITTLE.
LOOK OUT!!
THE ELEVATOR SHAFT IS CAVING IN!
AND THAT, TOO...THERE'S ...nnhf...NOTHING UNUSUAL ABOUT THAT...JUST LIGHT-WEIGHT BUILDING MATERIALS, I'M SURE...
GOTHIC COWBOY
KR-KRAASSSHH
LOOK OUT!!
THE THIRD-FLOOR ROOF IS COLLAPSING INTO THE ELEVATOR SHAFT!
KRA-BOOOMM
OH, COME ON!

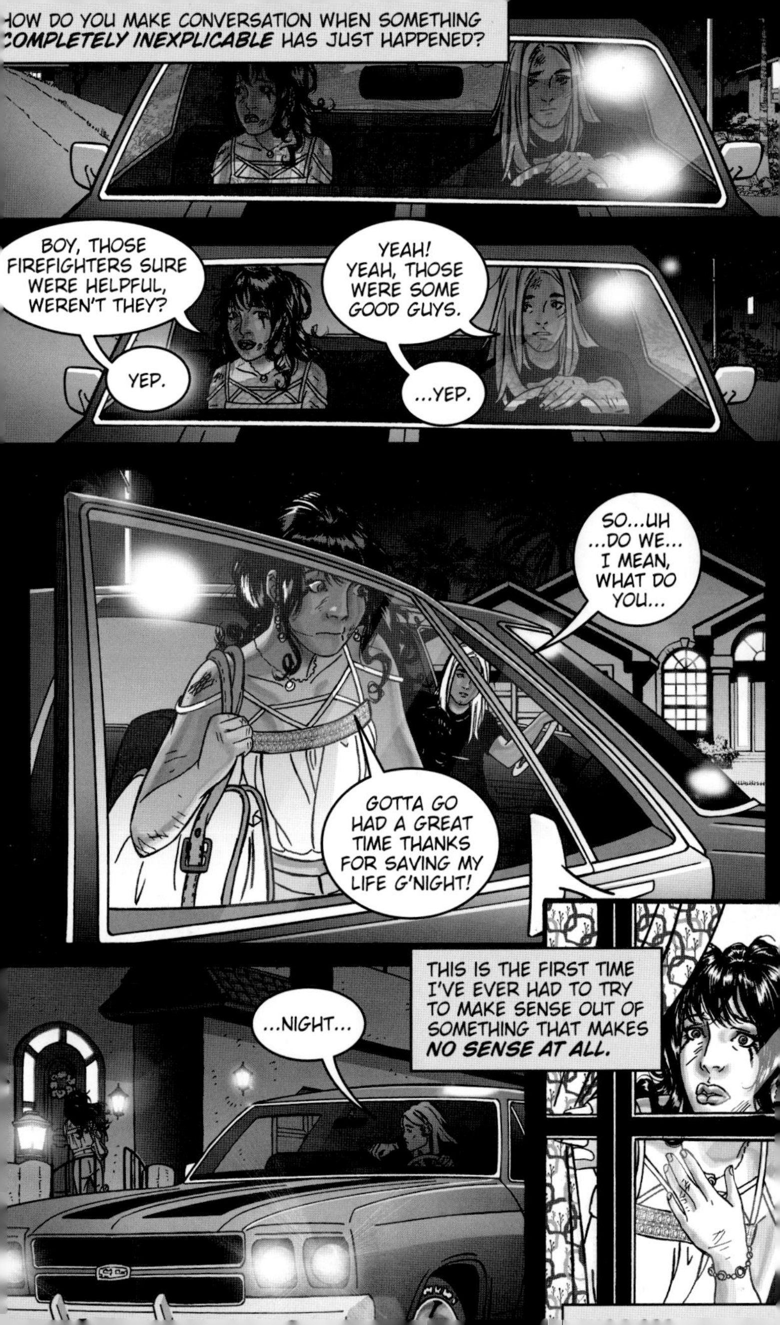
HOW DO YOU MAKE CONVERSATION WHEN SOMETHING COMPLETELY INEXPLICABLE HAS JUST HAPPENED?
BOY, THOSE FIREFIGHTERS SURE WERE HELPFUL, WEREN'T THEY?
YEP.
YEAH! YEAH, THOSE WERE SOME GOOD GUYS.
...YEP.
SO...UH ...DO WE... I MEAN, WHAT DO YOU...
GOTTA GO HAD A GREAT TIME THANKS FOR SAVING MY LIFE G'NIGHT!
...NIGHT...
THIS IS THE FIRST TIME I'VE EVER HAD TO TRY TO MAKE SENSE OUT OF SOMETHING THAT MAKES NO SENSE AT ALL.

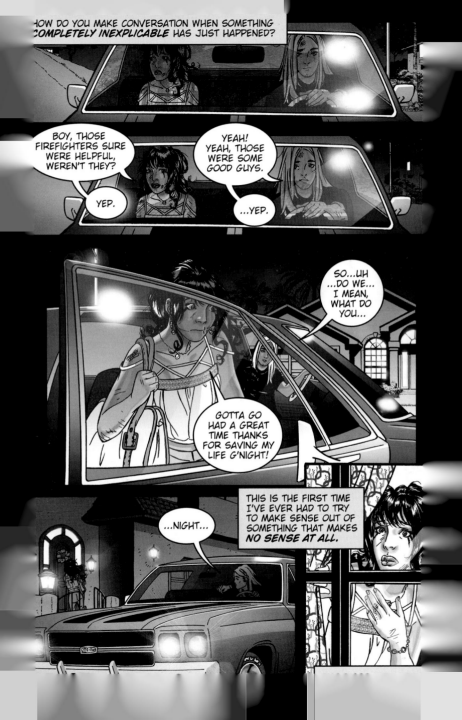

Chapter 2
Personal Grooming

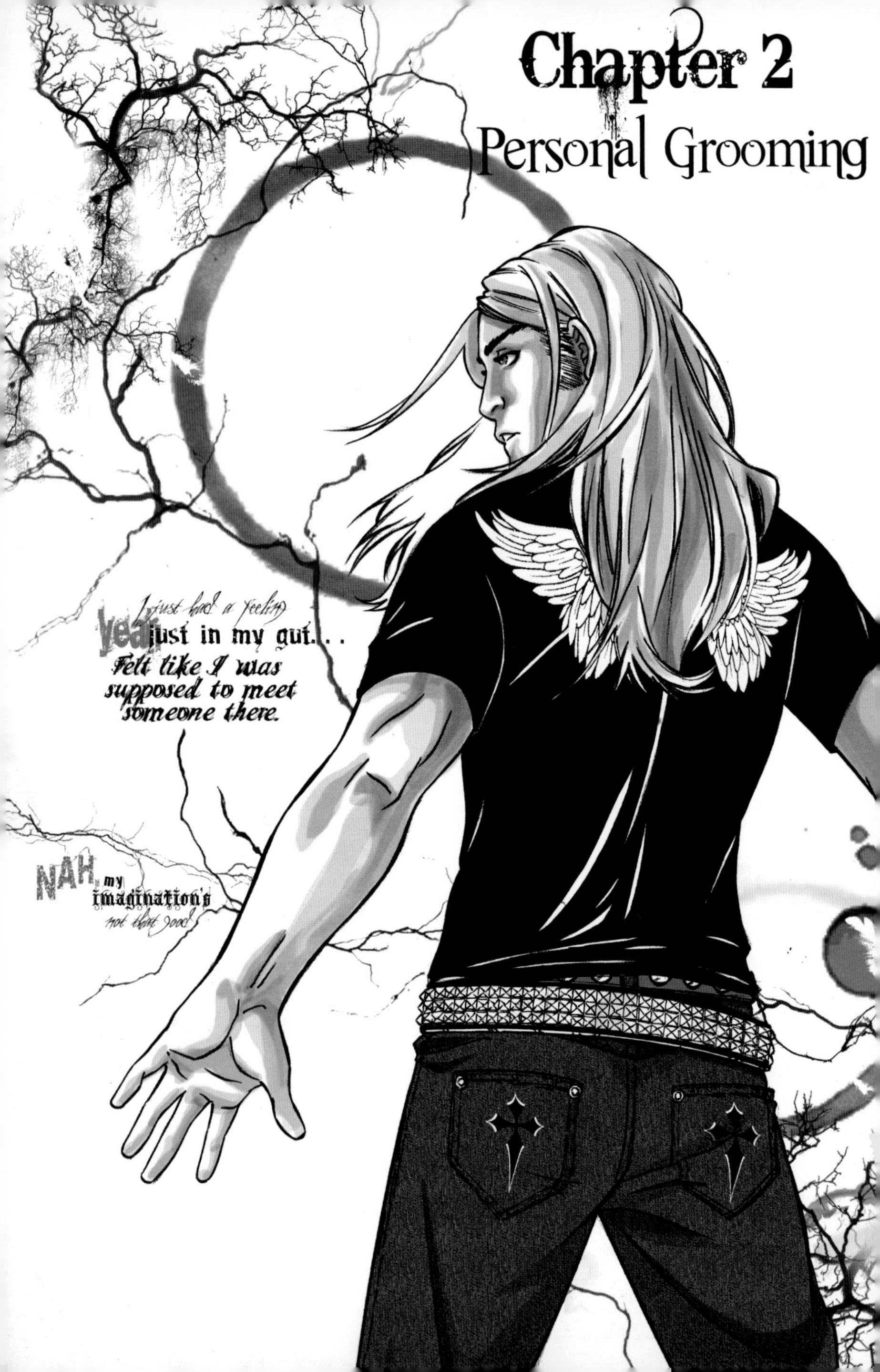
Yeah
I just had a feeling
just in my gut. . .
Felt like I was supposed to meet someone there.
NAH, my imagination's not that good.

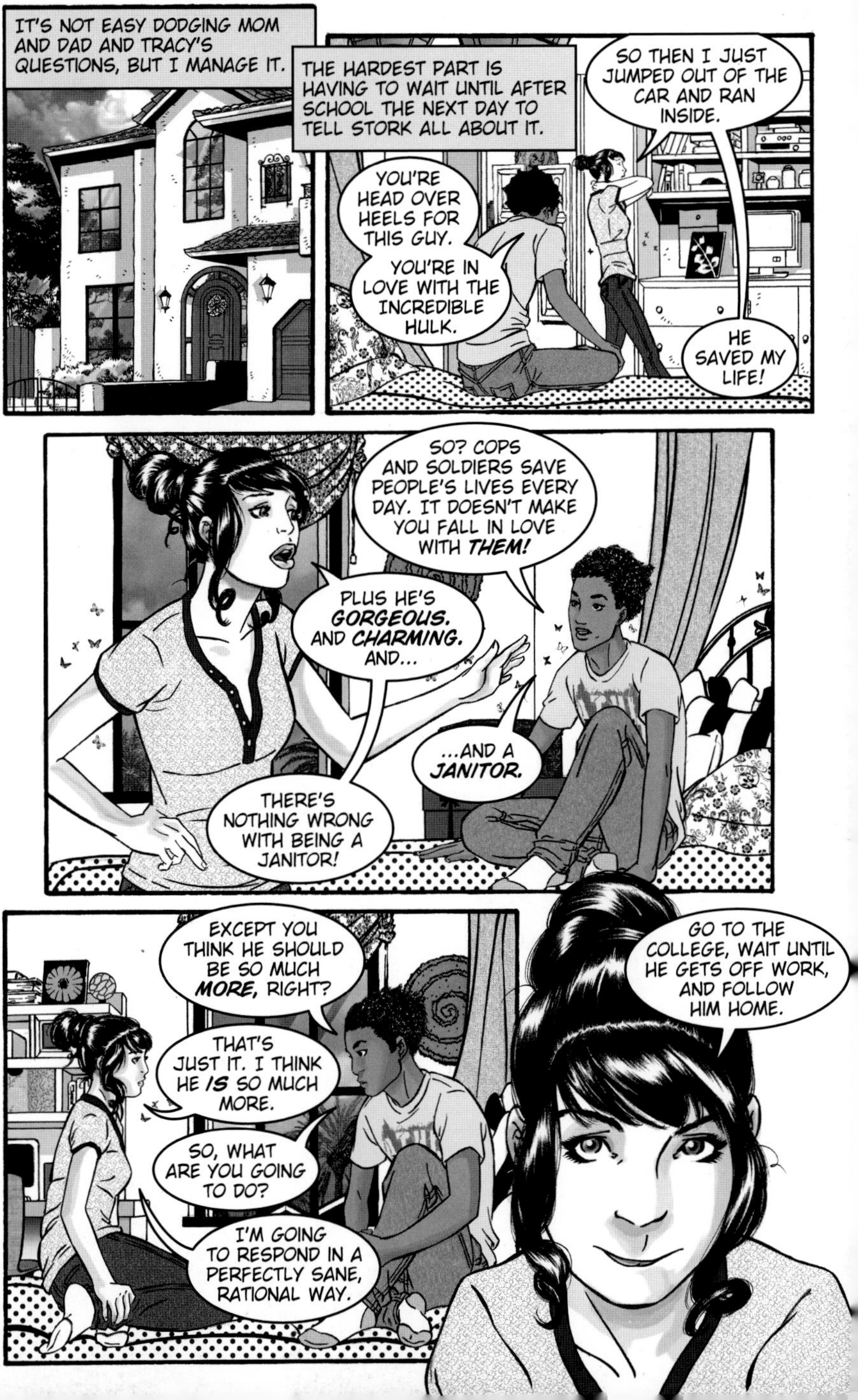
IT'S NOT EASY DODGING MOM AND DAD AND TRACY'S QUESTIONS, BUT I MANAGE IT.
THE HARDEST PART IS HAVING TO WAIT UNTIL AFTER SCHOOL THE NEXT DAY TO TELL STORK ALL ABOUT IT.
SO THEN I JUST JUMPED OUT OF THE CAR AND RAN INSIDE.
YOU'RE HEAD OVER HEELS FOR THIS GUY.
YOU'RE IN LOVE WITH THE INCREDIBLE HULK.
HE SAVED MY LIFE!
SO? COPS AND SOLDIERS SAVE PEOPLE'S LIVES EVERY DAY. IT DOESN'T MAKE YOU FALL IN LOVE WITH *THEM!*
PLUS HE'S *GORGEOUS.* AND *CHARMING.* AND...
...AND A *JANITOR.*
THERE'S NOTHING WRONG WITH BEING A JANITOR!
EXCEPT YOU THINK HE SHOULD BE SO MUCH *MORE,* RIGHT?
THAT'S JUST IT. I THINK HE *IS* SO MUCH MORE.
SO, WHAT ARE YOU GOING TO DO?
I'M GOING TO RESPOND IN A PERFECTLY SANE, RATIONAL WAY.
GO TO THE COLLEGE, WAIT UNTIL HE GETS OFF WORK, AND FOLLOW HIM HOME.

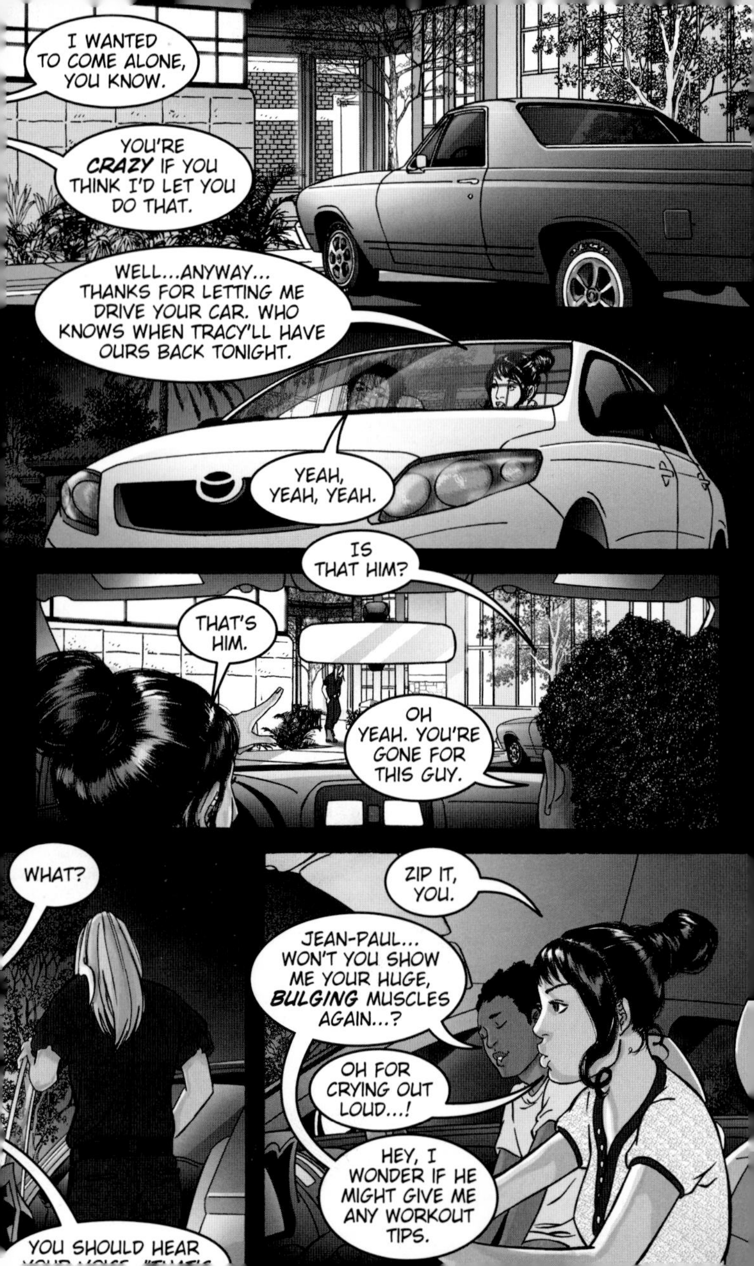
I WANTED TO COME ALONE, YOU KNOW.
YOU'RE **CRAZY** IF YOU THINK I'D LET YOU DO THAT.
WELL...ANYWAY... THANKS FOR LETTING ME DRIVE YOUR CAR. WHO KNOWS WHEN TRACY'LL HAVE OURS BACK TONIGHT.
YEAH, YEAH, YEAH.
IS THAT HIM?
THAT'S HIM.
OH YEAH. YOU'RE GONE FOR THIS GUY.
WHAT?
ZIP IT, YOU.
JEAN-PAUL... WON'T YOU SHOW ME YOUR HUGE, **BULGING** MUSCLES AGAIN...?
OH FOR CRYING OUT LOUD...!
HEY, I WONDER IF HE MIGHT GIVE ME ANY WORKOUT TIPS.
YOU SHOULD HEAR

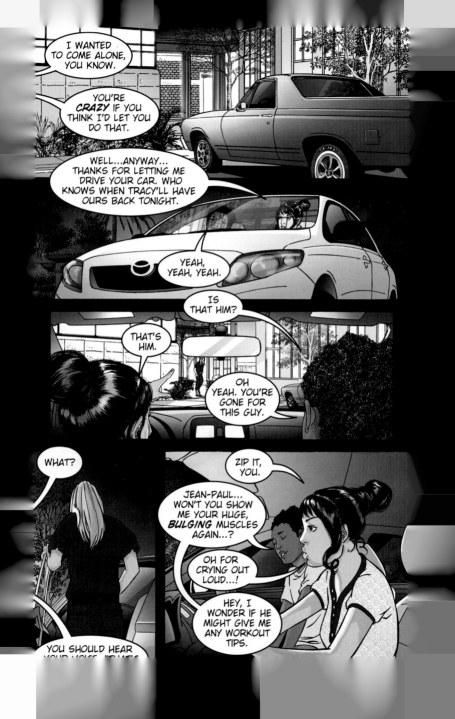

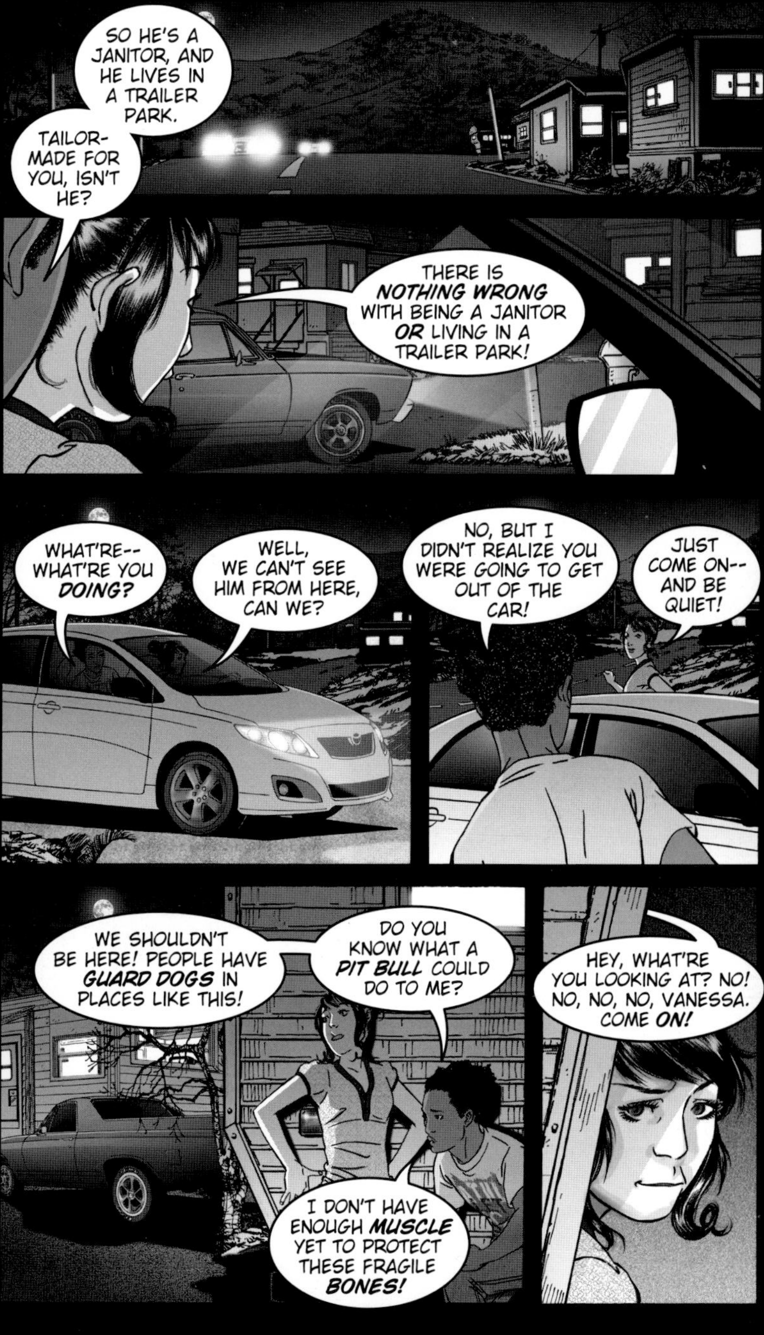
SO HE'S A JANITOR, AND HE LIVES IN A TRAILER PARK.
TAILOR-MADE FOR YOU, ISN'T HE?
THERE IS NOTHING WRONG WITH BEING A JANITOR OR LIVING IN A TRAILER PARK!
WHAT'RE--WHAT'RE YOU DOING?
WELL, WE CAN'T SEE HIM FROM HERE, CAN WE?
NO, BUT I DIDN'T REALIZE YOU WERE GOING TO GET OUT OF THE CAR!
JUST COME ON--AND BE QUIET!
WE SHOULDN'T BE HERE! PEOPLE HAVE GUARD DOGS IN PLACES LIKE THIS!
DO YOU KNOW WHAT A PIT BULL COULD DO TO ME?
I DON'T HAVE ENOUGH MUSCLE YET TO PROTECT THESE FRAGILE BONES!
HEY, WHAT'RE YOU LOOKING AT? NO! NO, NO, NO, VANESSA. COME ON!

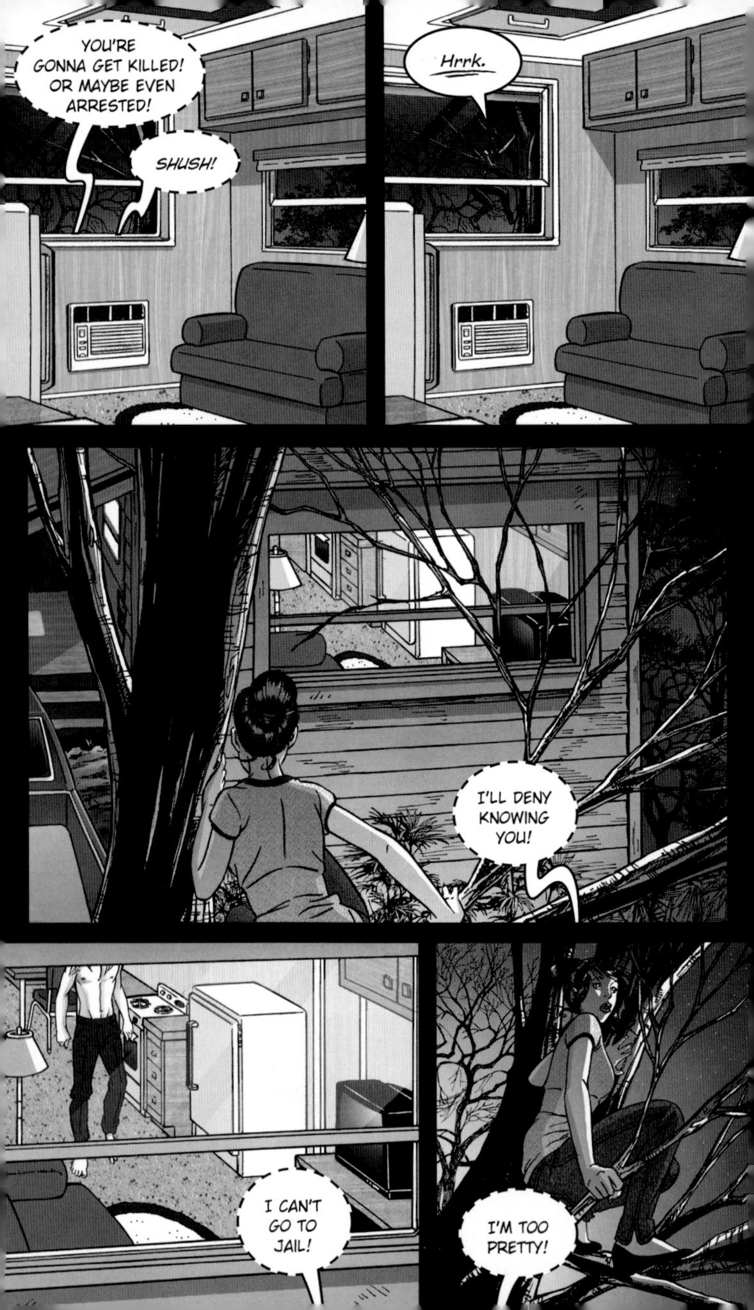
YOU'RE GONNA GET KILLED! OR MAYBE EVEN ARRESTED!
SHUSH!
Hrrk.
I'LL DENY KNOWING YOU!
I CAN'T GO TO JAIL!
I'M TOO PRETTY!

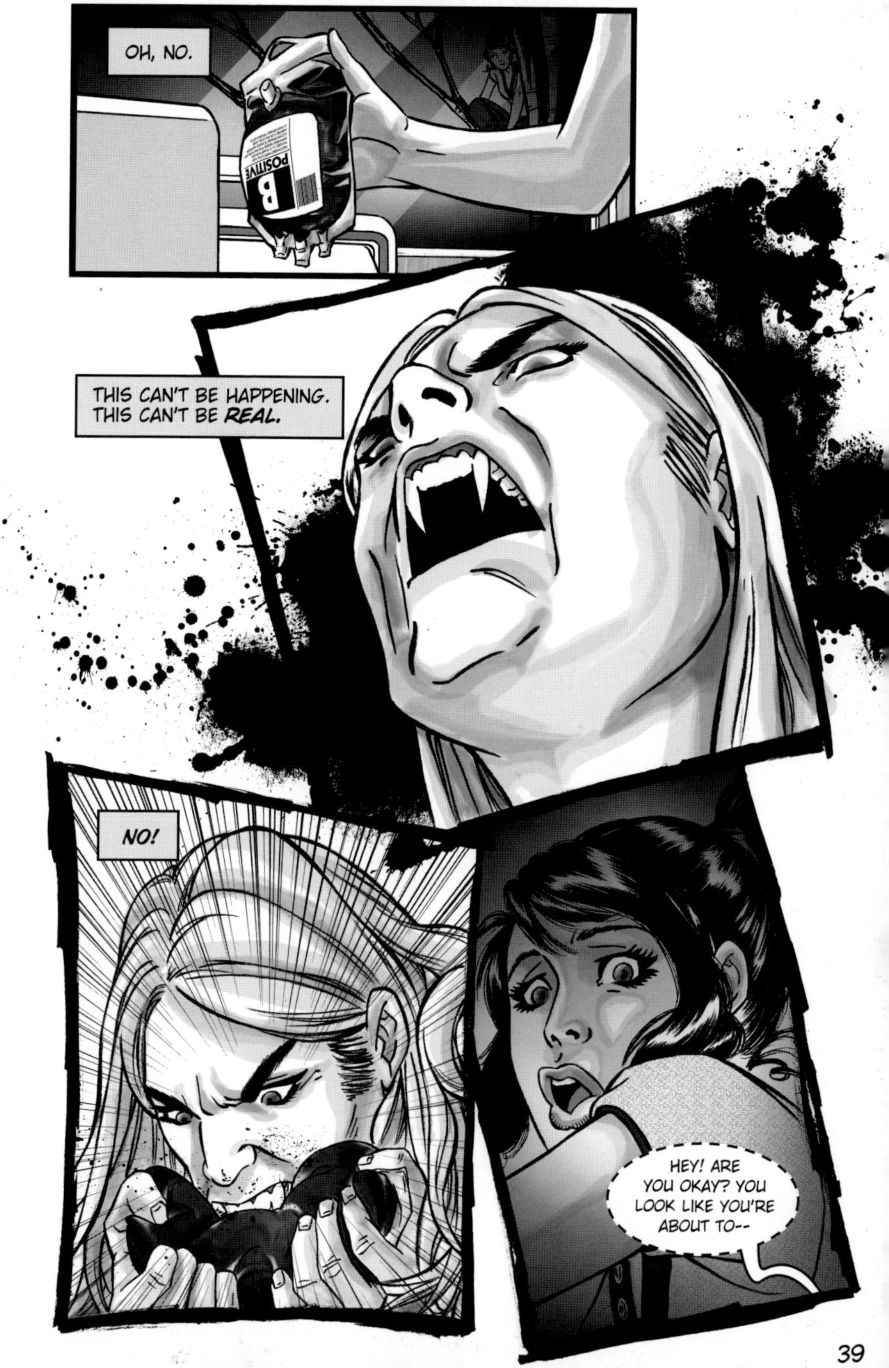
OH, NO.
B POSITIVE
THIS CAN'T BE HAPPENING. THIS CAN'T BE *REAL.*
NO!
HEY! ARE YOU OKAY? YOU LOOK LIKE YOU'RE ABOUT TO--

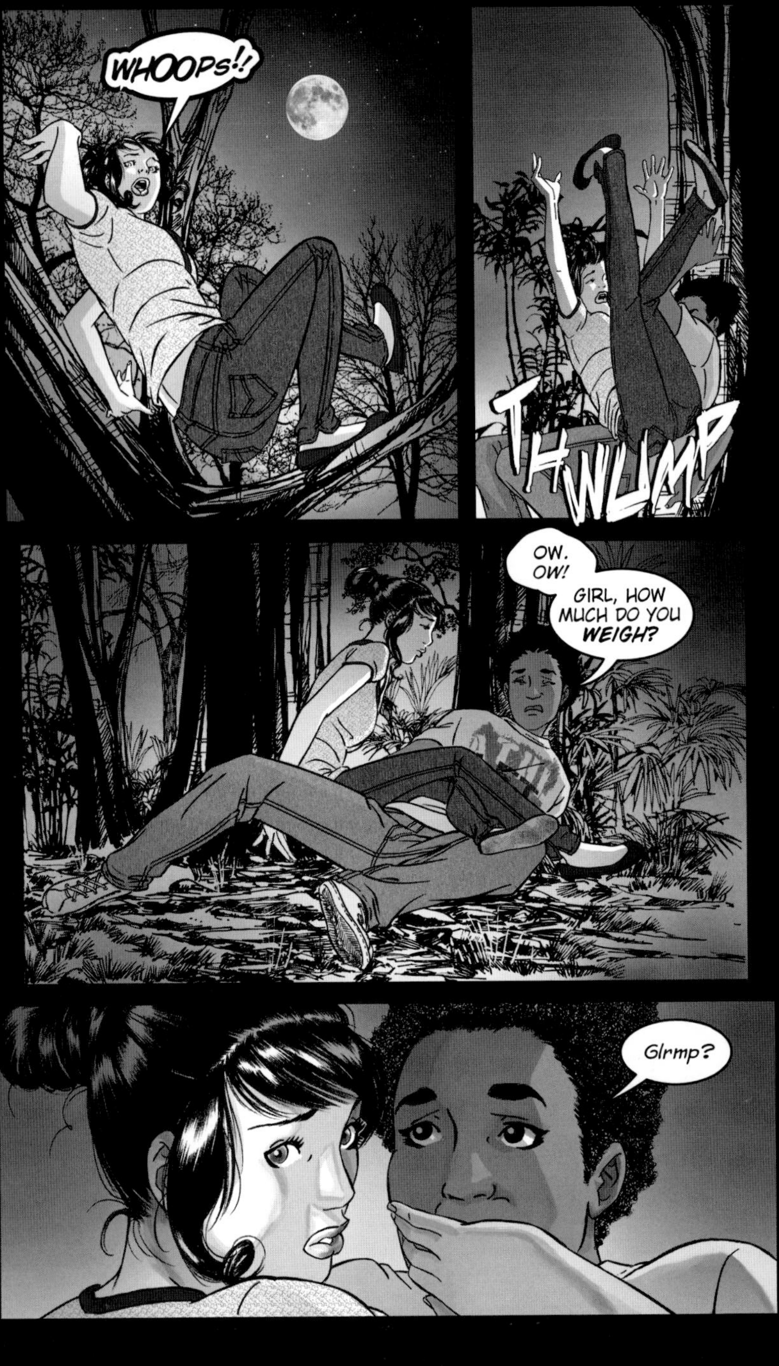
WHOOPS!!
THWUMP
OW. OW!
GIRL, HOW MUCH DO YOU WEIGH?
Glrmp?

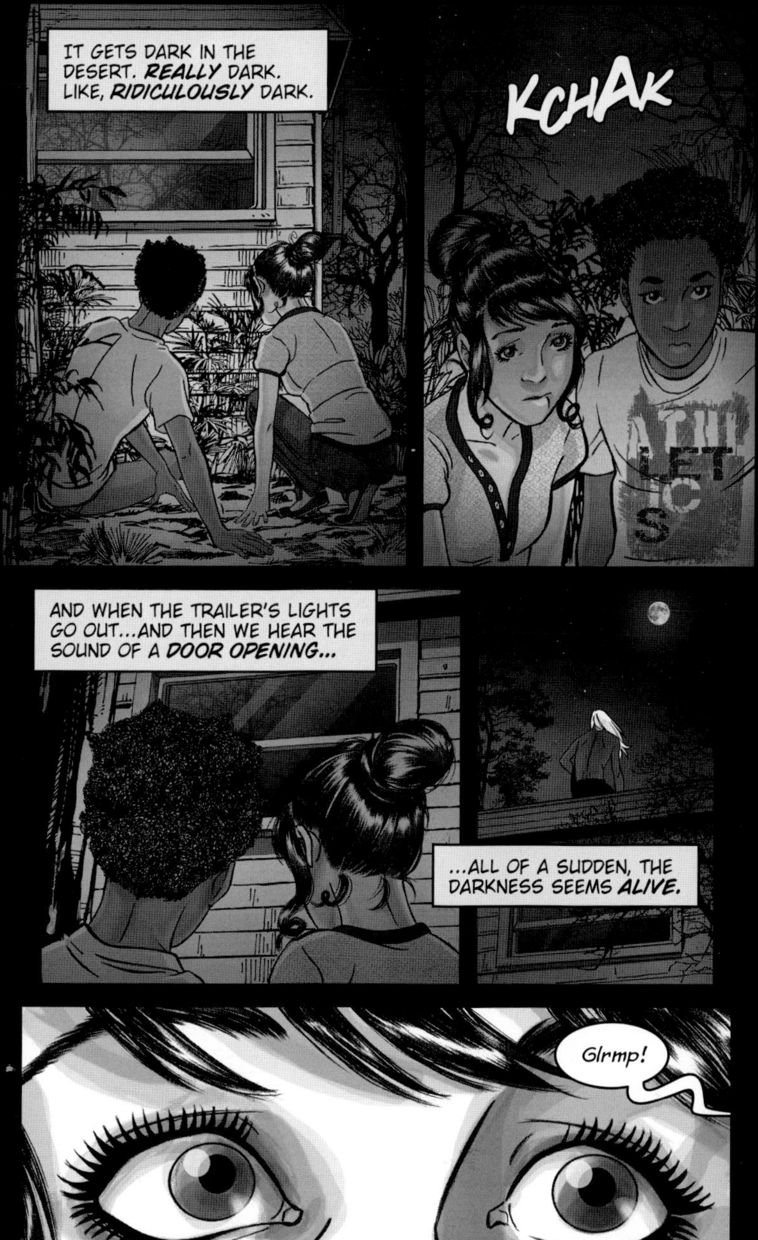
IT GETS DARK IN THE DESERT. **REALLY** DARK. LIKE, **RIDICULOUSLY** DARK.
KCHAK
ATHLETICS
AND WHEN THE TRAILER'S LIGHTS GO OUT...AND THEN WE HEAR THE SOUND OF A **DOOR OPENING...**
...ALL OF A SUDDEN, THE DARKNESS SEEMS **ALIVE.**
Glrmp!

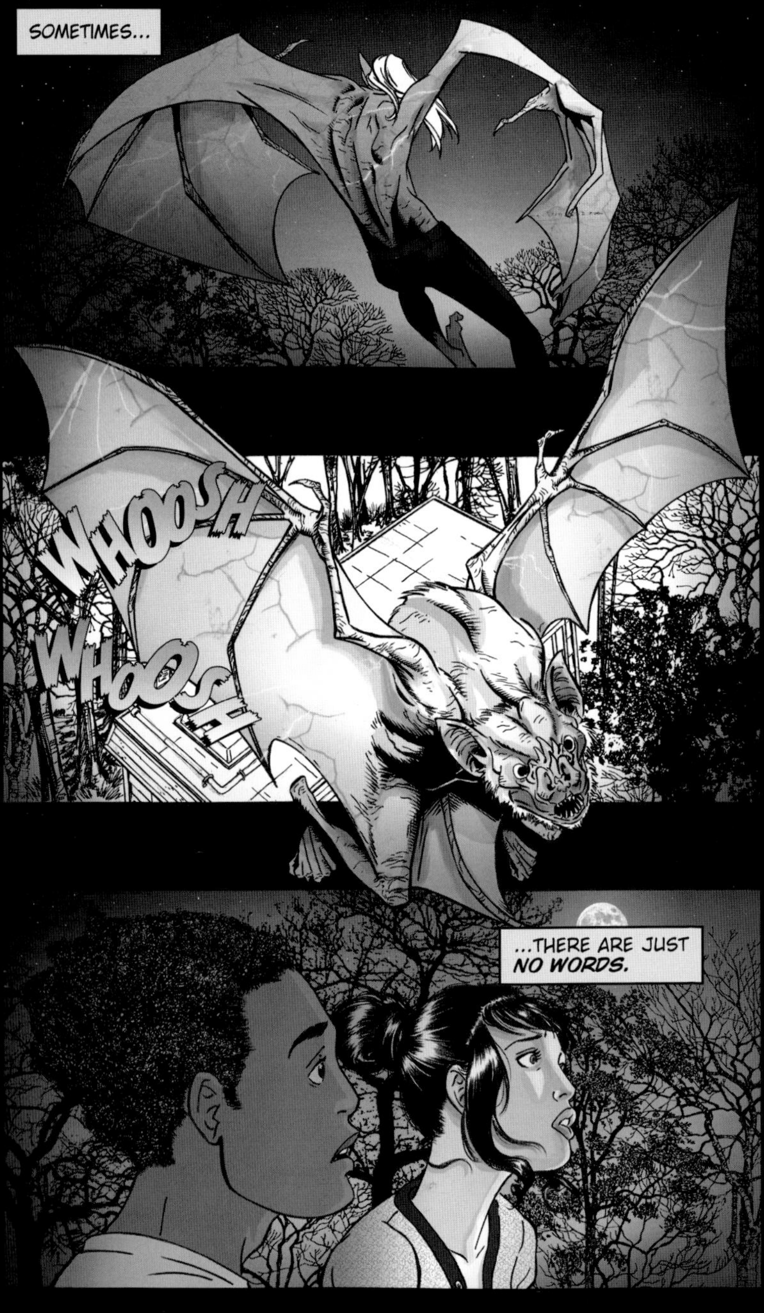
SOMETIMES...
WHOOSH
WHOOSH
...THERE ARE JUST NO WORDS.

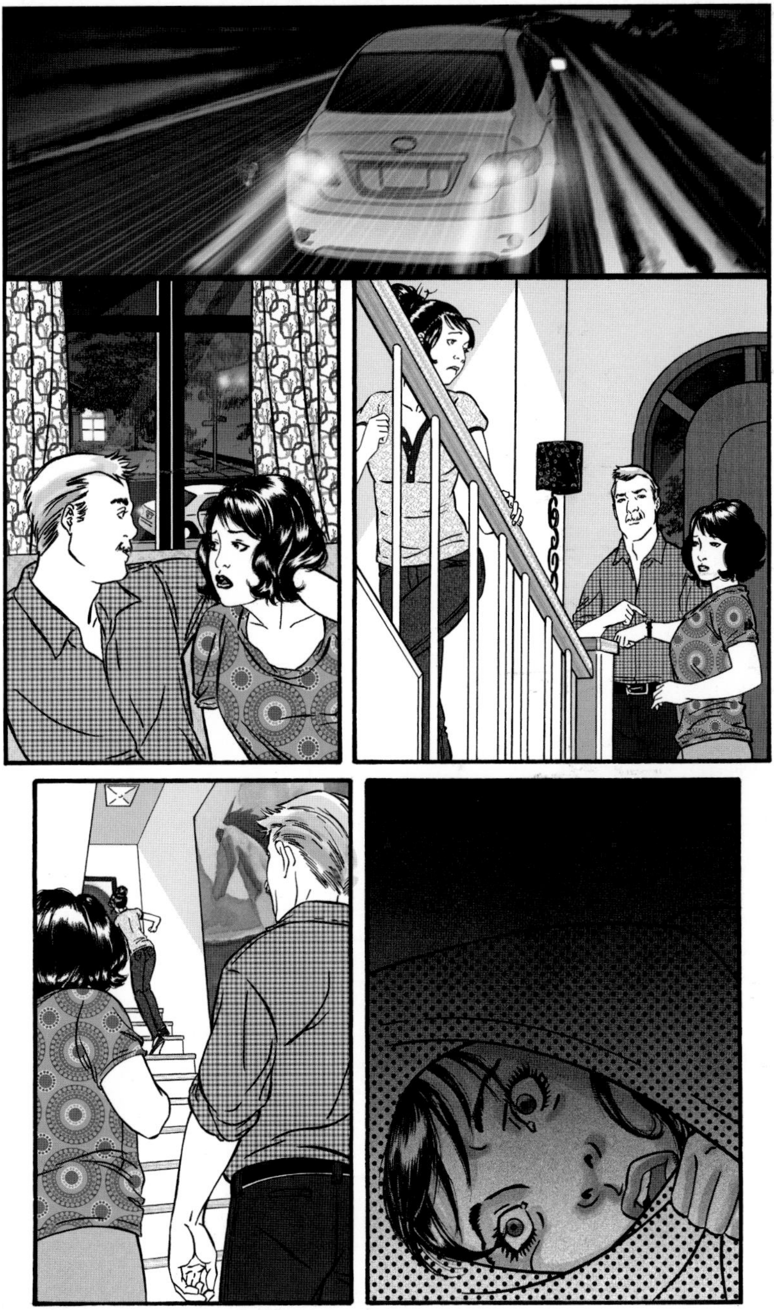

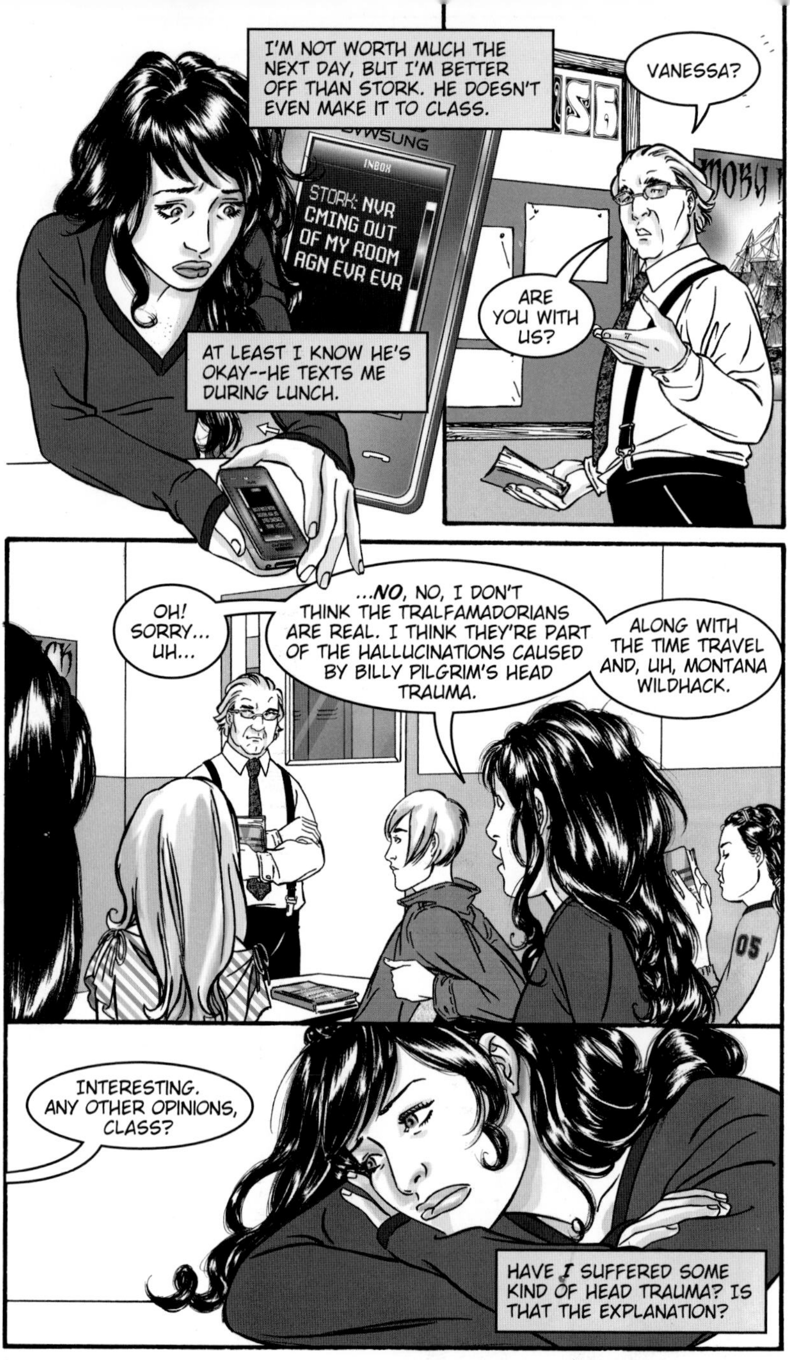
I'M NOT WORTH MUCH THE NEXT DAY, BUT I'M BETTER OFF THAN STORK. HE DOESN'T EVEN MAKE IT TO CLASS.
INBOX
STORK: NVR CMING OUT OF MY ROOM AGN EVR EVR
AT LEAST I KNOW HE'S OKAY--HE TEXTS ME DURING LUNCH.
VANESSA?
ARE YOU WITH US?
OH! SORRY... UH...
...NO, NO, I DON'T THINK THE TRALFAMADORIANS ARE REAL. I THINK THEY'RE PART OF THE HALLUCINATIONS CAUSED BY BILLY PILGRIM'S HEAD TRAUMA.
ALONG WITH THE TIME TRAVEL AND, UH, MONTANA WILDHACK.
INTERESTING. ANY OTHER OPINIONS, CLASS?
HAVE I SUFFERED SOME KIND OF HEAD TRAUMA? IS THAT THE EXPLANATION?

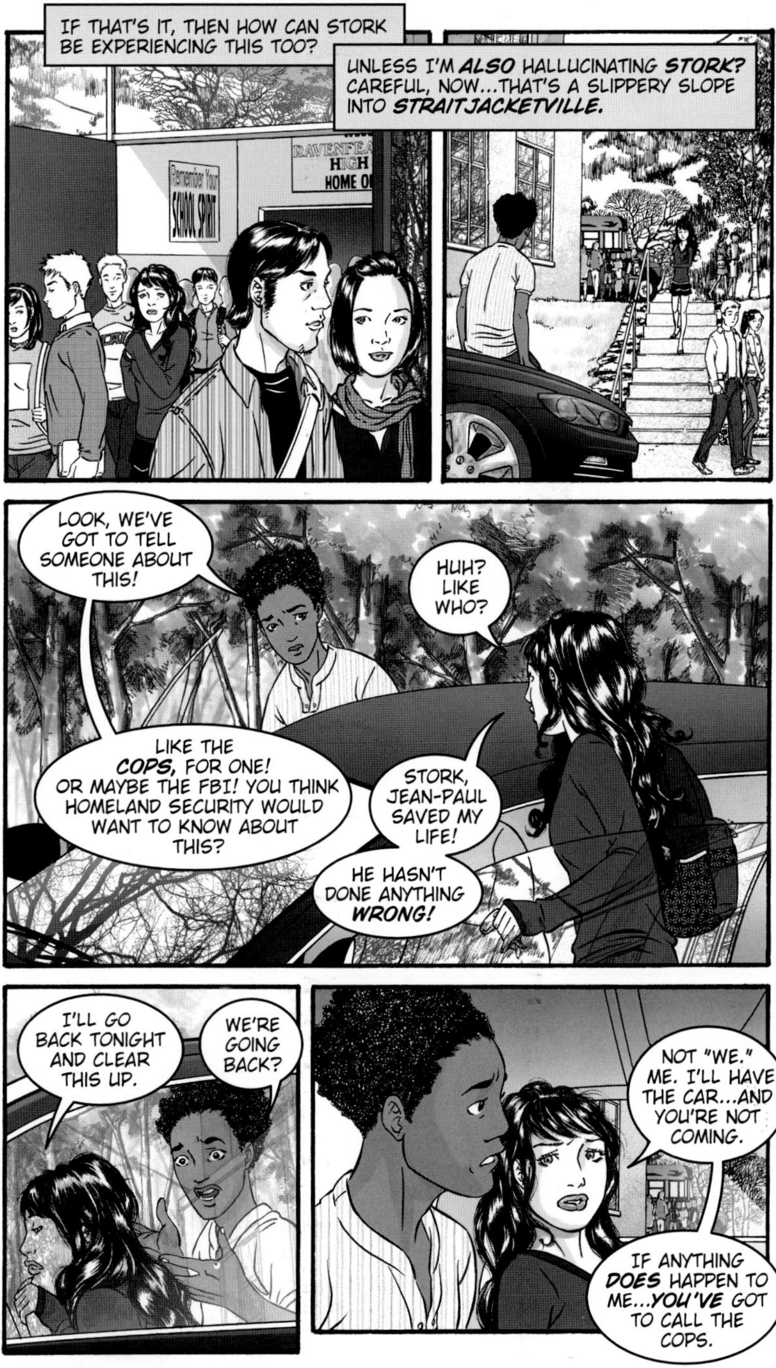
IF THAT'S IT, THEN HOW CAN STORK BE EXPERIENCING THIS TOO?
UNLESS I'M ALSO HALLUCINATING STORK? CAREFUL, NOW...THAT'S A SLIPPERY SLOPE INTO STRAITJACKETVILLE.
Remember Your SCHOOL SPIRIT
HIGH
HOME O
LOOK, WE'VE GOT TO TELL SOMEONE ABOUT THIS!
HUH? LIKE WHO?
LIKE THE COPS, FOR ONE! OR MAYBE THE FBI! YOU THINK HOMELAND SECURITY WOULD WANT TO KNOW ABOUT THIS?
STORK, JEAN-PAUL SAVED MY LIFE!
HE HASN'T DONE ANYTHING WRONG!
I'LL GO BACK TONIGHT AND CLEAR THIS UP.
WE'RE GOING BACK?
NOT "WE." ME. I'LL HAVE THE CAR...AND YOU'RE NOT COMING.
IF ANYTHING DOES HAPPEN TO ME...YOU'VE GOT TO CALL THE COPS.

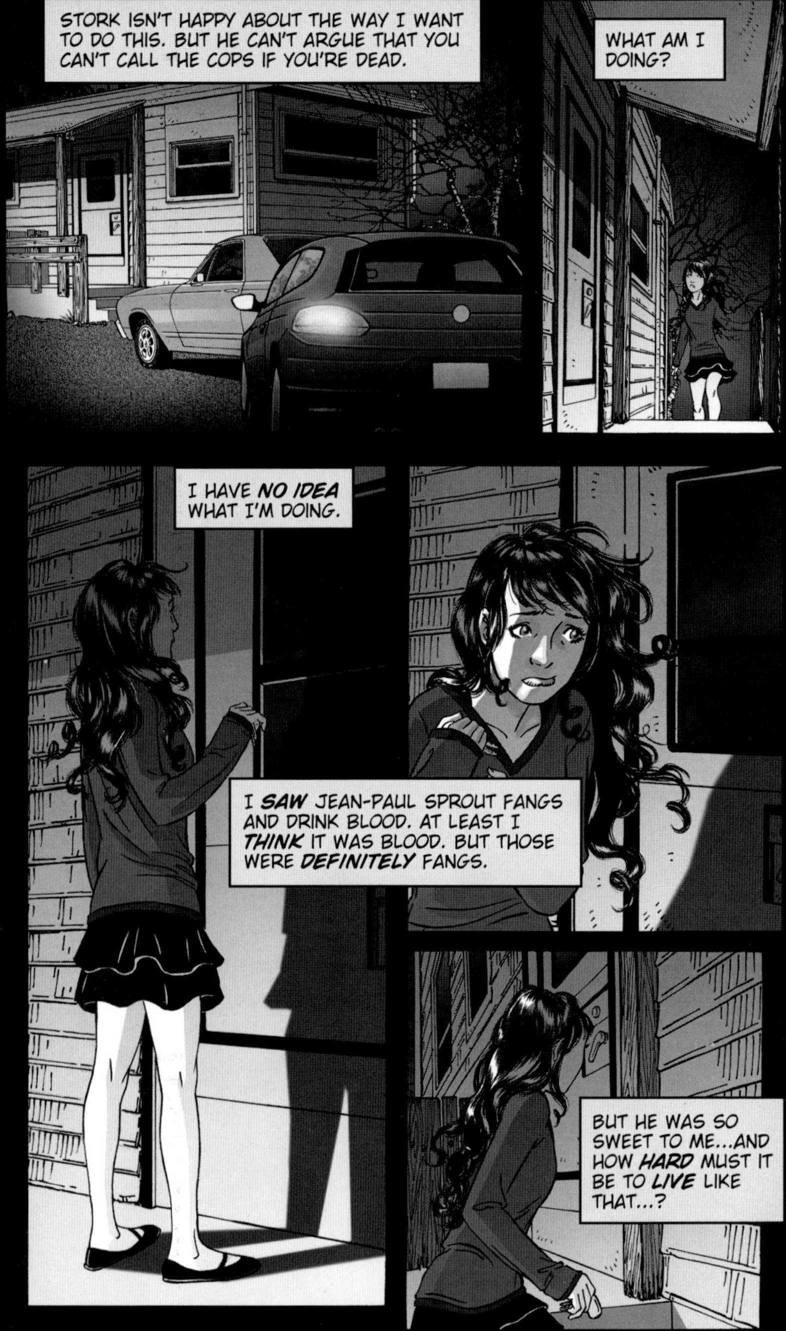
STORK ISN'T HAPPY ABOUT THE WAY I WANT TO DO THIS. BUT HE CAN'T ARGUE THAT YOU CAN'T CALL THE COPS IF YOU'RE DEAD.
WHAT AM I DOING?
I HAVE NO IDEA WHAT I'M DOING.
I SAW JEAN-PAUL SPROUT FANGS AND DRINK BLOOD. AT LEAST I THINK IT WAS BLOOD. BUT THOSE WERE DEFINITELY FANGS.
BUT HE WAS SO SWEET TO ME...AND HOW HARD MUST IT BE TO LIVE LIKE THAT...?

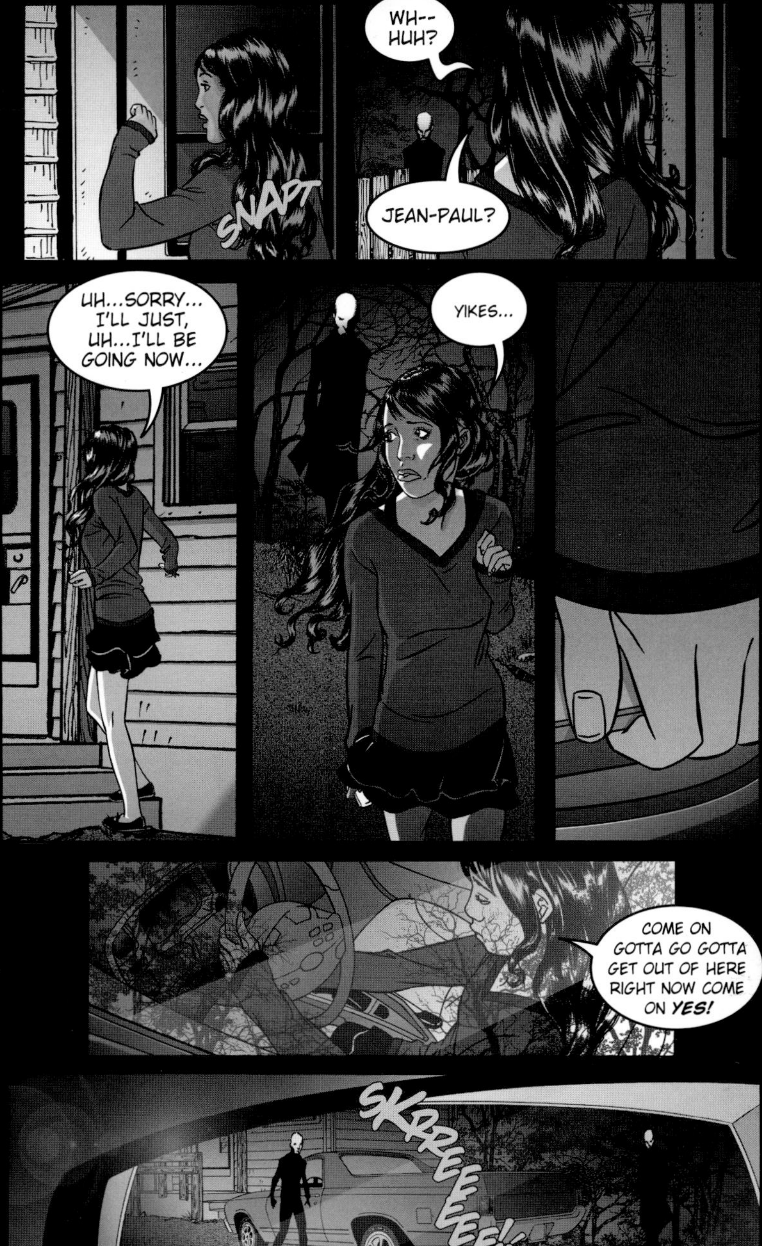
SNAP!
WH--
HUH?
JEAN-PAUL?
UH...SORRY... I'LL JUST, UH...I'LL BE GOING NOW...
YIKES...
COME ON GOTTA GO GOTTA GET OUT OF HERE RIGHT NOW COME ON **YES!**
SKRREEEEEE!!

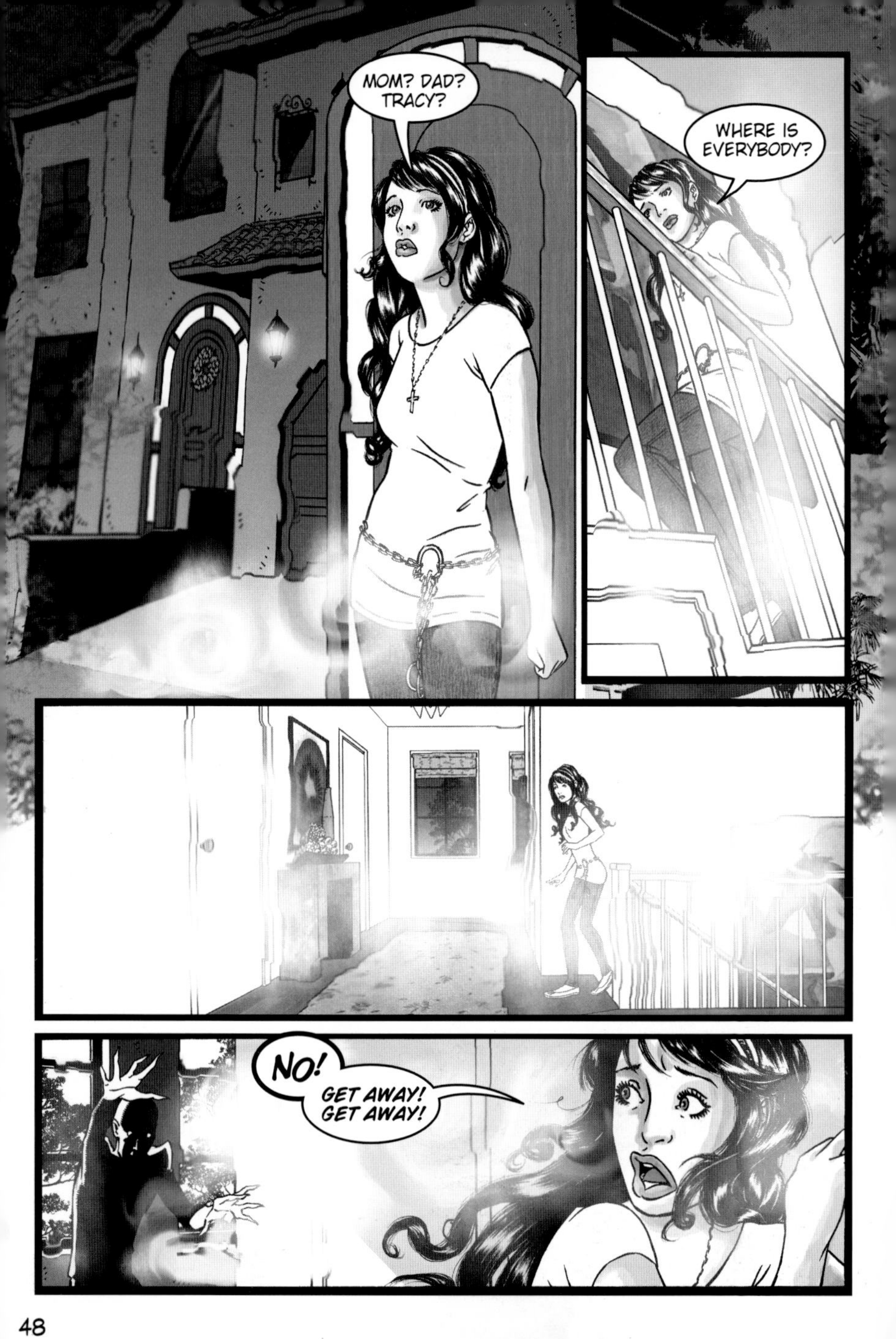
MOM? DAD? TRACY?
WHERE IS EVERYBODY?
NO!
GET AWAY! GET AWAY!

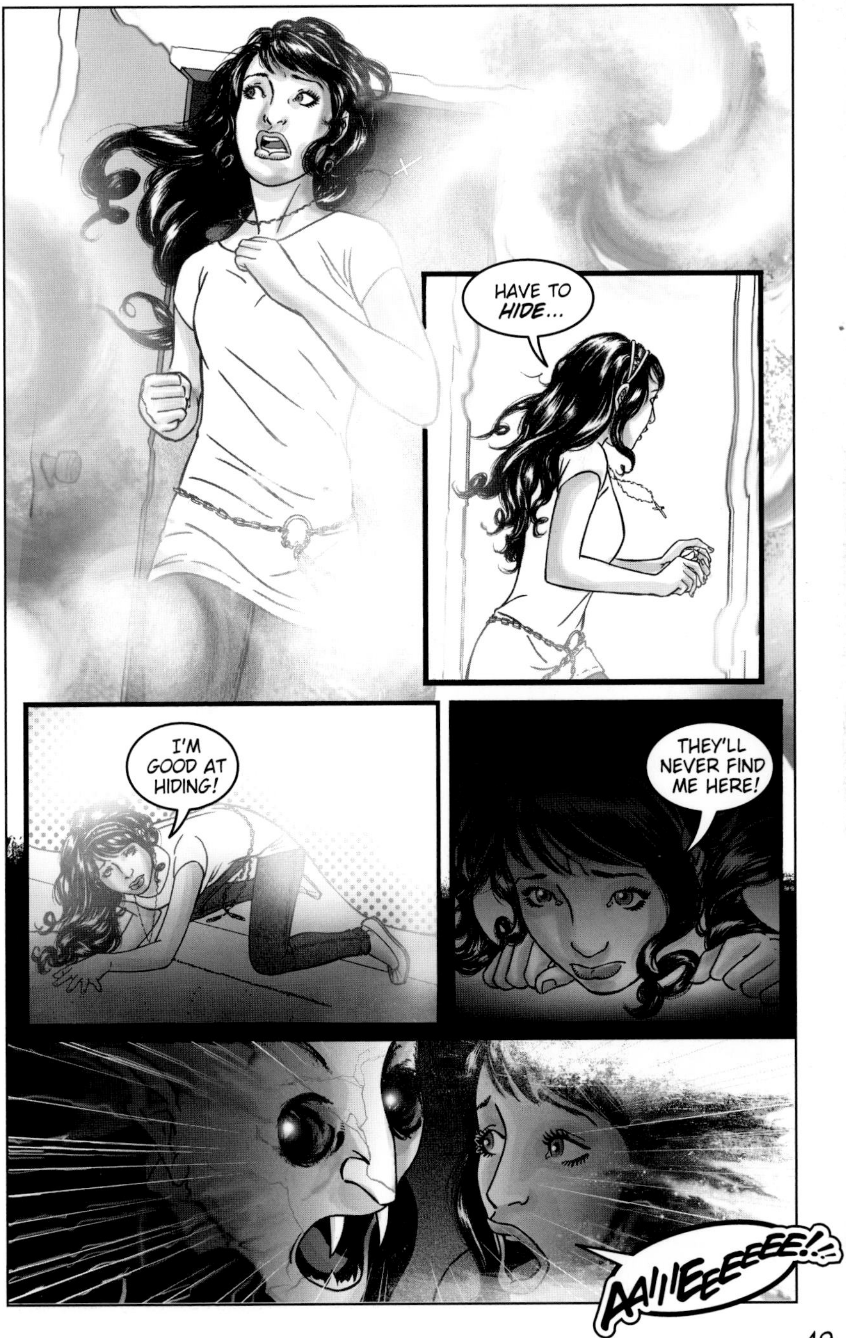
HAVE TO HIDE...
I'M GOOD AT HIDING!
THEY'LL NEVER FIND ME HERE!
AAIIIEEEEEEE!!

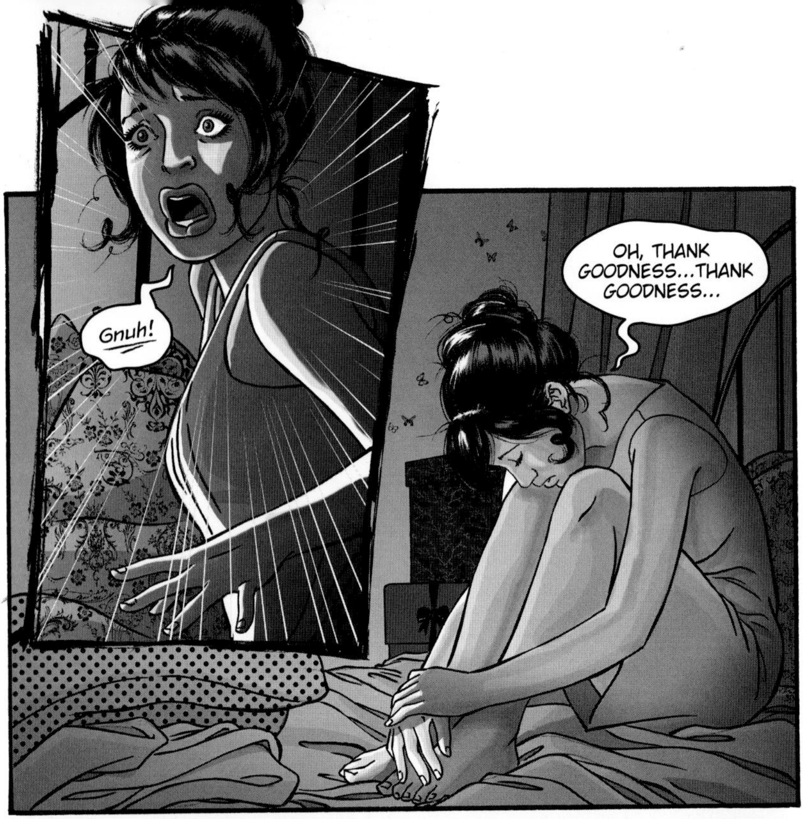
Gnuh!
OH, THANK GOODNESS...THANK GOODNESS...

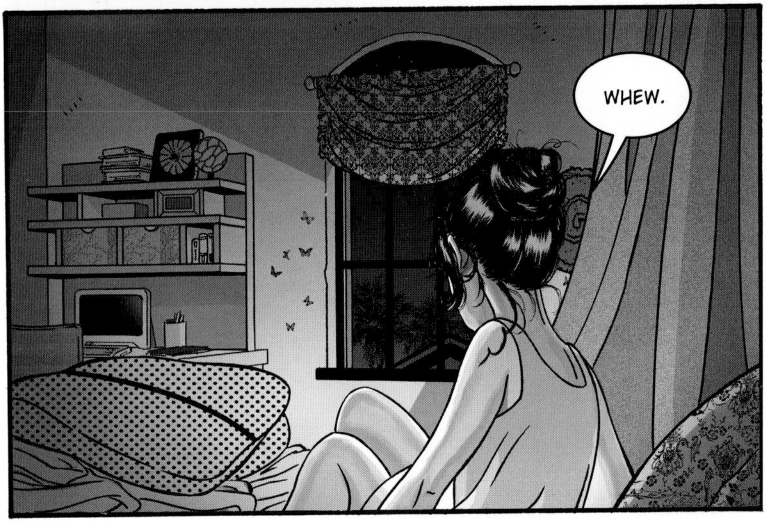
WHEW.

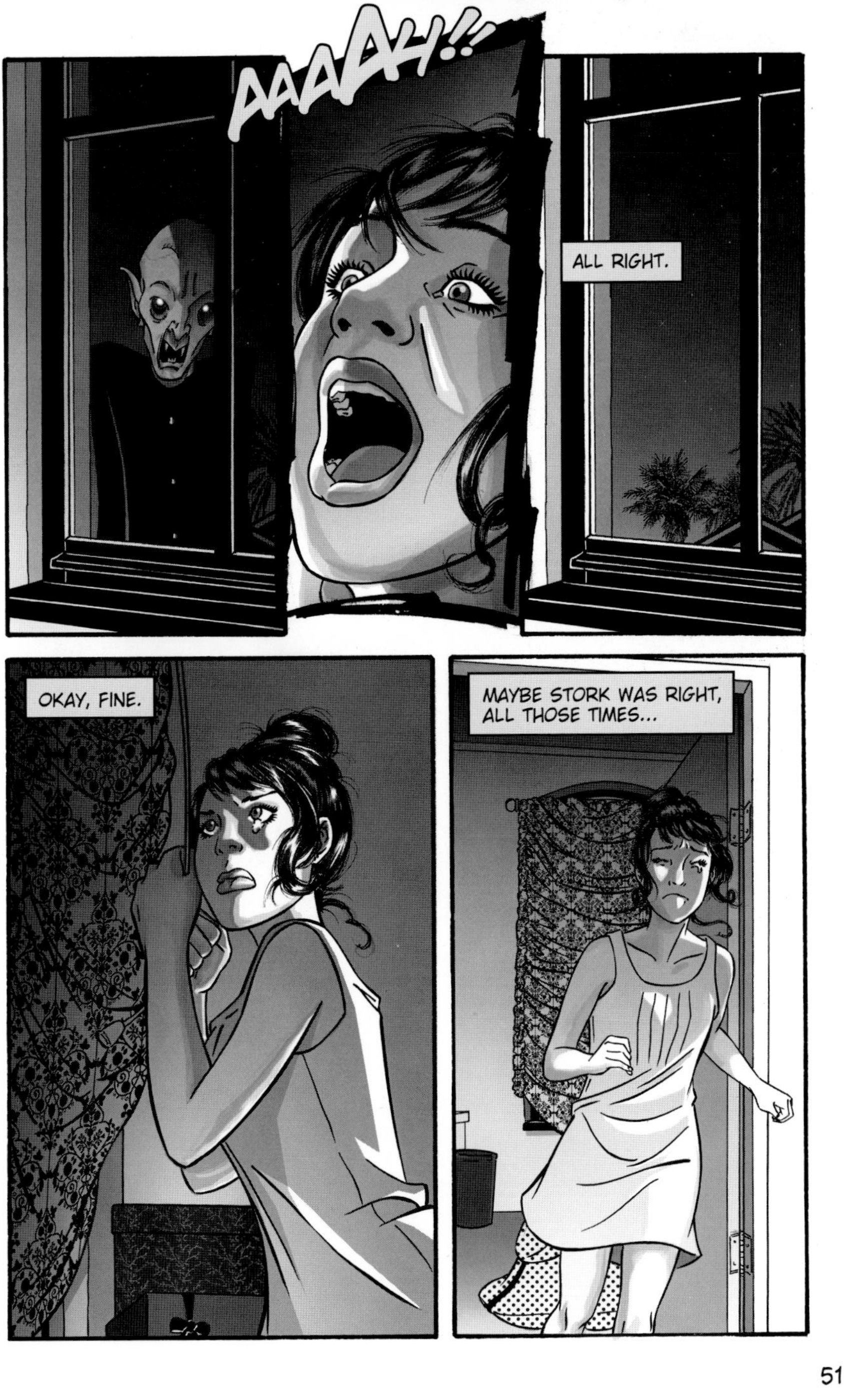
AAAAH!!
ALL RIGHT.
OKAY, FINE.
MAYBE STORK WAS RIGHT, ALL THOSE TIMES...

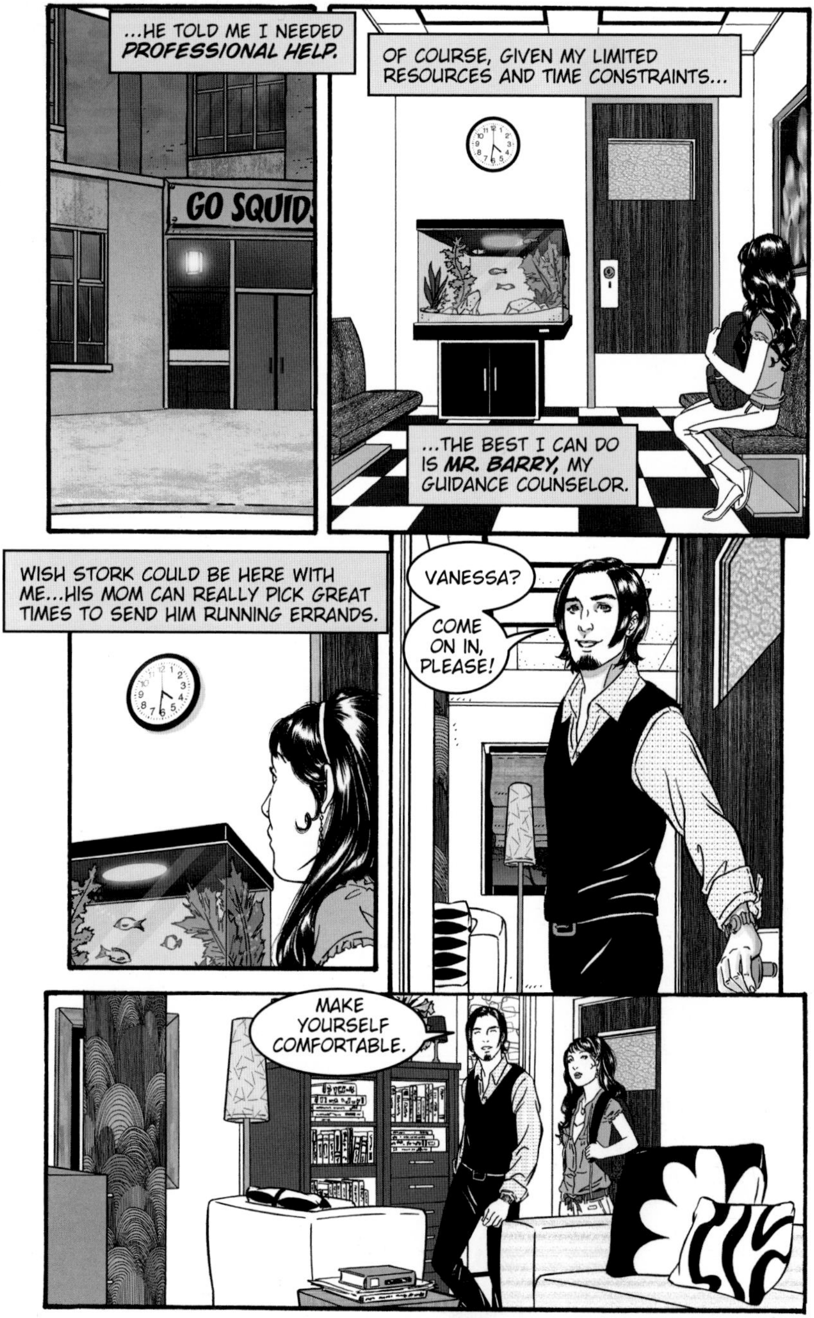

...HE TOLD ME I NEEDED PROFESSIONAL HELP.
GO SQUID
OF COURSE, GIVEN MY LIMITED RESOURCES AND TIME CONSTRAINTS...
...THE BEST I CAN DO IS MR. BARRY, MY GUIDANCE COUNSELOR.
WISH STORK COULD BE HERE WITH ME...HIS MOM CAN REALLY PICK GREAT TIMES TO SEND HIM RUNNING ERRANDS.
VANESSA?
COME ON IN, PLEASE!
MAKE YOURSELF COMFORTABLE.

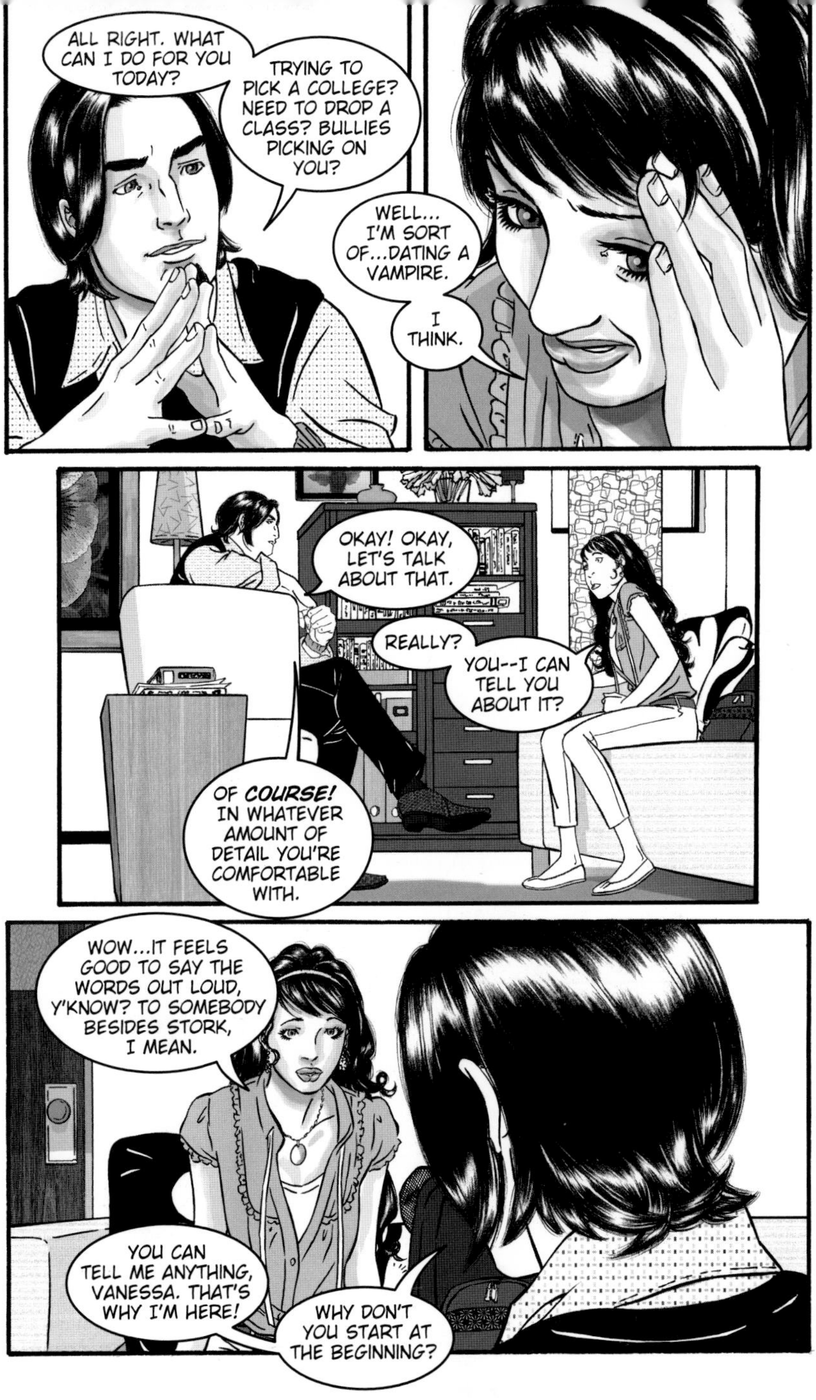
ALL RIGHT. WHAT CAN I DO FOR YOU TODAY?
TRYING TO PICK A COLLEGE? NEED TO DROP A CLASS? BULLIES PICKING ON YOU?
WELL... I'M SORT OF...DATING A VAMPIRE.
I THINK.
OKAY! OKAY, LET'S TALK ABOUT THAT.
REALLY?
YOU--I CAN TELL YOU ABOUT IT?
OF **COURSE!** IN WHATEVER AMOUNT OF DETAIL YOU'RE COMFORTABLE WITH.
WOW...IT FEELS GOOD TO SAY THE WORDS OUT LOUD, Y'KNOW? TO SOMEBODY BESIDES STORK, I MEAN.
YOU CAN TELL ME ANYTHING, VANESSA. THAT'S WHY I'M HERE!
WHY DON'T YOU START AT THE BEGINNING?

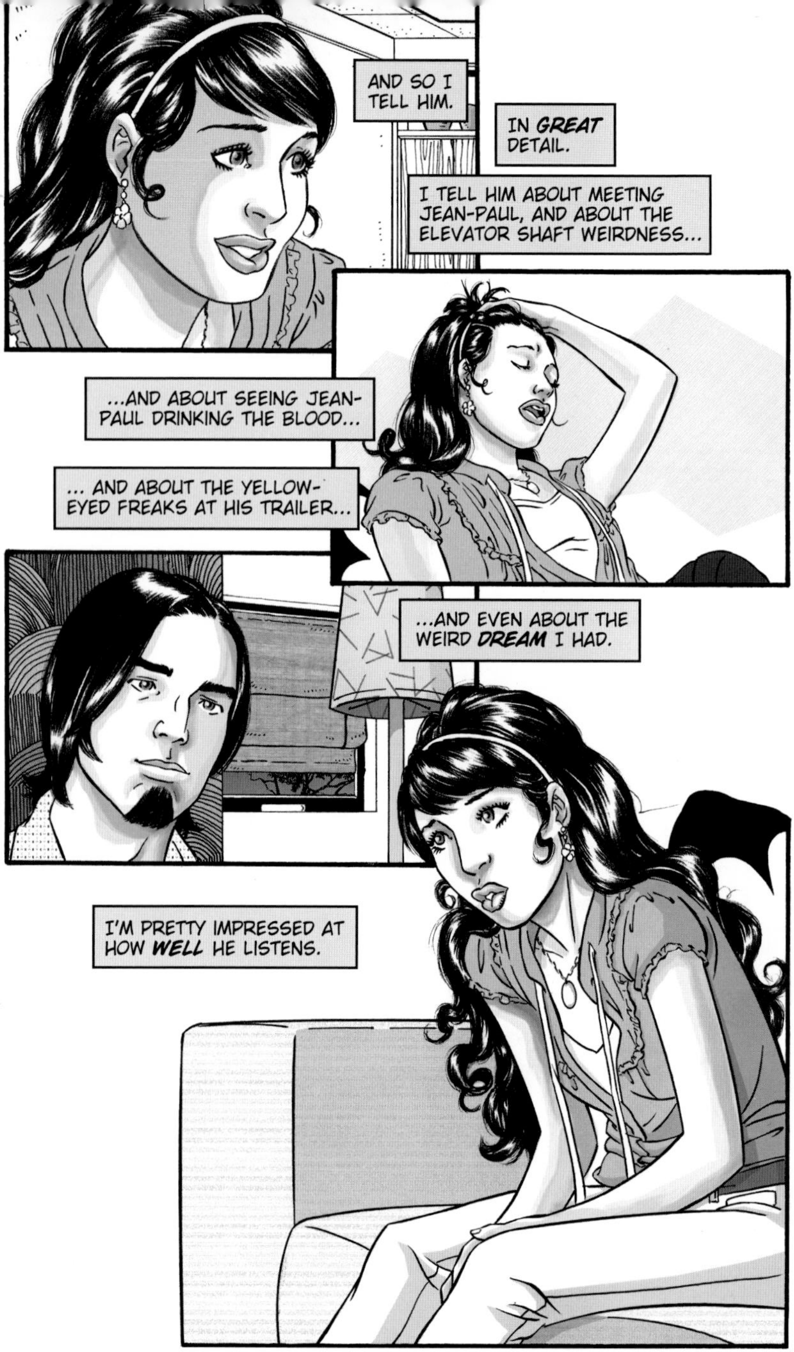
AND SO I TELL HIM.
IN GREAT DETAIL.
I TELL HIM ABOUT MEETING JEAN-PAUL, AND ABOUT THE ELEVATOR SHAFT WEIRDNESS...
...AND ABOUT SEEING JEAN-PAUL DRINKING THE BLOOD...
... AND ABOUT THE YELLOW-EYED FREAKS AT HIS TRAILER...
...AND EVEN ABOUT THE WEIRD DREAM I HAD.
I'M PRETTY IMPRESSED AT HOW WELL HE LISTENS.

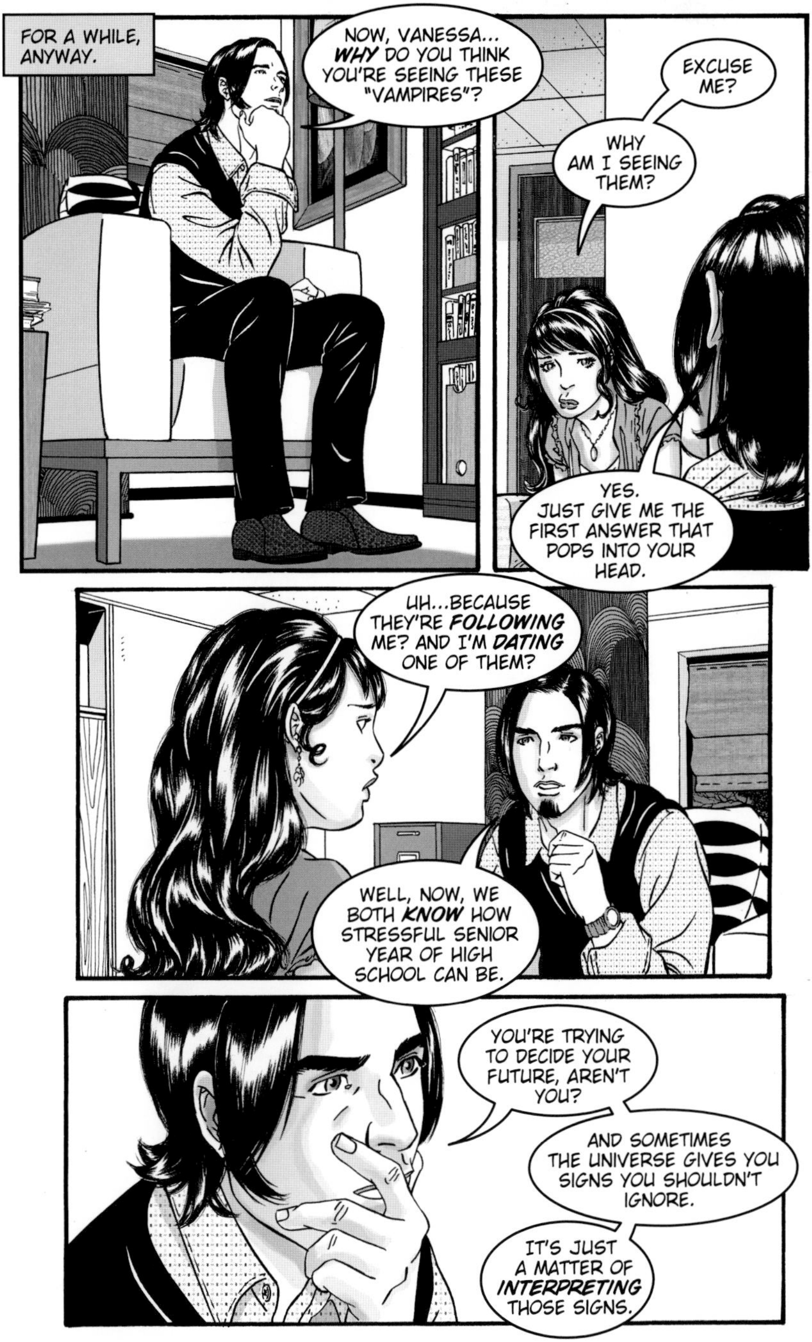
FOR A WHILE, ANYWAY.
NOW, VANESSA... *WHY* DO YOU THINK YOU'RE SEEING THESE "VAMPIRES"?
EXCUSE ME?
WHY AM I SEEING THEM?
YES. JUST GIVE ME THE FIRST ANSWER THAT POPS INTO YOUR HEAD.
UH...BECAUSE THEY'RE *FOLLOWING* ME? AND I'M *DATING* ONE OF THEM?
WELL, NOW, WE BOTH *KNOW* HOW STRESSFUL SENIOR YEAR OF HIGH SCHOOL CAN BE.
YOU'RE TRYING TO DECIDE YOUR FUTURE, AREN'T YOU?
AND SOMETIMES THE UNIVERSE GIVES YOU SIGNS YOU SHOULDN'T IGNORE.
IT'S JUST A MATTER OF *INTERPRETING* THOSE SIGNS.

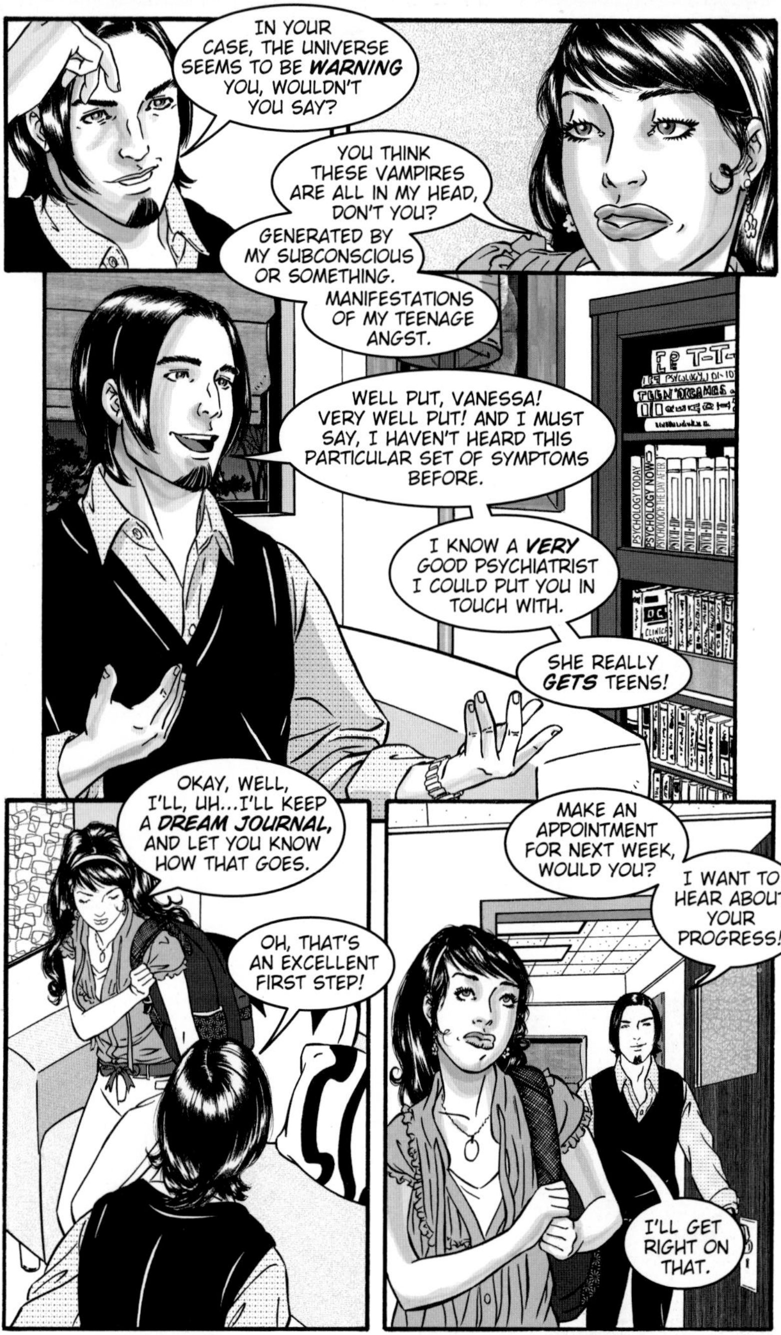
IN YOUR CASE, THE UNIVERSE SEEMS TO BE WARNING YOU, WOULDN'T YOU SAY?
YOU THINK THESE VAMPIRES ARE ALL IN MY HEAD, DON'T YOU?
GENERATED BY MY SUBCONSCIOUS OR SOMETHING.
MANIFESTATIONS OF MY TEENAGE ANGST.
WELL PUT, VANESSA! VERY WELL PUT! AND I MUST SAY, I HAVEN'T HEARD THIS PARTICULAR SET OF SYMPTOMS BEFORE.
I KNOW A VERY GOOD PSYCHIATRIST I COULD PUT YOU IN TOUCH WITH.
SHE REALLY GETS TEENS!
PSYCHOLOGY TODAY
PSYCHOLOGY NOW
PSYCHOLOGY: THE DAY AFTER
OKAY, WELL, I'LL, UH...I'LL KEEP A DREAM JOURNAL, AND LET YOU KNOW HOW THAT GOES.
OH, THAT'S AN EXCELLENT FIRST STEP!
MAKE AN APPOINTMENT FOR NEXT WEEK, WOULD YOU?
I WANT TO HEAR ABOUT YOUR PROGRESS!
I'LL GET RIGHT ON THAT.

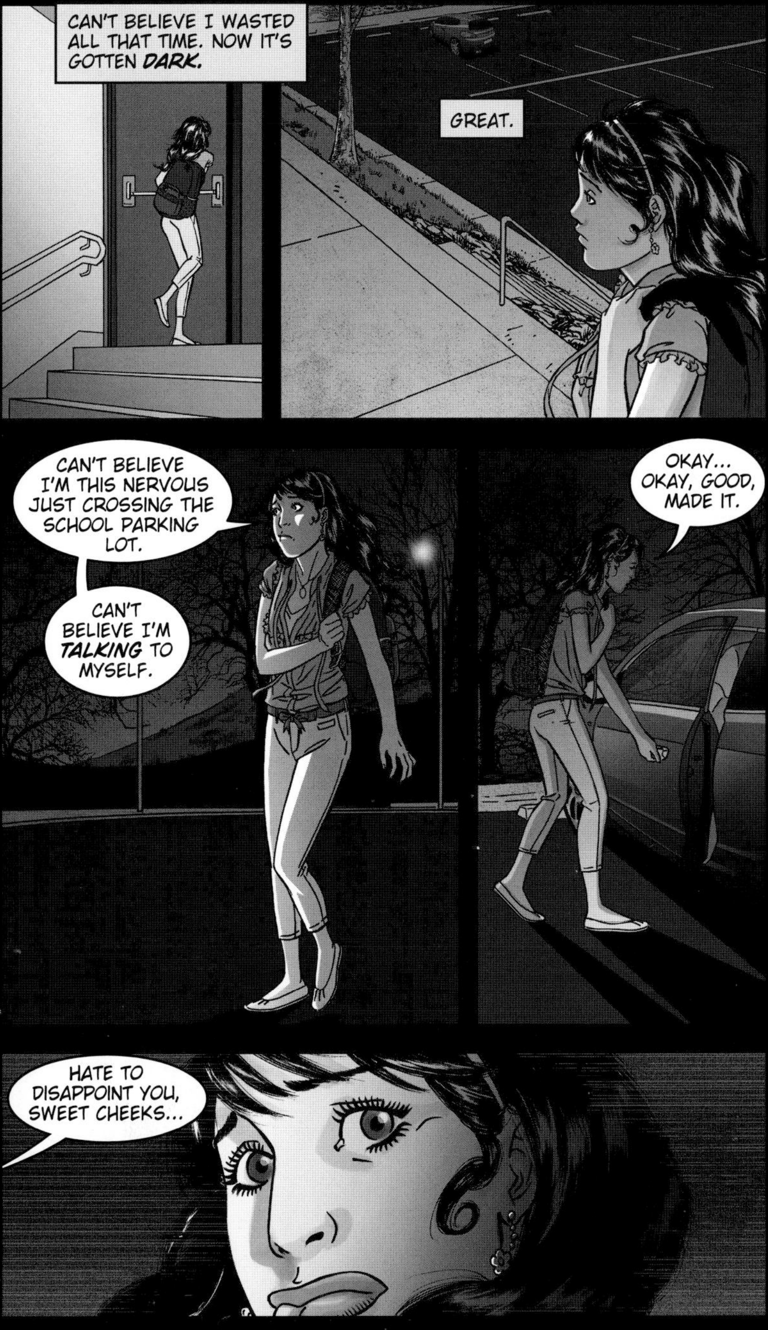
CAN'T BELIEVE I WASTED ALL THAT TIME. NOW IT'S GOTTEN DARK.
GREAT.
CAN'T BELIEVE I'M THIS NERVOUS JUST CROSSING THE SCHOOL PARKING LOT.
CAN'T BELIEVE I'M TALKING TO MYSELF.
OKAY... OKAY, GOOD, MADE IT.
HATE TO DISAPPOINT YOU, SWEET CHEEKS...

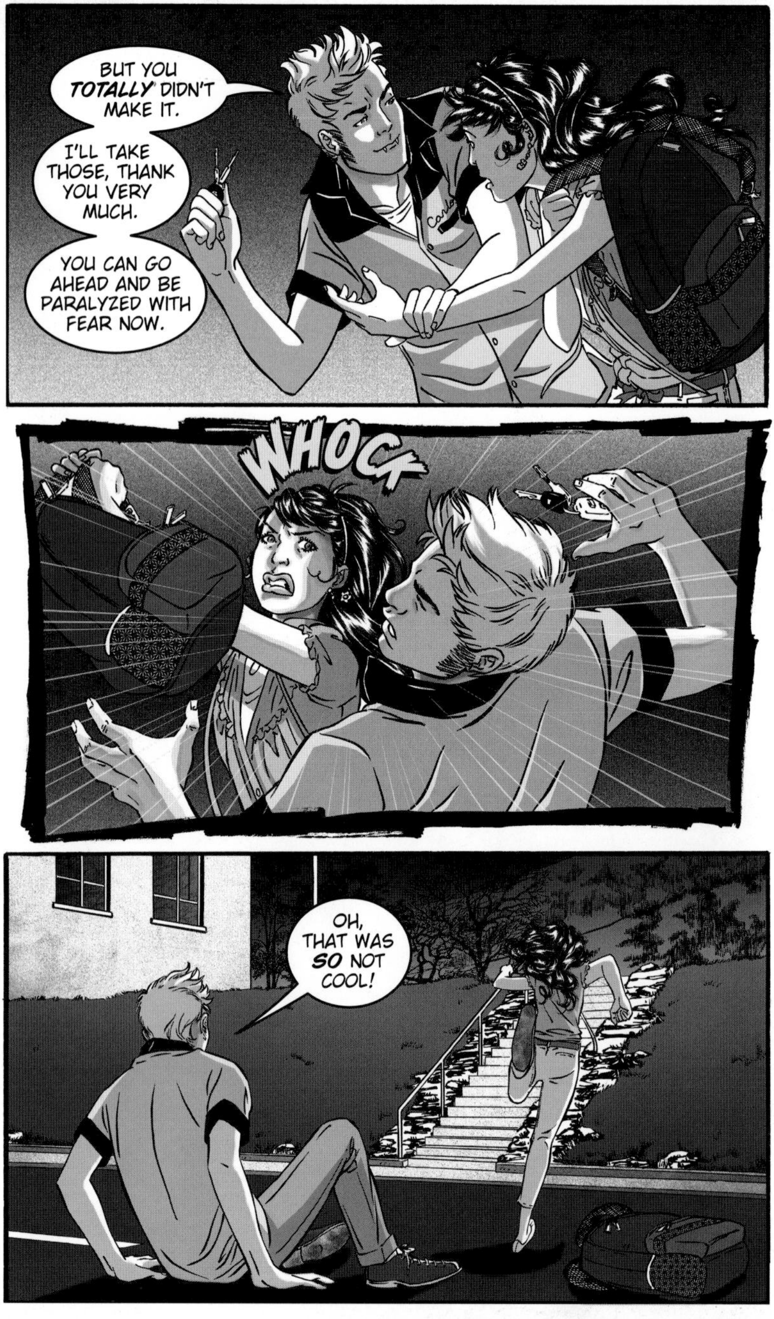

BUT YOU TOTALLY DIDN'T MAKE IT.
I'LL TAKE THOSE, THANK YOU VERY MUCH.
YOU CAN GO AHEAD AND BE PARALYZED WITH FEAR NOW.
WHOCK
OH, THAT WAS SO NOT COOL!

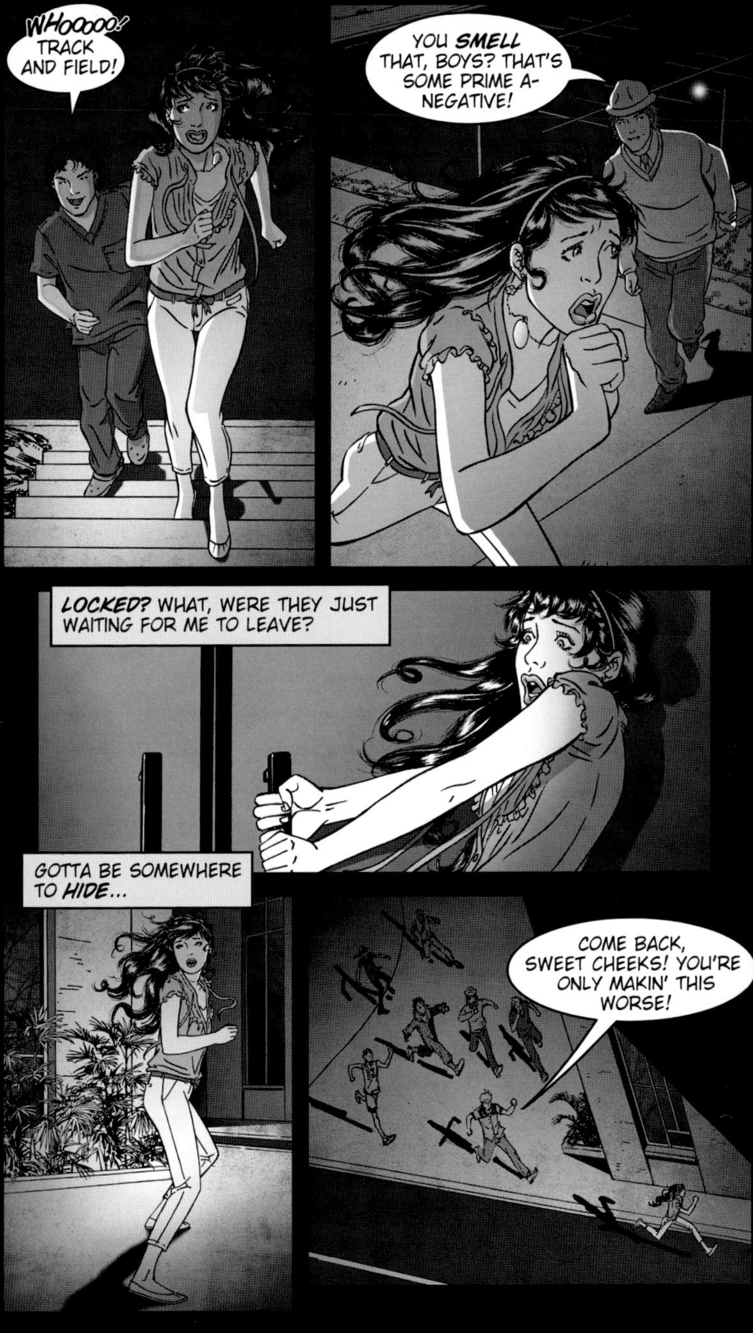
WHOooooo! TRACK AND FIELD!
YOU SMELL THAT, BOYS? THAT'S SOME PRIME A-NEGATIVE!
LOCKED? WHAT, WERE THEY JUST WAITING FOR ME TO LEAVE?
GOTTA BE SOMEWHERE TO HIDE...
COME BACK, SWEET CHEEKS! YOU'RE ONLY MAKIN' THIS WORSE!

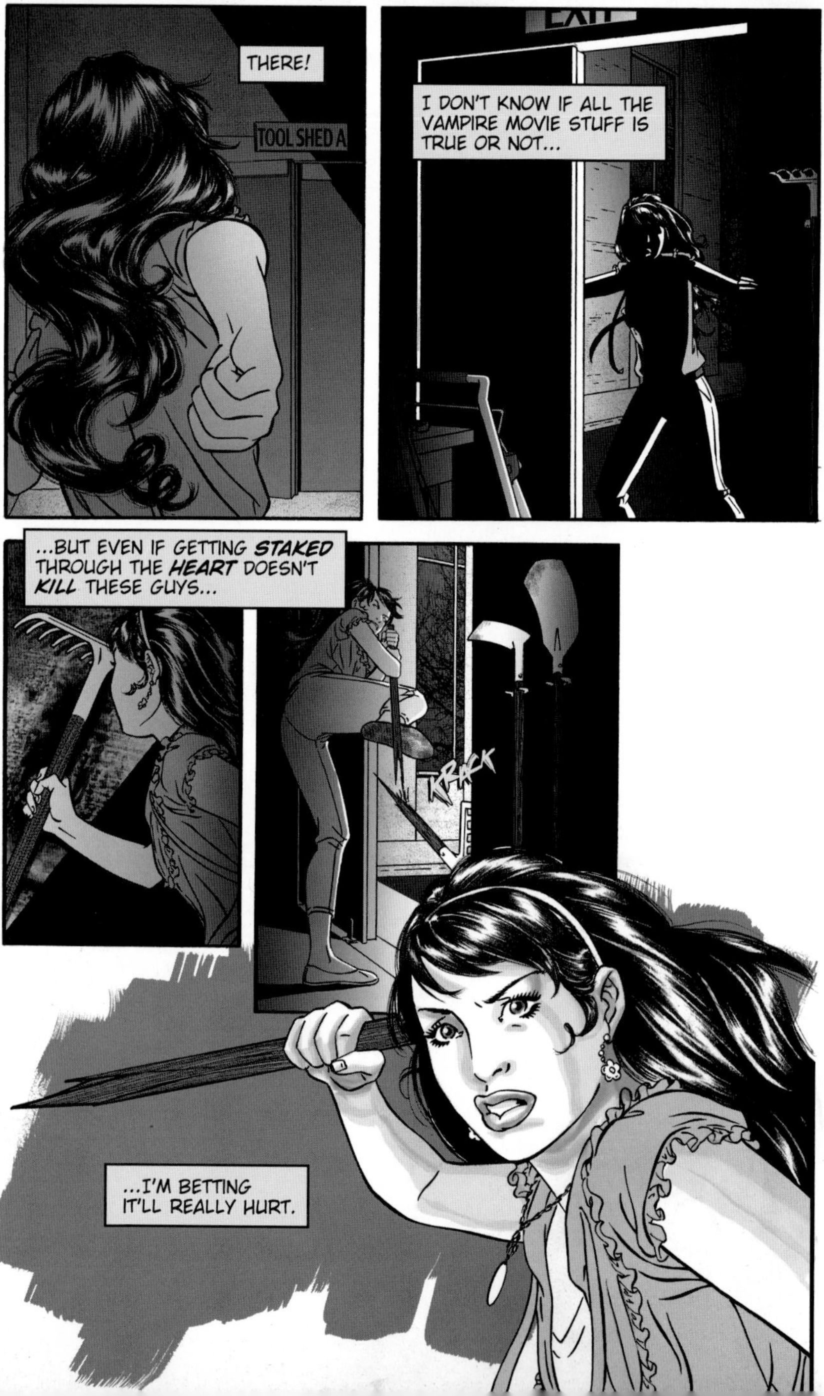
THERE!
TOOL SHED A
EXIT
I DON'T KNOW IF ALL THE VAMPIRE MOVIE STUFF IS TRUE OR NOT...
...BUT EVEN IF GETTING STAKED THROUGH THE HEART DOESN'T KILL THESE GUYS...
KRACK
...I'M BETTING IT'LL REALLY HURT.

OH
BOY
...

WOW. THAT'S
A *TOTALLY* POINTY
STICK YOU'VE GOT
THERE.

NOBODY CAN
STAKE SEVEN
VAMPS
AT ONE TIME,
VANESSA.

NOT EVEN
YOU.

Chapter 3
Painful Truths

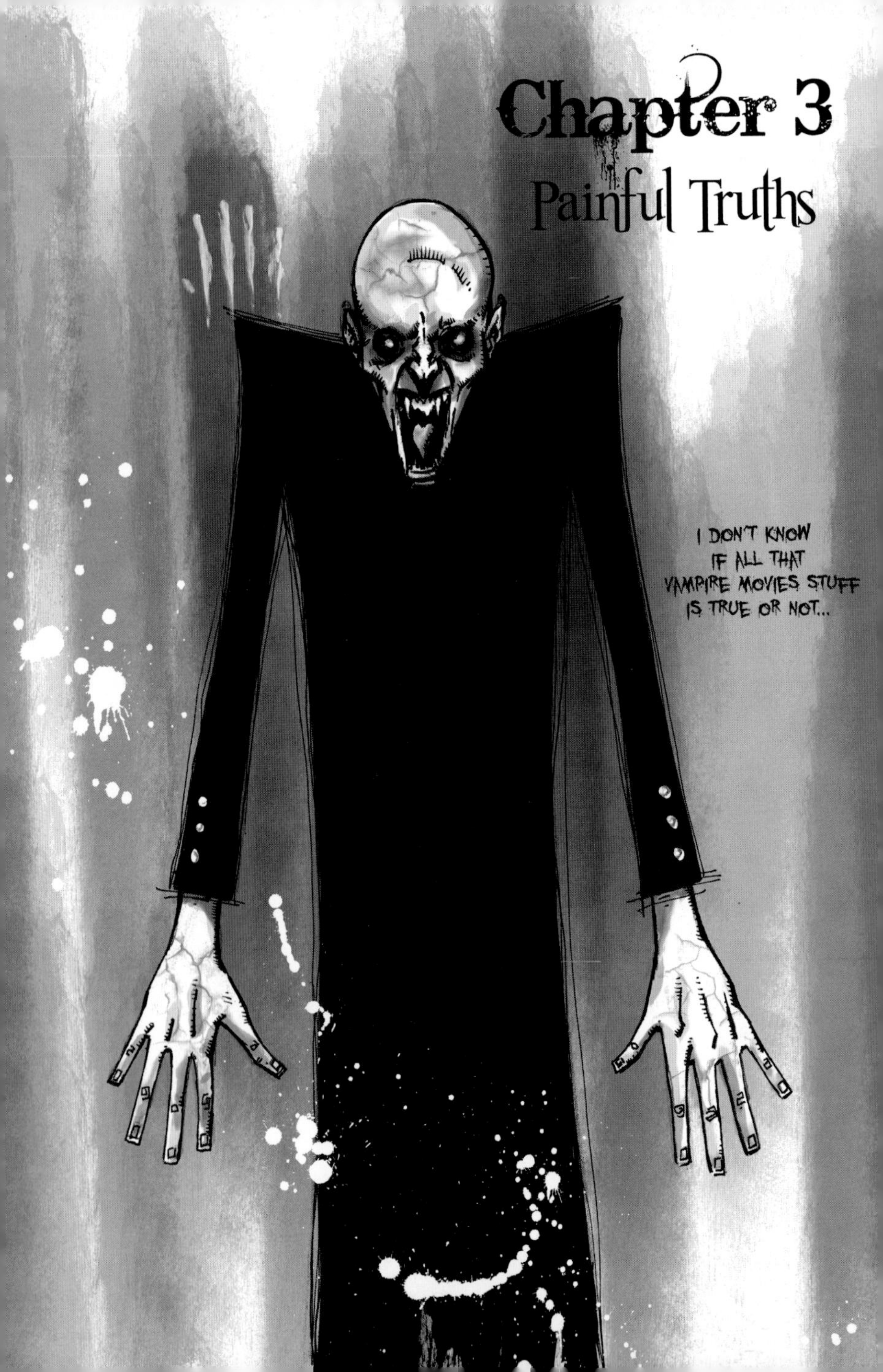
I DON'T KNOW IF ALL THAT VAMPIRE MOVIES STUFF IS TRUE OR NOT...

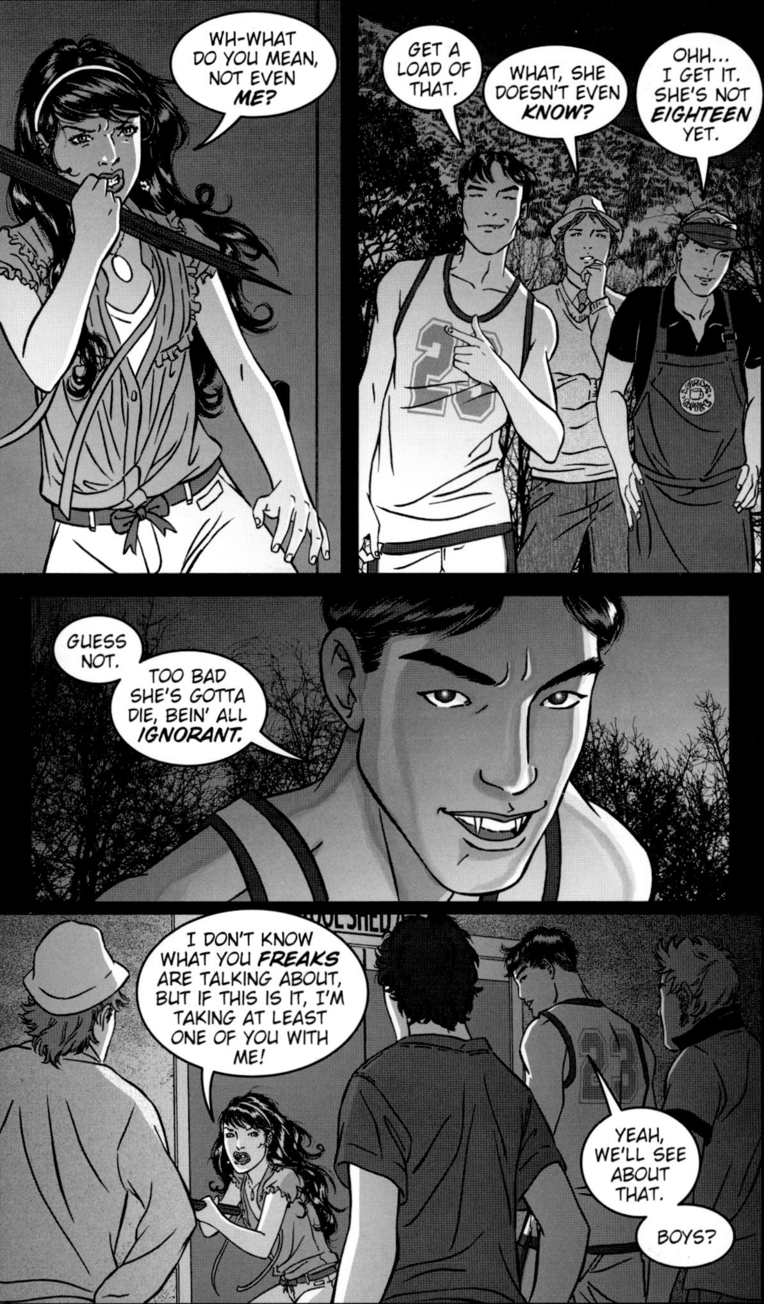
WH-WHAT DO YOU MEAN, NOT EVEN ME?
GET A LOAD OF THAT.
WHAT, SHE DOESN'T EVEN KNOW?
OHH... I GET IT. SHE'S NOT EIGHTEEN YET.
GUESS NOT.
TOO BAD SHE'S GOTTA DIE, BEIN' ALL IGNORANT.
I DON'T KNOW WHAT YOU FREAKS ARE TALKING ABOUT, BUT IF THIS IS IT, I'M TAKING AT LEAST ONE OF YOU WITH ME!
YEAH, WE'LL SEE ABOUT THAT.
BOYS?

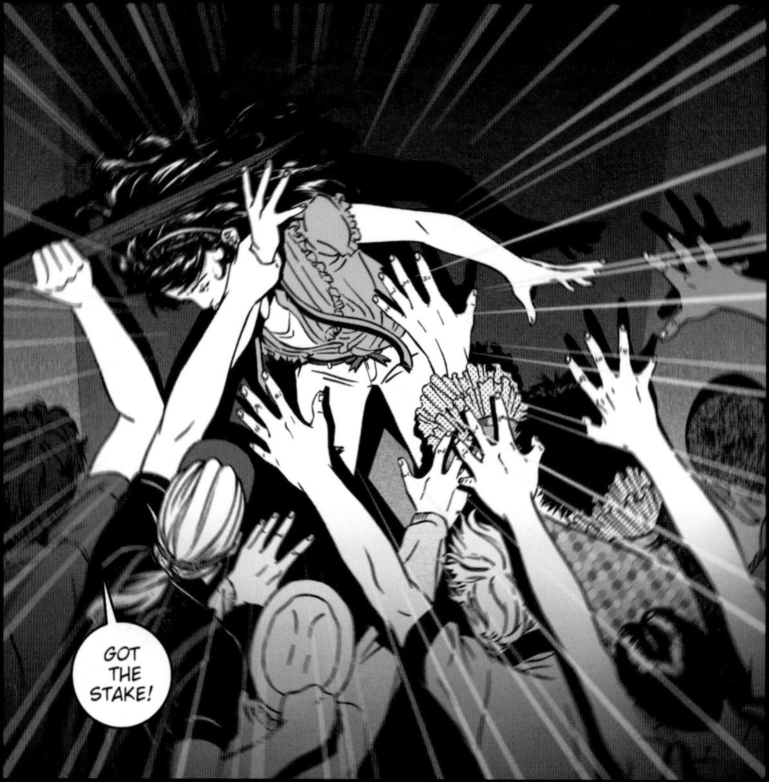
GOT THE STAKE!

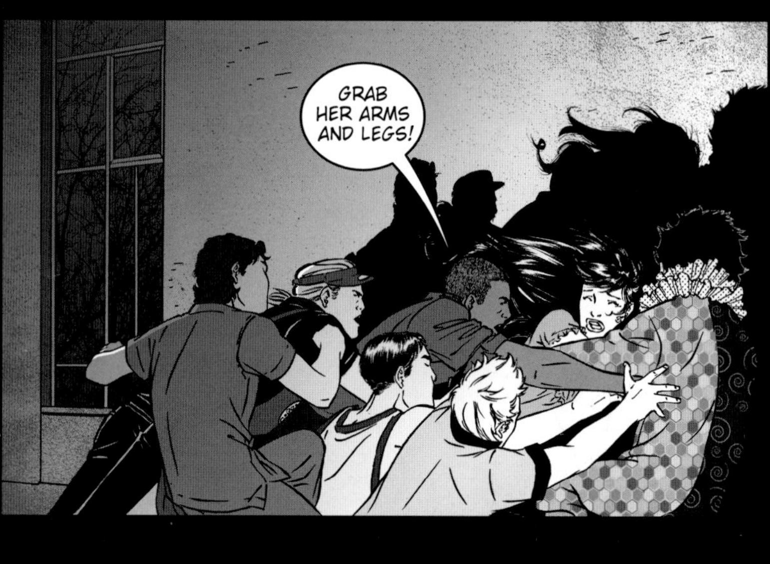
GRAB HER ARMS AND LEGS!

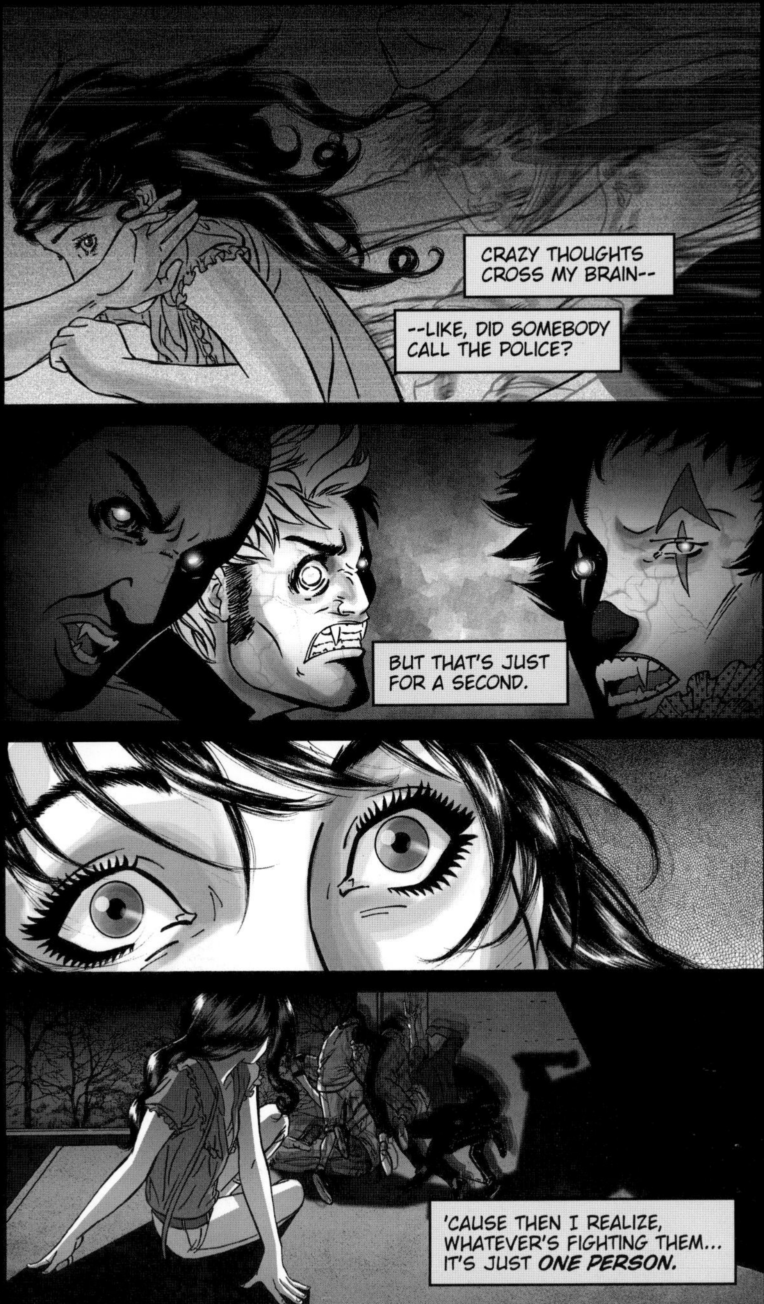
CRAZY THOUGHTS CROSS MY BRAIN--
--LIKE, DID SOMEBODY CALL THE POLICE?
BUT THAT'S JUST FOR A SECOND.
'CAUSE THEN I REALIZE, WHATEVER'S FIGHTING THEM... IT'S JUST **ONE PERSON.**

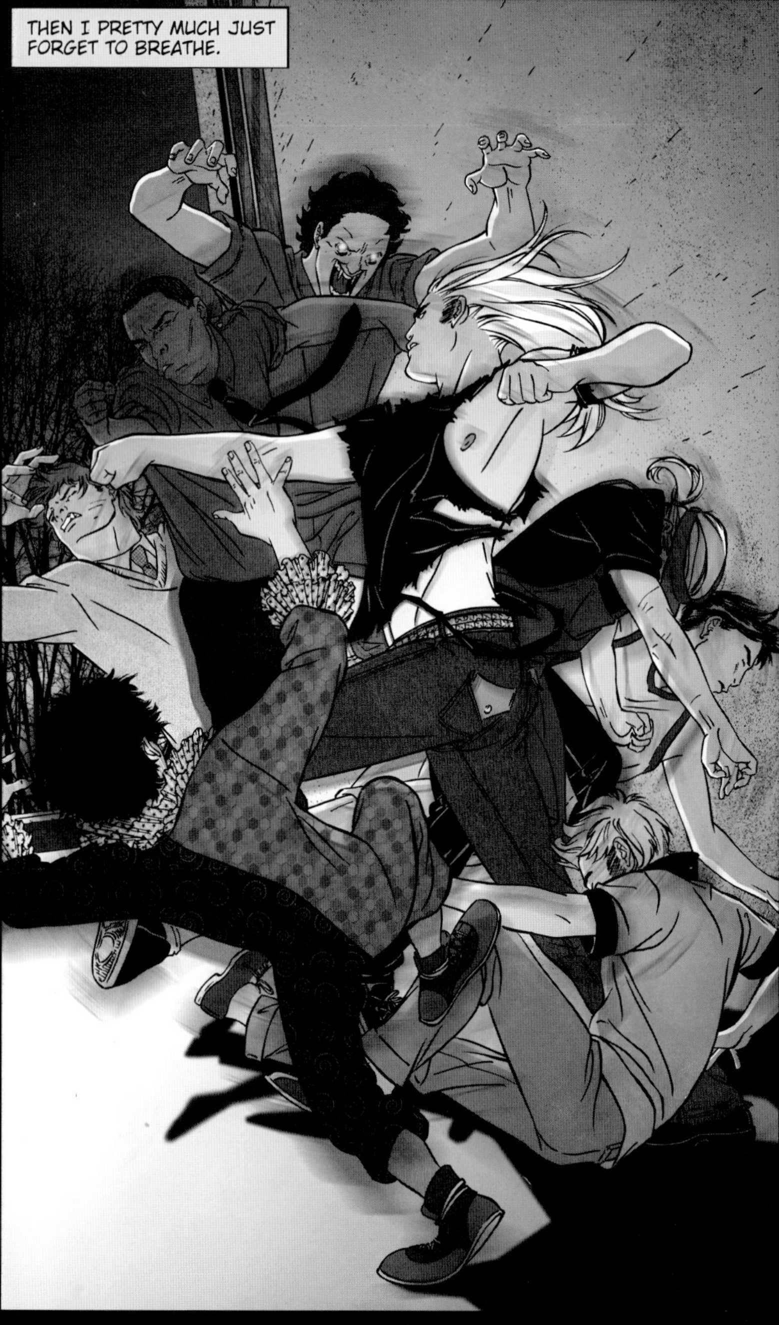
THEN I PRETTY MUCH JUST
FORGET TO BREATHE.

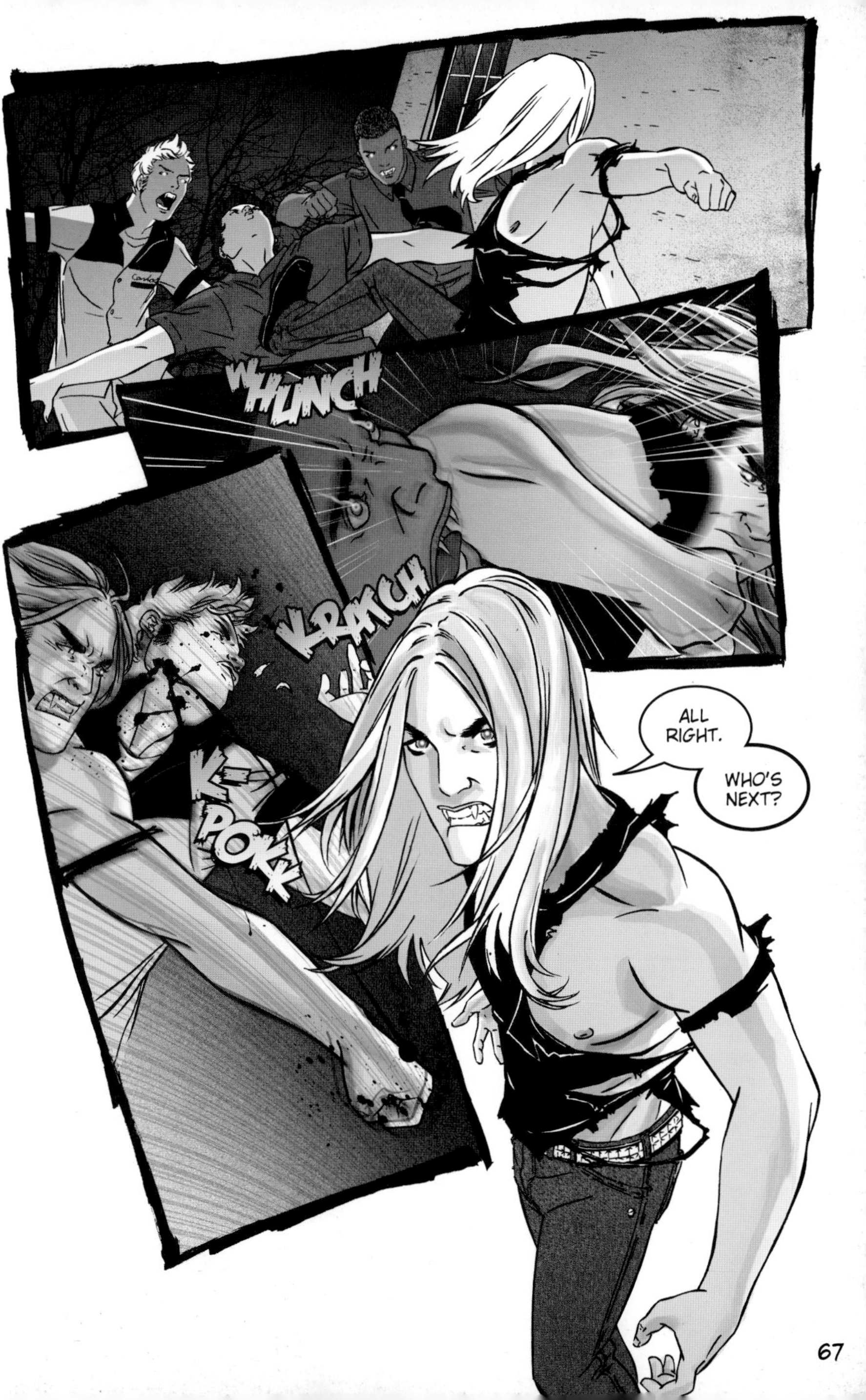
WHUNCH
KRATCH
K-POKK
ALL RIGHT.
WHO'S NEXT?

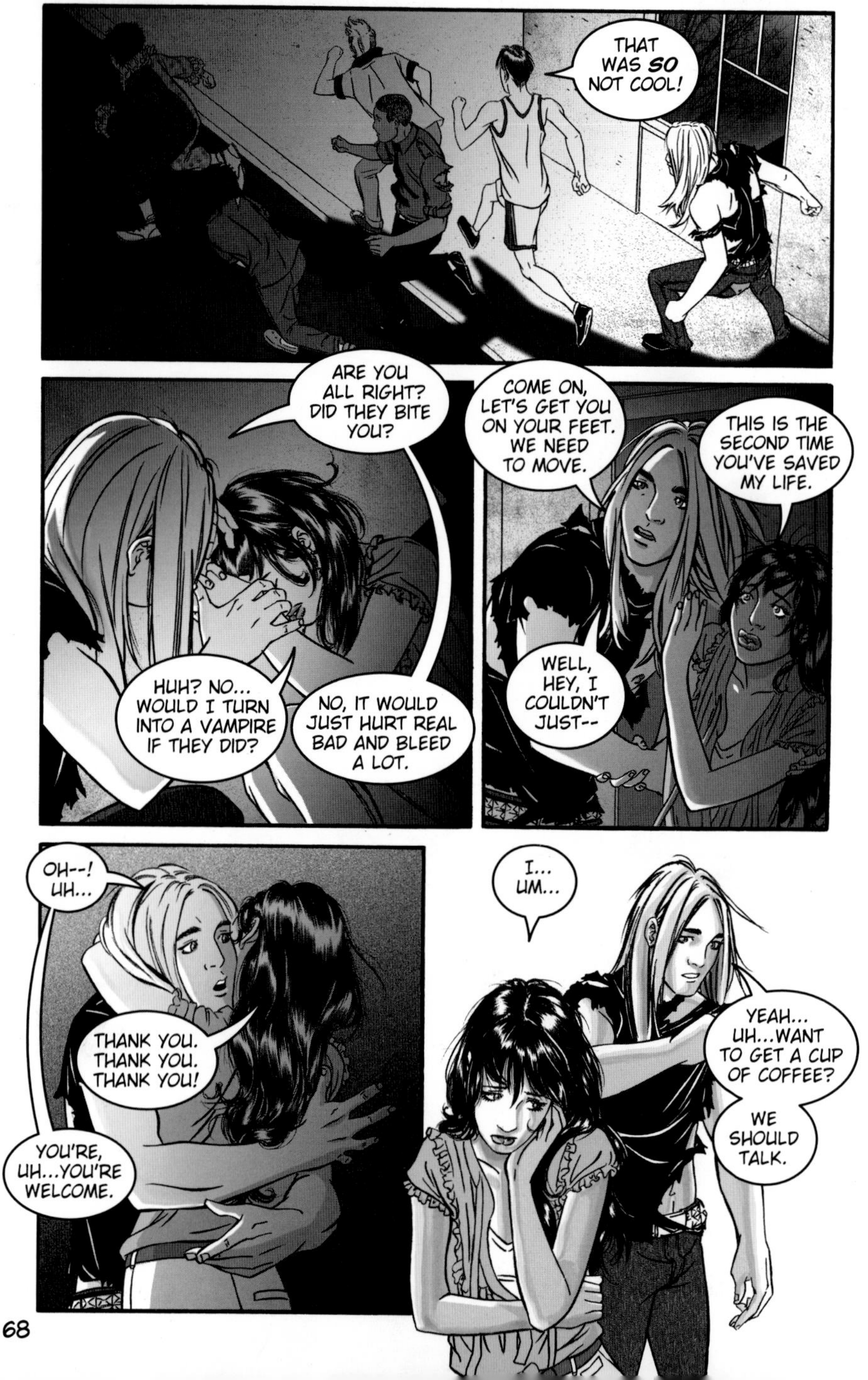
THAT WAS **SO** NOT COOL!
ARE YOU ALL RIGHT? DID THEY BITE YOU?
HUH? NO... WOULD I TURN INTO A VAMPIRE IF THEY DID?
NO, IT WOULD JUST HURT REAL BAD AND BLEED A LOT.
COME ON, LET'S GET YOU ON YOUR FEET. WE NEED TO MOVE.
THIS IS THE SECOND TIME YOU'VE SAVED MY LIFE.
WELL, HEY, I COULDN'T JUST--
OH--! UH...
THANK YOU. THANK YOU. THANK YOU!
YOU'RE, UH...YOU'RE WELCOME.
I... UM...
YEAH... UH...WANT TO GET A CUP OF COFFEE?
WE SHOULD TALK.

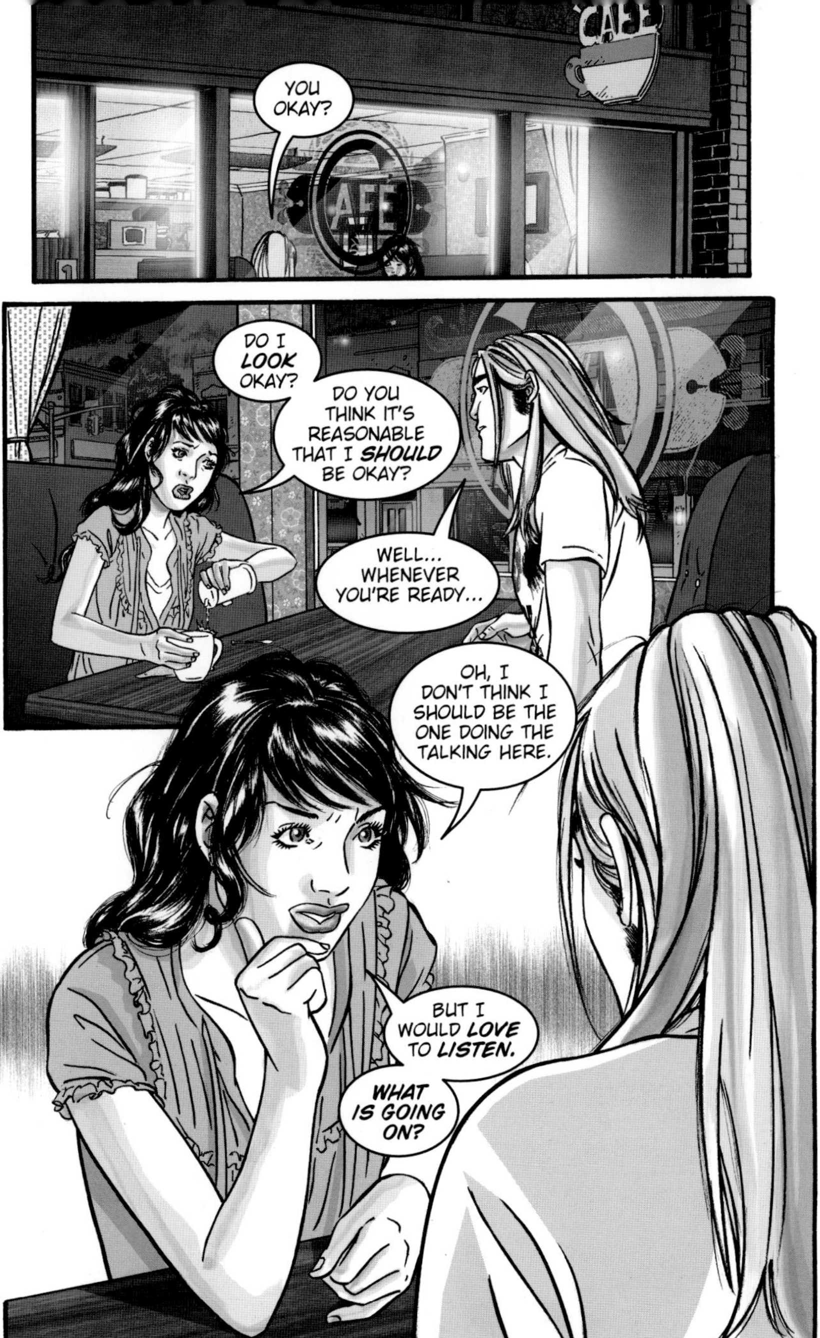

CAFE
YOU OKAY?
DO I *LOOK* OKAY?
DO YOU THINK IT'S REASONABLE THAT I *SHOULD* BE OKAY?
WELL... WHENEVER YOU'RE READY...
OH, I DON'T THINK I SHOULD BE THE ONE DOING THE TALKING HERE.
BUT I WOULD *LOVE* TO *LISTEN.*
WHAT IS GOING ON?

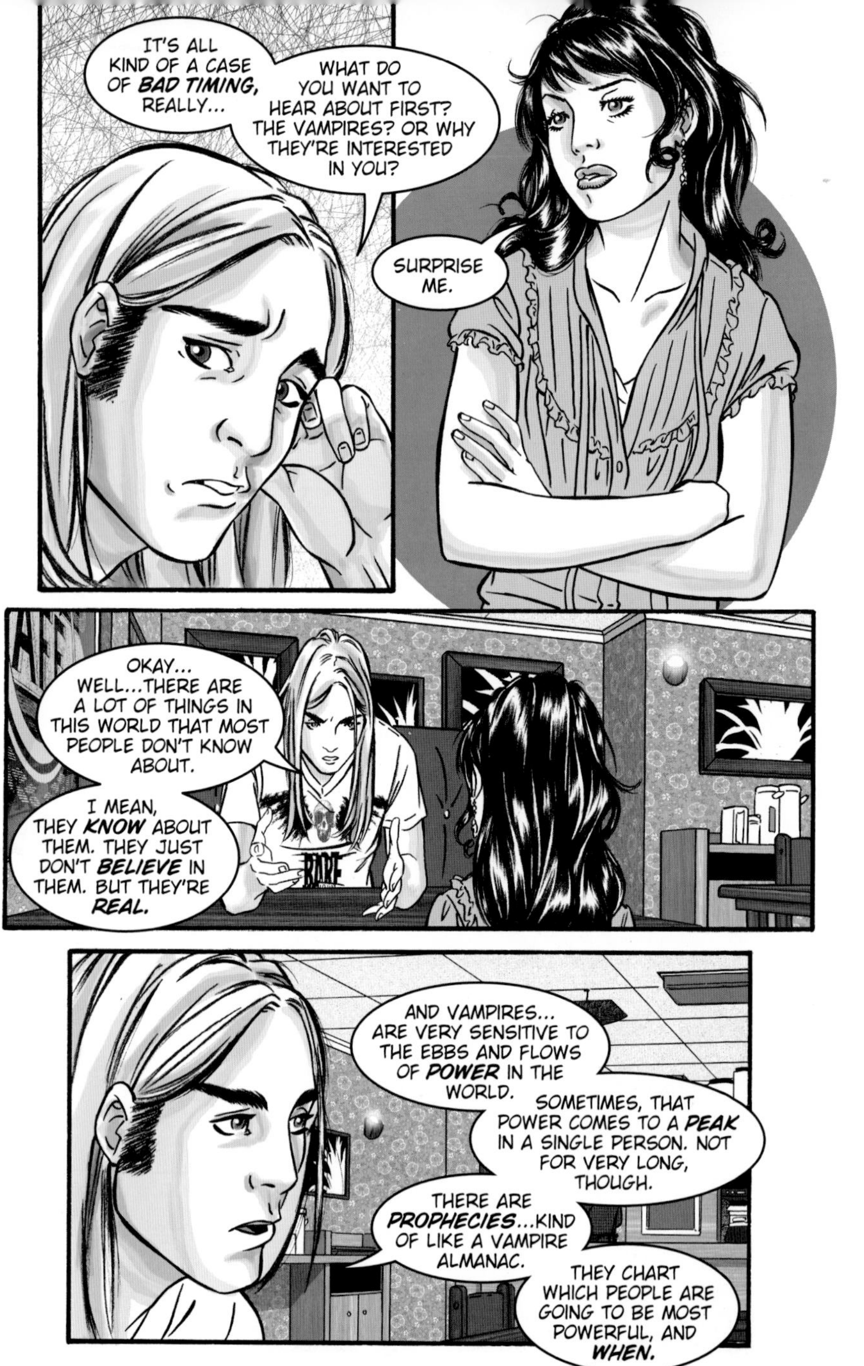
IT'S ALL KIND OF A CASE OF BAD TIMING, REALLY...
WHAT DO YOU WANT TO HEAR ABOUT FIRST? THE VAMPIRES? OR WHY THEY'RE INTERESTED IN YOU?
SURPRISE ME.
OKAY... WELL...THERE ARE A LOT OF THINGS IN THIS WORLD THAT MOST PEOPLE DON'T KNOW ABOUT.
I MEAN, THEY KNOW ABOUT THEM. THEY JUST DON'T BELIEVE IN THEM. BUT THEY'RE REAL.
AND VAMPIRES... ARE VERY SENSITIVE TO THE EBBS AND FLOWS OF POWER IN THE WORLD.
SOMETIMES, THAT POWER COMES TO A PEAK IN A SINGLE PERSON. NOT FOR VERY LONG, THOUGH.
THERE ARE PROPHECIES...KIND OF LIKE A VAMPIRE ALMANAC.
THEY CHART WHICH PEOPLE ARE GOING TO BE MOST POWERFUL, AND WHEN.

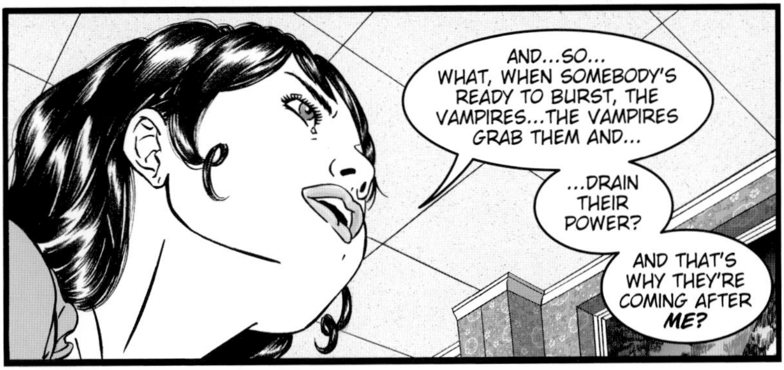
AND...SO...
WHAT, WHEN SOMEBODY'S READY TO BURST, THE VAMPIRES...THE VAMPIRES GRAB THEM AND...
...DRAIN THEIR POWER?
AND THAT'S WHY THEY'RE COMING AFTER ***ME?***

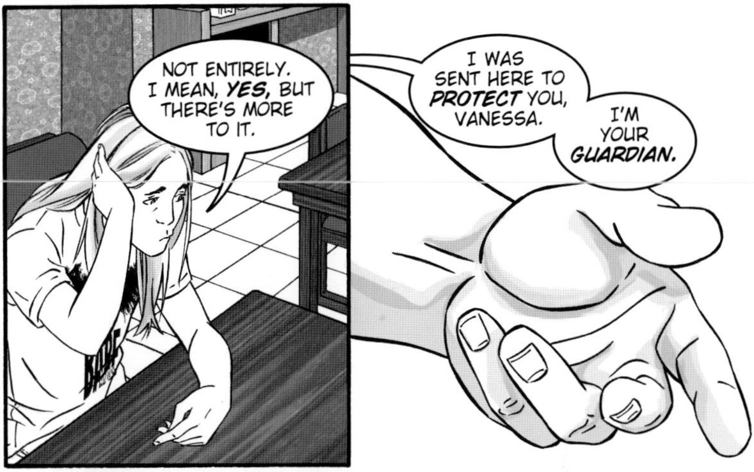
NOT ENTIRELY. I MEAN, ***YES,*** BUT THERE'S MORE TO IT.
I WAS SENT HERE TO ***PROTECT*** YOU, VANESSA.
I'M YOUR ***GUARDIAN.***

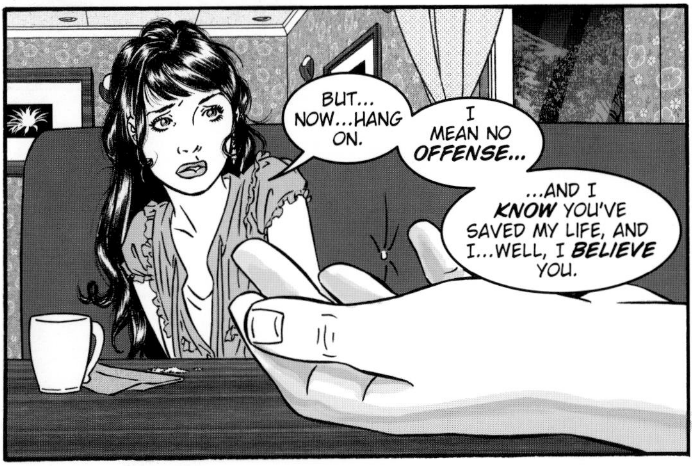
BUT... NOW...HANG ON.
I MEAN NO ***OFFENSE...***
...AND I ***KNOW*** YOU'VE SAVED MY LIFE, AND I...WELL, I ***BELIEVE*** YOU.

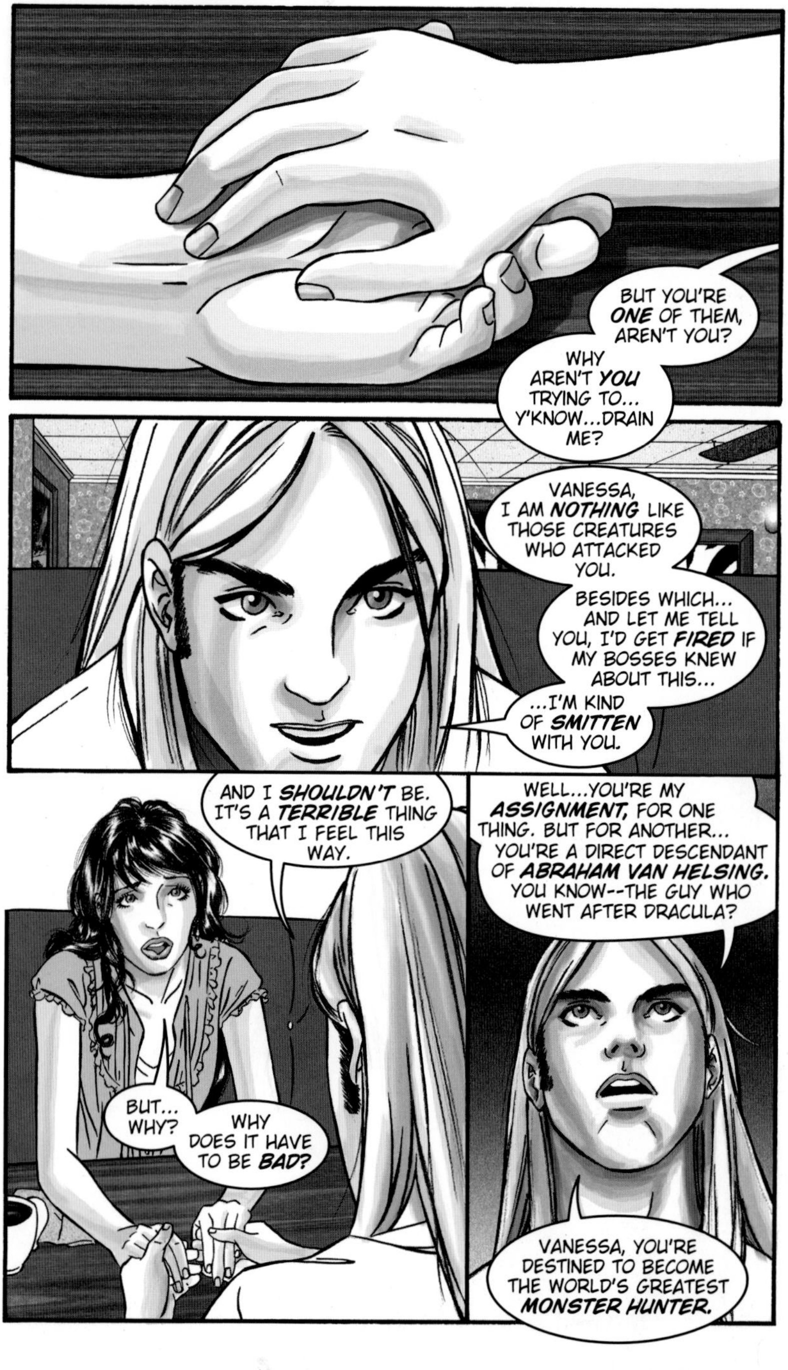
BUT YOU'RE ONE OF THEM, AREN'T YOU?
WHY AREN'T YOU TRYING TO... Y'KNOW...DRAIN ME?
VANESSA, I AM NOTHING LIKE THOSE CREATURES WHO ATTACKED YOU.
BESIDES WHICH... AND LET ME TELL YOU, I'D GET FIRED IF MY BOSSES KNEW ABOUT THIS...
...I'M KIND OF SMITTEN WITH YOU.
AND I SHOULDN'T BE. IT'S A TERRIBLE THING THAT I FEEL THIS WAY.
BUT... WHY?
WHY DOES IT HAVE TO BE BAD?
WELL...YOU'RE MY ASSIGNMENT, FOR ONE THING. BUT FOR ANOTHER... YOU'RE A DIRECT DESCENDANT OF ABRAHAM VAN HELSING. YOU KNOW--THE GUY WHO WENT AFTER DRACULA?
VANESSA, YOU'RE DESTINED TO BECOME THE WORLD'S GREATEST MONSTER HUNTER.

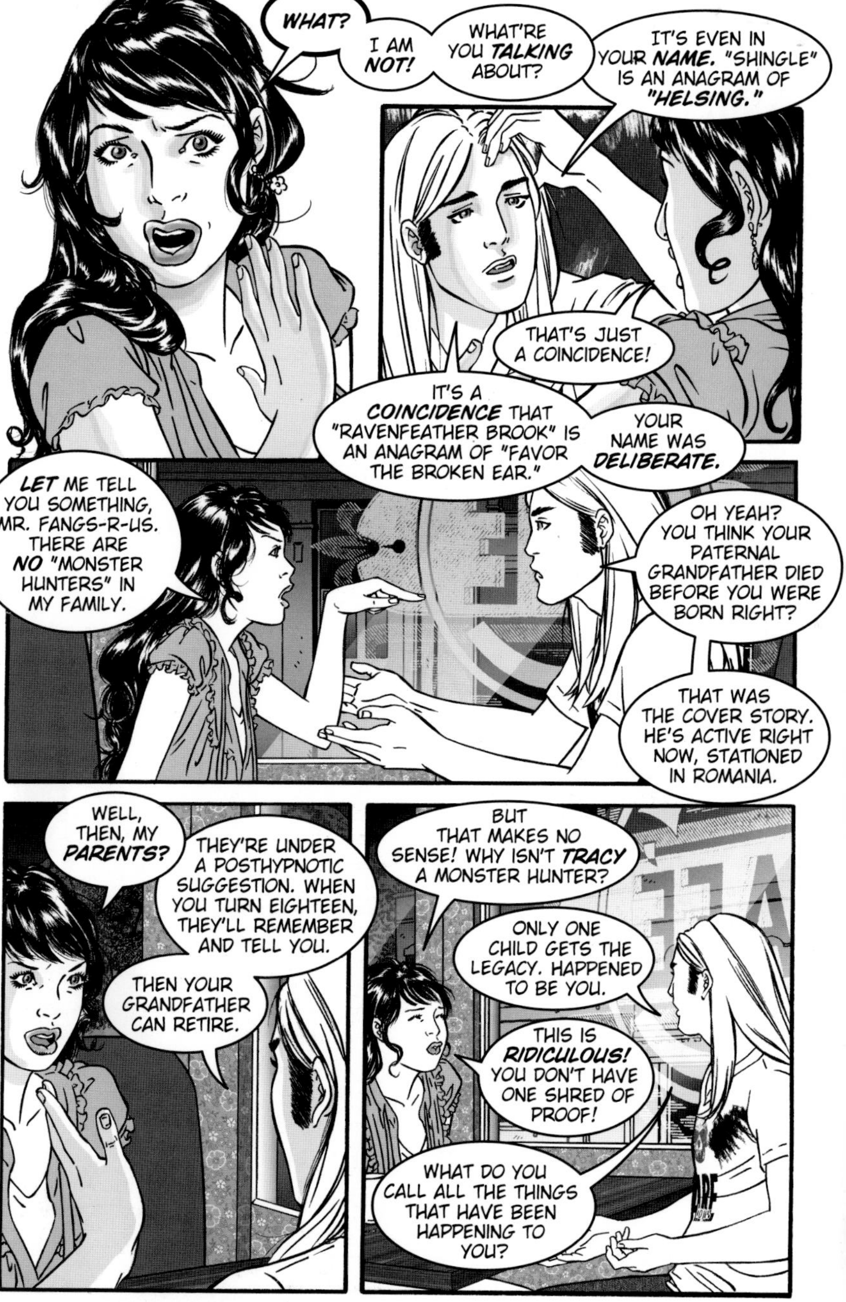
WHAT?
I AM NOT!
WHAT'RE YOU TALKING ABOUT?
IT'S EVEN IN YOUR NAME. "SHINGLE" IS AN ANAGRAM OF "HELSING."
THAT'S JUST A COINCIDENCE!
IT'S A COINCIDENCE THAT "RAVENFEATHER BROOK" IS AN ANAGRAM OF "FAVOR THE BROKEN EAR."
YOUR NAME WAS DELIBERATE.
LET ME TELL YOU SOMETHING, MR. FANGS-R-US. THERE ARE NO "MONSTER HUNTERS" IN MY FAMILY.
OH YEAH? YOU THINK YOUR PATERNAL GRANDFATHER DIED BEFORE YOU WERE BORN RIGHT?
THAT WAS THE COVER STORY. HE'S ACTIVE RIGHT NOW, STATIONED IN ROMANIA.
WELL, THEN, MY PARENTS?
THEY'RE UNDER A POSTHYPNOTIC SUGGESTION. WHEN YOU TURN EIGHTEEN, THEY'LL REMEMBER AND TELL YOU.
THEN YOUR GRANDFATHER CAN RETIRE.
BUT THAT MAKES NO SENSE! WHY ISN'T TRACY A MONSTER HUNTER?
ONLY ONE CHILD GETS THE LEGACY. HAPPENED TO BE YOU.
THIS IS RIDICULOUS! YOU DON'T HAVE ONE SHRED OF PROOF!
WHAT DO YOU CALL ALL THE THINGS THAT HAVE BEEN HAPPENING TO YOU?

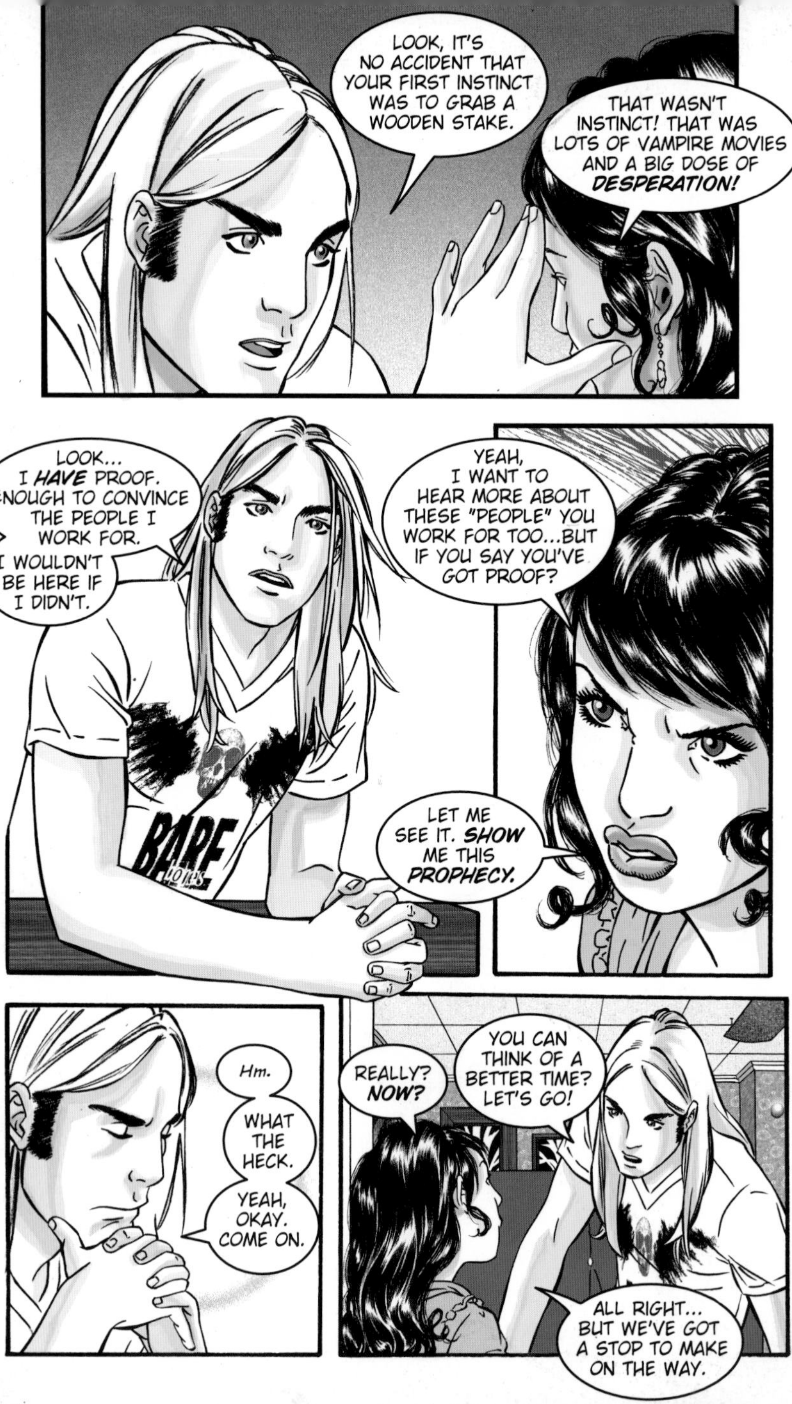
LOOK, IT'S NO ACCIDENT THAT YOUR FIRST INSTINCT WAS TO GRAB A WOODEN STAKE.
THAT WASN'T INSTINCT! THAT WAS LOTS OF VAMPIRE MOVIES AND A BIG DOSE OF DESPERATION!
LOOK... I HAVE PROOF. ENOUGH TO CONVINCE THE PEOPLE I WORK FOR.
I WOULDN'T BE HERE IF I DIDN'T.
YEAH, I WANT TO HEAR MORE ABOUT THESE "PEOPLE" YOU WORK FOR TOO...BUT IF YOU SAY YOU'VE GOT PROOF?
LET ME SEE IT. SHOW ME THIS PROPHECY.
Hm.
WHAT THE HECK.
YEAH, OKAY. COME ON.
REALLY? NOW?
YOU CAN THINK OF A BETTER TIME? LET'S GO!
ALL RIGHT... BUT WE'VE GOT A STOP TO MAKE ON THE WAY.

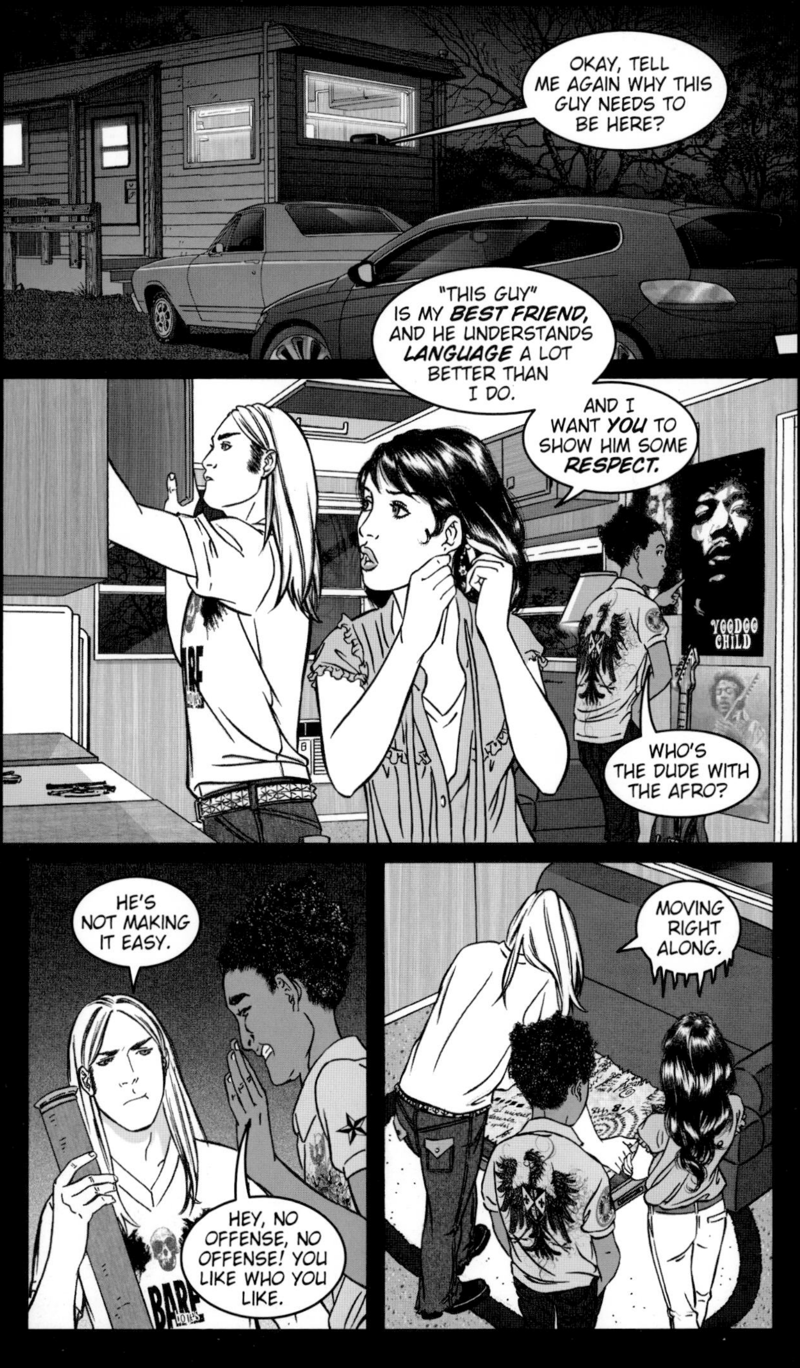
OKAY, TELL ME AGAIN WHY THIS GUY NEEDS TO BE HERE?
"THIS GUY" IS MY **BEST FRIEND,** AND HE UNDERSTANDS **LANGUAGE** A LOT BETTER THAN I DO.
AND I WANT **YOU** TO SHOW HIM SOME **RESPECT.**
VOODOO CHILD
WHO'S THE DUDE WITH THE AFRO?
HE'S NOT MAKING IT EASY.
HEY, NO OFFENSE, NO OFFENSE! YOU LIKE WHO YOU LIKE.
MOVING RIGHT ALONG.

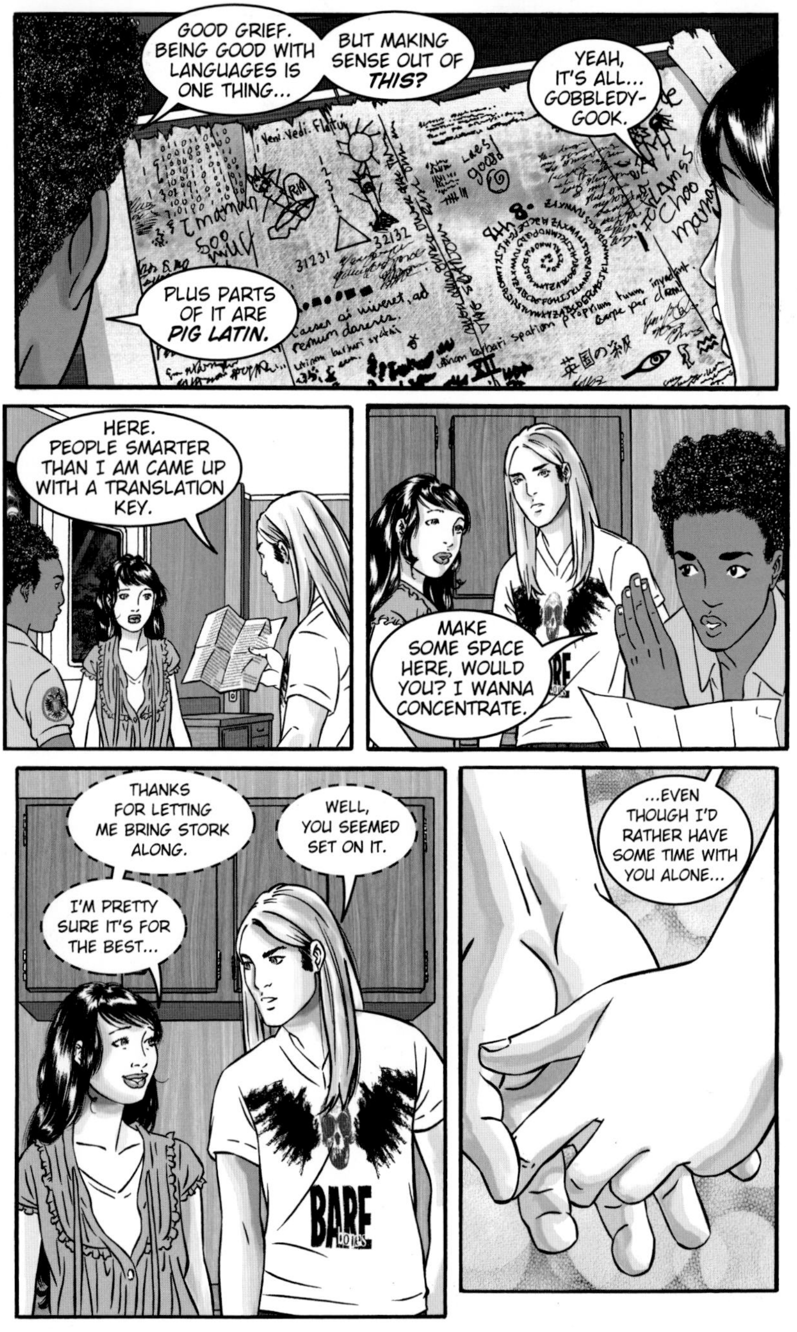
GOOD GRIEF. BEING GOOD WITH LANGUAGES IS ONE THING...
BUT MAKING SENSE OUT OF *THIS?*
YEAH, IT'S ALL... GOBBLEDY-GOOK.
PLUS PARTS OF IT ARE *PIG LATIN.*
HERE. PEOPLE SMARTER THAN I AM CAME UP WITH A TRANSLATION KEY.
MAKE SOME SPACE HERE, WOULD YOU? I WANNA CONCENTRATE.
THANKS FOR LETTING ME BRING STORK ALONG.
I'M PRETTY SURE IT'S FOR THE BEST...
WELL, YOU SEEMED SET ON IT.
...EVEN THOUGH I'D RATHER HAVE SOME TIME WITH YOU ALONE...

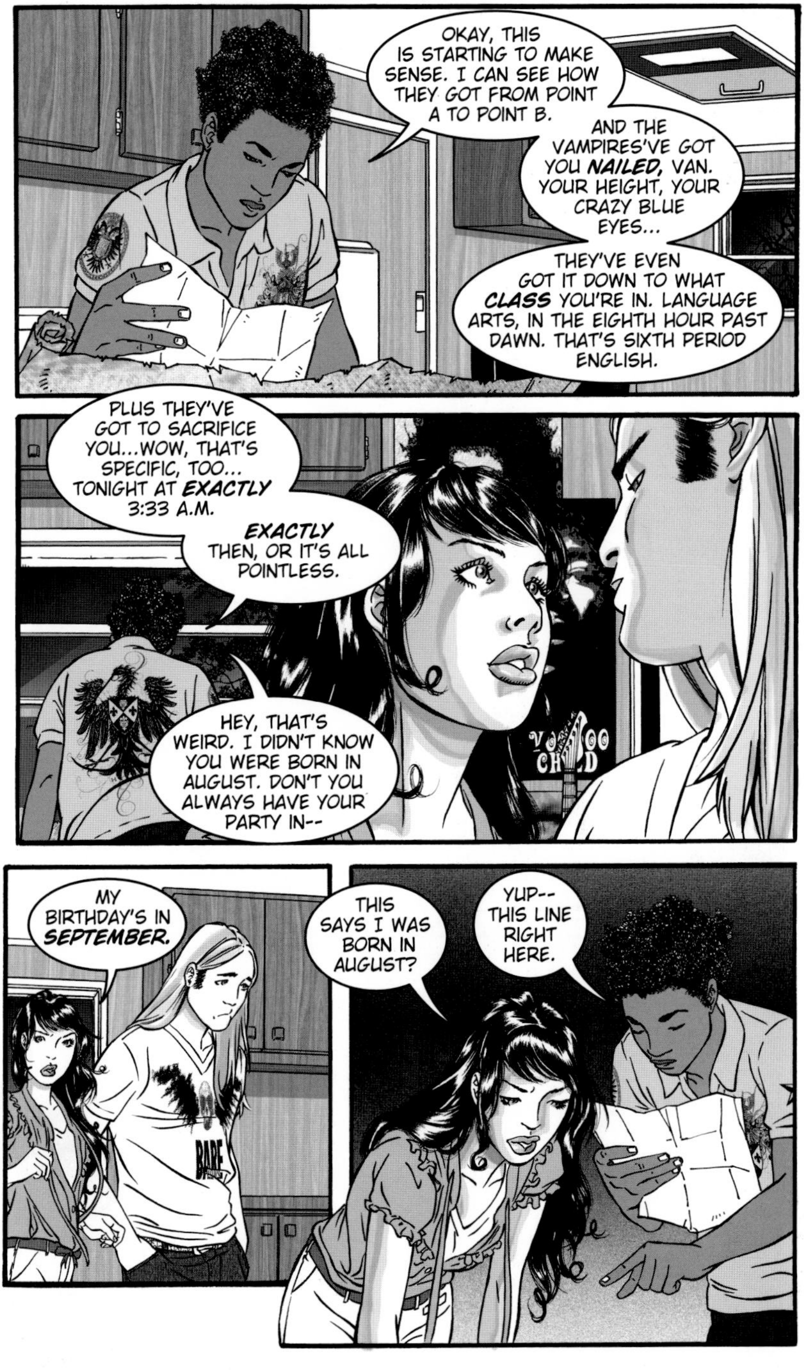
OKAY, THIS IS STARTING TO MAKE SENSE. I CAN SEE HOW THEY GOT FROM POINT A TO POINT B.
AND THE VAMPIRES'VE GOT YOU NAILED, VAN. YOUR HEIGHT, YOUR CRAZY BLUE EYES...
THEY'VE EVEN GOT IT DOWN TO WHAT CLASS YOU'RE IN. LANGUAGE ARTS, IN THE EIGHTH HOUR PAST DAWN. THAT'S SIXTH PERIOD ENGLISH.
PLUS THEY'VE GOT TO SACRIFICE YOU...WOW, THAT'S SPECIFIC, TOO... TONIGHT AT EXACTLY 3:33 A.M.
EXACTLY THEN, OR IT'S ALL POINTLESS.
HEY, THAT'S WEIRD. I DIDN'T KNOW YOU WERE BORN IN AUGUST. DON'T YOU ALWAYS HAVE YOUR PARTY IN--
MY BIRTHDAY'S IN SEPTEMBER.
THIS SAYS I WAS BORN IN AUGUST?
YUP-- THIS LINE RIGHT HERE.

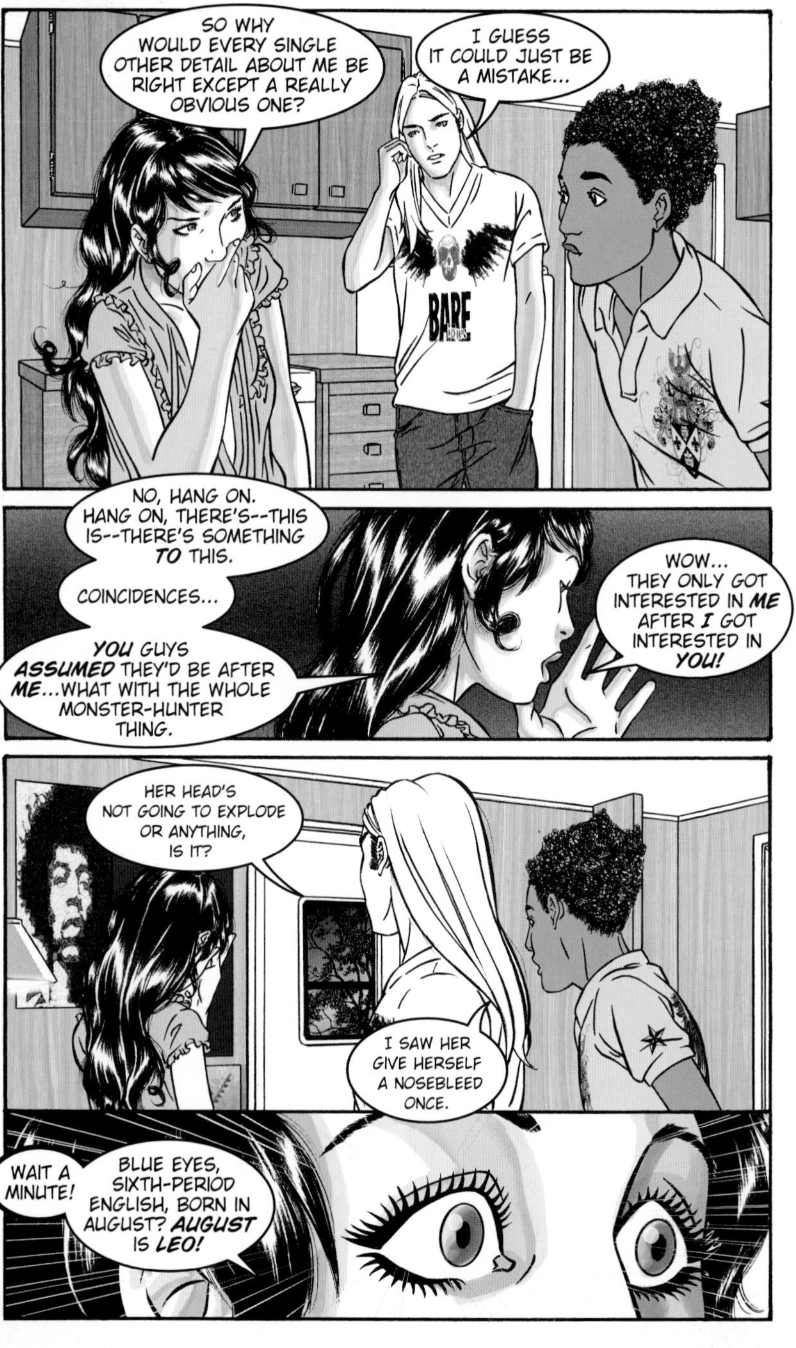
SO WHY WOULD EVERY SINGLE OTHER DETAIL ABOUT ME BE RIGHT EXCEPT A REALLY OBVIOUS ONE?
I GUESS IT COULD JUST BE A MISTAKE...
BARE
NO, HANG ON. HANG ON, THERE'S--THIS IS--THERE'S SOMETHING TO THIS.
COINCIDENCES...
YOU GUYS ASSUMED THEY'D BE AFTER ME...WHAT WITH THE WHOLE MONSTER-HUNTER THING.
WOW... THEY ONLY GOT INTERESTED IN ME AFTER I GOT INTERESTED IN YOU!
HER HEAD'S NOT GOING TO EXPLODE OR ANYTHING, IS IT?
I SAW HER GIVE HERSELF A NOSEBLEED ONCE.
WAIT A MINUTE!
BLUE EYES, SIXTH-PERIOD ENGLISH, BORN IN AUGUST? AUGUST IS LEO!

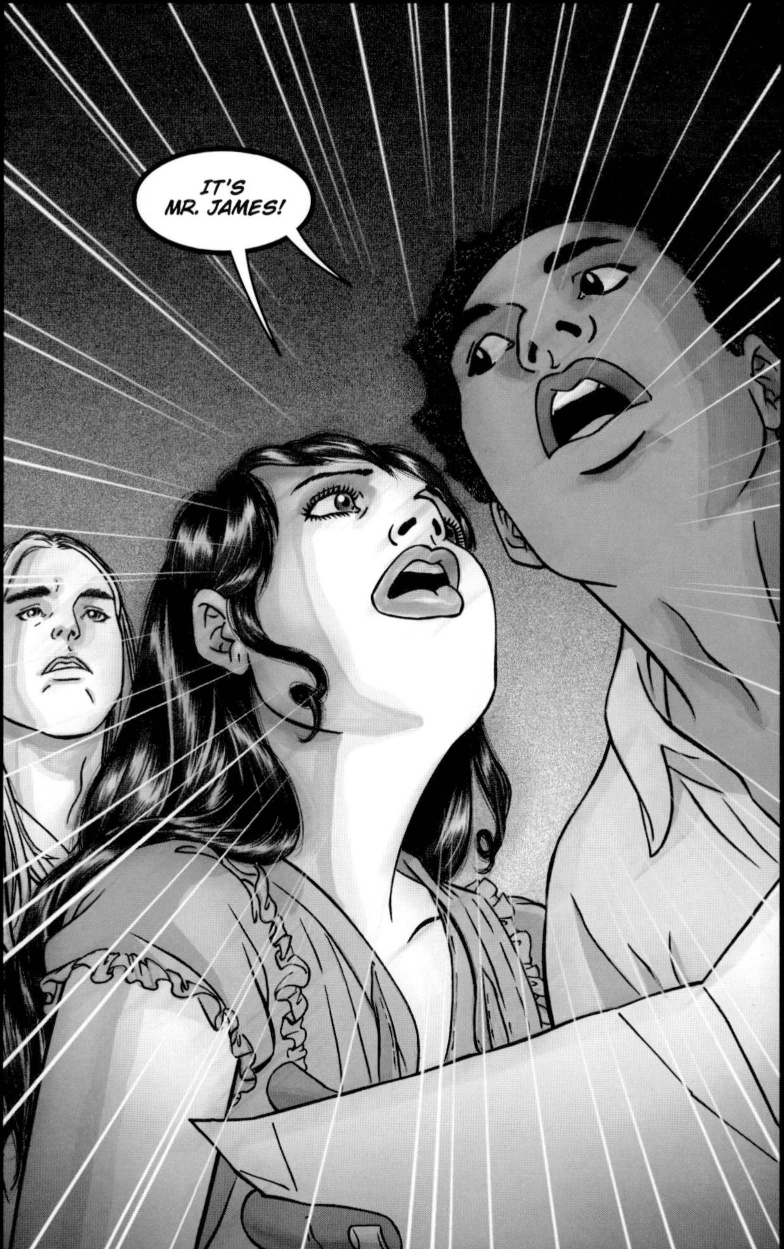
IT'S MR. JAMES!

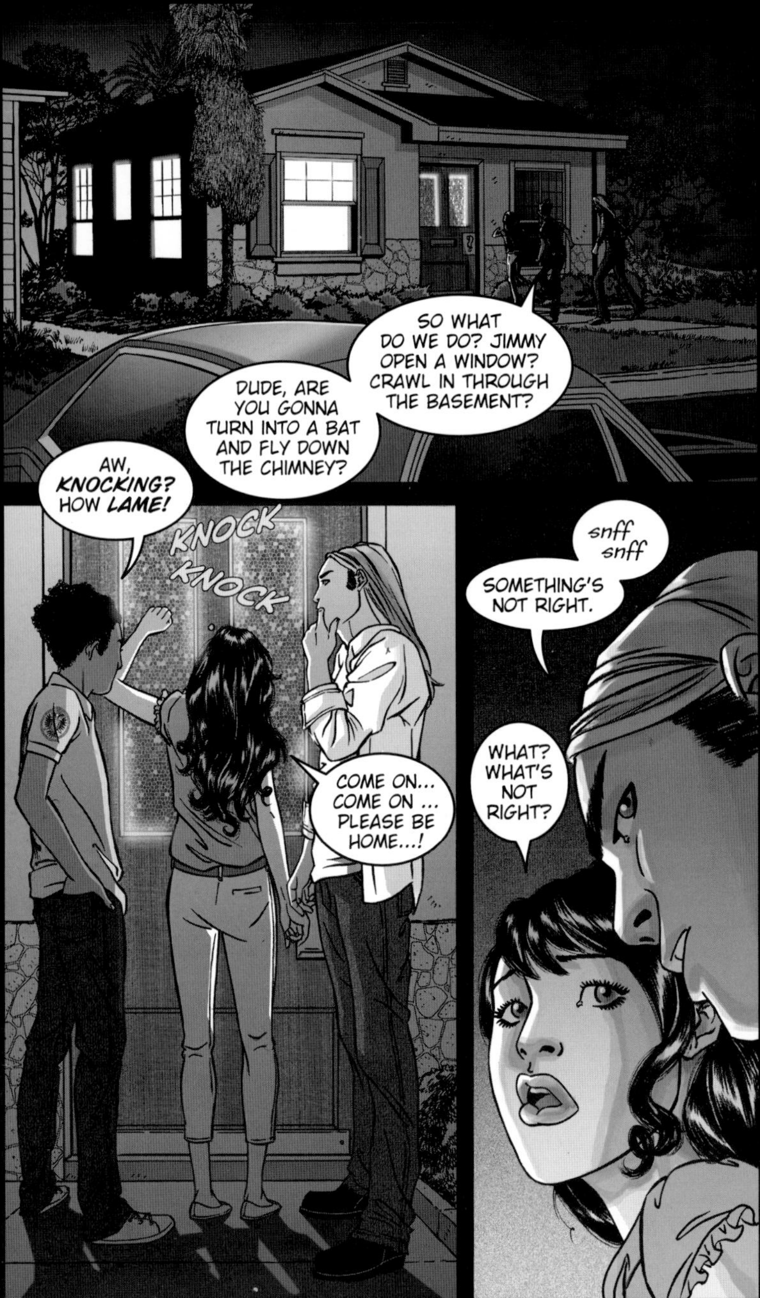
SO WHAT DO WE DO? JIMMY OPEN A WINDOW? CRAWL IN THROUGH THE BASEMENT?
DUDE, ARE YOU GONNA TURN INTO A BAT AND FLY DOWN THE CHIMNEY?
AW, ***KNOCKING?*** HOW ***LAME!***
KNOCK KNOCK
COME ON... COME ON ... PLEASE BE HOME...!
snff snff
SOMETHING'S NOT RIGHT.
WHAT? WHAT'S NOT RIGHT?

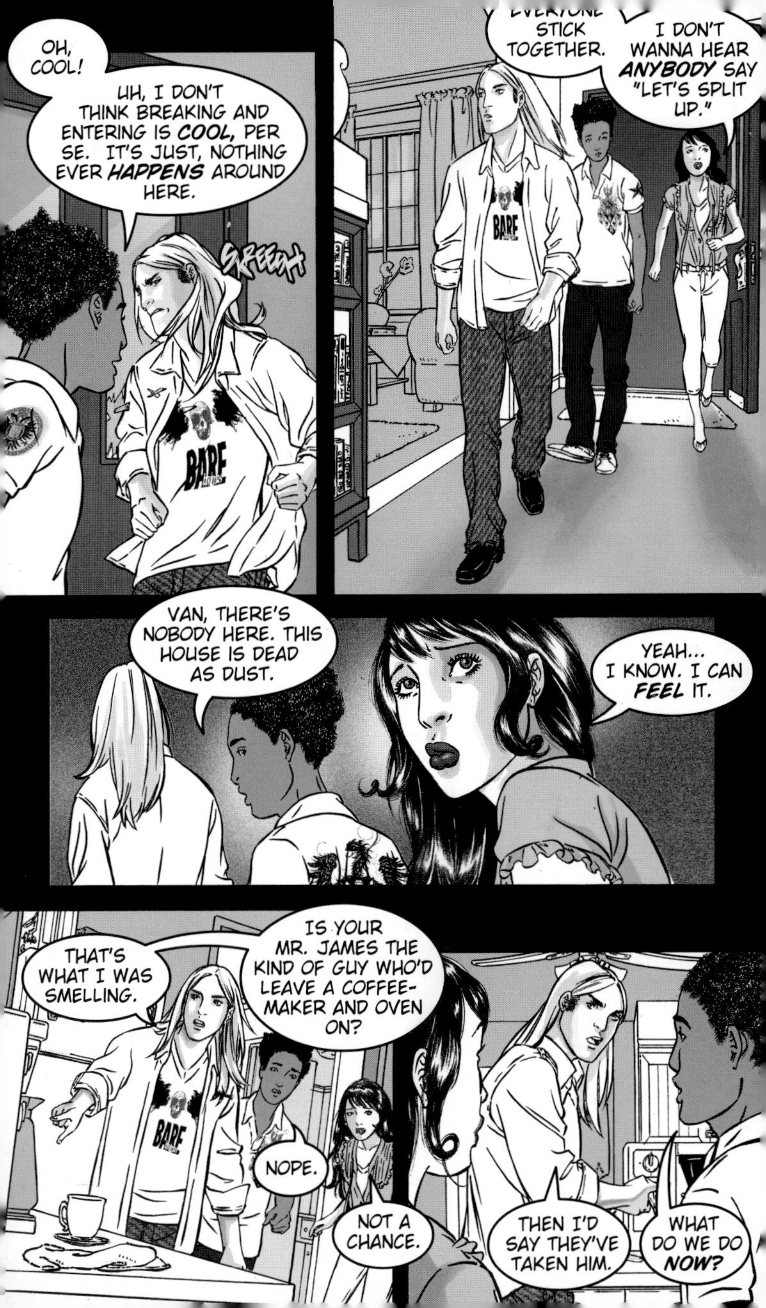
OH, COOL!
UH, I DON'T THINK BREAKING AND ENTERING IS *COOL,* PER SE. IT'S JUST, NOTHING EVER *HAPPENS* AROUND HERE.
SKREEGH
STICK TOGETHER.
I DON'T WANNA HEAR *ANYBODY* SAY "LET'S SPLIT UP."
VAN, THERE'S NOBODY HERE. THIS HOUSE IS DEAD AS DUST.
YEAH... I KNOW. I CAN *FEEL* IT.
THAT'S WHAT I WAS SMELLING.
IS YOUR MR. JAMES THE KIND OF GUY WHO'D LEAVE A COFFEE-MAKER AND OVEN ON?
NOPE.
NOT A CHANCE.
THEN I'D SAY THEY'VE TAKEN HIM.
WHAT DO WE DO *NOW?*

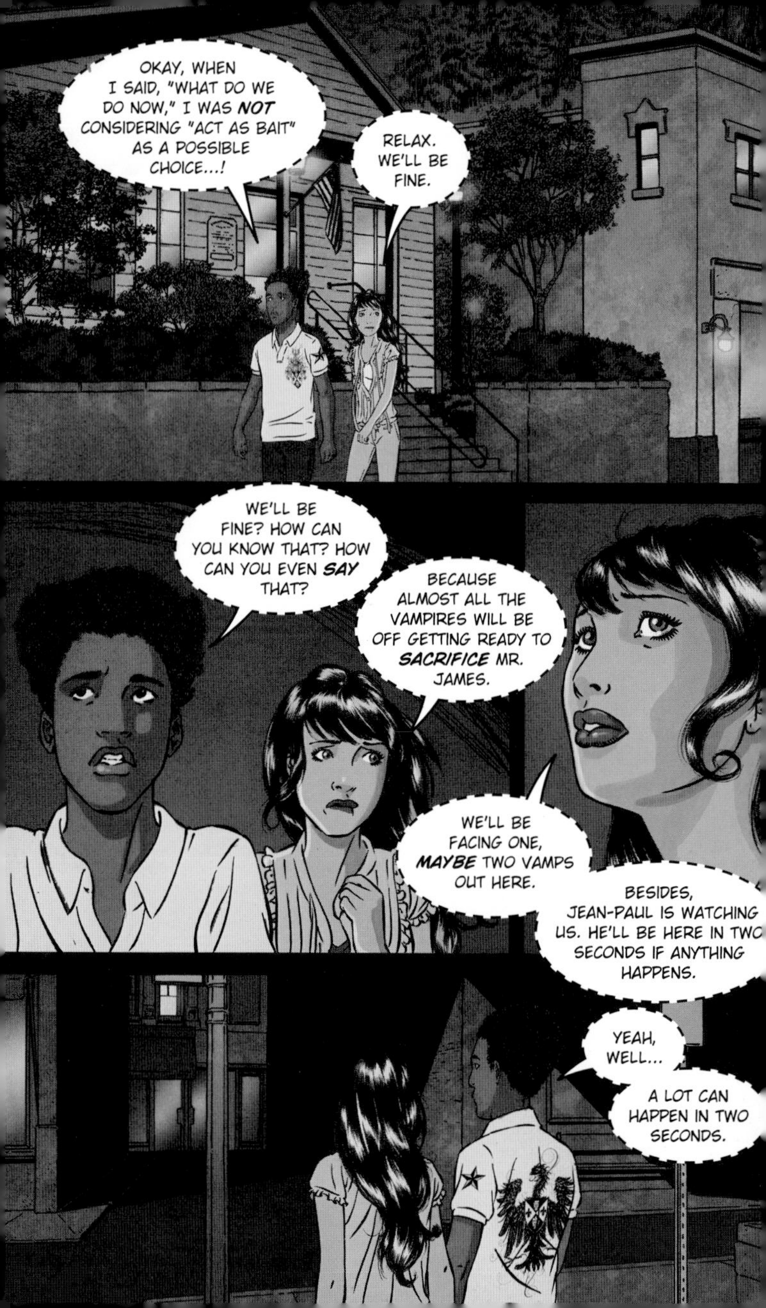
OKAY, WHEN I SAID, "WHAT DO WE DO NOW," I WAS NOT CONSIDERING "ACT AS BAIT" AS A POSSIBLE CHOICE...!
RELAX. WE'LL BE FINE.
WE'LL BE FINE? HOW CAN YOU KNOW THAT? HOW CAN YOU EVEN SAY THAT?
BECAUSE ALMOST ALL THE VAMPIRES WILL BE OFF GETTING READY TO SACRIFICE MR. JAMES.
WE'LL BE FACING ONE, MAYBE TWO VAMPS OUT HERE.
BESIDES, JEAN-PAUL IS WATCHING US. HE'LL BE HERE IN TWO SECONDS IF ANYTHING HAPPENS.
YEAH, WELL...
A LOT CAN HAPPEN IN TWO SECONDS.

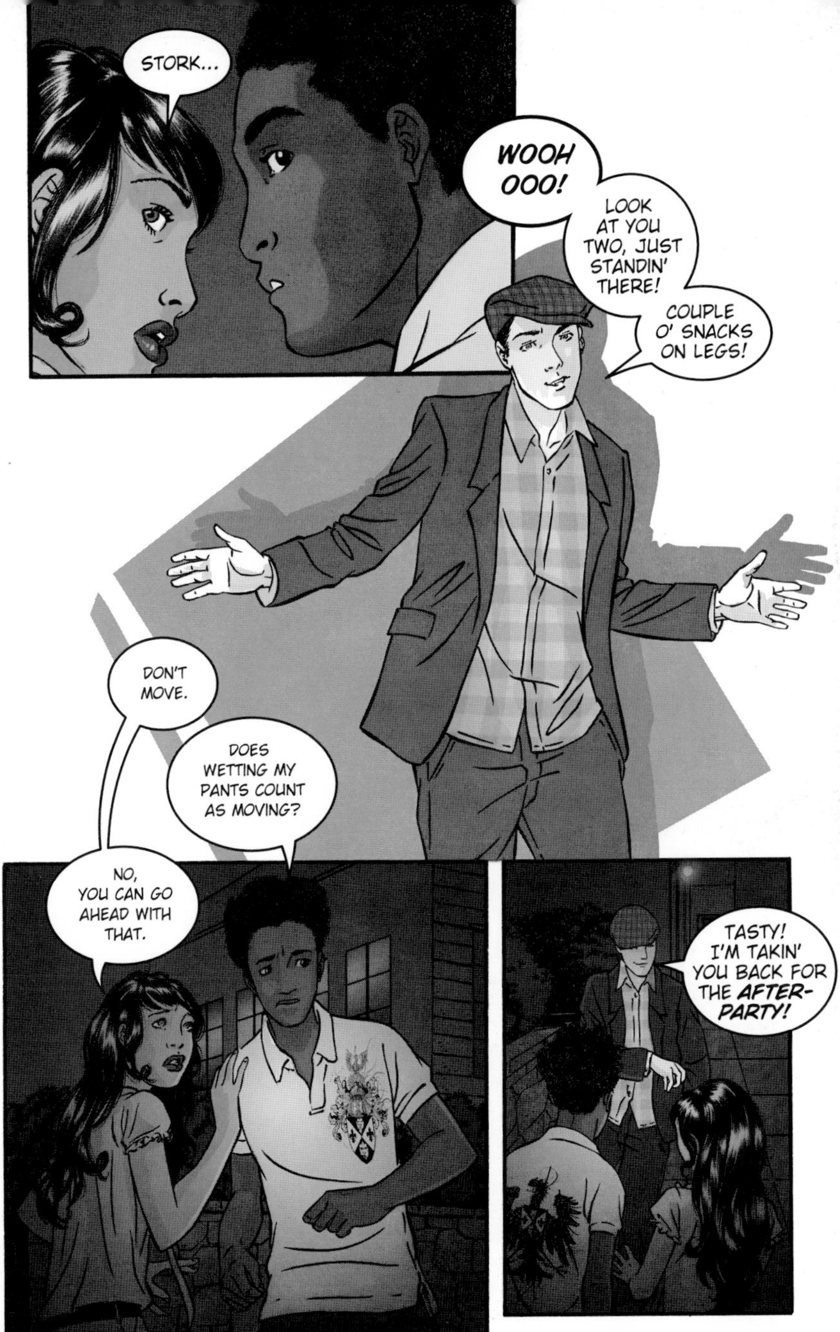
STORK...
WOOH OOO!
LOOK AT YOU TWO, JUST STANDIN' THERE!
COUPLE O' SNACKS ON LEGS!
DON'T MOVE.
DOES WETTING MY PANTS COUNT AS MOVING?
NO, YOU CAN GO AHEAD WITH THAT.
TASTY! I'M TAKIN' YOU BACK FOR THE **AFTER-PARTY!**

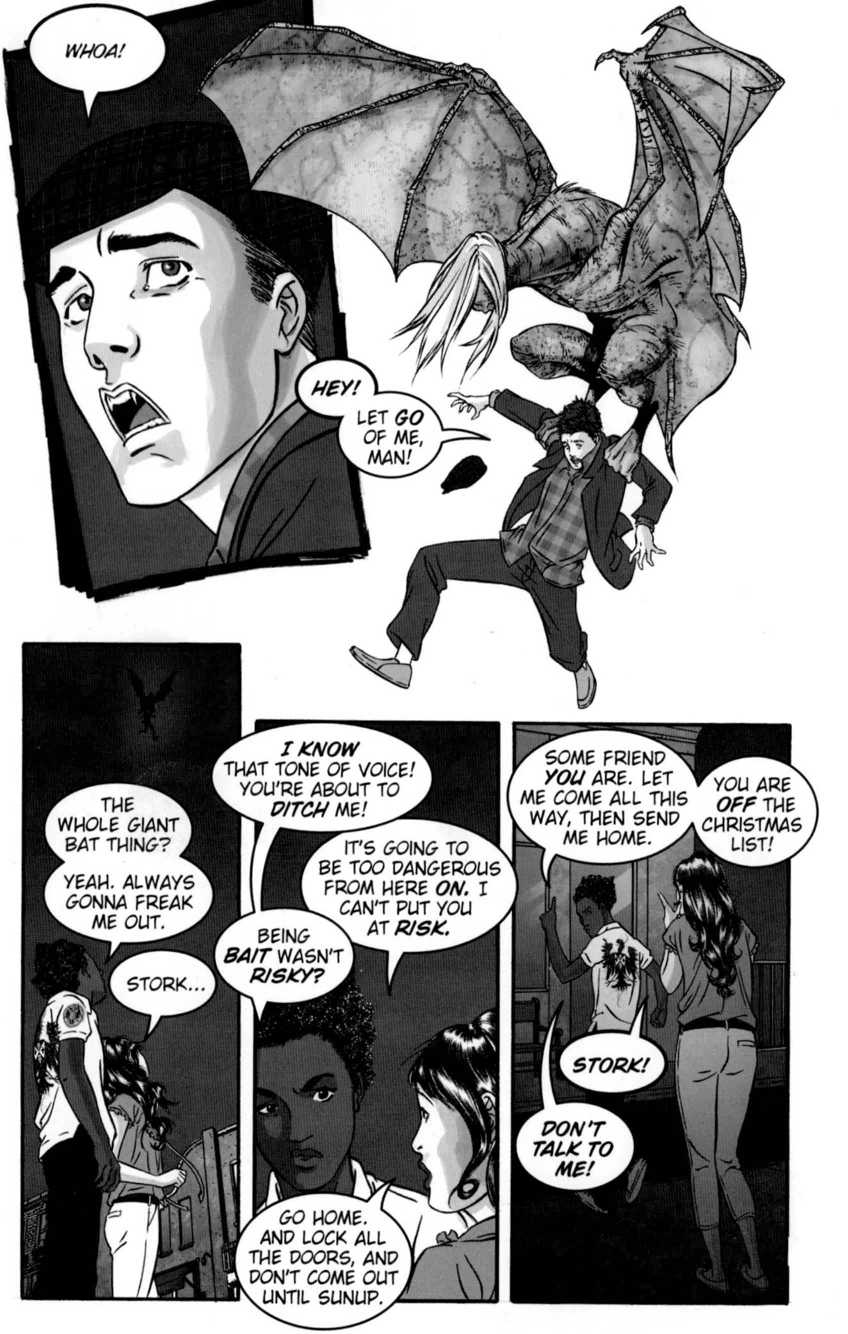
WHOA!
HEY!
LET GO OF ME, MAN!
THE WHOLE GIANT BAT THING?
YEAH. ALWAYS GONNA FREAK ME OUT.
STORK...
I KNOW THAT TONE OF VOICE! YOU'RE ABOUT TO DITCH ME!
IT'S GOING TO BE TOO DANGEROUS FROM HERE ON. I CAN'T PUT YOU AT RISK.
BEING BAIT WASN'T RISKY?
GO HOME. AND LOCK ALL THE DOORS, AND DON'T COME OUT UNTIL SUNUP.
SOME FRIEND YOU ARE. LET ME COME ALL THIS WAY, THEN SEND ME HOME.
YOU ARE OFF THE CHRISTMAS LIST!
STORK!
DON'T TALK TO ME!

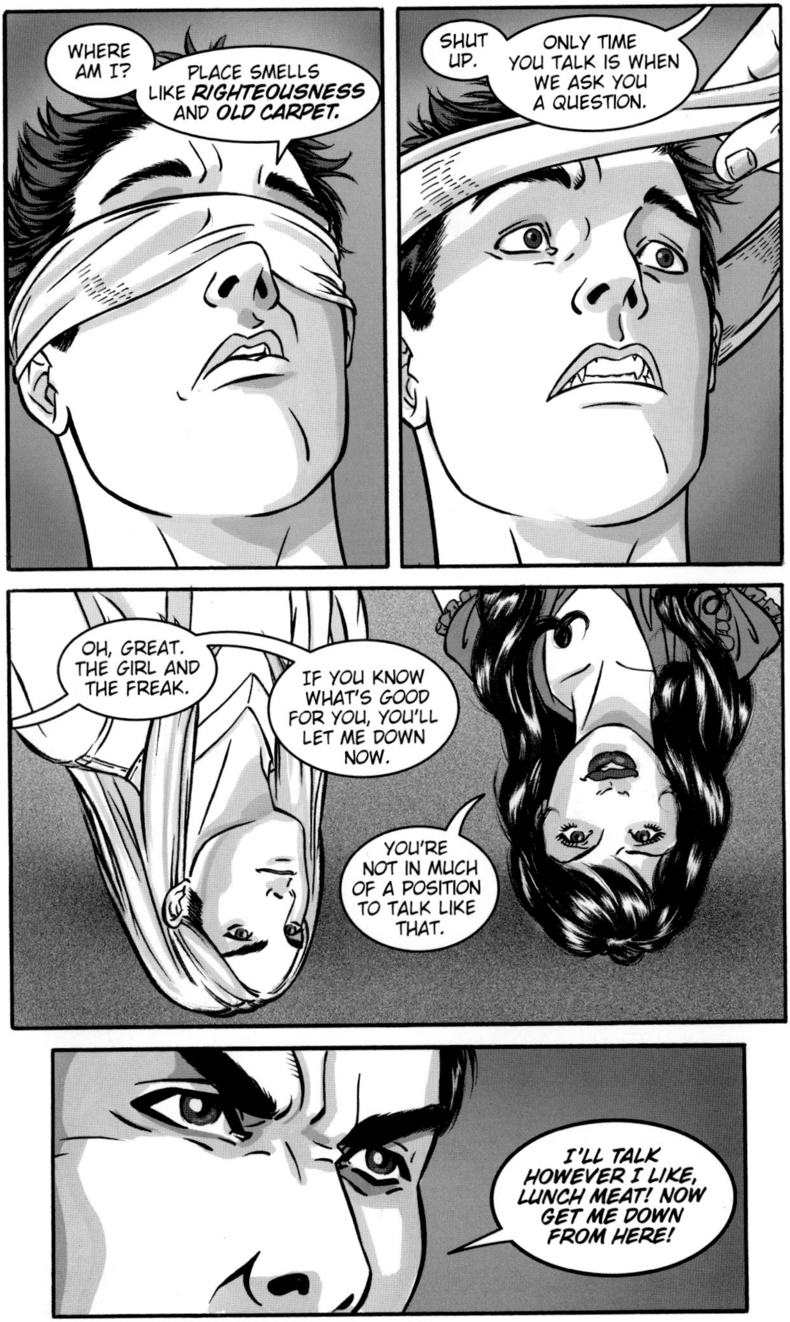
WHERE AM I?
PLACE SMELLS LIKE RIGHTEOUSNESS AND OLD CARPET.
SHUT UP.
ONLY TIME YOU TALK IS WHEN WE ASK YOU A QUESTION.
OH, GREAT. THE GIRL AND THE FREAK.
IF YOU KNOW WHAT'S GOOD FOR YOU, YOU'LL LET ME DOWN NOW.
YOU'RE NOT IN MUCH OF A POSITION TO TALK LIKE THAT.
I'LL TALK HOWEVER I LIKE, LUNCH MEAT! NOW GET ME DOWN FROM HERE!

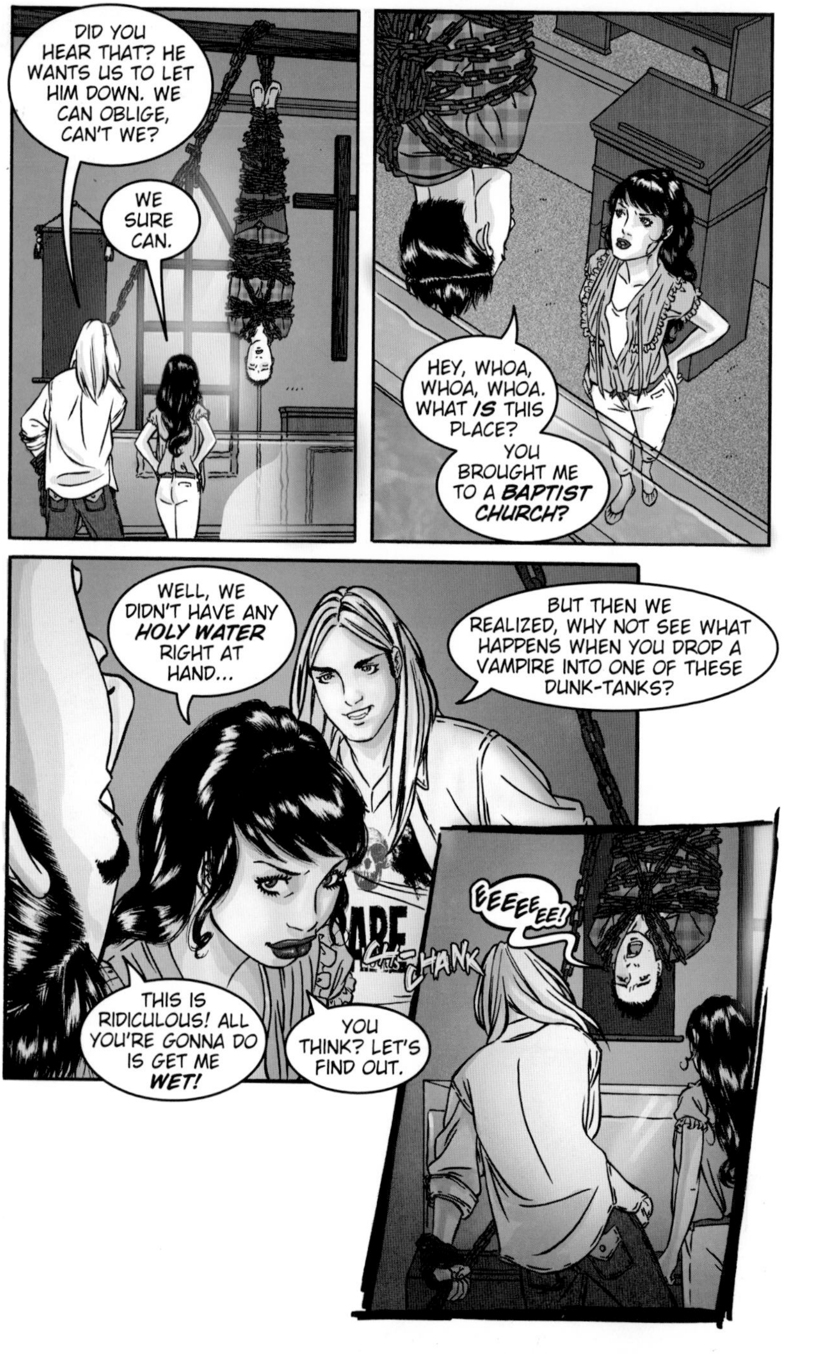
DID YOU HEAR THAT? HE WANTS US TO LET HIM DOWN. WE CAN OBLIGE, CAN'T WE?
WE SURE CAN.
HEY, WHOA, WHOA, WHOA. WHAT IS THIS PLACE?
YOU BROUGHT ME TO A BAPTIST CHURCH?
WELL, WE DIDN'T HAVE ANY HOLY WATER RIGHT AT HAND...
BUT THEN WE REALIZED, WHY NOT SEE WHAT HAPPENS WHEN YOU DROP A VAMPIRE INTO ONE OF THESE DUNK-TANKS?
THIS IS RIDICULOUS! ALL YOU'RE GONNA DO IS GET ME WET!
YOU THINK? LET'S FIND OUT.
CHANK
EEEEEEE!

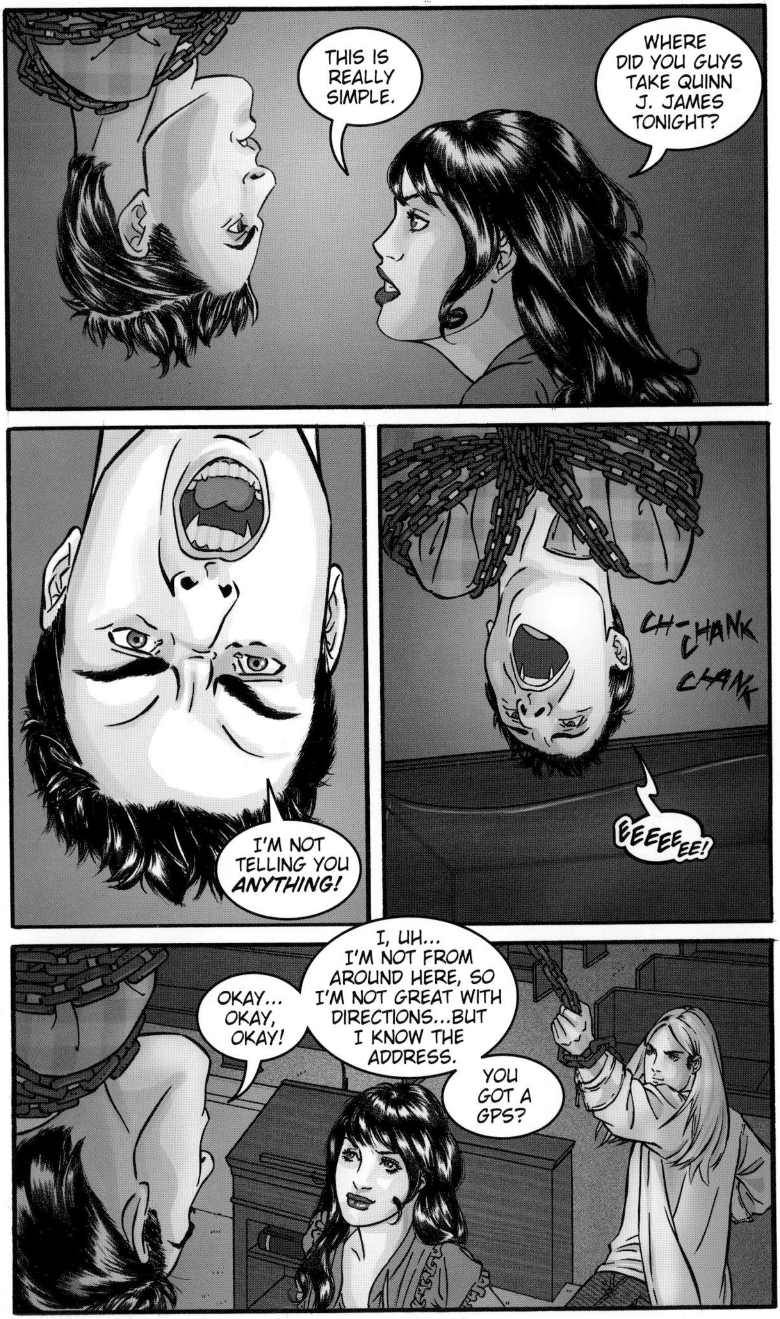
THIS IS REALLY SIMPLE.
WHERE DID YOU GUYS TAKE QUINN J. JAMES TONIGHT?
I'M NOT TELLING YOU *ANYTHING!*
CH-CHANK
CHANK
EEEEEEE!
OKAY... OKAY, OKAY!
I, UH... I'M NOT FROM AROUND HERE, SO I'M NOT GREAT WITH DIRECTIONS...BUT I KNOW THE ADDRESS.
YOU GOT A GPS?

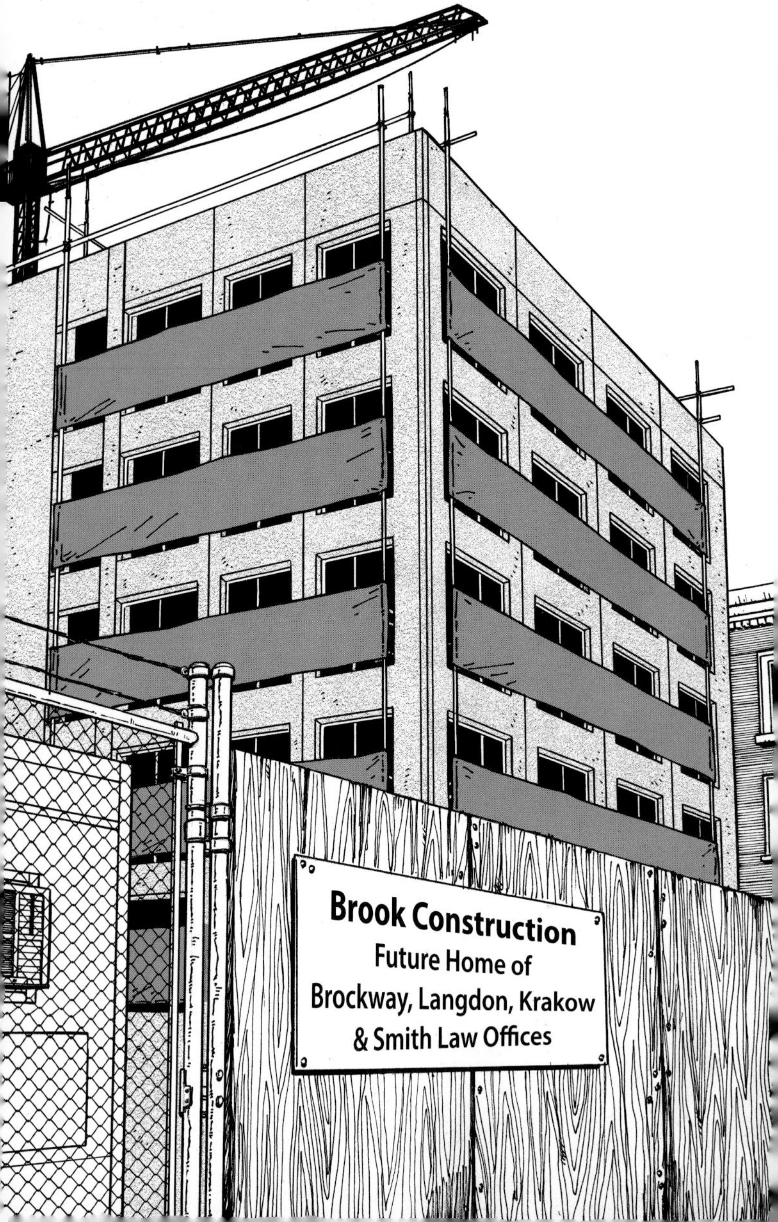
Brook Construction
Future Home of
Brockway, Langdon, Krakow
& Smith Law Offices

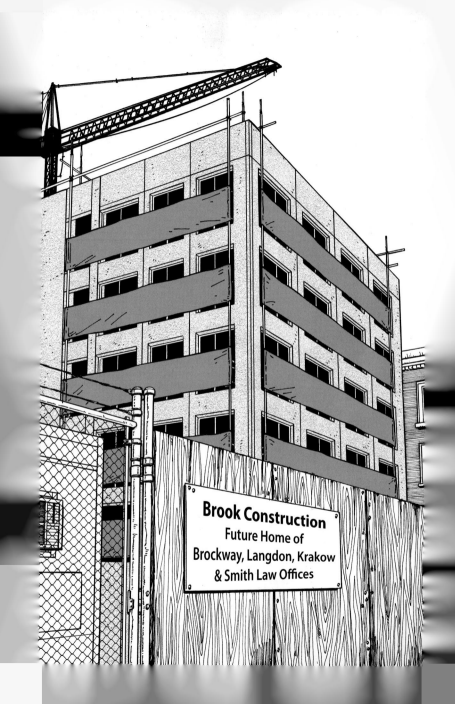

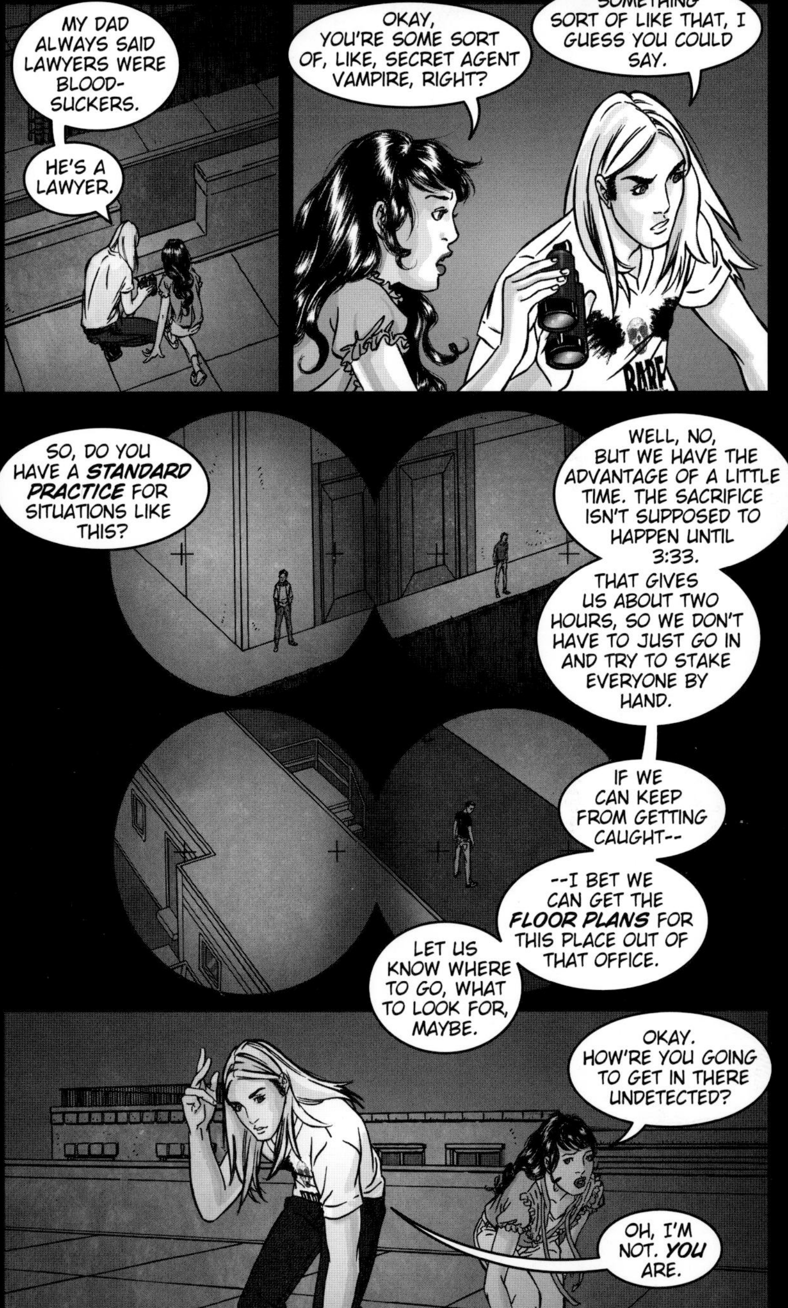
MY DAD ALWAYS SAID LAWYERS WERE BLOOD-SUCKERS.
HE'S A LAWYER.
OKAY, YOU'RE SOME SORT OF, LIKE, SECRET AGENT VAMPIRE, RIGHT?
SOMETHING SORT OF LIKE THAT, I GUESS YOU COULD SAY.
RARE
SO, DO YOU HAVE A **STANDARD PRACTICE** FOR SITUATIONS LIKE THIS?
WELL, NO, BUT WE HAVE THE ADVANTAGE OF A LITTLE TIME. THE SACRIFICE ISN'T SUPPOSED TO HAPPEN UNTIL 3:33.
THAT GIVES US ABOUT TWO HOURS, SO WE DON'T HAVE TO JUST GO IN AND TRY TO STAKE EVERYONE BY HAND.
IF WE CAN KEEP FROM GETTING CAUGHT--
--I BET WE CAN GET THE **FLOOR PLANS** FOR THIS PLACE OUT OF THAT OFFICE.
LET US KNOW WHERE TO GO, WHAT TO LOOK FOR, MAYBE.
OKAY. HOW'RE YOU GOING TO GET IN THERE UNDETECTED?
OH, I'M NOT. ***YOU*** ARE.

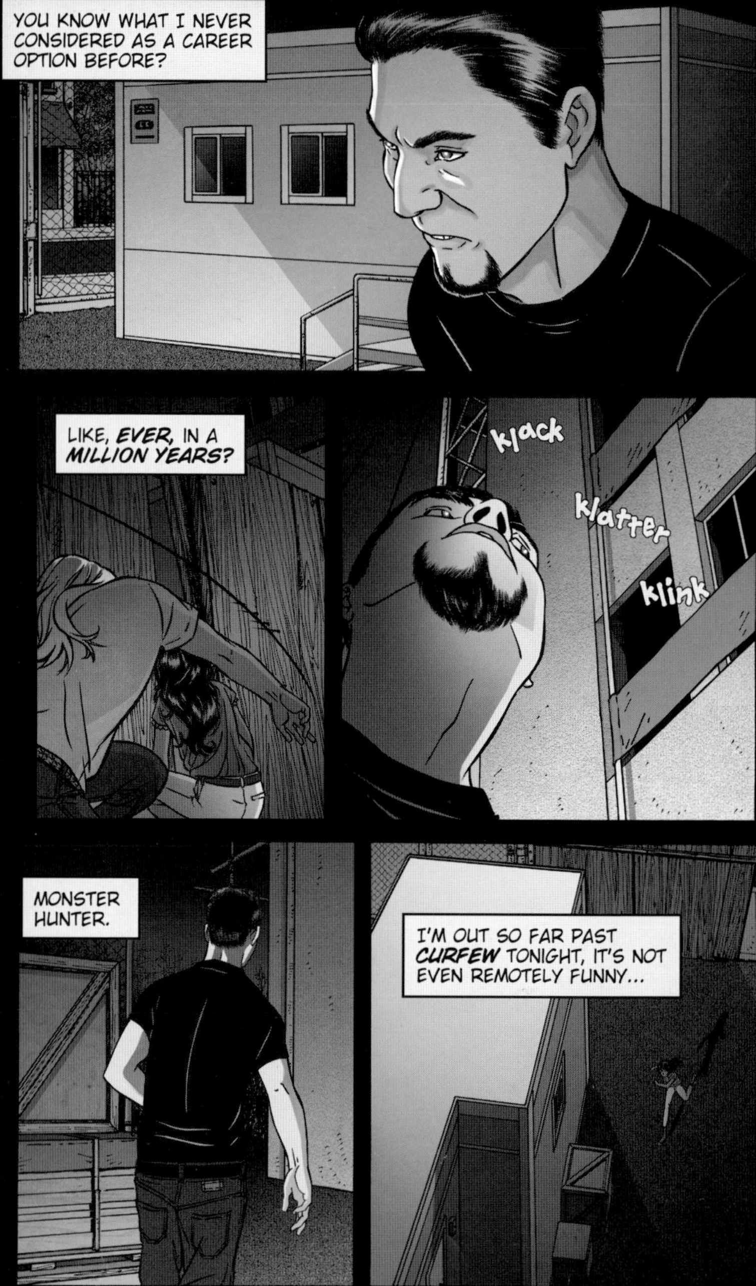
YOU KNOW WHAT I NEVER CONSIDERED AS A CAREER OPTION BEFORE?
LIKE, EVER, IN A MILLION YEARS?
klack
klatter
klink
MONSTER HUNTER.
I'M OUT SO FAR PAST CURFEW TONIGHT, IT'S NOT EVEN REMOTELY FUNNY...

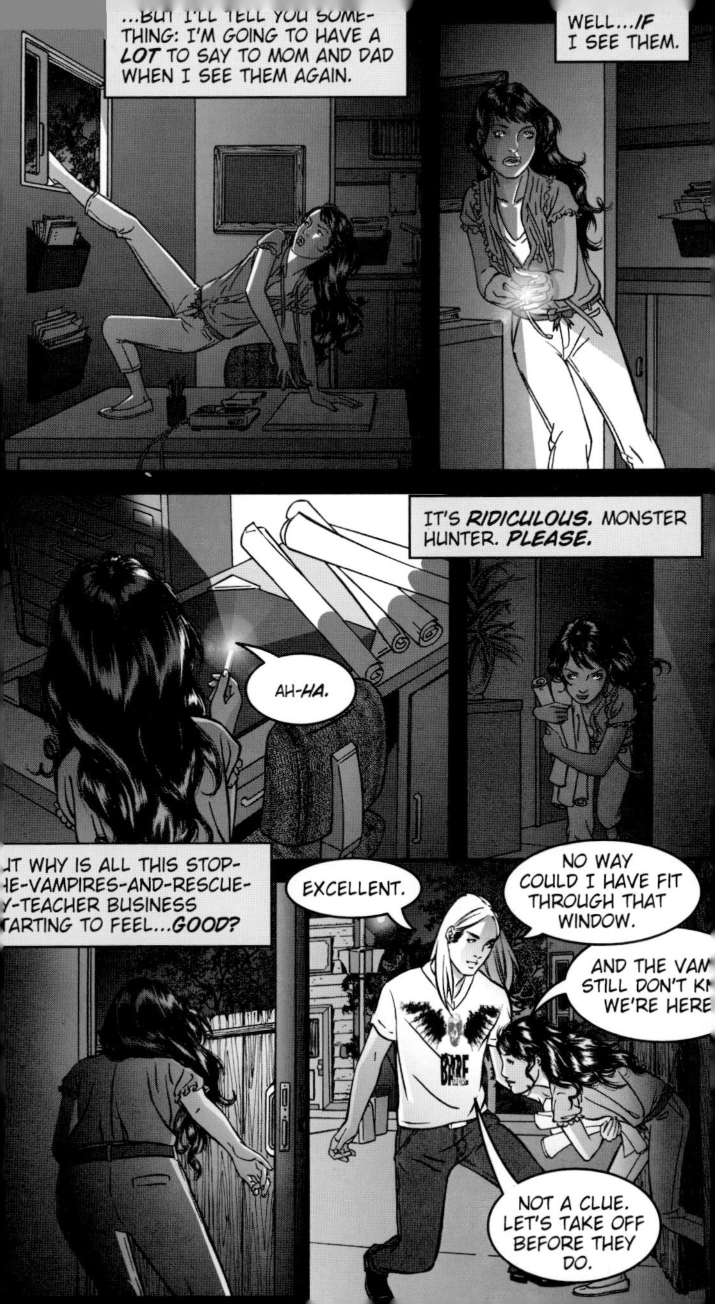
...BUT I'LL TELL YOU SOMETHING: I'M GOING TO HAVE A LOT TO SAY TO MOM AND DAD WHEN I SEE THEM AGAIN.
WELL...IF I SEE THEM.
IT'S RIDICULOUS. MONSTER HUNTER. PLEASE.
AH-HA.
UT WHY IS ALL THIS STOP-HE-VAMPIRES-AND-RESCUE-Y-TEACHER BUSINESS TARTING TO FEEL...GOOD?
EXCELLENT.
NO WAY COULD I HAVE FIT THROUGH THAT WINDOW.
AND THE VAM STILL DON'T K WE'RE HERE
NOT A CLUE. LET'S TAKE OFF BEFORE THEY DO.

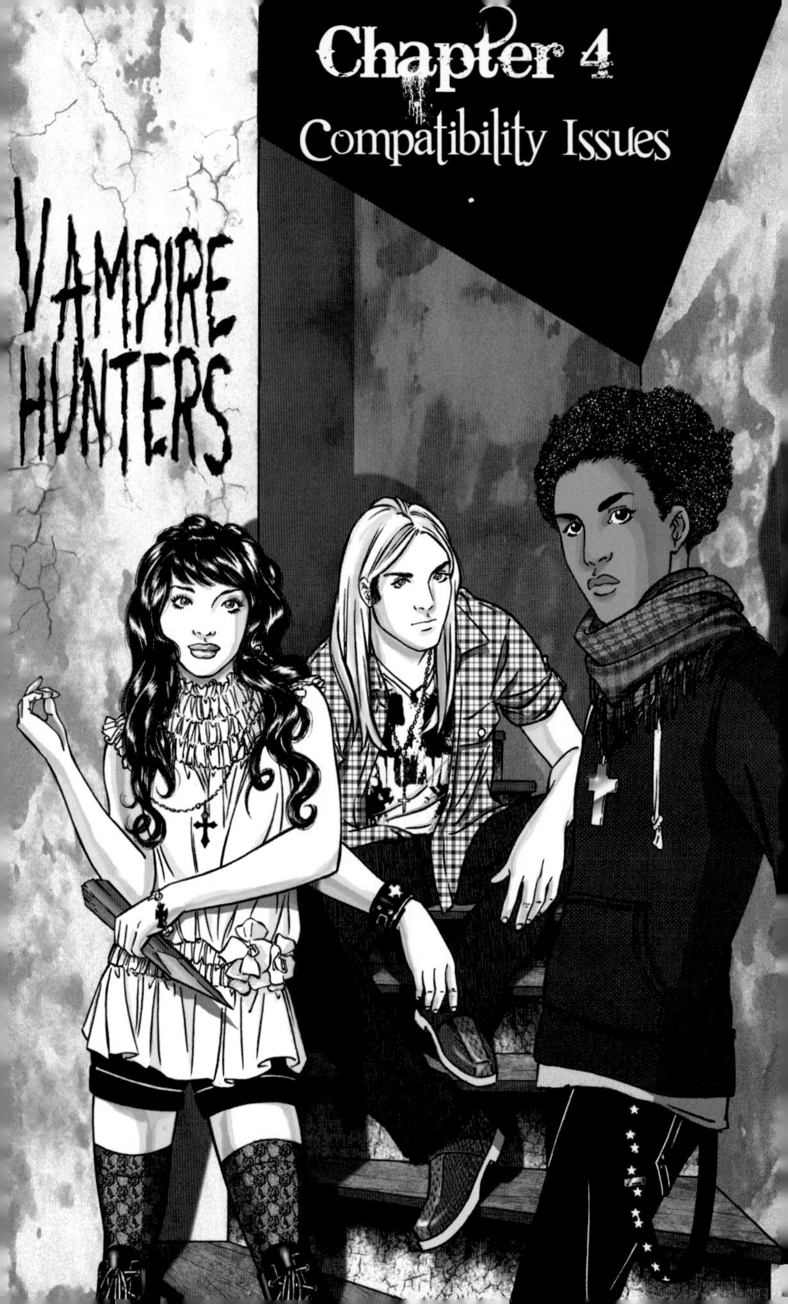
Chapter 4
Compatibility Issues
VAMPIRE HUNTERS

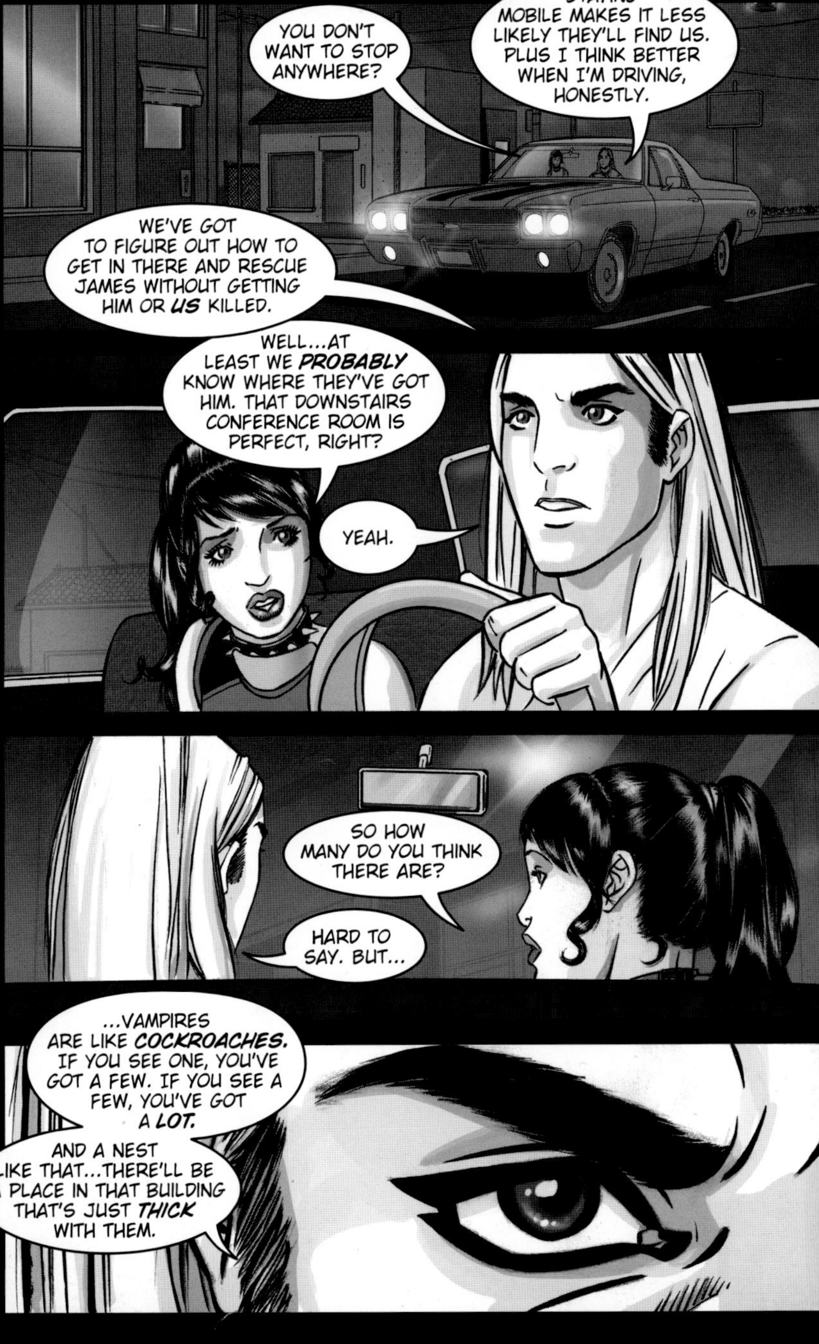
YOU DON'T WANT TO STOP ANYWHERE?
STAYING MOBILE MAKES IT LESS LIKELY THEY'LL FIND US. PLUS I THINK BETTER WHEN I'M DRIVING, HONESTLY.
WE'VE GOT TO FIGURE OUT HOW TO GET IN THERE AND RESCUE JAMES WITHOUT GETTING HIM OR US KILLED.
WELL...AT LEAST WE PROBABLY KNOW WHERE THEY'VE GOT HIM. THAT DOWNSTAIRS CONFERENCE ROOM IS PERFECT, RIGHT?
YEAH.
SO HOW MANY DO YOU THINK THERE ARE?
HARD TO SAY. BUT...
...VAMPIRES ARE LIKE COCKROACHES. IF YOU SEE ONE, YOU'VE GOT A FEW. IF YOU SEE A FEW, YOU'VE GOT A LOT.
AND A NEST LIKE THAT...THERE'LL BE A PLACE IN THAT BUILDING THAT'S JUST THICK WITH THEM.

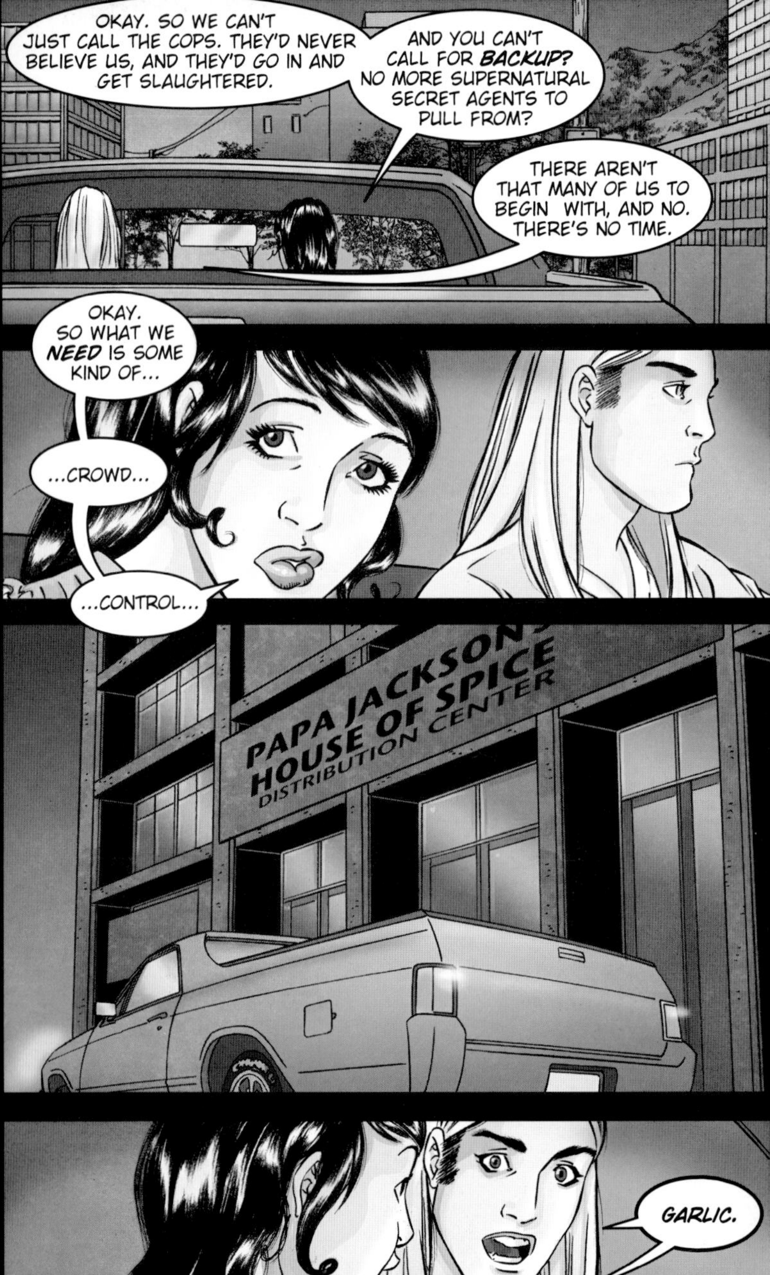
OKAY. SO WE CAN'T JUST CALL THE COPS. THEY'D NEVER BELIEVE US, AND THEY'D GO IN AND GET SLAUGHTERED.
AND YOU CAN'T CALL FOR BACKUP? NO MORE SUPERNATURAL SECRET AGENTS TO PULL FROM?
THERE AREN'T THAT MANY OF US TO BEGIN WITH, AND NO. THERE'S NO TIME.
OKAY. SO WHAT WE NEED IS SOME KIND OF...
...CROWD...
...CONTROL...
PAPA JACKSON'S HOUSE OF SPICE DISTRIBUTION CENTER
GARLIC.

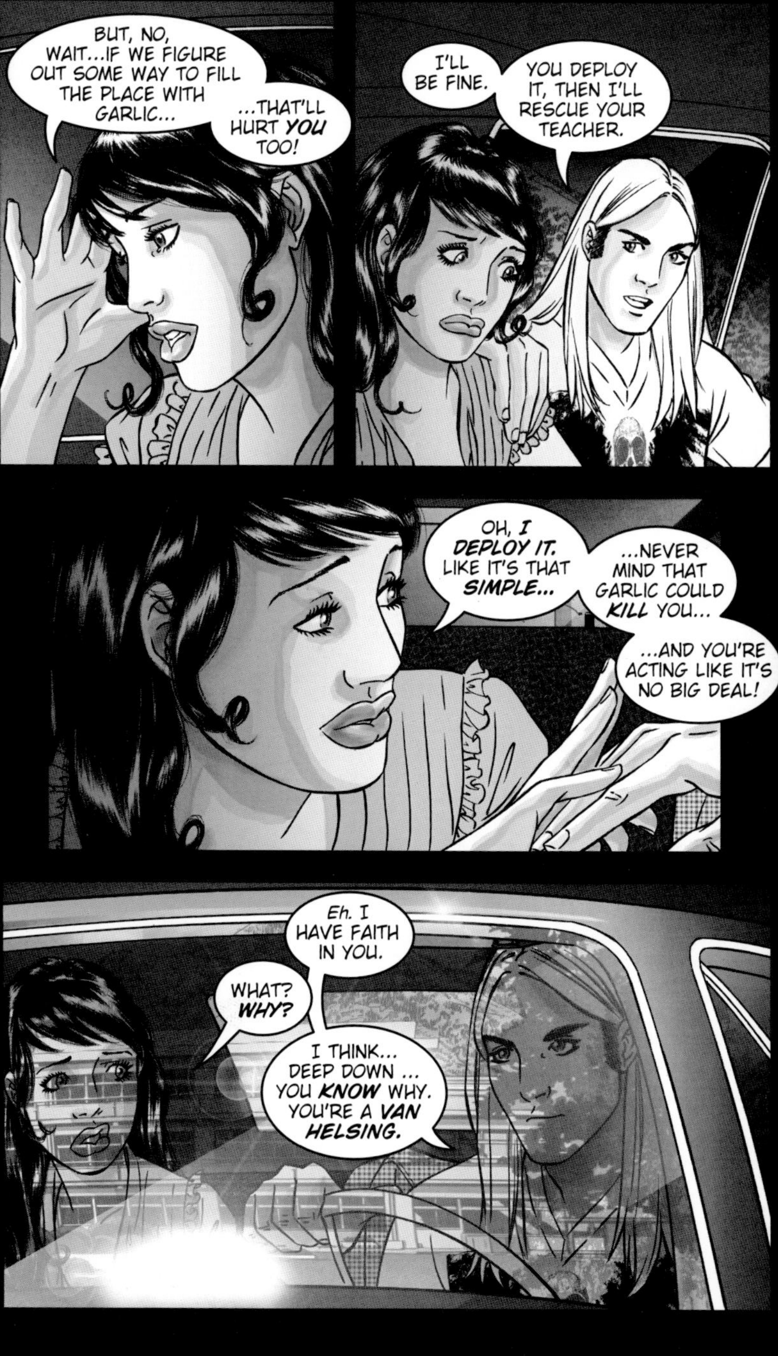
BUT, NO, WAIT...IF WE FIGURE OUT SOME WAY TO FILL THE PLACE WITH GARLIC...
...THAT'LL HURT ***YOU*** TOO!
I'LL BE FINE.
YOU DEPLOY IT, THEN I'LL RESCUE YOUR TEACHER.
OH, ***I DEPLOY IT.*** LIKE IT'S THAT ***SIMPLE...***
...NEVER MIND THAT GARLIC COULD ***KILL*** YOU...
...AND YOU'RE ACTING LIKE IT'S NO BIG DEAL!
Eh. I HAVE FAITH IN YOU.
WHAT? ***WHY?***
I THINK... DEEP DOWN ... YOU ***KNOW*** WHY. YOU'RE A ***VAN HELSING.***

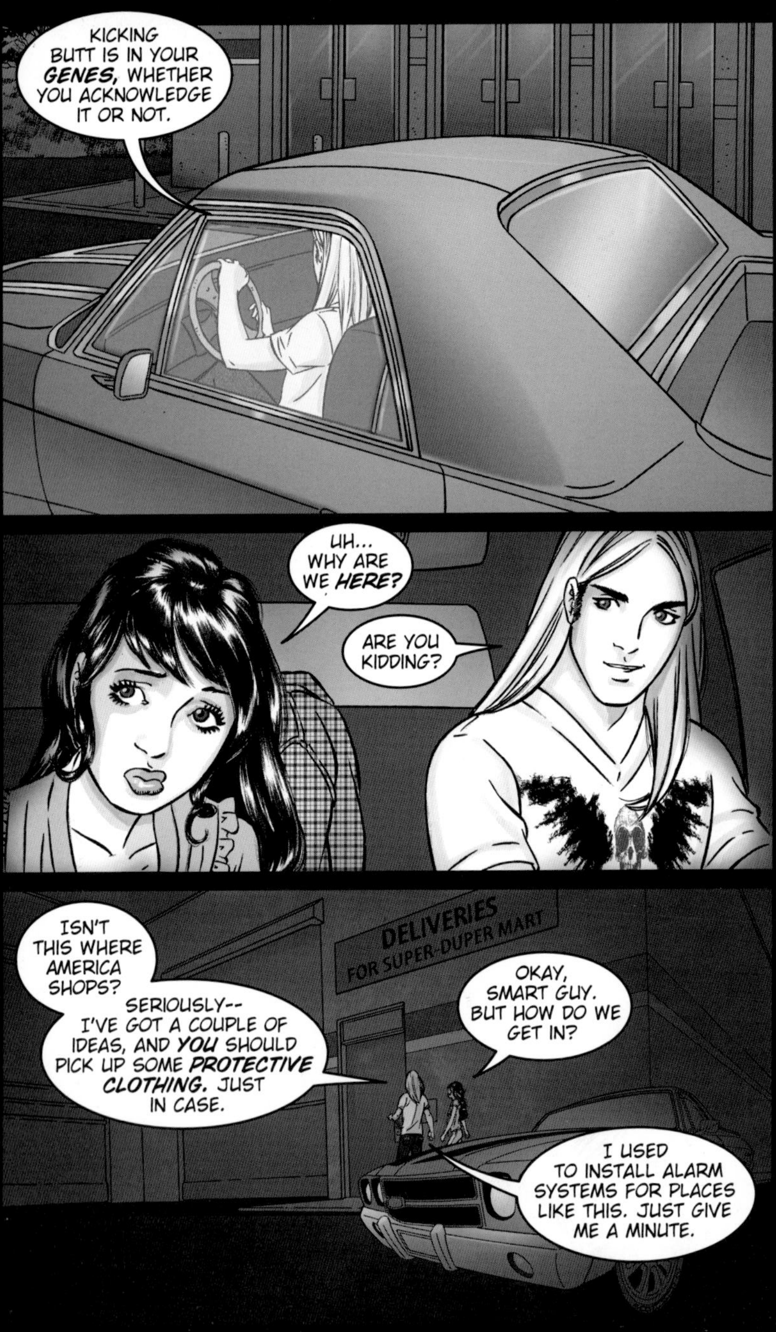
KICKING BUTT IS IN YOUR GENES, WHETHER YOU ACKNOWLEDGE IT OR NOT.
UH... WHY ARE WE HERE?
ARE YOU KIDDING?
ISN'T THIS WHERE AMERICA SHOPS?
SERIOUSLY-- I'VE GOT A COUPLE OF IDEAS, AND YOU SHOULD PICK UP SOME PROTECTIVE CLOTHING. JUST IN CASE.
DELIVERIES
FOR SUPER-DUPER MART
OKAY, SMART GUY. BUT HOW DO WE GET IN?
I USED TO INSTALL ALARM SYSTEMS FOR PLACES LIKE THIS. JUST GIVE ME A MINUTE.

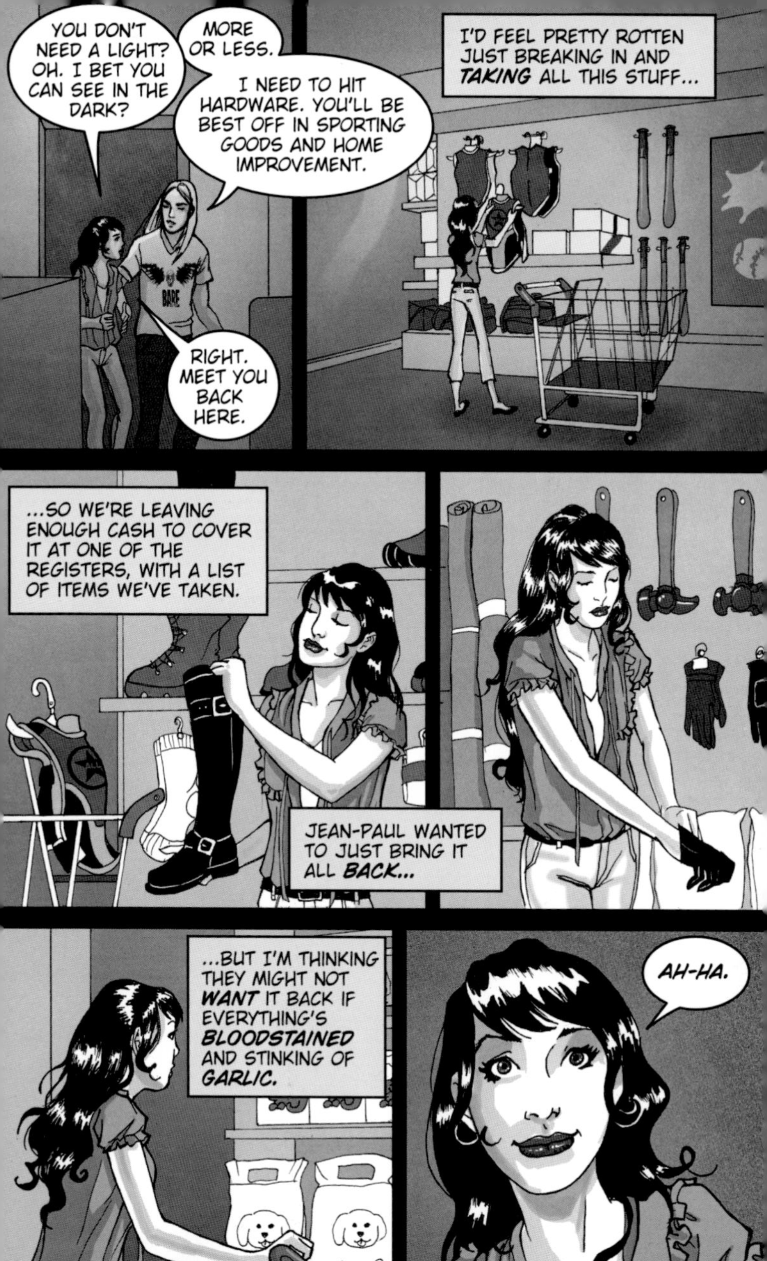
YOU DON'T NEED A LIGHT? OH. I BET YOU CAN SEE IN THE DARK?
MORE OR LESS.
I NEED TO HIT HARDWARE. YOU'LL BE BEST OFF IN SPORTING GOODS AND HOME IMPROVEMENT.
BARE
RIGHT. MEET YOU BACK HERE.
I'D FEEL PRETTY ROTTEN JUST BREAKING IN AND TAKING ALL THIS STUFF...
...SO WE'RE LEAVING ENOUGH CASH TO COVER IT AT ONE OF THE REGISTERS, WITH A LIST OF ITEMS WE'VE TAKEN.
JEAN-PAUL WANTED TO JUST BRING IT ALL BACK...
...BUT I'M THINKING THEY MIGHT NOT WANT IT BACK IF EVERYTHING'S BLOODSTAINED AND STINKING OF GARLIC.
AH-HA.

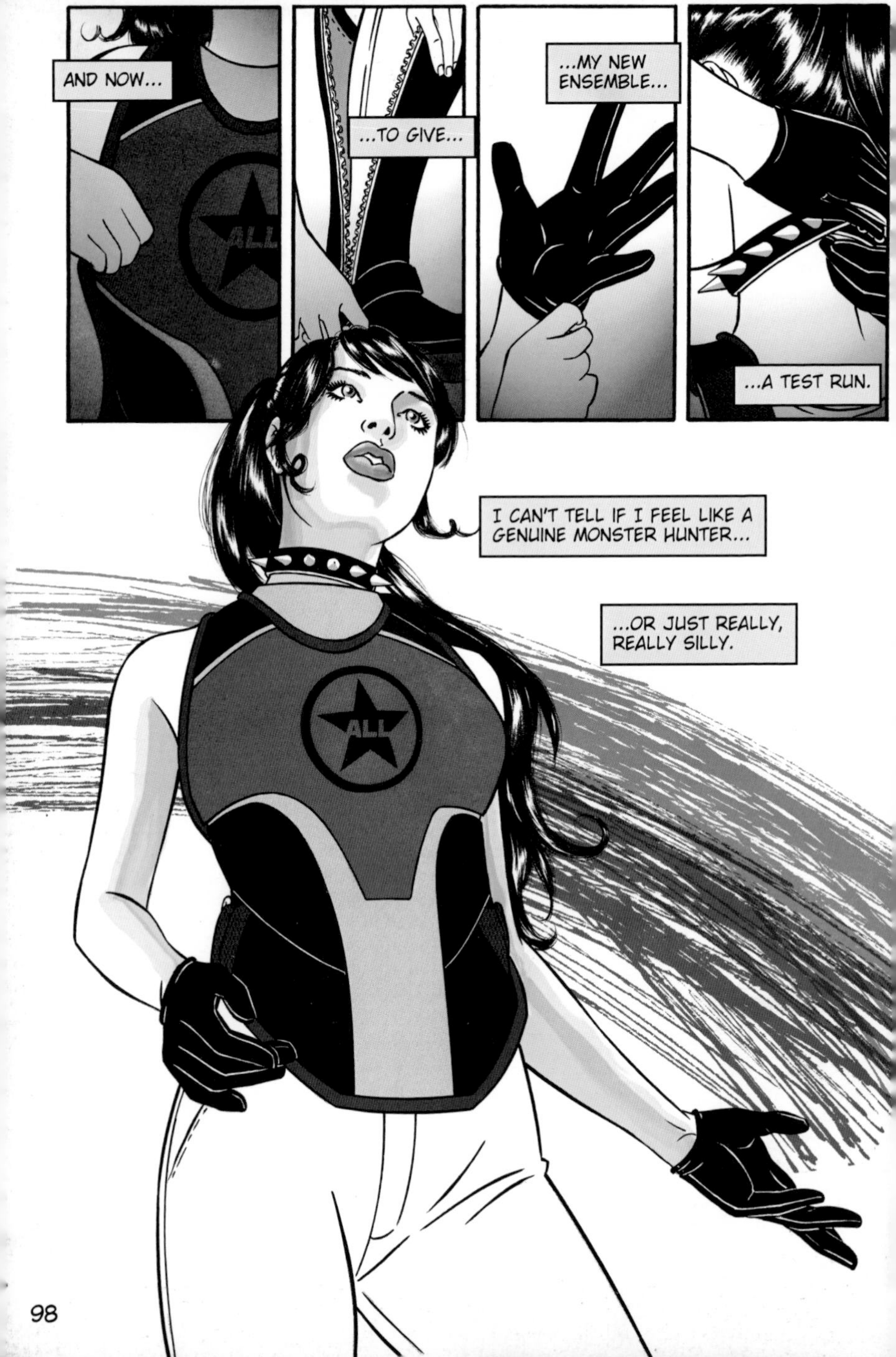
AND NOW...
...TO GIVE...
...MY NEW ENSEMBLE...
...A TEST RUN.
ALL
I CAN'T TELL IF I FEEL LIKE A GENUINE MONSTER HUNTER...
...OR JUST REALLY, REALLY SILLY.
ALL

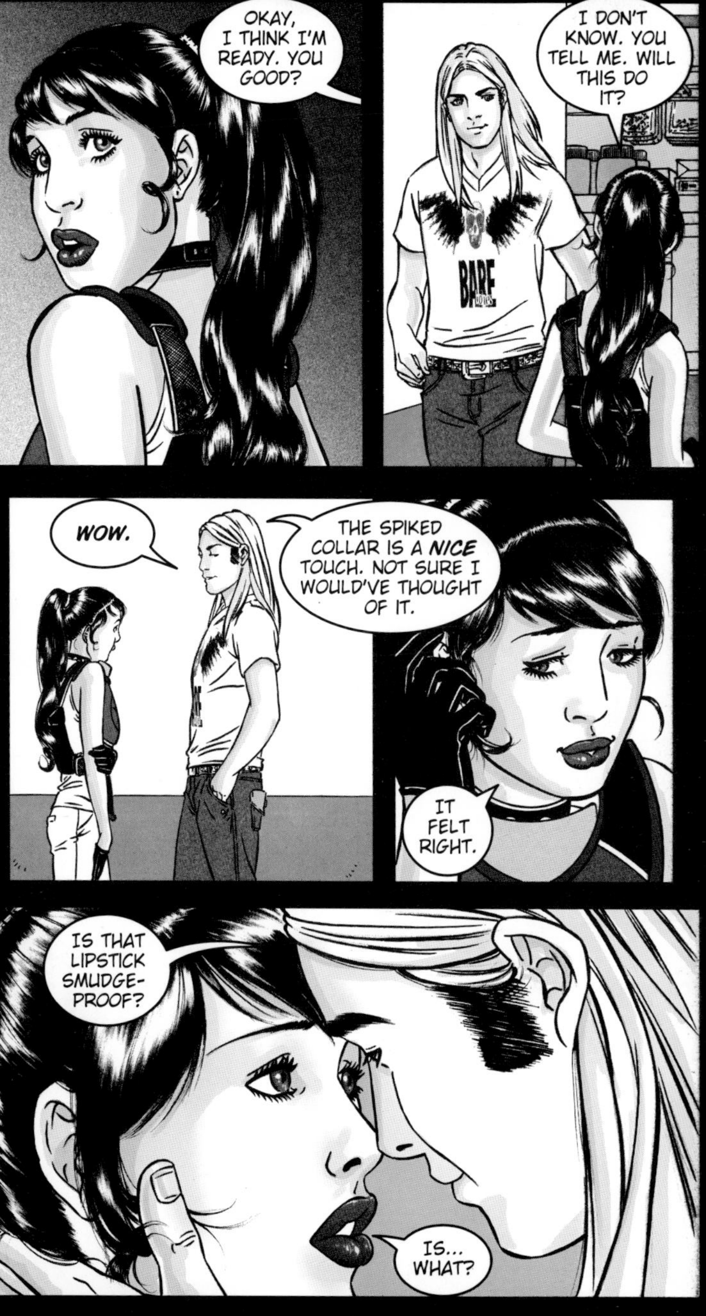
OKAY, I THINK I'M READY. YOU GOOD?
I DON'T KNOW. YOU TELL ME. WILL THIS DO IT?
BARF
WOW.
THE SPIKED COLLAR IS A *NICE* TOUCH. NOT SURE I WOULD'VE THOUGHT OF IT.
IT FELT RIGHT.
IS THAT LIPSTICK SMUDGE-PROOF?
IS... WHAT?

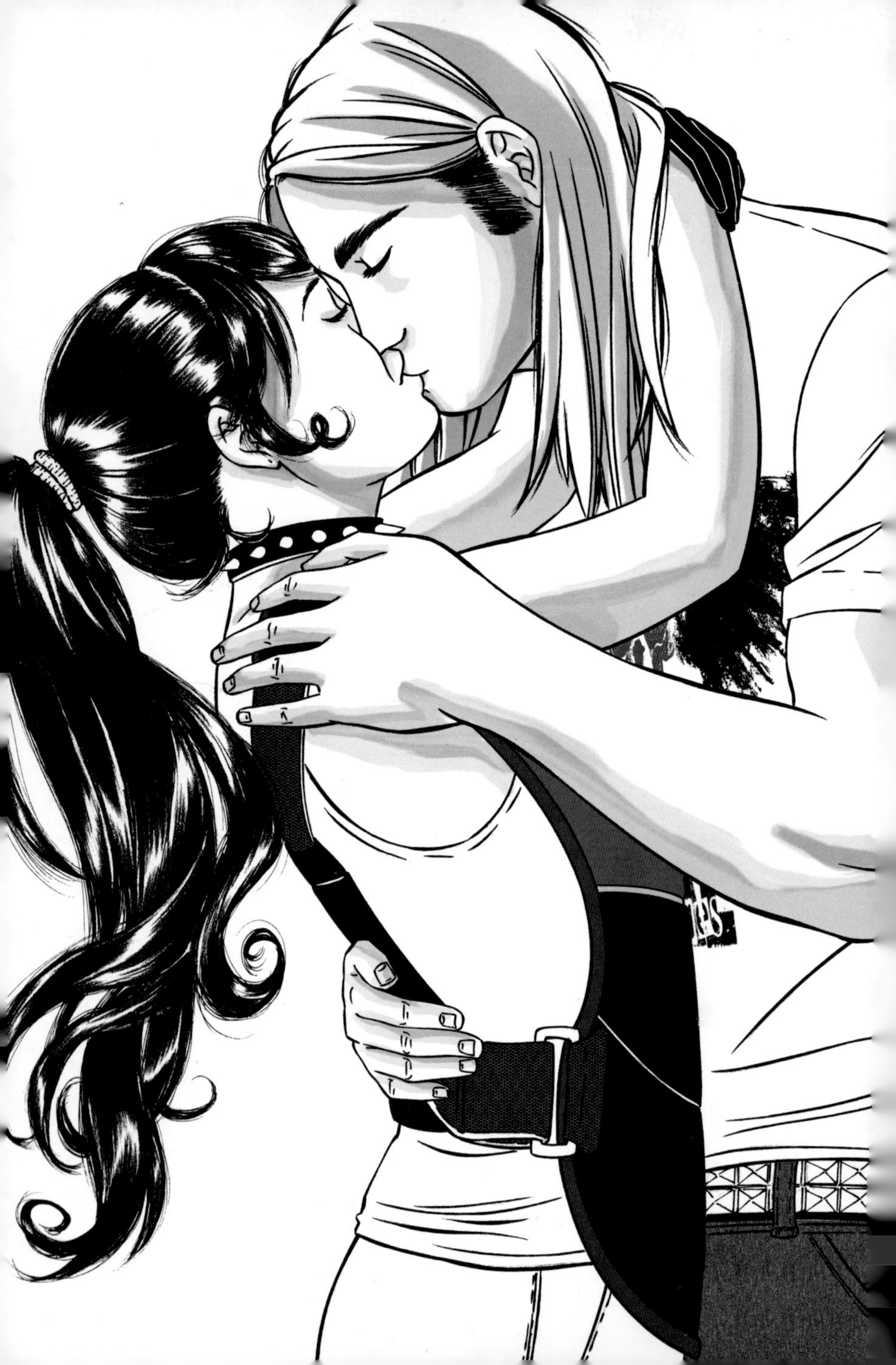

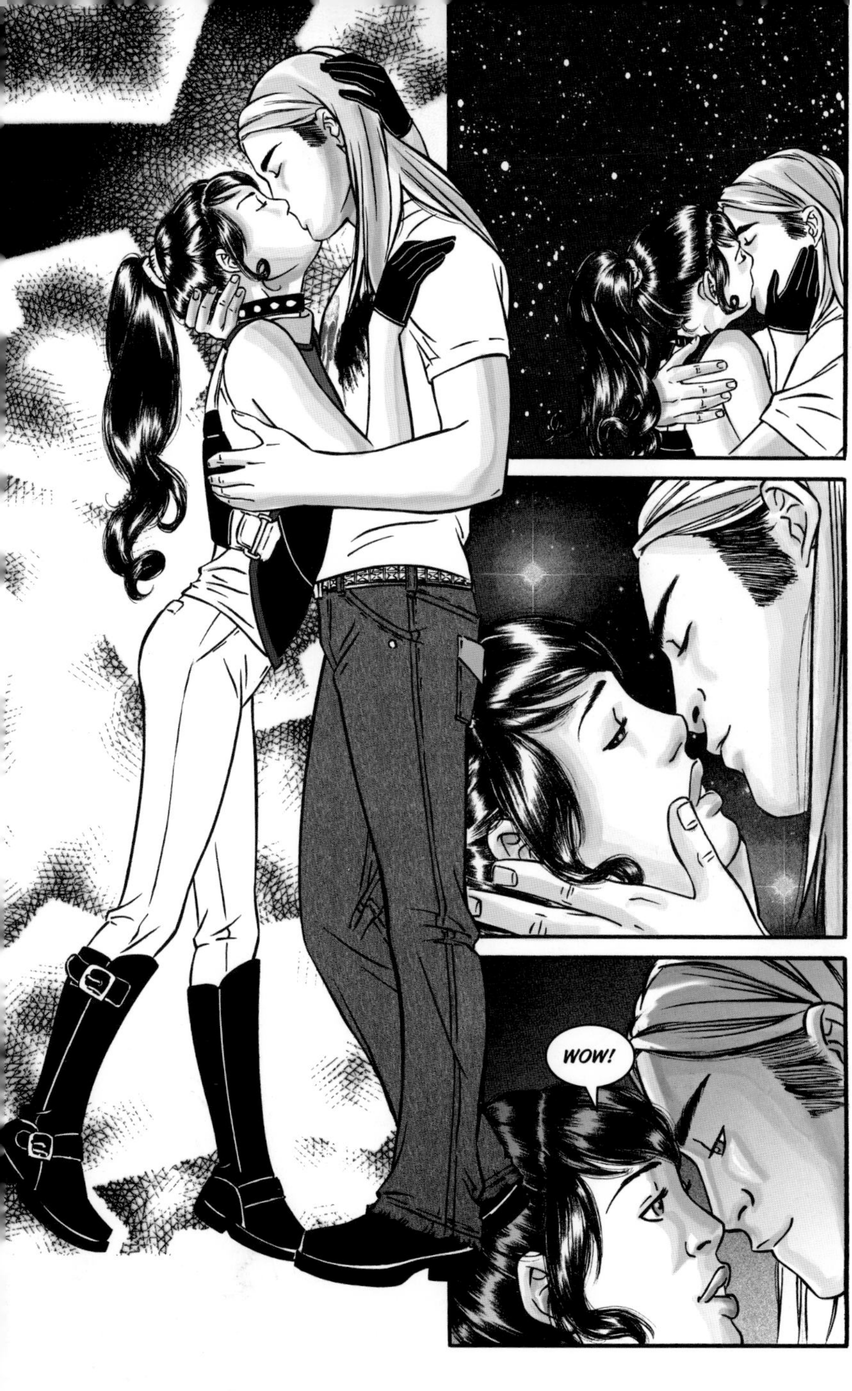
WOW!

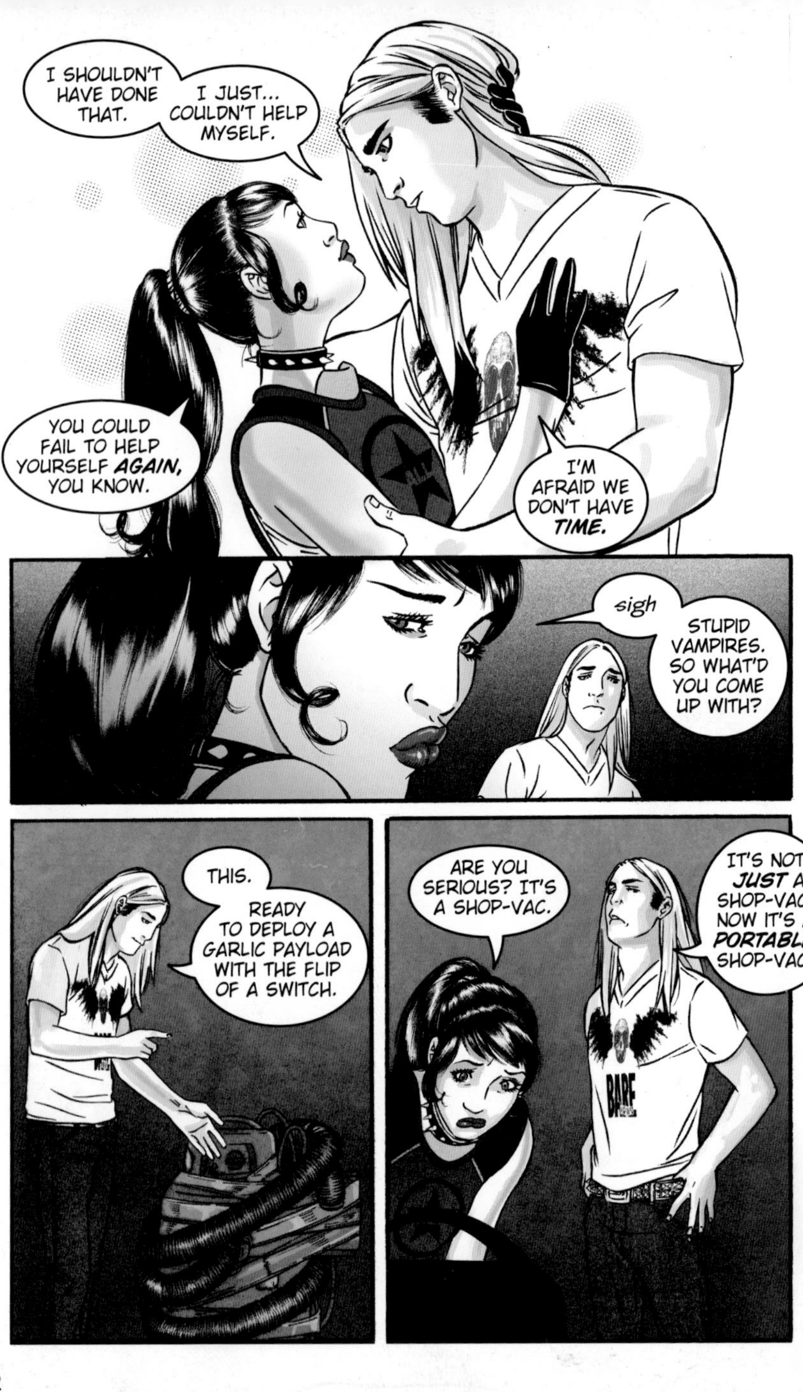
I SHOULDN'T HAVE DONE THAT.
I JUST... COULDN'T HELP MYSELF.
YOU COULD FAIL TO HELP YOURSELF AGAIN, YOU KNOW.
I'M AFRAID WE DON'T HAVE TIME.
sigh
STUPID VAMPIRES. SO WHAT'D YOU COME UP WITH?
THIS.
READY TO DEPLOY A GARLIC PAYLOAD WITH THE FLIP OF A SWITCH.
ARE YOU SERIOUS? IT'S A SHOP-VAC.
IT'S NOT JUST A SHOP-VAC. NOW IT'S A PORTABLE SHOP-VAC.
BARE

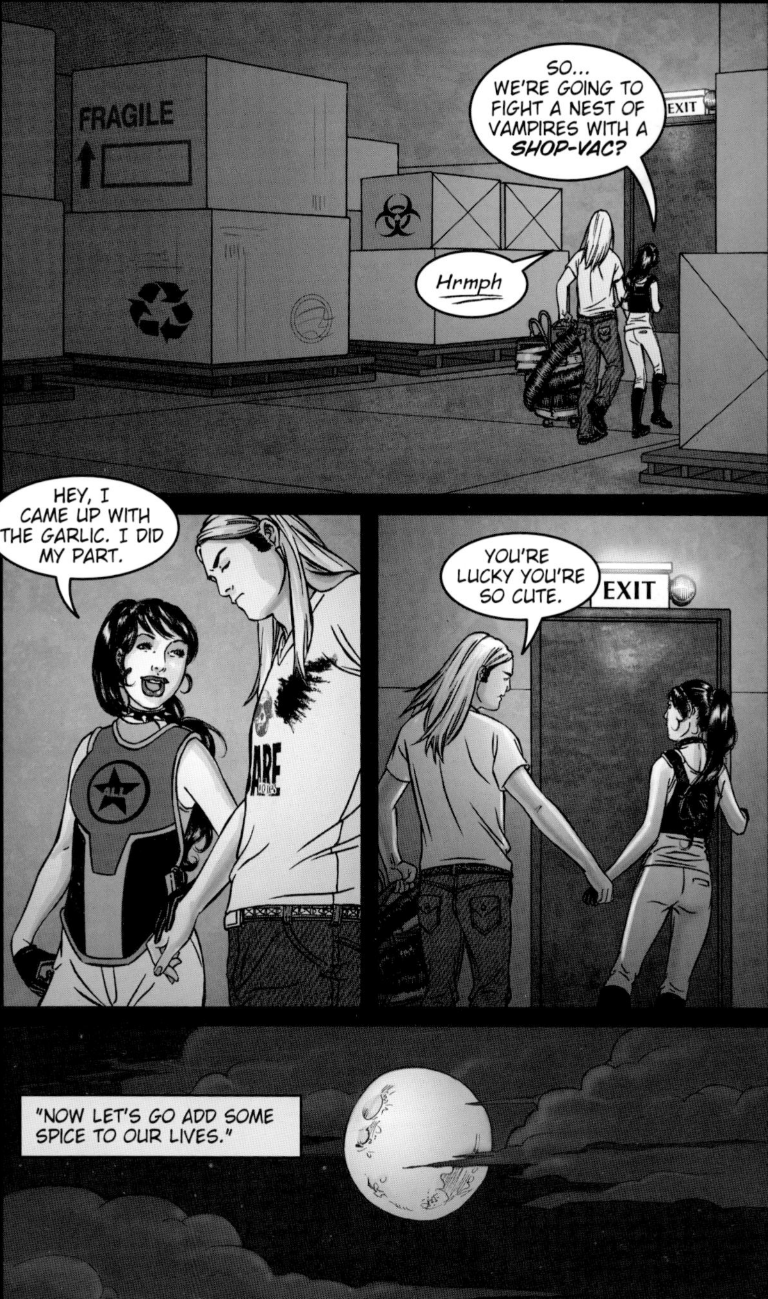
FRAGILE
EXIT
SO... WE'RE GOING TO FIGHT A NEST OF VAMPIRES WITH A *SHOP-VAC?*
Hrmph
HEY, I CAME UP WITH THE GARLIC. I DID MY PART.
YOU'RE LUCKY YOU'RE SO CUTE.
EXIT
"NOW LET'S GO ADD SOME SPICE TO OUR LIVES."

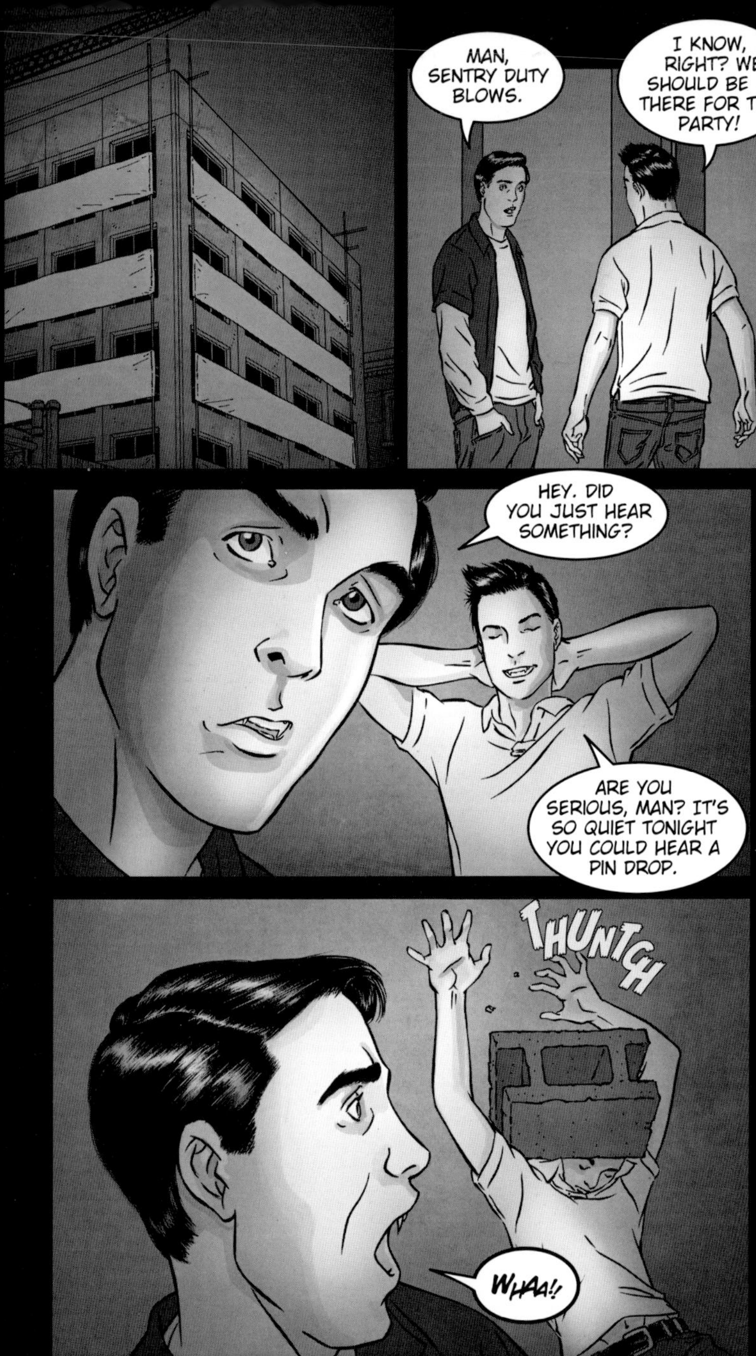
MAN, SENTRY DUTY BLOWS.
I KNOW, RIGHT? WE SHOULD BE IN THERE FOR THE PARTY!
HEY. DID YOU JUST HEAR SOMETHING?
ARE YOU SERIOUS, MAN? IT'S SO QUIET TONIGHT YOU COULD HEAR A PIN DROP.
THUNTCH
WHAA!!

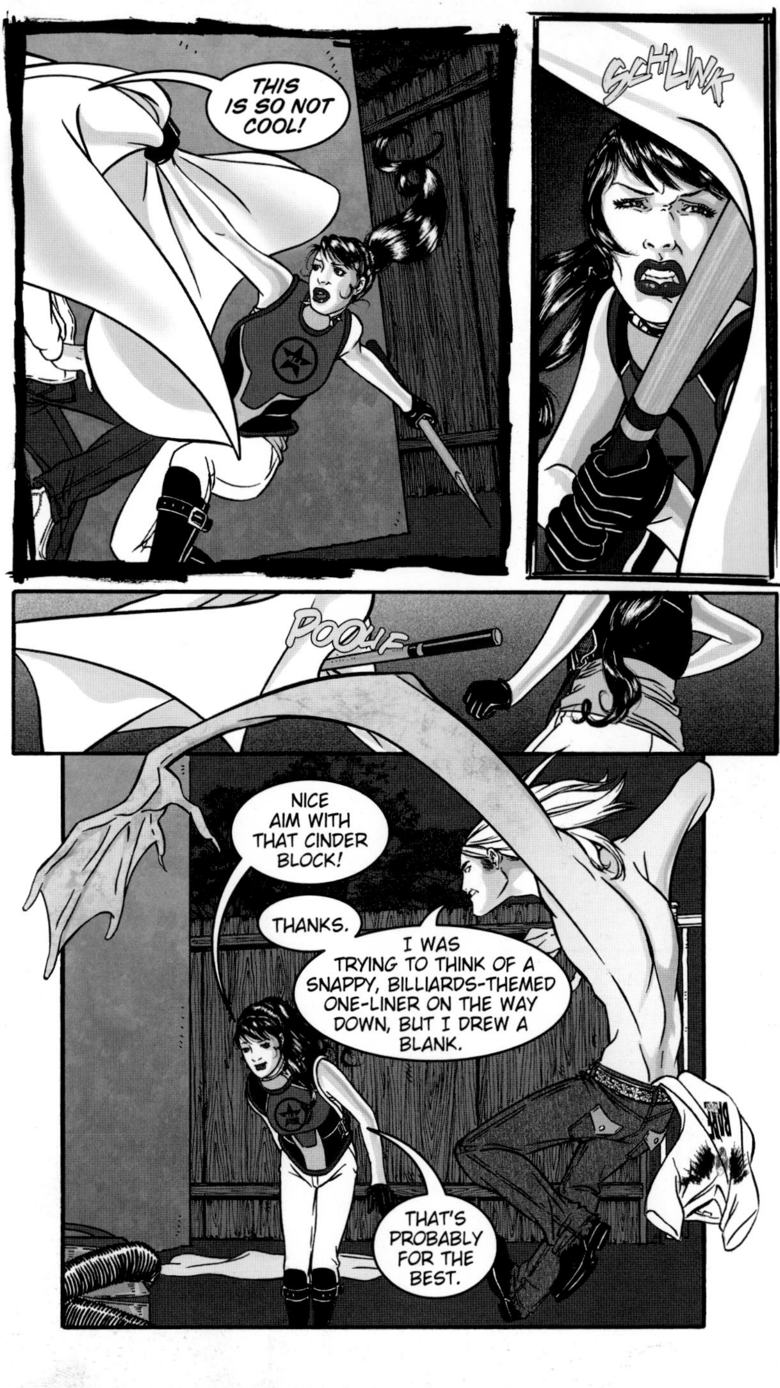
THIS IS SO NOT COOL!
SCHLINK
POOUF
NICE AIM WITH THAT CINDER BLOCK!
THANKS.
I WAS TRYING TO THINK OF A SNAPPY, BILLIARDS-THEMED ONE-LINER ON THE WAY DOWN, BUT I DREW A BLANK.
THAT'S PROBABLY FOR THE BEST.

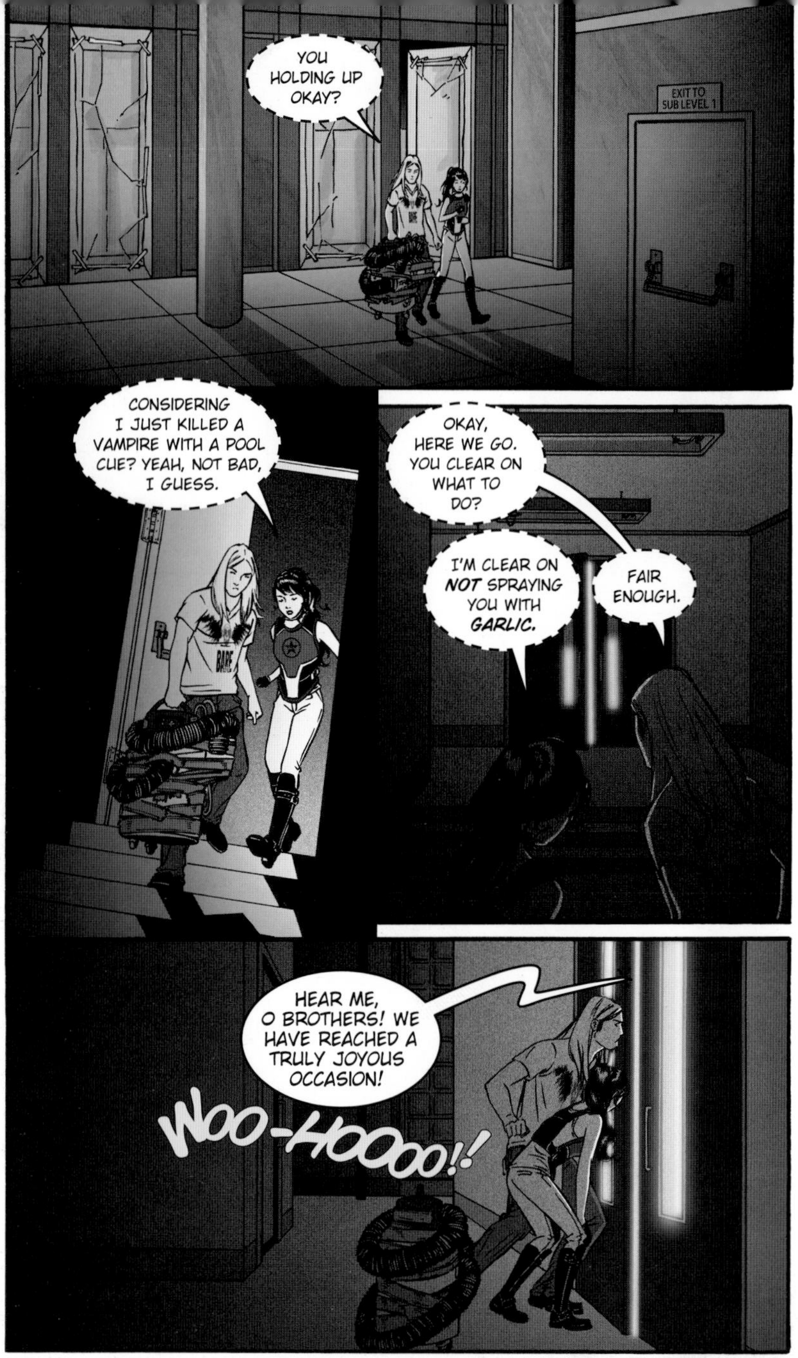
YOU HOLDING UP OKAY?
EXIT TO SUB LEVEL 1
CONSIDERING I JUST KILLED A VAMPIRE WITH A POOL CUE? YEAH, NOT BAD, I GUESS.
OKAY, HERE WE GO. YOU CLEAR ON WHAT TO DO?
I'M CLEAR ON **NOT** SPRAYING YOU WITH **GARLIC.**
FAIR ENOUGH.
HEAR ME, O BROTHERS! WE HAVE REACHED A TRULY JOYOUS OCCASION!
WOO-HOOOO!!

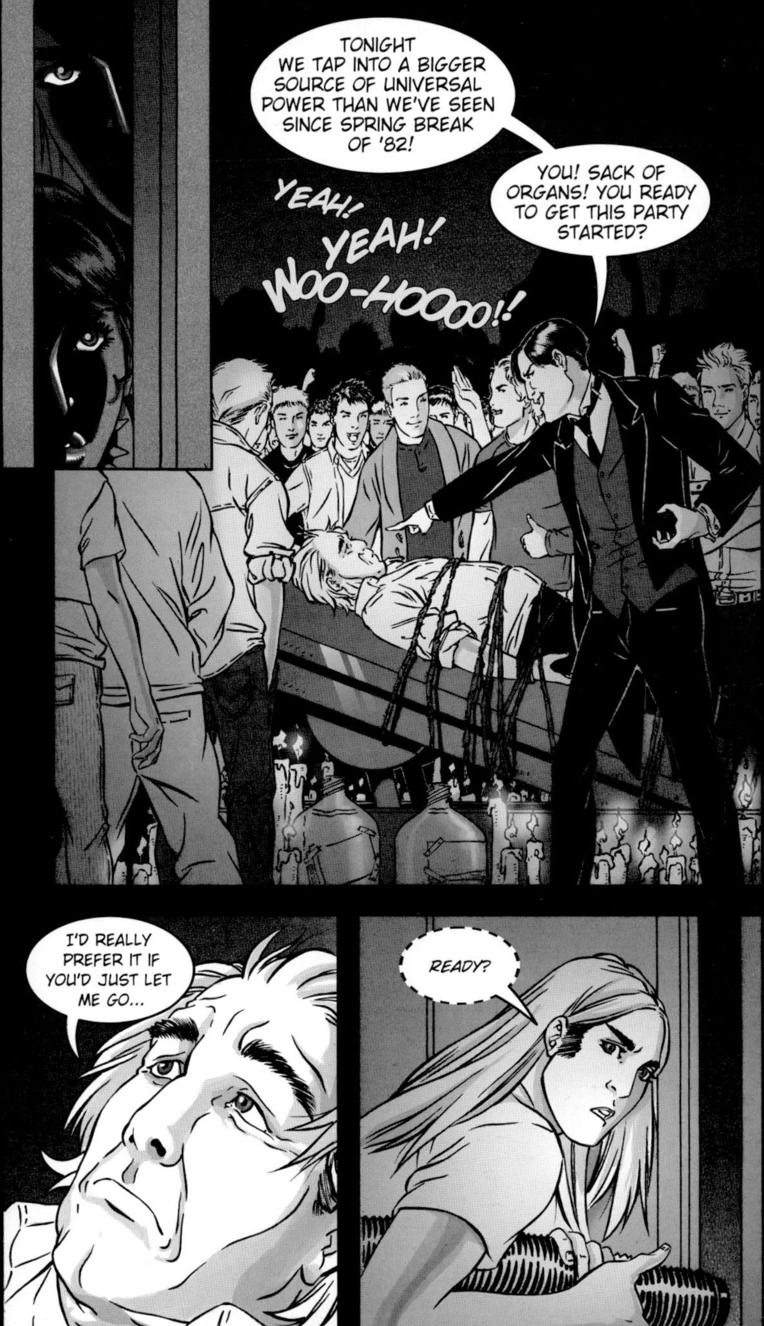
TONIGHT WE TAP INTO A BIGGER SOURCE OF UNIVERSAL POWER THAN WE'VE SEEN SINCE SPRING BREAK OF '82!
YOU! SACK OF ORGANS! YOU READY TO GET THIS PARTY STARTED?
YEAH! YEAH! WOO-HOOOO!!
I'D REALLY PREFER IT IF YOU'D JUST LET ME GO...
READY?

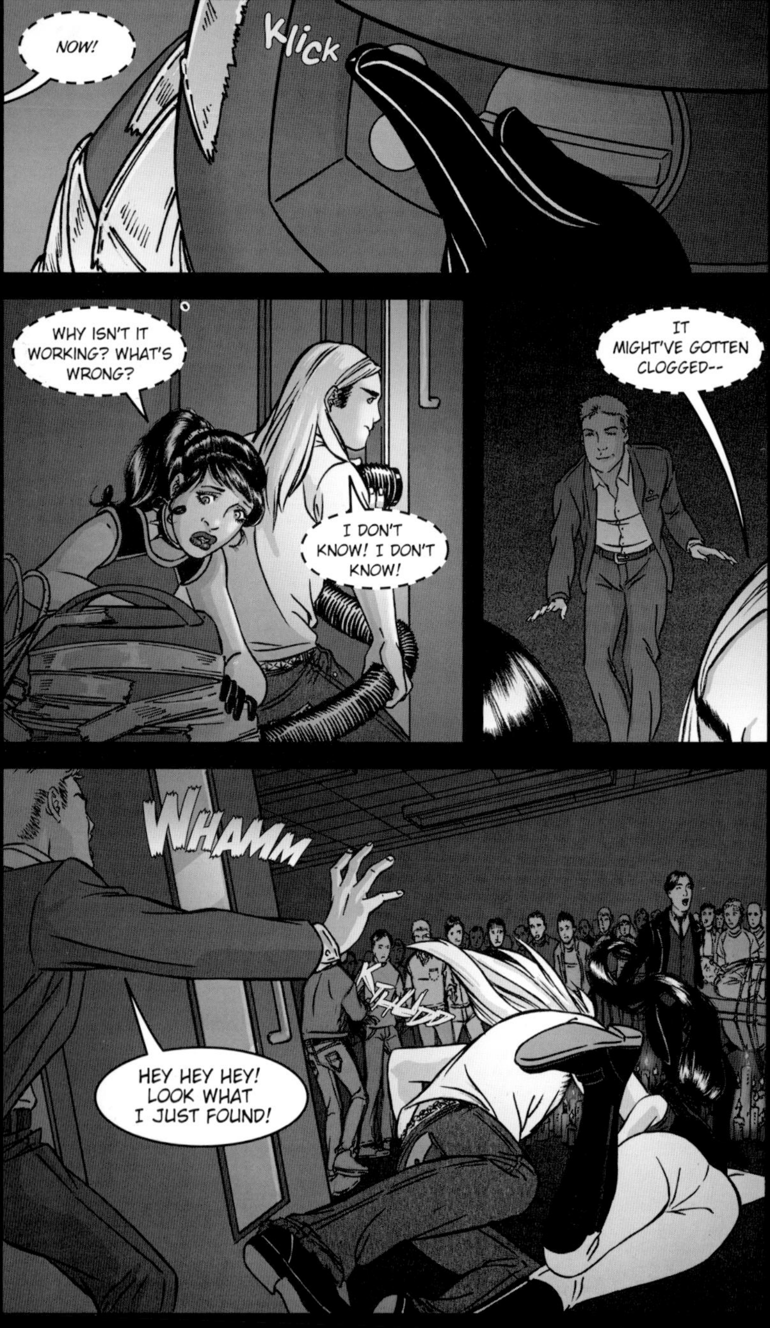
NOW!
Klick
WHY ISN'T IT WORKING? WHAT'S WRONG?
I DON'T KNOW! I DON'T KNOW!
IT MIGHT'VE GOTTEN CLOGGED--
WHAMM
HEY HEY HEY! LOOK WHAT I JUST FOUND!

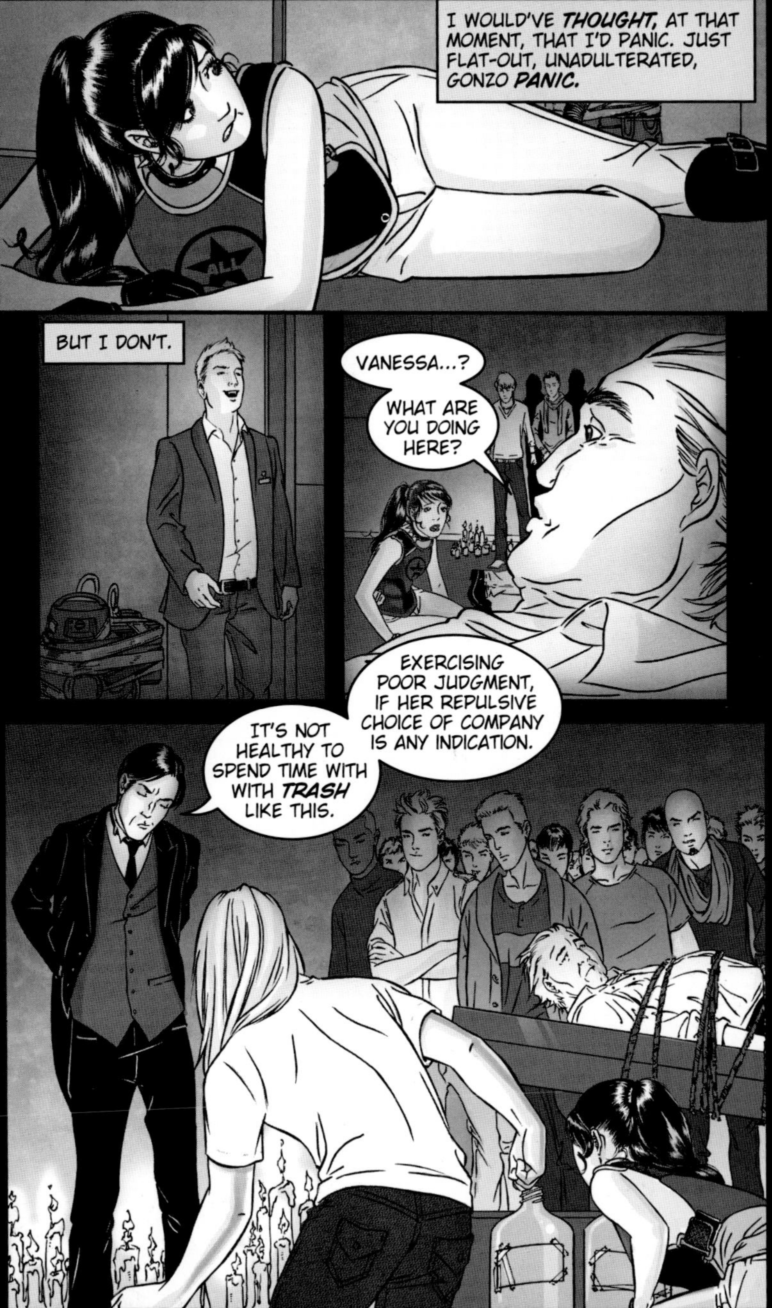
I WOULD'VE **THOUGHT,** AT THAT MOMENT, THAT I'D PANIC. JUST FLAT-OUT, UNADULTERATED, GONZO **PANIC.**
BUT I DON'T.
VANESSA...?
WHAT ARE YOU DOING HERE?
EXERCISING POOR JUDGMENT, IF HER REPULSIVE CHOICE OF COMPANY IS ANY INDICATION.
IT'S NOT HEALTHY TO SPEND TIME WITH WITH **TRASH** LIKE THIS.

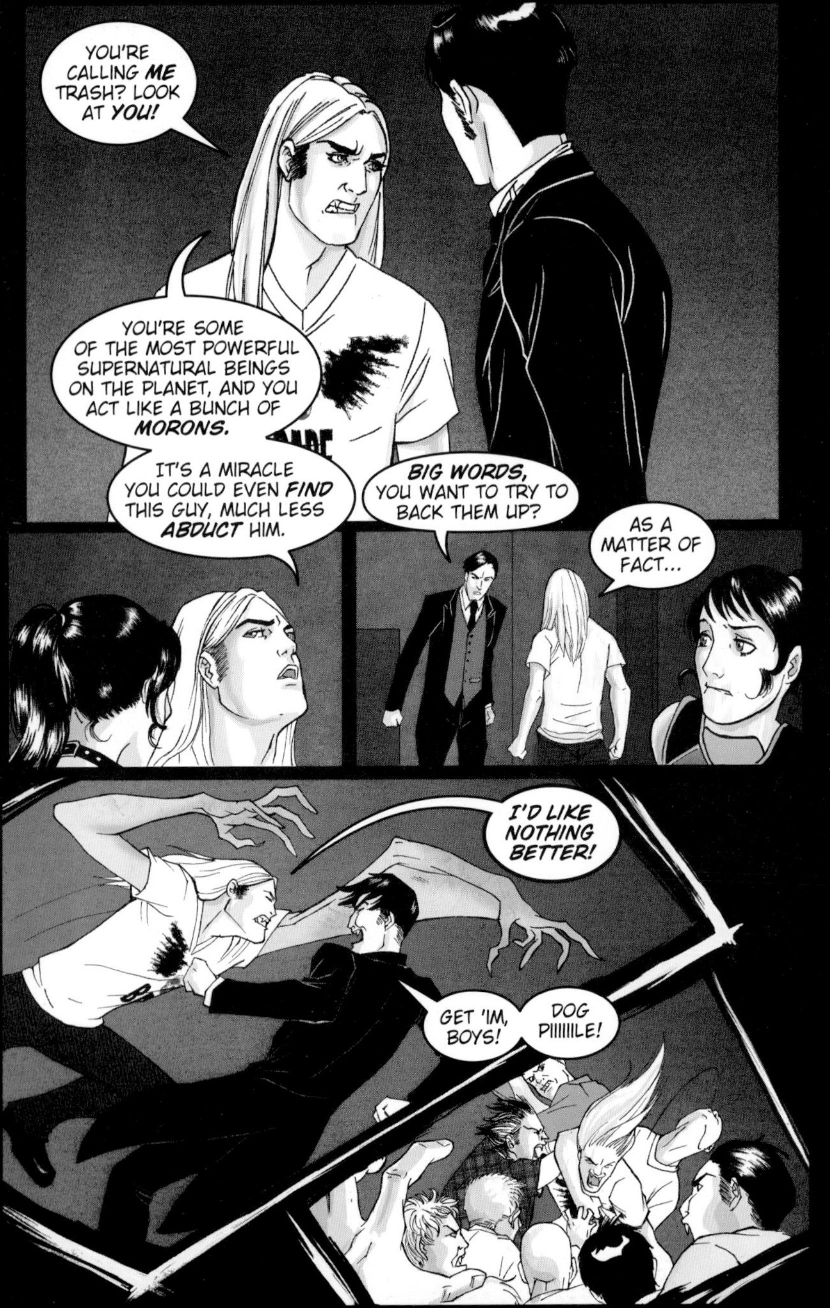
YOU'RE CALLING ME TRASH? LOOK AT YOU!
YOU'RE SOME OF THE MOST POWERFUL SUPERNATURAL BEINGS ON THE PLANET, AND YOU ACT LIKE A BUNCH OF MORONS.
IT'S A MIRACLE YOU COULD EVEN FIND THIS GUY, MUCH LESS ABDUCT HIM.
BIG WORDS, YOU WANT TO TRY TO BACK THEM UP?
AS A MATTER OF FACT...
I'D LIKE NOTHING BETTER!
GET 'IM, BOYS!
DOG PIIIIILE!

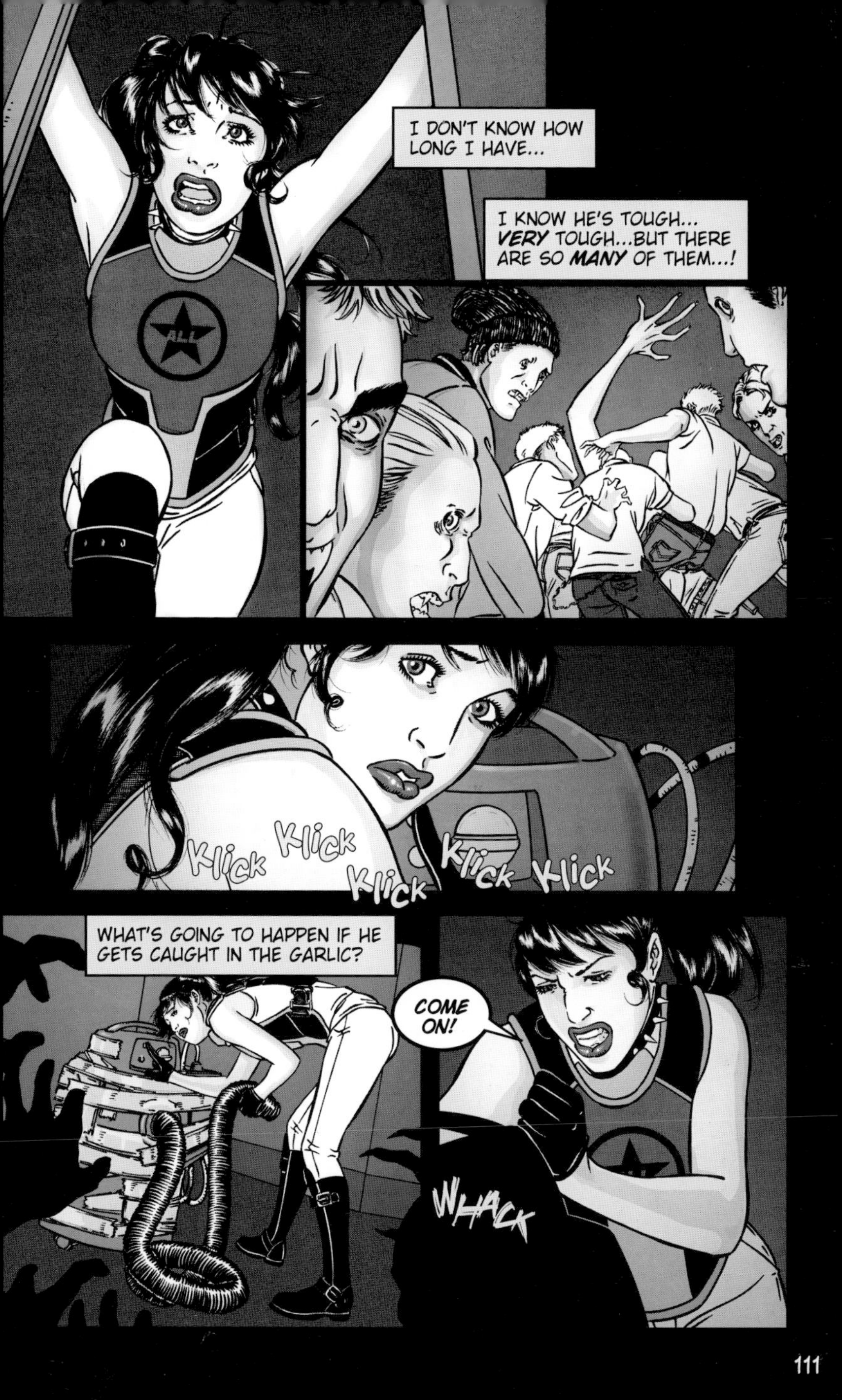
I DON'T KNOW HOW LONG I HAVE...
I KNOW HE'S TOUGH... **VERY** TOUGH...BUT THERE ARE SO **MANY** OF THEM...!
ALL
KLICK
KLICK
KLICK
KLICK
KLICK
WHAT'S GOING TO HAPPEN IF HE GETS CAUGHT IN THE GARLIC?
COME ON!
WHACK

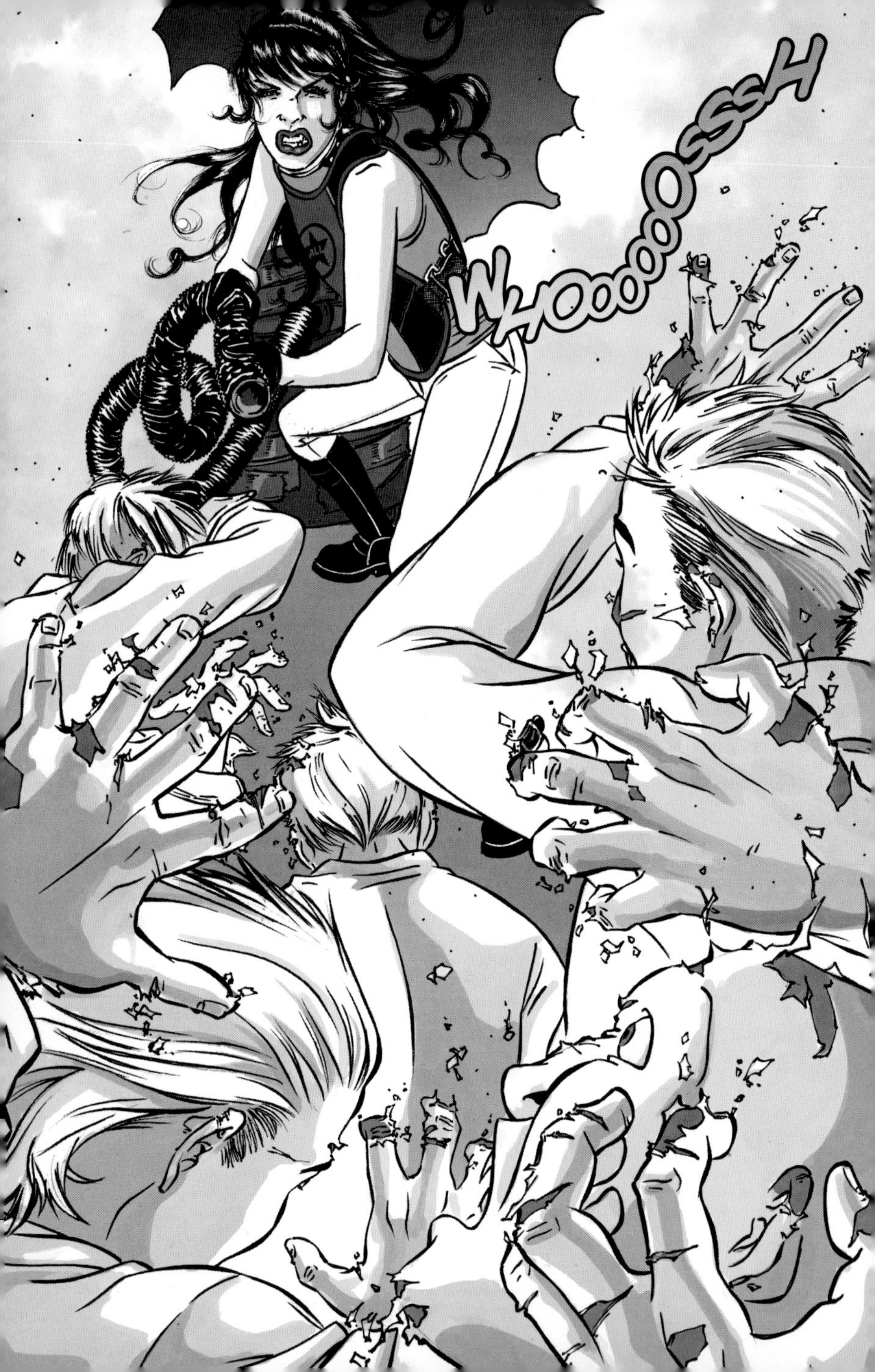
WHOOOOOSSSH

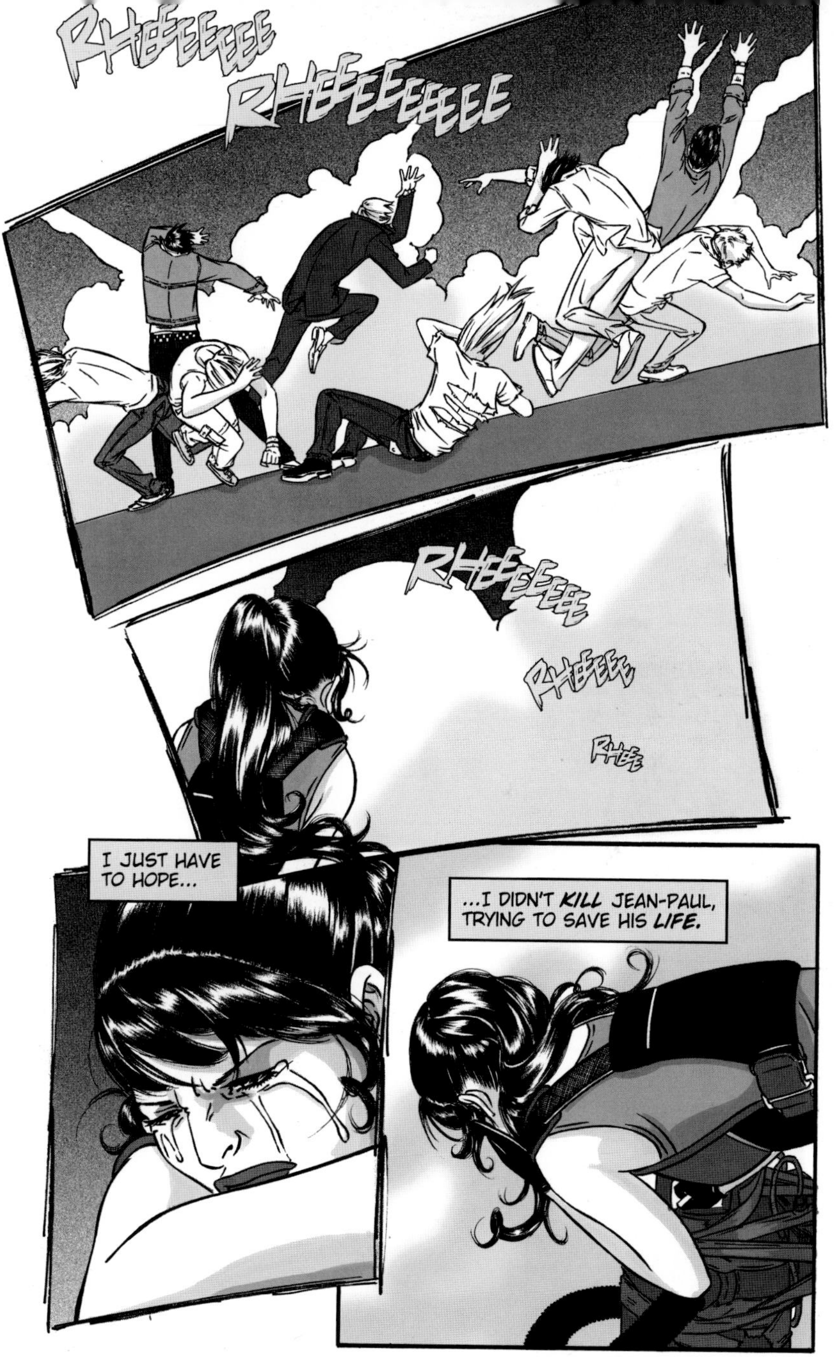
RHEEEEEEE
RHEEEEEEEEEE
RHEEEEEEE
RHEEEE
RHEE
I JUST HAVE TO HOPE...
...I DIDN'T KILL JEAN-PAUL, TRYING TO SAVE HIS LIFE.

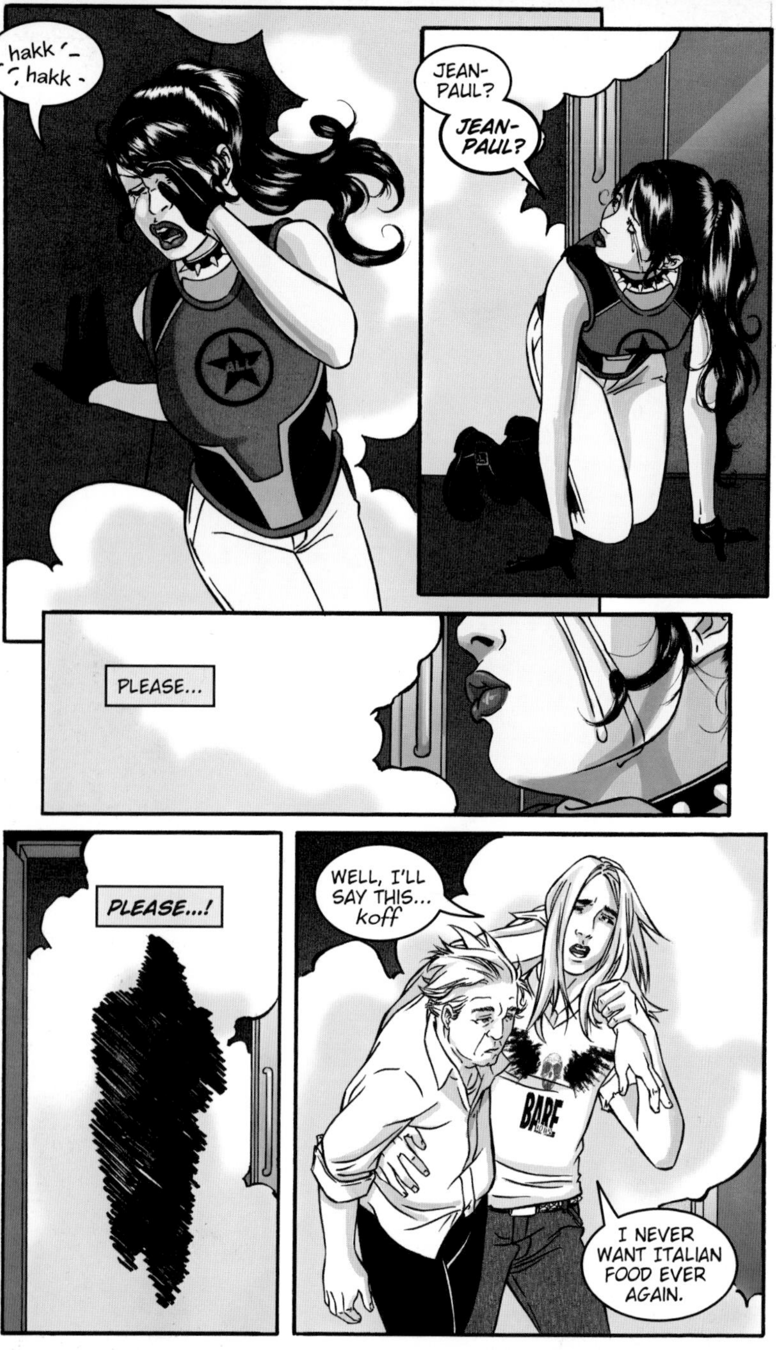
hakk hakk
JEAN-PAUL?
JEAN-PAUL?
PLEASE...
PLEASE...!
WELL, I'LL SAY THIS... koff
I NEVER WANT ITALIAN FOOD EVER AGAIN.

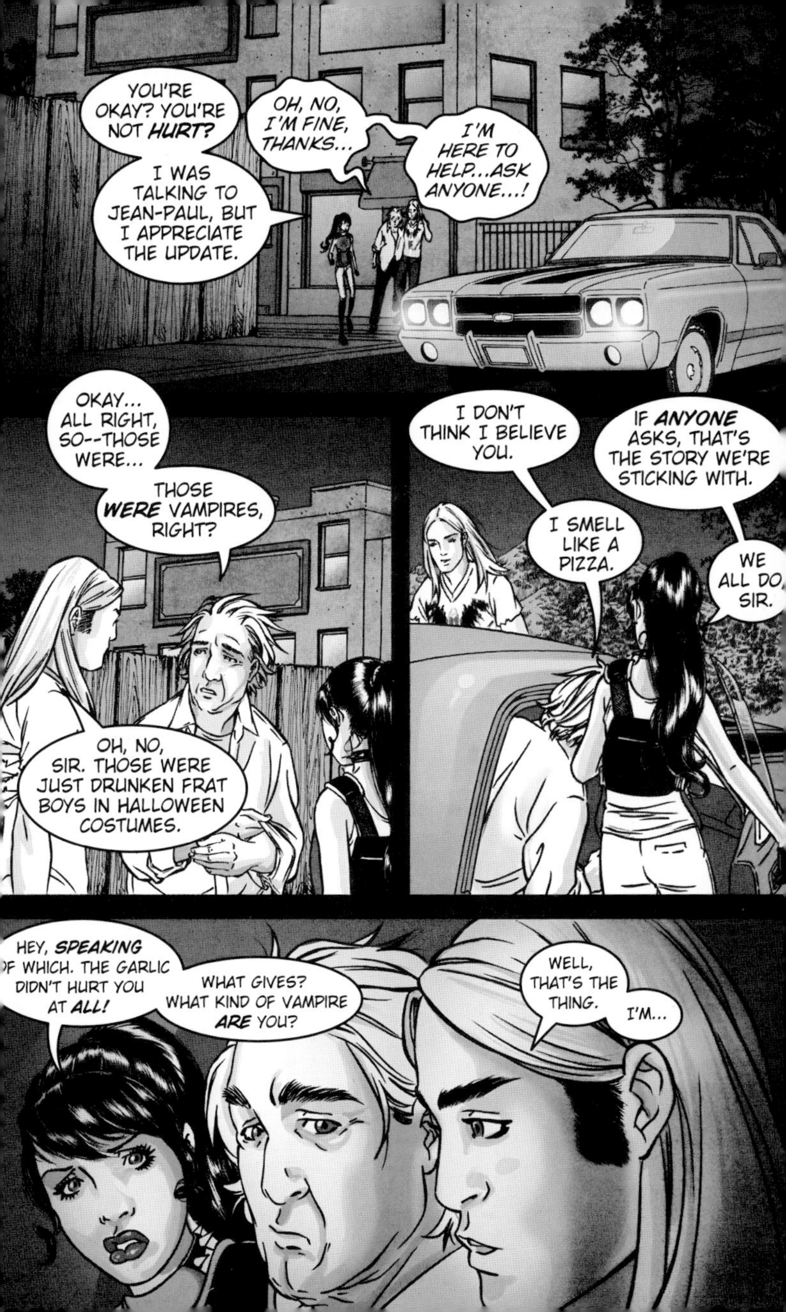
YOU'RE OKAY? YOU'RE NOT HURT?
I WAS TALKING TO JEAN-PAUL, BUT I APPRECIATE THE UPDATE.
OH, NO, I'M FINE, THANKS...
I'M HERE TO HELP...ASK ANYONE...!
OKAY... ALL RIGHT, SO--THOSE WERE...
THOSE WERE VAMPIRES, RIGHT?
OH, NO, SIR. THOSE WERE JUST DRUNKEN FRAT BOYS IN HALLOWEEN COSTUMES.
I DON'T THINK I BELIEVE YOU.
IF ANYONE ASKS, THAT'S THE STORY WE'RE STICKING WITH.
I SMELL LIKE A PIZZA.
WE ALL DO, SIR.
HEY, SPEAKING OF WHICH. THE GARLIC DIDN'T HURT YOU AT ALL!
WHAT GIVES? WHAT KIND OF VAMPIRE ARE YOU?
WELL, THAT'S THE THING.
I'M...

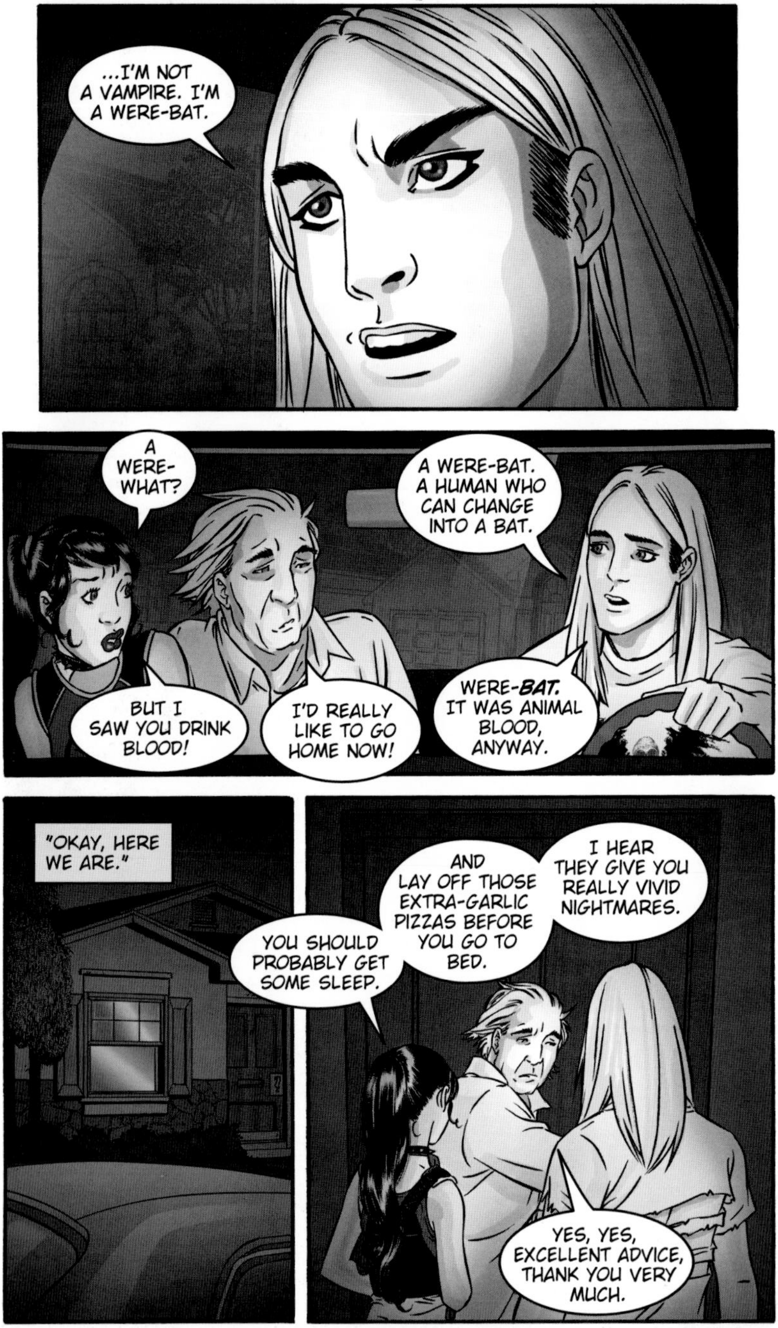
...I'M NOT A VAMPIRE. I'M A WERE-BAT.
A WERE-WHAT?
A WERE-BAT. A HUMAN WHO CAN CHANGE INTO A BAT.
BUT I SAW YOU DRINK BLOOD!
I'D REALLY LIKE TO GO HOME NOW!
WERE-BAT. IT WAS ANIMAL BLOOD, ANYWAY.
"OKAY, HERE WE ARE."
YOU SHOULD PROBABLY GET SOME SLEEP.
AND LAY OFF THOSE EXTRA-GARLIC PIZZAS BEFORE YOU GO TO BED.
I HEAR THEY GIVE YOU REALLY VIVID NIGHTMARES.
YES, YES, EXCELLENT ADVICE, THANK YOU VERY MUCH.

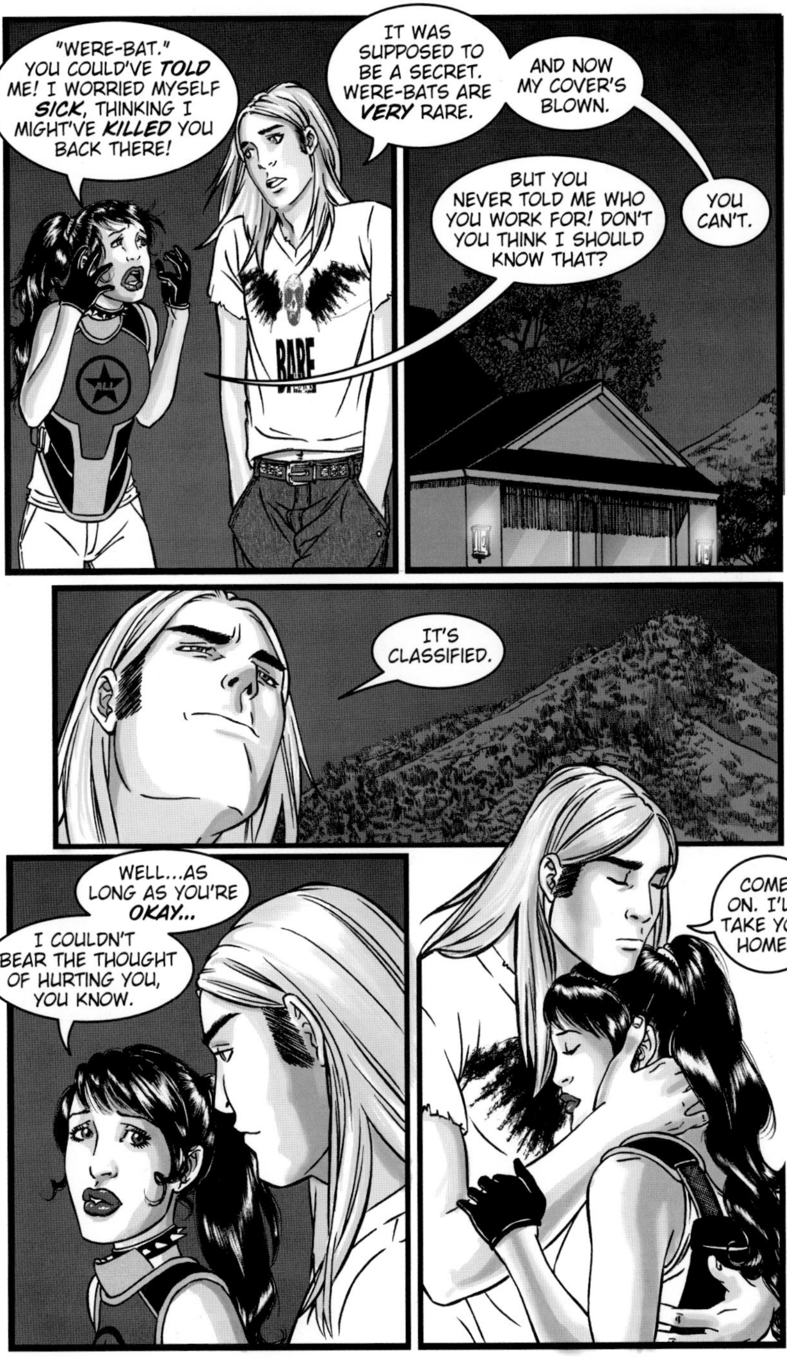
"WERE-BAT." YOU COULD'VE TOLD ME! I WORRIED MYSELF SICK, THINKING I MIGHT'VE KILLED YOU BACK THERE!
IT WAS SUPPOSED TO BE A SECRET. WERE-BATS ARE VERY RARE.
AND NOW MY COVER'S BLOWN.
RARE
BUT YOU NEVER TOLD ME WHO YOU WORK FOR! DON'T YOU THINK I SHOULD KNOW THAT?
YOU CAN'T.
IT'S CLASSIFIED.
WELL...AS LONG AS YOU'RE OKAY...
I COULDN'T BEAR THE THOUGHT OF HURTING YOU, YOU KNOW.
COME ON. I'LL TAKE YOU HOME.

DO YOU REALIZE THE KINDS OF *PLANS* WE CAN MAKE NOW? THIS IS GOING TO BE *AWESOME!*

...PLANS?

FOR DEALING WITH YOUR LYCANTHROPY! OR IS IT STILL LYCANTHROPY IF YOU DON'T TURN INTO A WOLF? BATANTHROPY?

WE NEED TO FIND A BETTER PLACE FOR YOU TO LIVE...

...MAYBE A LITTLE MORE ISOLATED, SO IT'S NOT AS EASY TO SPOT YOU WHEN YOU FLY...

VANESSA...

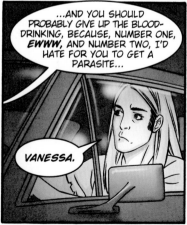

...AND YOU SHOULD PROBABLY GIVE UP THE BLOOD-DRINKING, BECAUSE, NUMBER ONE, *EWWW,* AND NUMBER TWO, I'D HATE FOR YOU TO GET A PARASITE...

VANESSA.

...AND IF YOU *HAVE* TO CHANGE, WHEN IT'S A FULL MOON? I BET WE COULD FIND SOME PLACE TO KEEP YOU *LOCKED UP...*

...WOULDN'T WANT YOU TO GO OUT ON ANY *RAMPAGES!* DO YOU LIKE BELFRIES? WE COULD--

VANESSA!

118

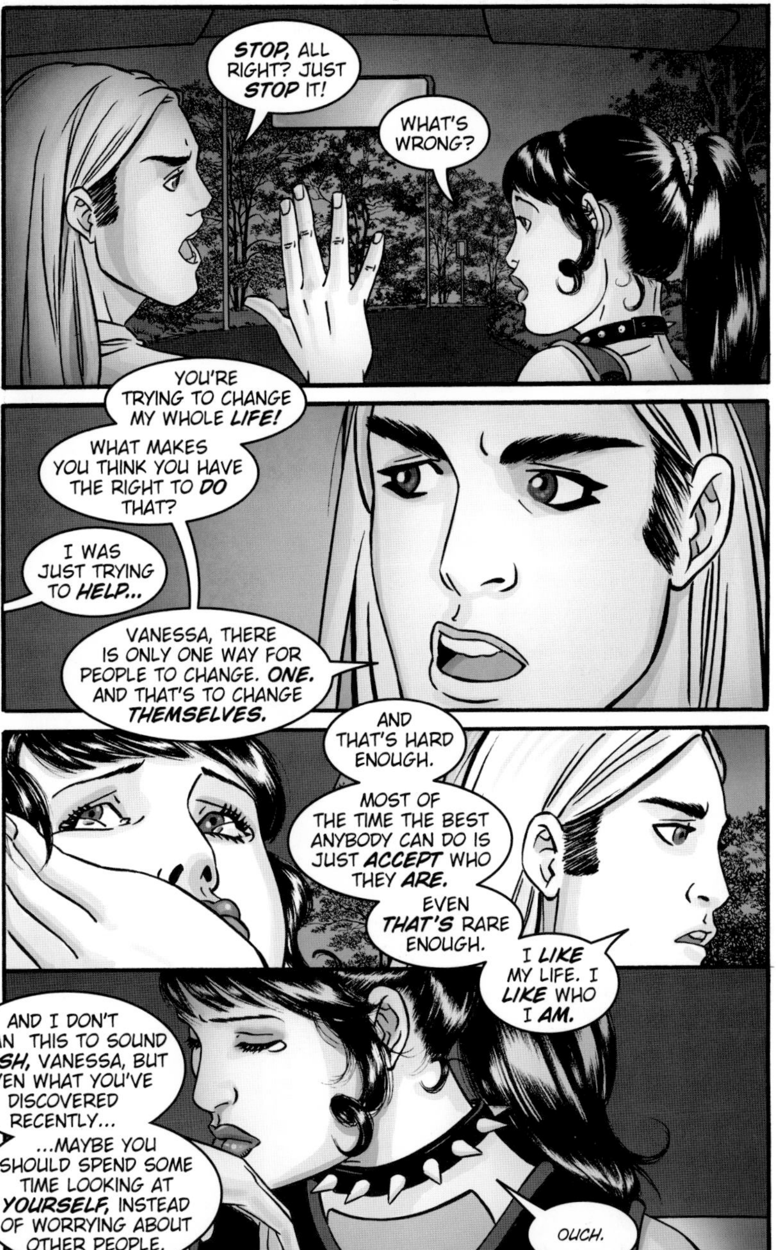
STOP, ALL RIGHT? JUST STOP IT!
WHAT'S WRONG?
YOU'RE TRYING TO CHANGE MY WHOLE LIFE!
WHAT MAKES YOU THINK YOU HAVE THE RIGHT TO DO THAT?
I WAS JUST TRYING TO HELP...
VANESSA, THERE IS ONLY ONE WAY FOR PEOPLE TO CHANGE. ONE. AND THAT'S TO CHANGE THEMSELVES.
AND THAT'S HARD ENOUGH.
MOST OF THE TIME THE BEST ANYBODY CAN DO IS JUST ACCEPT WHO THEY ARE.
EVEN THAT'S RARE ENOUGH.
I LIKE MY LIFE. I LIKE WHO I AM.
AND I DON'T MEAN THIS TO SOUND HARSH, VANESSA, BUT GIVEN WHAT YOU'VE DISCOVERED RECENTLY...
...MAYBE YOU SHOULD SPEND SOME TIME LOOKING AT YOURSELF, INSTEAD OF WORRYING ABOUT OTHER PEOPLE.
OUCH.

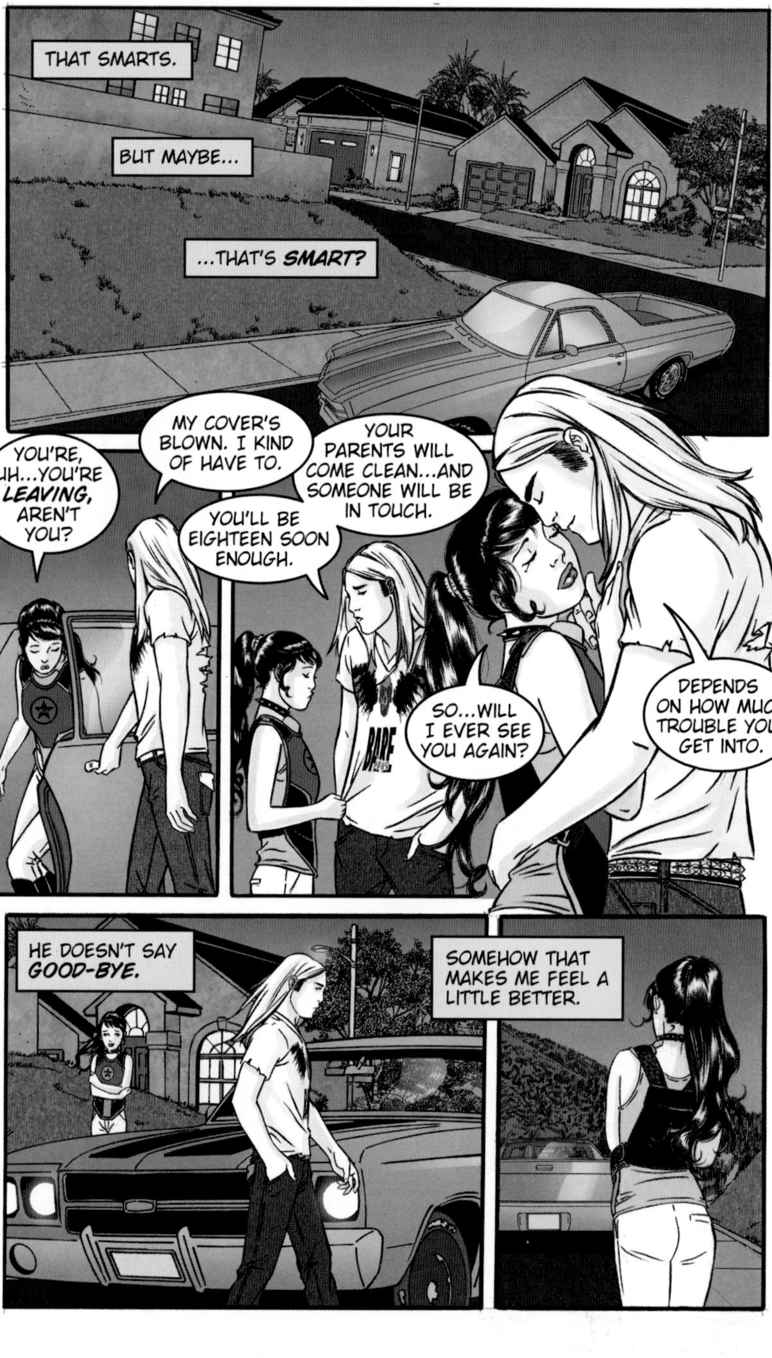
THAT SMARTS.
BUT MAYBE...
...THAT'S SMART?
YOU'RE, UH...YOU'RE LEAVING, AREN'T YOU?
MY COVER'S BLOWN. I KIND OF HAVE TO.
YOUR PARENTS WILL COME CLEAN...AND SOMEONE WILL BE IN TOUCH.
YOU'LL BE EIGHTEEN SOON ENOUGH.
BARE
SO...WILL I EVER SEE YOU AGAIN?
DEPENDS ON HOW MUCH TROUBLE YOU GET INTO.
HE DOESN'T SAY GOOD-BYE.
SOMEHOW THAT MAKES ME FEEL A LITTLE BETTER.

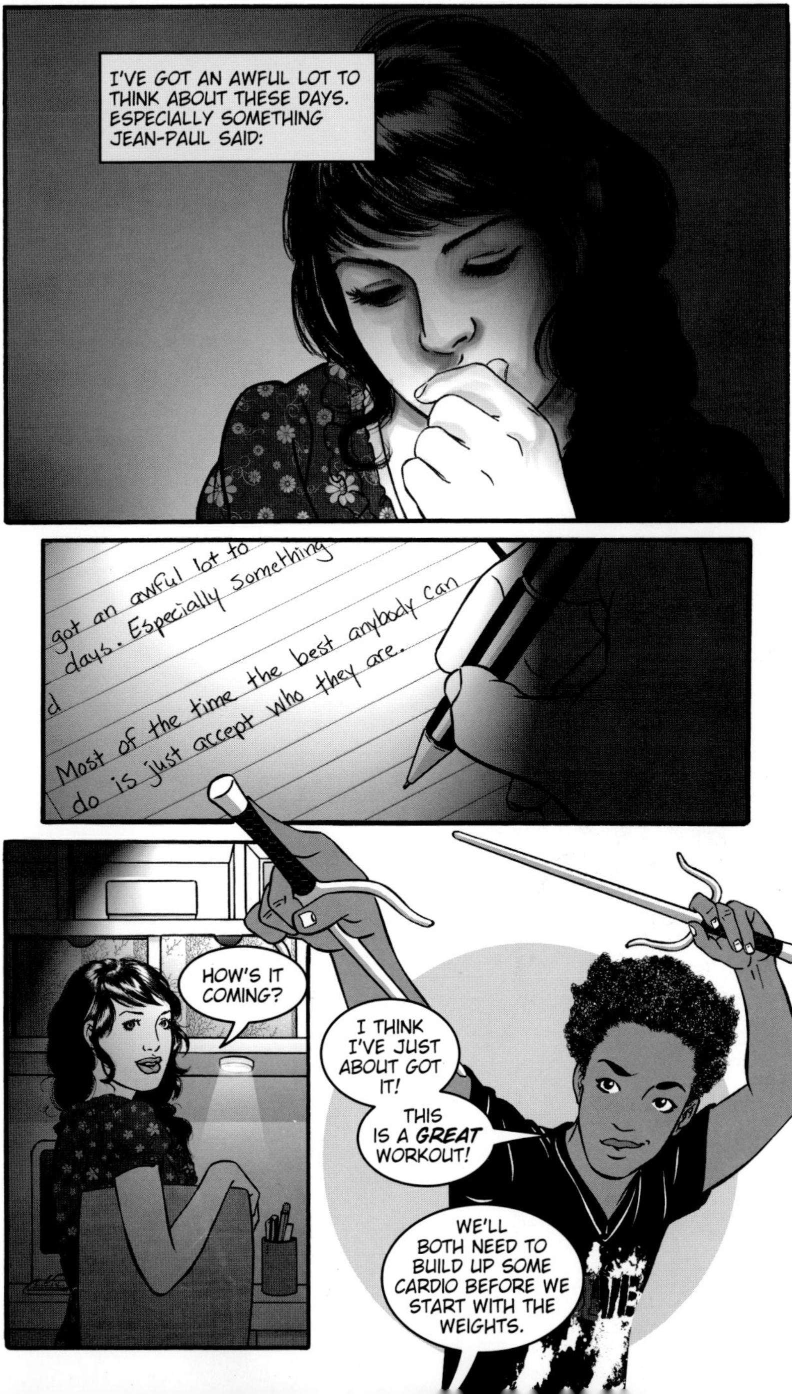

I'VE GOT AN AWFUL LOT TO THINK ABOUT THESE DAYS. ESPECIALLY SOMETHING JEAN-PAUL SAID:
got an awful lot to
days. Especially something
d
Most of the time the best anybody can
do is just accept who they are.
HOW'S IT COMING?
I THINK I'VE JUST ABOUT GOT IT!
THIS IS A **GREAT** WORKOUT!
WE'LL BOTH NEED TO BUILD UP SOME CARDIO BEFORE WE START WITH THE WEIGHTS.

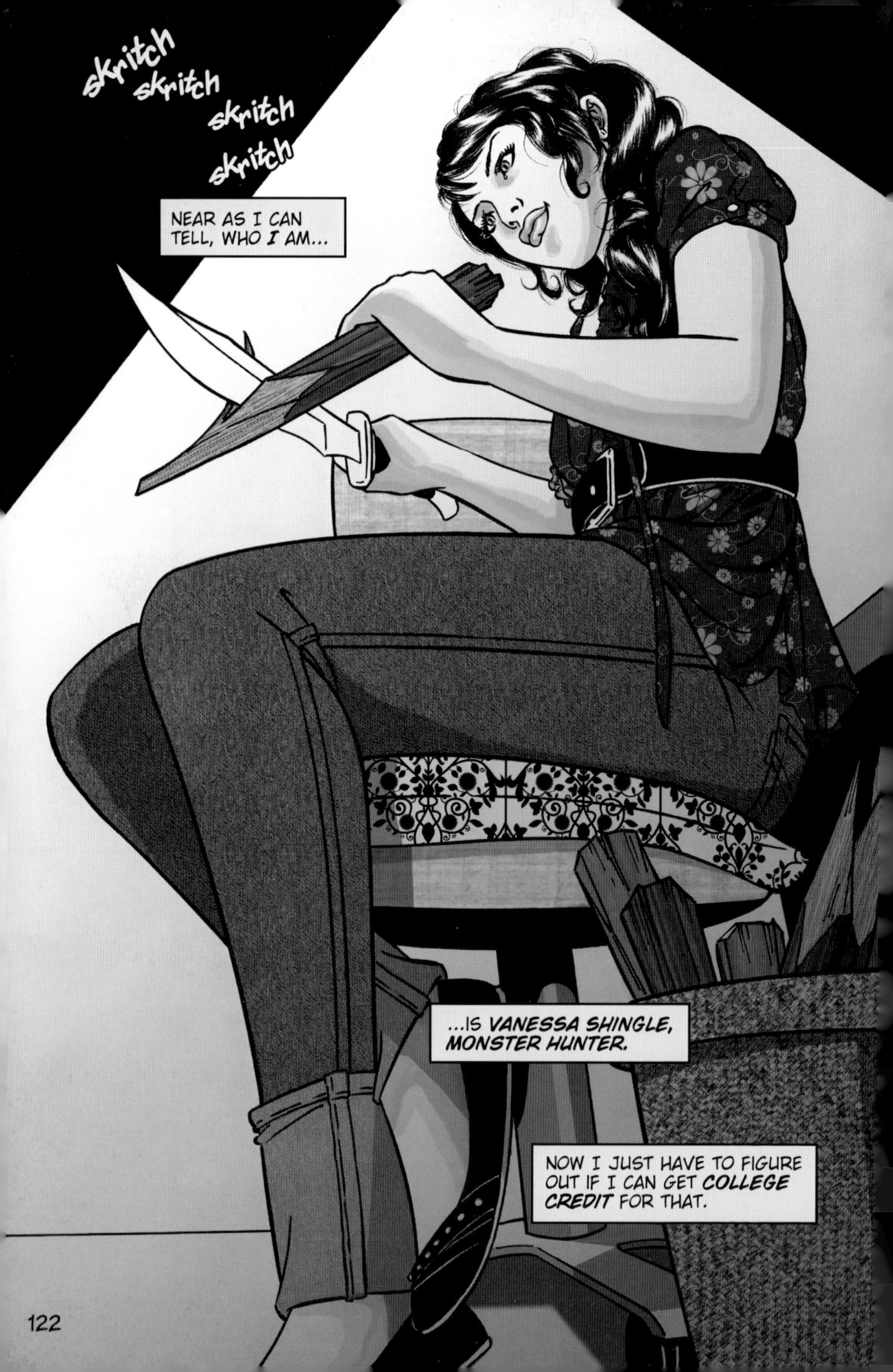
skritch skritch skritch skritch
NEAR AS I CAN TELL, WHO I AM...
...IS VANESSA SHINGLE, MONSTER HUNTER.
NOW I JUST HAVE TO FIGURE OUT IF I CAN GET COLLEGE CREDIT FOR THAT.

VANESSA SHINGLE, MONSTER HUNTER

MONSTERS EXPUNGED
ALL QUERIES WELCOME

Q. I heard you fought a vampire dressed as a clown! Clowns are terrifying.

A. Well, there was a clown convention in Hackensack, and some of the attendees started disappearing, and then some bodies started turning up, and let me tell you, it's not easy dealing with a dead guy who's wearing a rainbow wig and a big red nose. I tried to feel for a pulse, and his big plastic lapel flower squirted me in the face. So I'm thinking, "Okay, what's the best way to figure out who the clown-killer vamp is?" and Stork was like, "You could go undercover," which was a pretty good idea—being a clown decoy, vamp bait to draw out the killer. So I did the whole thing with all the makeup and these enormous shoes, and it took a whole night of waiting around, but then—

—wait, are you talking about the *vampire* who was dressed like a clown? Because that's a whole other thing. Terrifying.

Q. Aren't there any girl vampires?

A. Plenty. They're generally more subtle about it than the guys are, because, y'know, guys can get dumb sometimes. Okay, okay, not all guys. But a lot of guys don't think clearly once something like *I'm a vampire now!* happens to them. A guy gets turned into a vampire, and suddenly his skin clears up and he's standing taller and his muscles get big, and I tell you, it's like a switch gets flipped in his head and he's all, "Whooo! Look what I can do! High five, bro!" A lot of the girl vamps take more time to think about how they've changed, you know? What it means? They're more like, "Now what can I accomplish with all this? What's next?"

Between you and me, those girl vamps are a lot scarier.

Q. Did your boyfriend get bitten by a were-bat?

A. Ugh. He won't tell me. Or, I mean, he did tell me, but his story changes every time! One day it's, "I was walking down the street one night, and a truck full of radioactive bats was driving by and hit a pothole, and the bats spilled out and chewed all over me." But then

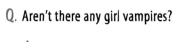

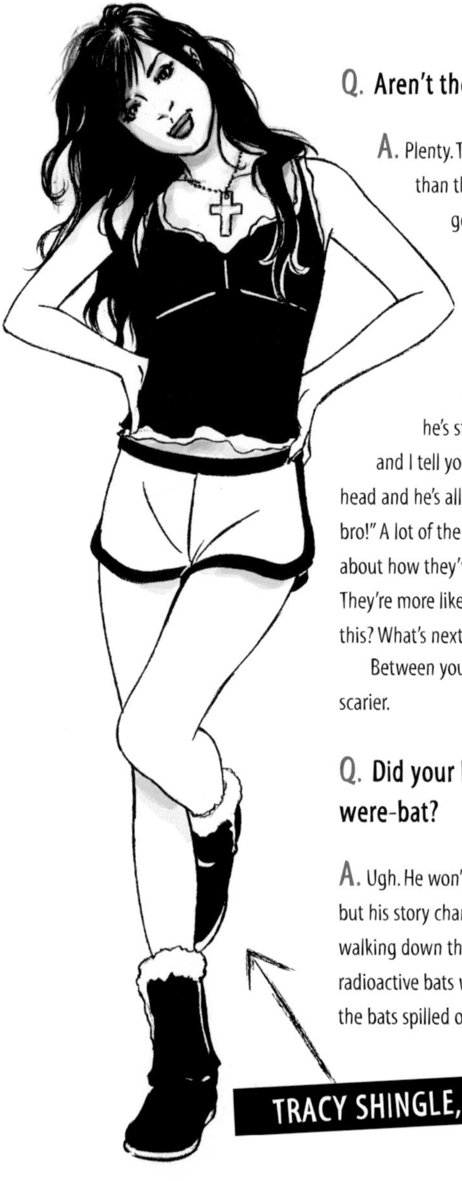

TRACY SHINGLE, VANESSA'S SISTER

the next day it's, "The McClellan clan have been were-bats as far back as anybody can remember," like it's a hereditary thing or a family curse. Then I overheard him talking to what I'm pretty sure was his mom on the phone one day, and he said something like, "Ha ha, yeah, that was a really funny practical joke, you got me good with the whole bat thing." But maybe I misheard him.

Q. What happened to Mr. James?!! Is he all right? He didn't come back to school and he was the most decent teacher we had.

A. I was worried about him to begin with. I thought he should talk to a therapist or something, and I think he did have a talk with Mr. Barry, the school counselor. But it turns out he's pretty resilient. He just wanted to get away from town for a while. He sent me a couple of postcards, and I love his sense of humor, like, "Fresno is beautiful, despite the recently unearthed nest of ancient chthonic monsters. Wish you were here."

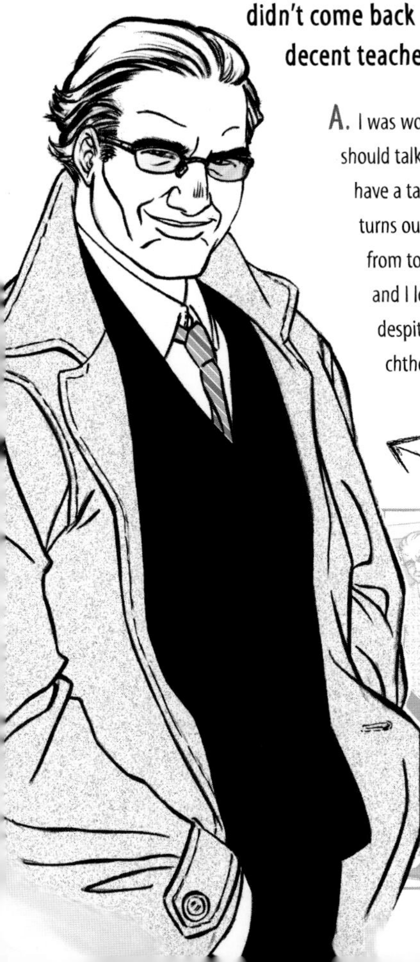

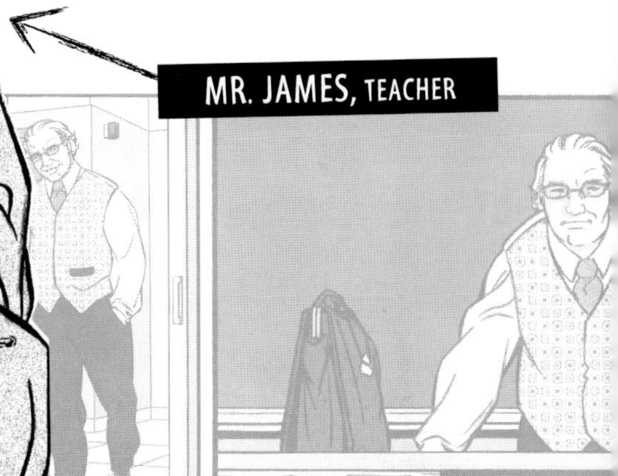
MR. JAMES, TEACHER

Q. I know vampires are bloodsucking monsters, but are they super hot?

A. I guess it depends on your point of view. They do tend to have really great hair and super-fit bodies, and they usually drive nice cars. And if you've got six or seven hundred years to work on it, you can really figure out what makes your date tick. But this is something that Stork and I talk about sometimes: how important it is not to ignore *red flags*. A red flag is something that you know is going to stop a relationship from moving forward, no matter how great everything else about it is. Say you meet a guy, and he's terrific, but then you find out he steals cars on the weekends. Red flag! Maybe you want to tell yourself, "Everything else about him is so great, I can overlook a little grand larceny." Take it from me, no, you can't. A red flag will ruin the relationship sooner or later. It can be exciting and all, but it's best not even to get involved in the first place. So you meet this tall, dark, handsome, rich, suave guy, and you tell yourself, "Maybe it's not such a big deal that he kills people and drinks their blood." RED FLAG! RED FLAG!

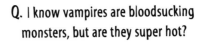

GARY BARRY, GUIDANCE COUNSELOR

126

Q. Is Jean-Paul your boyfriend? Isn't being a were-bat a red flag?

A. Maybe. Wait—I mean "maybe" about "is he my boyfriend," not the red flag. His *job* is to help people, he never hurts anybody but bad guys . . . so, no, being a were-bat is not a red flag. It's even like dating a cop. Um . . . *if* we were dating. I'm traveling all over the place, and he's all over the place too . . . but I guess we *are* dating, because whenever we wind up in the same city at the same time, we do hang out. Is he my boyfriend? Is my boyfriend a monster? I don't know! Next question!

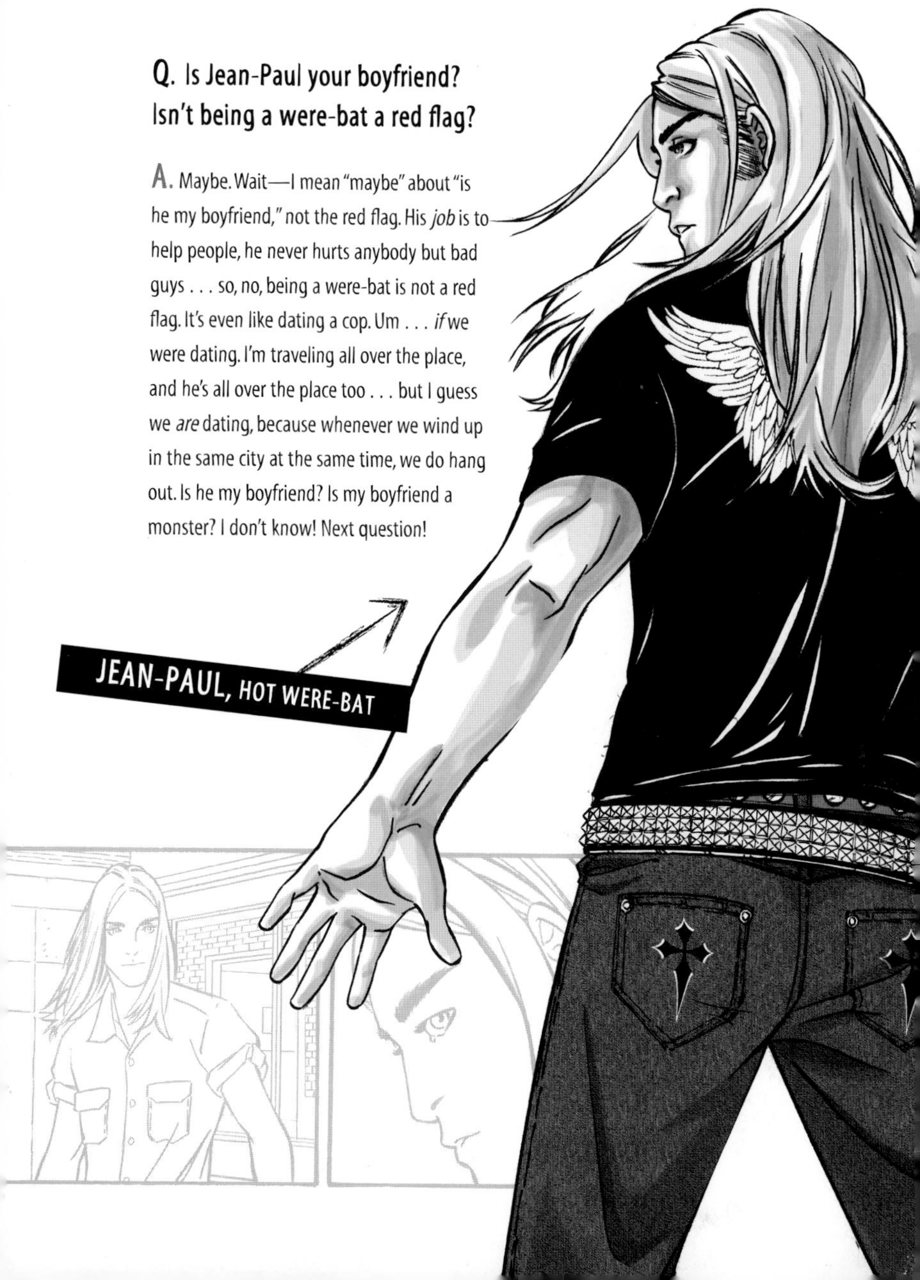
JEAN-PAUL, HOT WERE-BAT

ABOUT THE AUTHOR
AND THE ARTIST

Comic book author and video game writer DAN JOLLEY has created work for Marvel, DC, Dark Horse, and TokyoPop and for game developers including Activision and Ubisoft. He is also the author of several Graphic Myths and Legends titles including *Odysseus*, *Pigling* (a Korean Cinderella story), and *The Hero Twins: Against the Lords of Death* (a Mayan myth). Among his Twisted Journeys® titles are *Vampire Hunt*, *Escape from Pyramid X*, and *Agent Mongoose and the Hypno-Beam Scheme*. He lives in Georgia with his wife Tracy and three cats.

ALITHA MARTINEZ is a veteran in the world of mainstream American superhero comics who has ventured into manga as well. Her work can be found in issues of *Black Panther*, *Iron Man*, *Spider-Girl Battlebook: Streets of Fire*, *Shi*, *X-Men: Black Sun*, *Marvel Age: Fantastic Four*, *Voltron: Defender of the Universe*, and NBC's *Heroes*, as well as in her self-published series *Yume and Ever*. She is also the illustrator of Twisted Journeys® *Kung Fu Masters* and *The Quest for Dragon Mountain*. She lives in New York City.